To Joe—
Continued blessings
on you and yours
for many years to
come. Your Pal,

Patrick M
K

Behind the Mask

by

Patrick Kennedy

RoseDog 🐾 Books

PITTSBURGH, PENNSYLVANIA 15222

The contents of this work including, but not limited to, the accuracy of events, people, and places depicted; opinions expressed; permission to use previously published materials included; and any advice given or actions advocated are solely the responsibility of the author, who assumes all liability for said work and indemnifies the publisher against any claims stemming from publication of the work.

ISBN: 978-1-4349-8238-4
eISBN: 978-1-4349-4482-5
Printed in the United States of America

First Printing

For more information or to order additional books, please contact:
RoseDog Books
701 Smithfield Street
Pittsburgh, Pennsylvania 15222
U.S.A.
1-800-834-1803
www.rosedogbookstore.com

To my parents John and Connie Kennedy,
my brother Chris and sister Andrea,
and all my family and friends for inspiring my need to write.

Table of Contents

Chapter One

Guardian Angel

The air held a cold chill. Add in a slight icy breeze just to make matters worse. It was abnormally cold for an October night in Kansas. Then again, abnormal weather was the norm for the Sunflower State. Weather such as this would have driven the citizens of Derby indoors on a normal night, but this was no normal night. The beloved Derby High School football Wolves, having just won a game against their heated rivals from Haysville, gave the town reason to celebrate. For the students of the school, only one venue would properly reflect the magnitude of the festivity to come.

There were many reasons the Smith's place had become the number one party spot for Derby teens. The main reason was its countryside view. The party animals could be as loud as they pleased, but they would never receive any complaint about the noise. Just a short drive beyond city limits, about five miles or so, and there it was. The house, being the largest in the area, was impossible to overlook. Covering well over five-thousand square-feet, this partier's refuge stood two stories tall and featured a full basement. As daunting a structure as the house was from the outside, its true amazement was contained within its walls.

On the ground floor, the area beyond the front door opened into a spacious living room. A series of couches and chairs lined the walls to provide amble seating. While a few coffee tables complemented the furniture, most of the floor remained exposed, creating a makeshift dance floor. Artwork adorned the walls with the exception of one area, which served as the entertainment center. It housed the works: full on surround sound with 52-inch flat screen TV, DVD player, and MP3 player hooked into the speakers. Towards the rear of the room was an archway that segued to a kitchen housing a full range with a large refrigerator and an island in the middle of the room. While there were several other rooms on the ground floor, including a formal dining room down the hall from the kitchen, the only other room that drew any attention from partygoers was the den. Cornered in between the kitchen and the living room, the den was more of a quiet place for people to get together and chat. The furniture was all leather and it was the only carpeted room on the floor. It, along with the hallway on the other side of the kitchen, also had staircases leading to the other stories of the house.

The basement served as an arcade room than anything else. Featuring another big screen TV, this one had video game systems hooked into it. There was also a card table and foosball table to entertain guests. All of these proved to be enough to keep guests disinterested in the other rooms down there, but they were just storage and spare rooms anyway. Similarly, the upstairs typically went unexplored. There was a string of bedrooms up there, but they held no importance to those who didn't reside in them. The only room upstairs that consistently saw visitors was the bathroom.

As usual, the party commenced around nine-thirty. Within five minutes of the first car arriving, the living room was alive with the sounds of 3 Doors Down's newest album. A small group huddled around the TV to wait for the news report on the recently ended game and to hear the latest on what else had happened around the state in football news. A mess of students gathered outside with cell phones in hand calling either their parents or their friends. Everyone knew it would be a long night. The kitchen island had transformed into a buffet-line of chips, dips, pizza, and candy. The fridge, which was already half stocked with sodas, bottled water, and Gatorades, was filled up with more soda and a few alcoholic beverages. It wasn't ten minutes more before the house filled with exuberant teens celebrating sweet victory and the hours began to fly.

For Maggie, the party could not have happened at a better time. The five days of the school week seemed to have dragged on for two weeks. Although the weekend only guaranteed a short two-day reprieve from the classroom, it would be sufficient time to get her recharged for another go around. Though disappointed that she had failed to convince her neighbor and best friend Trick to take part in the festivities, Maggie wasn't about to let that small shortcoming get her down. Trick always shied away from the social spotlight after all. He'd just as likely host his own soiree before he'd show up here. Besides, the night still had unlimited potential, and the promise of time alone with her boyfriend Eric.

With a drink in hand, Eric was currently sitting in the kitchen staring past the glass door out to the lake. A boy of average height and build, his blonde hair trickled just over his eyes. A toss of his head to the right flipped his hair out of his vision to give him a lucid view of his escape. The porch outside the kitchen wandered out about twenty feet before giving way to a dirt path. About fifty yards further, it ended at a pier that extended out over a lake. The pier was relatively new, built nearly seven years ago. Carefully crafted and reinforced, it was sporting a sturdy oak construct. From the edge of the lake, the pier stretched out fifty feet or so and hovered ten feet above the crystal waters. Below the surface, the water was about the same distance deep. Bordered by trees all around, the lake covered about three acres. In some areas, the trees went on for miles.

Ice already frosted the tips of the trees, and the lake was beginning to freeze over. Eric gazed out at the clear sky, seeing the full moon and twinkling stars. For as long as the party had been going, he'd barely spent any time alone with Maggie. He had to be up early the next morning and with midnight fast approaching, he desperately wanted to break away for a little while. Perhaps, the party wasn't the best place to come to be alone, but there were definitely opportunities available for the advantageous.

With the lake utterly unoccupied, Eric found such an opportunity; he just needed to grab Maggie and persuade her to slip away. He finished what was left of his drink and began hunting for her in the living room. His quest would not last long. Maggie was perched on a couch conversing with her friends Katie, Ashley, and a couple others as well. Before interrupting her, Eric watched speechlessly as she teased her shoulder length curly blond hair. Her soft blue eyes held the sky and a peaceful haven for anyone who gazed in them. A bright smile shined against her pale skin. Even dressed casually in jeans and a T-shirt, her clothes accentuated her perfect body.

Still astounded by his unmerited luck at having a girl like her, Eric gently took her hand and whispered in her ear that the two of them should go stargazing out at the pier. At first, Maggie protested, insisting that it was much too cold to be venturing outside, but Eric procured a quilt as a pledge that he wouldn't let her get cold. Trusting Eric's word and with a longing look in her eyes, Maggie agreed to join him. They swiftly made their way to the kitchen door, hesitating before making their break. Wanting so dearly to be alone, the extra precaution proved imperative. Once assured that no one would pursue them, they snuck out the door. Eric carefully closed the door behind them as Maggie playfully started running for the pier. Eric would soon begin to chase after her.

Maggie reached the pier first. Stopping for but a moment, she glanced over her shoulder to see how far behind Eric was. He was unexpectedly close and assured her that he'd catch her soon enough. Maggie laughed as she continued down the pier. As she looked over the lake, she could just make out the icy rim forming around the bank. A moment later, she glanced back again to see how well Eric's pursuit was coming along. Close, but he had yet to reach the wooden platform. With an attentive eye on him, Maggie became oblivious to the ice patch at the pier's edge. As she approached, she slowed—unfortunately, not quickly enough. Slipping on the ice, she lost her balance. Her feet flew up in the air as her head slammed against the oak boards. The force of the collision knocked her out, and she dropped helplessly into the icy murk below.

As Eric witnessed these distressing events unfold, his playful disposition morphed into a dreadful panic. The quilt fell from his hand as he broke into a full sprint toward the pier. A few steps onto the pier, Eric slipped on a patch of ice as well and landed hard on his head. Attempting to regain his wits, Eric stretched his hand toward the end of the pier before it harmlessly dropped to the ground. The last thing Eric heard was the frenzied stomping of feet coming from behind him. His vision blurred, Eric could barely make out a figure that whisked past him, leapt from the pier, and crashed into the water. After that, everything went black.

In the water, the figure swam to the bottom of the lake to catch the rapidly sinking damsel. Unable to see her with his eyes, he grabbed wildly for anything substantial and eventually caught hold of Maggie's arm. Securing Maggie by the chest in one arm, he pulled her back to the surface, desperately trying to remove her from the arctic hazard. Once she was clear of the water, he dashed after the quilt that Eric left on the ground. It was only when he returned that he realized Maggie wasn't breathing.

Reacting on pure impulse, he ripped her soaked jacket from her motionless body. Tossing it carelessly to the side, he started franticly pushing on her chest and administering CPR. Finally, she convulsed, coughing up some water but breathing.

Slowly, Maggie regained her senses. It took a minute before she could realize where exactly she was, but she couldn't figure out what had transpired. Wrapped around her body, she could feel the quilt Eric had been holding. She could also feel the tight, yet tender, embrace of a pair of arms she sensed did not belong to Eric. After an initial jolt of apprehension shot through her, she felt a sense of comfort and ease in these arms. Her head rested against the stranger's chest as he knelt down on one knee rubbing her arms in an attempt to get her circulation going. Maggie suddenly felt herself shivering from the lingering dampness of the water. Just as she remembered hitting her head, it began to throb in waves of pain.

She moaned, which resulted in the arms around her loosening their grip. Whoever had been holding her must have been startled as he began to retreat. Still panicky from the experience, Maggie struggled to grasp hold of him before he went too far. She grabbed hold of some cloth, but it ripped leaving a small scrap of the clothing in her hand. The sound only escalated her anxiety as she frantically grabbed for him again. This time, she managed to snag his arm, but he already had his arms around her in an effort to calm her.

"Don't leave me," she pleaded, distress still prevalent in her tone.

"I won't," he replied. "I'd never leave you if you needed me."

When Maggie heard his voice, she couldn't quite recognize it though it sounded eerily familiar. It eased her trepidation and even momentarily numbed her head. As she searched her memory attempting to match the voice to a face, the stranger lifted her to her feet. Once she was stable, he gradually removed the support of his arm and stepped aside.

With her vision still distorted and the incessant pounding of her head almost ringing in her ears, Maggie couldn't get a proper look at the person who had pulled her from the lake. She wiped her face with the quilt, hoping her eyes could reclaim enough of their focus so she could address her hero.

To her disappointment, when her eyes did reset, all they set upon was a pair of eyes that belonged to a face hidden behind the black confines of a ski mask. One cheek was significantly thinner than the other. Still clutching the small black cloth in her hand, she realized his mask was apparently what had torn previously.

From what Maggie could see, he was about a head taller than she was, athletically thin, and covered head to toe in black. Whoever he was, Maggie wouldn't uncover any clues from looking at him. More important than his identity, his body was noticeably shivering, though he forced his arms to his sides in an attempt to mask his discomfort.

Maggie was quick to voice her concern, "You're freezing."

"I'll be fine, thanks," he quickly replied. "Are you alright?"

Still troubled by his predicament, Maggie rubbed her head. "My head really hurts but at least I'll live now—thanks to you."

Saying nothing more, the masked man nodded in acknowledgement. Apparently satisfied, he moved past her, heading for the trees. Astounded that he was departing now, Maggie went after him. For one, he did need to get inside where it was warm, but more importantly, she needed to thank him properly and know who had saved her.

"Wait!" Maggie yelled.

He yielded. He didn't confront her…just tilted his head to hear her better.

"You're not going to just leave me here are you?" Maggie asked taking a step towards him.

"Do you need any help getting back inside the house?" he asked.

Maggie knew that she could make it, so she scrambled to think of something that would force him to stay. But as hard as she thought, nothing came.

"No," she finally replied.

"Then, yes, I am going," he said walking towards the trees again.

Opportunity slipping away, Maggie blurted out the first thing that came to her.

"What about Eric? Where's Eric?"

Unwilling to break his stride, he pointed indistinctly toward the pier. "He's up there. Like you, he'll have a horrible headache, but once he sees you're okay, he'll be fine."

Maggie looked to the pier and saw Eric motionlessly lying there. Normally, she'd be at his side without hesitation, but this night had proven to be anything but normal. Trusting that he was indeed okay, Maggie refocused on the figure disappearing in front of her.

"Don't leave like this."

"Nothing personal," he said, "but I need to get somewhere warm soon."

"Then come inside." Maggie offered.

"No thanks, I got somewhere else to go."

Maggie dropped her arms in frustration, almost losing the quilt draped around her. She wrapped back up to prevent a trip as she pursued him. "How am I supposed to thank you when I don't know who you are?" she asked.

He curtly responded. "You don't need to thank me or know who I am."

Before Maggie could think of what to say, the stranger breached the tree line and began to fade into the cover of the limbs. Even as the rustling of the branches fell silent, Maggie refused to halt her efforts to detain him.

"But you saved my life!" she yelled. "At least tell me who you are."

"Just think of me as a guardian angel," she heard from within the trees.

Maggie couldn't fathom the necessity for such secrecy. "Why won't you tell me who you are?"

"I have my reasons."

Maggie had neither the time nor the patience to decipher these cryptic responses. Clearly, he wouldn't resurface unless there was good reason, and she detested him leaving like this. At that moment, she wished she had lied earlier.

"Will I ever see you again?" she asked when all other options were exhausted.

A silence settled over the scene; even the trees mutely awaited a response. He had stopped—conceivably contemplating a curtain call. Maggie intently scanned over the trees looking for any sign of him, but he didn't emerge. She accepted that he wasn't coming back and turned to walk away, wondering what a person would have to hide from her. Still clenched in her fist was the clump of cloth she'd ripped from his cloak. It was the only part of him she managed to retain—the only hint to his identity. She looked aimlessly into the trees a while longer, hoping that whoever had saved her would give up this charade. With each passing second, the silence stole her hope away.

"Maybe someday you'll see me again," she heard resounding from the trees. "And maybe someday…," he hesitated, unsure whether he should guarantee anything or not, "maybe I'll tell you who I am."

Maggie glared at the torn shard in her palm and shook her head in exasperation. "And what am I supposed to do until then?"

Another short period of silence set in. For all she knew, he hadn't even heard her inquiry and he was already long gone. Just as she abandoned her last hope, she heard his voice resonate from the trees one final time.

"Just know that I love you…that is all you ever need to know."

Before she could react, Maggie heard the cracking of twigs and frantic rustling of branches, which she assumed to be the stranger taking his leave. Seconds later, the sounds dissipated and were gone. Maggie scanned the trees one final time and then turned her attention to the pier. Tucking away the cloth in one of her pockets, the gravity of the situation shifted in her mind, and Eric's current state became her sole focus. Hating herself for having kept Eric's well-being on the back burner, she ran to the pier. He was still unconscious when she reached him. Gently placing a hand on his shoulder, she tried to nudge him back to consciousness.

"Eric," she said, "come on, wake up."

Maggie gently held his face in her hand. Eric slowly opened his eyes and then sat up. Extremely groggy, he began rubbing his head to ease the throbbing pain. As his memories reformed in his mind, a jolt of fear pulsed through him. When his eyes eventually settled on Maggie's face, an immense feeling of relief swarmed over him, and he threw his arms around her.

"Oh, my gosh," he exclaimed, "you're okay!"

Maggie hugged him back but she didn't say anything about the stranger or getting pulled out of the lake. "Yeah, I'm a little cold, and I've got a pretty big headache, but I'm fine," Maggie replied. "What about you?"

"Well, I'm with you in the headache department," Eric replied. "Who pulled you out?"

At first, Maggie was concerned that Eric overheard the self-proclaimed 'guardian angel' professing his love for her. It seemed unlikely, but there was the possibility that Eric could place the voice she had been unable to indentify. Still, the last thing she wanted was Eric fretting over some spontaneous admittance of love by a masked knight in shining armor.

"I don't know," Maggie finally admitted. "Did you see him?"

"No," Eric replied getting to his feet. "I heard him go running by and saw him jump off the pier, but that was it for me."

Maggie sighed. "Oh, well he was gone shortly after I woke up."

Eric wrapped his arm around Maggie's shoulders, and they slowly walked back towards the house. As they were walking, Maggie turned to the area where the stranger disappeared. She hoped to see some sign of him, but it was all too clear that her angel had spread his wings and flown away. Eric noticed her diverted attention.

"Hey, you alright?" he asked.

"Yeah," Maggie replied turning away from the trees. "Yeah, I'm fine. I was just wondering who would be out there on a night like this."

"It is kind of weird when you think about it, isn't it?"

Eric chuckled a little bit, doing anything to lighten the mood. Maggie wasn't quite ready to laugh this off, however. She glanced back at the trees and then at Eric. After a sigh, she smiled and nodded in agreement.

"Yeah, it is."

Eric threw open the door and guided Maggie inside. Katie was getting a drink as they walked in. She saw that Maggie was soaking wet and concern immediately gripped her. She carelessly sat the drink down, almost spilling it as she approached them. Ashley and a couple others noticed too, and a small crowd swarmed around Maggie and Eric.

"Eric, what happened out there?" Katie yelled.

Eric explained, "She fell in the lake."

"I hit my head on the pier, too," Maggie added.

With no consideration given to the headache, Katie turned to the living room and yelled as loud as she could. "Jordan!" Eric and Maggie both cringed, knowing Katie was only worried about them. "Get some blankets and Advil over here now!"

Katie tended to Maggie, taking the wet quilt from her and grabbing a dry towel. Meanwhile, a friend of Eric's noticed Eric rubbing his head, too. Not wanting to draw any attention from Maggie who was obviously worse off, Eric exercised discretion.

"Eric," Brian asked, "are you alright?"

"Yeah, I'm cool," replied Eric. "I just need some Advil. I hit my head on the pier, too."

A few seconds passed before two lanky teens, Jordan and Scott, came charging in with the blankets and Advil. Katie impatiently grabbed the pill bottle and tore the top off. Pouring a handful of pills out, she quickly seized two and gave them to Maggie. Ashley already had a glass of water in Maggie's hand. Katie also snatched a blanket from Jordan and draped it over Maggie. Katie wrapped her arms around Maggie once she was in the dry blanket and placed a hand gently on Maggie's head, which she rested on Katie's chest.

"What took so long, Jordan?" Katie asked.

Jordan took offense. "Forgo the decibel level in here; I was on the phone with Trick. I didn't exactly hear you at first."

Though totally unsubstantiated, the notion of Trick being the 'angel' suddenly hit Maggie. "Where is Trick?" she asked.

"Where he always is," Scott replied, "in his garage playing pool."

Maggie sighed. It was silly to think that way anyway she told herself. The more she thought about it, the more it didn't make any sense whatsoever. Trick would never hide behind a mask nor was he in love with her. So who was? Ashley, who had taken a seat in front of Maggie, tried to get Maggie to just relax from her whole ordeal.

"Don't worry about that now, Maggie," she said. "Just get warmed up."

As Maggie tucked herself in the blanket, she closed her eyes and tried to relax. Now that the excitement had diminished, Jordan took a seat on the island. He grabbed a handful of chips before he noticed that Eric was next to him sloped over with his head in his hands. It was clear he was disappointed with himself. Jordan attempted to alleviate Eric's anxiety, but his friendly pat on the back caused Eric to jump. Jordan threw up his hands to show he meant no harm, and Eric only slumped back down when he saw who it was.

"First mention of Trick and she has to know where he is," Eric grumbled. "Sometimes, I think she's in love with that guy."

Jordan chomped down on some chips. "Trick?" he repeated in shock. "Come on, man, be serious. They've lived next to each other their whole lives. If something was gonna happen, it would have already."

"Ah, you're right."

It hadn't struck Jordan as odd, but once he thought it through, it was quite peculiar. "Hey, how come your clothes are dry?"

"I didn't pull her out of the lake," Eric admitted.

Jordan stopped mid-chew before swallowing. "Then, who did?"

Eric shrugged his shoulders. "I don't know. She doesn't either. She said he left before she was awake."

Maggie heard the two talking and got uncomfortable when Eric said 'he left before she was awake.' She had lied to him. All in all, it wasn't that big of a deal, especially since she doubted she'd ever see him again. Still, she wanted to drop the matter and go home. Eric agreed to take her since he needed to get home, too. Katie was cautious at first about letting Eric drive after hitting his head, but eventually, she rescinded her objection. While Eric went to get the car to leave, Maggie sat alone in the kitchen to collect herself.

Since the crowd around her had dispersed, she examined her lone clue. It was a simple piece of cloth, nothing distinct about it. Had she not seen the tear herself, she wouldn't have known the fabric belonged to a mask. It was such a minute, indistinct clue, but coupled with the vague remembrance of his voice, it was all she had. How she would get answers from this point on was uncertain, but she was determined to get them somehow.

Away from the party, down the road little more than three miles, Kenny had been in a dead sprint for a couple miles already. He was exhausted, he was out of breath, but he didn't dare slow down. He desperately needed to get in-doors and out of his soaked clothes. He had finally arrived at Trick's house situated in a development outside of town. After bolting through the yard up to the door, he rang the bell fervently. Kenny shivered by the door as the seconds slowly ticked by. When no one came to the door, he began looking over the other houses in the neighborhood. No lights were on. Frantically searching for somewhere to escape from the bitter cold, he noticed a light on in Trick's garage. He wasted no time getting to the door and banged on it relentlessly.

"Come on, Trick!" he yelled jumping up and down to get warm. "Let me in!"

Trick, who had been squarely focused on his game of pool before he heard the knocking at the door, contemplated who would be visiting him at this time of night. At first, he thought about not answering but decided against it since whoever was out there knew him. Doing what he could to err on the safe side, Trick slowly turned the door handle with a pool cue in his hand.

Kenny burst through the door as soon as there was a sliver of light. "Dude, let me in," he whined as he knocked past Trick.

Trick looked at Kenny and saw him dripping wet and shivering from the frigid air. His shoes, blue jeans, and green shirt were all soaked, and his hair matted down on his head. Trick dropped the cue and slammed the door shut.

"Come on, hurry up," Trick said. "Get over to the heater before you're frozen stiff."

Kenny scooted past the pool table and plopped down in front of the heater. Still shivering uncontrollably, Kenny started ferociously rubbing his chest. He also searched the room for anything that would help him warm up, but couldn't find anything.

"Is the heat up all the way?" Kenny asked.

"As high as it'll go," Trick assured him. "What happened to you?"

"I was down by Miller's lake," Kenny explained. "Just walking around killing time...."

As he talked, he walked around the room looking for a towel or some-thing. Aside from the pool table, there wasn't much to this part of the garage.

In the corner was a small dorm room refrigerator along with a card table and two old recliners. The side door was ajar, showing a bit of the laundry room and car side of the garage. On the floor inside the door, Kenny could just spot a towel on the ground and grabbed it to dry off. As soon as he touched it, it secreted water. He immediately dropped it and turned towards Trick.

"What's with the wet towel, dude?" Kenny asked.

"Sorry, I spilled something earlier," Trick replied. "I'll get you another one, hang on."

Trick scooped up the wet towel as he walked into the laundry room. Kenny retreated to the heater as the stubborn cold refused to release its grip on him. Moments later, Trick appeared with a dry towel and change of clothes for Kenny.

"Here," Trick said, setting it all on the card table. "You can change in the other room whenever you're ready."

"Thanks," Kenny replied. "Like I was saying, I was walking around the lake up on one of the high banks and stopped for a second to look at the sky. The ground under me must have been really weak or something because before I realized it, it gave out right under me and I fell in. I got out as quick as I could, and then I started running until I ended up here. I went up to your house but no one was there."

"Yeah, my dad's been gone since yesterday," Trick said.

"Good thing I saw the light on out here."

Trick closed the laundry room door to keep the heat from escaping. Once he felt warm enough, Kenny grabbed the clothes and stepped into the other room. Trick wiped up what water he could before refocusing on his game. When Kenny reentered the room, Trick was setting up a shot as he arched himself over the table.

"Now, I need something to do with these," Kenny said with his wet clothes in hand.

"Throw them in the dryer," Trick instructed pointing to the other room. "I'm doing a load of wash right now...shouldn't be too long."

Kenny walked back into the garage. He took a glance at the washer to see exactly how much time remained. Despite his declaration that the dryer would start soon, Trick had pretty much just started the wash. Tired of wet hands, Kenny opened the dryer and threw his clothes in before returning to the other room and taking his seat by the heater.

"So...how often do you go to the lake to 'kill time'?" Trick asked.

"Not that often," Kenny replied. "Why?"

"Oh, nothing really," Trick said walking around the table to his next shot. "It just sounds a little strange going out to the lake by yourself to kill time."

Kenny offered his rebuttal. "You stay out here by yourself all the time."

"That's true," said Trick eyeing the eight ball. "But here, I'm inside, got some fun things to do, and there's no risk of falling in a lake."

Trick smiled coyly at his friend before taking his shot and ending the game. Kenny rolled his eyes, not agreeing with Trick's timing for jokes. "Well, I usually work at the gas station until about ten or so," Kenny explained. "Sometimes, I walk over to the lake, takes like half an hour to forty-five minutes."

Trick patronized as he reset the table. "Oh, sure, I could see that."

Kenny continued ignoring the attitude. "After that, I usually walk over to the Smith's house since they got a party there just about every Friday. Then, I usually get a ride home with someone."

"Still can't drive, huh?"

"No," Kenny said the disappointment ringing in his voice.

"Man, you have got to get another car," Trick said as he lifted the rack.

"Tell me about it," Kenny concurred. "But I don't have enough money. If my old car hadn't gotten totaled last month, I could trade it in, but that's how it goes."

Trick sympathized as he set his cue on the table and ventured into the garage. He started the dryer before returning. Kenny finally warmed up and moved away from the heater. Now that his shivering had ceased, he was able to calm down a bit. For his part, Trick shook a pop can, only to discover it was empty.

"You warm enough for a drink yet?" Trick asked opening the fridge.

"I could go for a Mountain Dew," Kenny replied.

Trick grabbed two drinks and shut the refrigerator door. He tossed one to Kenny as he scrambled back to his feet. Once standing, he took the pool cue in hand and went back to the table. Kenny opened the can and took a drink.

"So, you just didn't go to the party tonight I take it?" Trick asked.

"What?" Kenny replied startled by the question.

Trick repeated himself. "You didn't go to the party tonight? You said you normally go for a while."

"No," Kenny replied, "I guess I lost track of time."

"Yeah, staring at the lake will do that to ya."

Kenny shrugged off Trick's comment and grabbed a pool cue of his own. As Trick circled the table, Kenny challenged him to a game.

"Let's play."

"I racked 'em so I get to break 'em," Trick stipulated.

Kenny agreed, and Trick took his position at the front of the table. While he waited, Kenny grabbed a piece of chalk and scraped it across the tip of his cue. Once he coated it to his satisfaction, Kenny tossed the chalk aside and stood next to the table. Trick was carefully placing the cue ball on the table and lining up his break. It was always amazing to Kenny how seriously Trick took even a friendly game.

"Have you been here all night?" Kenny asked.

"As always," Trick replied with a casual smile. A second later, he struck the cue ball, sending it flying across the table into the pyramid of balls. The thundering crack of the break echoed briefly before dying out.

"You should go to the games," Kenny suggested as he surveyed the damage.

"Every week you tell me this," Trick said seeing he got a ball in on the break. "Every week I ignore you."

"Oh, but we killed the Falcons," Kenny informed while awaiting his turn.

"Yeah, I know. I saw the report on the news," Trick said shooting and missing. "I didn't know you could get good reception out at the lake."

Kenny examined the table for his shot. "I listened to the game at work."

"I'm sure your boss was happy about that."

"He was listening, too," Kenny said.

"He does have a kid on the team," Trick remembered. "And it is a good team."

"You bet it is and this year we're gonna win state." Kenny proclaimed while taking his next shot. It missed badly and Trick just laughed.

"Let's hope that's not an omen. What makes you say we're gonna win?"

"It's our senior year, we have to win."

"Oh, please," moaned Trick as he made his next shot. "That is the lamest reason I've ever heard. As if one thing could have anything to do with the other."

"Well, if you're not gonna go to the games, then you should at least go to the party afterwards."

"I do just fine here," Trick assured him, knocking in another ball.

"Come on," Kenny pleaded grabbing the cue ball off the table. Trick rolled his eyes, upset that Kenny interrupted the game. Perhaps more upset that Kenny wouldn't drop such a worn out discussion. "Think about it, five hours of playing pool by yourself or a party that goes all night long while you're surrounded by beautiful girls."

Trick sauntered over to Kenny and yanked the cue ball from his grip. "A: I happen to like playing pool and B: while your idea sounds good in theory, the odds that I'd just end up sitting by myself are astronomical." Trick purposefully turned his back and returned to the table. He put the ball back on its spot and took a shot. Kenny wasn't about to let the discussion die there.

"Well, I could change all of that," Kenny offered.

Before Trick could shoot, he had to drop his head and laugh. Once he composed himself, he sarcastically remarked. "Alright! With your unbelievable track record, I've got nothing to worry about."

"What does that mean?" Kenny asked defensively.

"What do you think it means?" Trick asked. "You haven't been on a date in three years."

Kenny lined up his shot and knocked it in. "You haven't been on a date in your entire life. Now what do ya gotta say?"

Trick didn't say anything for a minute, just waited for Kenny to miss a shot and then chalked up for his next run. A very sly smile creeping across his face as he approached the table, he ran the barrel of the cue up and down in his circled fingers a few times before he voiced his carefully crafted reply.

"While I do understand how bringing up my track record in the realm of dating would make sense at this juncture, I must inform you that your attempt to tear down my self-esteem based on that fact has failed miserably because I feel no ill sentiment towards that truth. Rather, I acknowledge that to this point, it has been a voluntary choice to remain single and not venture to that aspect of life. So it's not that I've failed, I just haven't tried."

After saying his peace, Trick took his cue and ran the table, knocking in every one of his balls left on the table. After finishing off the eight-ball, he pocketed the rest of Kenny's balls just to show off. As soon as the last ball had fallen, Trick flipped the cue down on the table and strutted from the table to one of the recliners. Eyes intensely focused on Kenny, Trick snagged his pop and took a long sip of Mountain Dew.

"Rack 'em," was all he said.

Kenny grinned; though he admired Trick's ability, he despised being on the receiving end. "I hate it when you do that!"

He grabbed the rack and dropped it on the table. Still undaunted by Trick's vigorous defense, he started to pull the balls out of the pockets and align them properly. Trick sat serenely in his chair, the smile still gleaming on his face. While Kenny knew to save the conversation for a later date, he still had one avenue to explore.

"So, have you thought about trying to get a date for prom?"

"No, not really," Trick replied.

"Oh, come on," Kenny whined. "It's the biggest dance of high school."

"I've already missed all the little ones; it seems appropriate to miss the big one, too."

Kenny finished preparing the table and set the rack aside. Trick popped up from his seat and sauntered over to the table.

"Just trust me;" Kenny said with certainty, "you'll end up at prom this year."

"Sure," Trick replied sarcastically. "You and me will be on a double date."

"You never know, man," Kenny said with stern sincerity on his face. "It's amazing how quickly things change."

Trick gave Kenny a peculiar look and then broke for the next game. Over the next hour, they shot several games of pool and drank close to a case of pop. Kenny decided to stay the night given the late hour. No one else was home with Trick, so he appreciated the company. After they had exhausted all points of discussion and Kenny had had his fill of pool, they decided to watch a movie or two inside the house.

In the living room, they curled up on the floor in front of the TV. Trick popped some popcorn and put in the first movie. By five, they were rather tired, but neither could sleep because of the large doses of caffeine. Hoping that it would lull them to sleep, Trick threw in another movie. When it ended and both were still awake, they noticed the sun had risen. With the sun up, they agreed sleep would be impossible now.

About nine in the morning, Kenny conceded that he needed to be getting home. Trick stopped by the garage and grabbed Kenny's now dried clothes. Before going home, Kenny invited Trick out to breakfast to which Trick was happy to oblige. At the IHOP, the two talked more about school and whatever else was happening in their lives. When they finished, Kenny headed home and so did Trick. And while he knew he wouldn't have anything exciting to do this weekend, Trick couldn't begin to imagine everything that was going to happen once he got to school on Monday.

Chapter Two

The Rumor Starts

One of the biggest draws the city of Derby had was that it was home to the largest high school in the state. Standing two stories tall, the building encompassed over twenty-five thousand square feet and held an enrollment of over two thousand for grades nine through twelve. There were two parking lots on opposite sides of the building both on a hill so the main floor was actually the second level. The smaller of the two was strictly for faculty parking while the other was for students and visitors. Each parking lot funneled down to a set of double doors to enter the building.

All of these doors opened into the commons area, and the rest of the school branched out from there. From the student entrance, the administrative offices stretched along the right side wall. A hallway led down to the gyms and P.E. rooms from there. Another hallway split off from the commons to an adjacent building where the art rooms, drama rooms, and journalism hall were located.

To the left, a maze of interconnected hallways wrapped around the school with classrooms and lockers adorning the walls. The farthest hall led back out to the commons next to the faculty entrance. Downstairs, the halls held an identical pattern to the upper level. The only difference was the school library in the back room.

Given the size of the school, it would normally take some time for gossip to spread through its halls, but the events that transpired on Friday were anything but normal.

The rumors regarding that night shot through the school like wildfire. The only thing more amazing than the speed with which the rumors spread was the variety of stories going around. If five people questioned five students about that night, there might be five different stories.

For his part, Kenny remained oblivious to all of these rumors. Most of the reason for that revolved around his crucial involvement in the tales. Unbeknownst to him, Trick had mentioned their encounter to Katie who told Trick all about what had happened to Maggie. While not of all the pieces added up, it was enough for Katie to draw certain conclusions about why Kenny was really soaked. And now Kenny was about to get a crash course to those rumors.

"Hey, Kenny," Darren exclaimed slapping Kenny on the back.

"How's it going, Darren?" Kenny asked.

"Oh, I'm doing pretty good," responded Darren coyly. "Hey, I heard about Friday night, man. That's pretty cool for you."

A bit defensive, Kenny would only ask. "What are you talking about?"

Darren smiled. "Oh, like you don't know."

"No, I don't."

Darren rolled his eyes and chuckled. "Whatever…I'll see ya later, man."

Kenny stopped in the middle of the hallway and watched as Darren left waving a hand at him in disbelief. As Kenny stood there, still confused and concern mounting in his mind, his friends Danny and Avery passed him in the hall. As soon as Danny saw Kenny, he stopped dramatically in the hall, clutched his chest, and started singing.

"There goes my hero!"

"There he is, indeed," added Avery clapping for him. "Way to be, Kenny!"

As Danny and Avery continued their way down the hall, all Kenny could do was shake his head and continue on his own way. About that time, Trick came up from behind him and smacked him on the back. Normally not bothered by the physical nature of the salutation, Kenny couldn't take much more after his odd exchange only a few moments ago. For Trick's sake, Kenny buried the umbrage and forced a quick smile; surely, Trick would have answers for this odd turn of events.

"What's up?" Trick asked.

"Have you noticed anything strange going on lately?" Kenny asked.

"Define 'strange'."

No sooner had Trick finished his question when a group of girls came walking down the hall giggling and laughing at Kenny. Whenever Kenny made eye contact with them, they'd avert their eyes and laugh even harder. The closer they got, the more they laughed and whispered to each other. Finally, one of them, Sabrina, walked right up to Kenny and ran a finger up his chest.

"Hey, Kenny," she said stepping in between him and Trick. "Would you save me if I was in trouble?"

"I'm sure he would, Sabrina," Angela interjected. "He just needs a new mask first."

Sabrina and Angela walked on by and the rest of the girls burst out in laughter as they continued walking. Trick, now fully understanding what he was dealing with, could only scratch his head and draw in a deep breath in uneasiness. With a frown and a deep sigh, Kenny turned to Trick and held out an arm to put his argument on display.

"Consider 'strange' defined," Kenny stated.

"Geez," Trick muttered, ignoring Kenny's question, "ya tell a person to keep something on the down low and just look at what happens."

"That's not helping," said Kenny, trying to get back on topic.

"Just trust me on this." Trick went on like Kenny knew what he was talking about. "Never go into a confidentiality agreement with a girl on a subject as hot as this."

Kenny's interest peaked. "And what subject would this be?"

Trick sensed the hostility building in Kenny's voice and wanted things to be calm before he explained everything he knew. "Okay, just bear with me and you'll see how this all fits together."

"Okay," Kenny agreed, now saying anything to get to the answer. "Start explaining."

Trick played it coy. "Just give me a second."

Kenny's patience was running thin. "No, just start talking."

"I will," Trick assured him, "calm down."

"I am calm!"

Trick paused for a second while Kenny took a deep breath to appease Trick's anxiety. He could tell by now that whatever Trick had to say, he wasn't going to like it. Trick knew as much, too, but also knew he had to say whatever information he had. Finally, Trick gave in and told Kenny the truth. He began very calmly.

"Well, it has to do with the Smith's party and my house."

Kenny wasn't happy with the direction things were going and interrupted. "I don't get it."

Trick held up his hands to calm Kenny down. "I'm getting there, just cool your jets. Well, I'm guessing you wanted to keep this whole thing a secret...."

"What thing?" Kenny asked not following.

"Yeah, like you haven't figured that out by now," Trick replied, not believing Kenny couldn't follow. "Anyway, I stumbled on to your little secret. See, this morning, I was in the editing room with Katie, and she was going on and on about what had happened to Maggie at the Smith's place on Friday...."

"What happened to Maggie on Friday?" Kenny asked.

"Oh, you're classic," Trick chuckled. "I'll play along. It all went down at the party after the game. Maggie and Eric decided they'd go out by the lake and spend some time alone on the pier. As they're running out there, Maggie slips on the ice, bangs her head on the pier, and falls into the lake completely knocked out."

"Did Eric get her?" Kenny asked with concern.

"No, he slipped on some ice, too."

"So what happened, who got her?"

"Some mystery man in all black wearing a ski mask comes out of nowhere, dives in the lake, and saves her. So now, Maggie doesn't know who saved her, but she has part of the ski mask that the guy was wearing. She's also very interested in finding him for reasons that are unbeknownst to just about all of us."

Trick finished his explanation to allow Kenny to piece together the rest from there. However, Kenny couldn't quite connect the dots. "So, what does this have to do with me?" Kenny asked confused. "Is the mask my size or something?"

Trick raised an eyebrow at the notion. "A wool knit ski mask; it would not surprise me if it somehow fit your head," he said sarcastically. "No, see I remembered that on Friday a certain someone showed up at my door dripping wet from as he said 'falling in a lake.' So, I tell Katie about you, and she kinda derived her own conclusion from there. I told her to keep it just between the two of us for the time being, but you've seen for yourself how well that went."

Kenny's expression had gone from curiosity to anger to despair while Trick told his story. "How could you do that?" Kenny asked with his head in his hands.

"What? It was nothing," Trick assured him.

"Nothing!" Kenny exclaimed. "I told you I was over at Miller's lake, not Smith's lake."

"Yeah, I remember that," Trick said plainly. "Then I started thinking about it and it didn't make a whole lot of sense. Katie just decided that it was just a cover story and a pretty bad one too. I'd have defended the story, but I really didn't believe it."

"But I really did fall into Miller's lake, and that is something that you can't disprove." Kenny affirmed.

"True," Trick agreed with a smile, "but I could make a pretty good case against you."

"How so?" Kenny asked with both interest and concern.

"Well, for starters," Trick began, "you showed up at my house a little after twelve-thirty. As the story goes, Maggie fell in the lake just before midnight. So, let's say you leave the lake at about five after. That still gives you a good half-hour to get from the Smith's to my house; which, for you, would be plenty of time."

"What makes you so sure that I could run four miles in less than a half-hour?" Kenny asked thinking he had found a flaw in Trick's explanation.

Trick offered his rebuttal, "Well, you do run cross-country."

"Yeah, it's still like four miles," Kenny argued.

"Even so, I'm pretty sure you could easily do three miles in under twenty minutes. That gives you a two minute rest and another mile to run in ten minutes," Trick explained. "Plus, you're freezing cold from the icy water and that is going to keep the legs pumping on a cold night. Heck, I'll give you a five minute break and you'd still show up at about the right time."

Kenny conceded the point. "Okay, maybe you've got me there, but there isn't one person at that party that can say that they ever saw me there that night."

"And that's supposed to cement your alibi?" Trick asked in disbelief. "Come on, you were wearing a ski mask while dressed in black; you're not gonna go inside to hang out with the partygoers. Chances are you were hanging out outside the entire time—sneaking around in the trees and such. And, to be completely honest, the whole stalking around the woods is moderately creepy in and of itself."

"Okay, that really doesn't make any sense," Kenny said in his defense. "Why would I be sneaking around outside of the Smith's house for more than two hours?"

"Oh, sure," Trick said derisively, "and the whole idea of being at Miller's lake at midnight on a Friday night makes all the sense in the world now, doesn't it?"

Kenny dropped his head and let out a sigh. With only minutes before the next bell rang, Kenny knew he couldn't get all the answers to the questions he still had regarding this strain of rumors. He counted himself lucky that he didn't have a class with Maggie today—that little face-to-face would happen soon enough. The more pressing matter then concerned the extent of the reach of the rumors.

"Okay," he said with his hand still on his head, "so there's this wild rumor going around school about how I supposedly saved Maggie's life and hid the truth from her for whatever reason. Exactly how many people, in your expert opinion, would you say know about this?"

Tapping a finger on his lips, Trick crunched the numbers in his head. "Well, let's look at this realistically."

"Yes, let's do that." Kenny concurred.

Trick summed up the particulars. "We're looking at a juicy rumor about someone who's widely considered one of the hottest girls in this school being saved by a mysterious stranger. Now, this stranger may be some weirdo who just walks around the woods at night under the cover of darkness, so that puts even more emphasis on the rescue. Add the fact that this took place while her boyfriend of many years failed to come to her aid, and then consider that the rumor only started this morning, known by two people. It is now one-twenty in the afternoon...."

Trick paused for a moment as Kenny grew impatient and barked, "And all that means what exactly, Sherlock?"

"It means that you're looking at seventy-five to eighty percent of the student body having knowledge of this rumor."

"Seventy-five to eighty percent!" Kenny exclaimed. "You've got to be kidding me!"

"The numbers don't lie."

"That's just great." Kenny said upset with this knowledge. "Maggie probably knows about the rumor already."

Trick attempted to alleviate Kenny's concerns by assuring him that Maggie won't know because it would ruin the rumor. If people loved a rumor, they especially loved one with some staying power; this rumor definitely had that. No one was going to broach the subject to Maggie, according to Trick, and for her to find out Kenny would have to address the issue directly. Since he wasn't about to do that, she would remain oblivious.

Kenny continued to voice his concern about Maggie finding out and him coming under scrutiny. Trick tried to think of a way to reassure Kenny that everything was going to be all right. Before he could think of anything, he glanced down the hallway and saw Maggie, Katie, and a few other girls walking towards them. When Maggie saw Trick, she waved at him and smiled. Trick slowly waved back and painted on a smile. He then nudged Kenny in the arm to warn him.

"Something tells me that you're gonna find out if she knows about the rumor pretty quick." Trick said, bracing himself for the confrontation.

"She's not." Kenny turned away pleading for Trick to be joking.

"She is," Trick replied dashing any hopes.

Kenny lost his nerve. "Is she coming up fast?"

Trick shrugged his shoulders. "She's walking," he replied bluntly.

"How fast?" Kenny asked trying to slow his doom.

"How am I supposed to know?"

"Just make a judgment call!"

"Oh, get out of here."

Kenny whipped around and faked a smile. His discomfort was noticeable to Trick, but the others didn't seem to pick up on it. Instead, they all kept walking while Maggie smiled and waved. As they got closer, Kenny grasped at the only legitimate chance he had to get out of this predicament.

"Maybe she'll just walk on by," Kenny whispered.

"Don't bet on it," Trick replied.

Just as Trick had guessed, Maggie stopped in front of them. The growing discomfort inside Kenny had grown to the point where he could no longer maintain motor functions. He just stood there making no movements with the forced smile still painted on his face. Trick, on the other hand, managed to compose himself and was pretty relaxed amid the tension.

"Hey, Kenny, how's it going?" Maggie asked.

At first, Kenny did not reply. Still standing there with the same expression on his face, Maggie and the other girls began to look at him very confused. After a roll of the eyes, Trick slowly swayed to the side and elbowed Kenny in the back, which jolted him back into coherence.

Kenny blurted out, "Oh, pretty good, I guess. How are you?"

Kenny's hurried response caused Trick to lean over and whisper, "Smooth!"

"Shut it." Kenny whispered back.

"I'm fine." Maggie replied looking at both of them with confusion.

Bothered by a short stint of silence, Kenny spoke up. "I heard about what happened on Friday," he stammered. "That's some pretty strange stuff."

"Yeah, no kidding," Maggie replied.

Kenny attempted to test the waters. "Any idea who the guy was?"

"No, I never saw his face," Maggie explained with disappointment. "I really wish I could've, though."

"Do you think you'll ever figure out who it was?" Kenny asked to keep her talking.

Maggie shrugged her shoulders. "I can't be sure either way about that, but I do think that it's someone I know…."

"You could say that," Trick muttered under his breath.

Though no one else heard Trick, Kenny responded instinctively by elbowing Trick in the side. Since Trick was unprepared for the shot, it did more damage than Kenny probably intended. Trick grimaced momentarily, fighting to mask his discomfort for Kenny's sake. Try as he might, Maggie caught a glimpse of the pained expression that crossed his face. Concerned, she looked over Kenny's shoulder to see what was wrong.

"Are you okay?" Maggie asked.

Trick quickly composed himself and stood up tall. "Of course," he wheezed.

Maggie shook her head. "Forget it. It's not likely that I'll ever see him again, so I doubt I'll find out who he really is."

Kenny sympathized though he felt relieved. "Well, that's how things go sometimes."

"Yeah, I guess so," Maggie agreed. After a short pause, she changed subjects. In two short days, it had quickly become habit for Maggie to engage everyone she came across in this particular line of questioning. "Hey, I don't remember seeing you at the party Friday. Don't you usually go?"

Trick coughed and rolled his eyes, "Here we go."

Kenny quickly responded to cover Trick's remark. "Oh, I had to work Friday. After I got off, I just went over to Trick's house to hang out since I knew he'd be alone." Kenny looked out of the corner of his eye to see Trick staring at him with an 'oh really' expression on his face. Maggie waited for Trick to say something, but when he didn't, she assumed he was agreeing with Kenny.

"Well, that is his typical MO, isn't it?" Maggie asked.

"Yeah, he would never admit it, but he likes the company," Kenny explained.

Trick looked at the two of them. "Standing right here, ya know?" he said.

Knowing that Kenny was lying about being with Trick right after work, Katie decided to poke a few holes in Kenny's explanation. Trick may have been okay with the lie, but Katie wasn't so accommodating. "With Trick all evening, huh, what did you guys do?"

Kenny's eyes got big as the unprovoked ambush caught him off guard. Realizing Katie's ploy, Trick answered before Kenny took the opportunity. "We were just playing pool, watched a movie, ya know, the usual guy stuff."

Kenny felt a weight lift off his shoulders as Trick provided a plausible backstory. Content for the moment, Katie relented. With a satisfied smile beaming, Katie stared at Trick, who glared right back at her. While the two engrossed themselves in their staring contest, Kenny provided further explanation to his change of plans.

"I was thinking of going to the party, but I didn't get off work until about ten. Knowing I'd have to go home and change, maybe even shower, I just said forget the whole party scene and went to hang out with Trick."

The mere mention of Trick's name vaulted him to the forefront of Maggie's thoughts. "Speaking of Trick," she said shifting the focus off Kenny, which he couldn't be more relieved about, "you weren't at the game or the party, either."

Not understanding the significance of the statement nor appreciating the sudden interest, Trick shrugged his shoulders. "Well, that's nothing new; I never go to the games—or the parties, for that matter."

"That wouldn't be stretching the truth a little would it?" Katie asked, letting her inquisitive nature continue to shine. Normally, she wouldn't take such an interest, but she wanted to remind Trick that she knew he wasn't being entirely honest with Maggie.

Understanding the game she was playing, Trick stared down Katie again, seemingly warning her with his eyes to back off. "Have you ever seen me there?"

Katie continued to play her part. "No."

"Well, there ya go."

Maggie glanced up at the clock and noticed they only had seconds left before the bell rang. "Okay, we gotta get going," she said. "See you guys later."

"See ya," Trick said.

"Ya, bye," Kenny said, glad it was over. For the first time since the conversation started, a genuine smile crept across his face. "Hope you find your mystery man!" he called out.

Maggie laughed. "Thanks, Kenny."

Maggie walked on ahead, but Katie lingered to have a brief word with Trick. He eyed her as she approached him with a sly smile stretched across her face the entire time. She was quite pleased with the way she almost tripped Kenny up.

"That was interesting," Katie commented innocently.

"Yeah, thanks for respecting the whole privacy thing we worked out earlier," Trick said. "It's nice to know who's standing on your side."

"This has nothing to do with you, and you know it. This is all about him, his lies, and his secrets."

"Yeah, well, you didn't have to let a rumor get this out of control," Trick replied, still a little perturbed by her actions.

Katie was quick to defend herself. "That is not my fault."

"No, of course not, why would it be?" Trick asked sarcastically. "It must have been everyone else who was in the editing room we told. Ya know, when it was just the two of us."

Trick got a little liberal with the volume of his voice, which startled Katie somewhat. "Well, at least she doesn't know about it," she whispered.

"Are you sure about that?"

"We'll talk more in class," Katie promised.

Trick watched as Katie trotted towards class, taunting him all the way. As Trick turned to talk to Kenny again, he almost ran into Ashley who had stepped in front of him. His sudden halt caused his backpack to fly off his shoulder, which Ashley found amusing. He quickly readjusted himself before facing up to her.

"Ya know, Trick, it's a shame you don't go to the parties every once and a while," she said. "It would give us a chance to hang out more."

Before he could say anything in reply, Ashley said goodbye and took off down the hall. As she walked away, Trick stared at her for a few seconds with a furrowed brow slightly confused by her remark. Normally, the two of them didn't converse that often and when they did, it dealt mostly with homework of some sort. He had never really done it before, but now he couldn't help but notice her. Her smile was electric and her adorable figure almost danced with his eyes as she walked away. Once he regained himself, he looked over at Kenny, who wasn't happy.

"What?" Trick asked.

"You know what," replied Kenny, not the least bit pleased with Trick's actions.

"Oh, I was joking around," Trick assured him. "She's none the wiser and besides, I went along with your alibi."

Kenny was still uneasy. "I don't care. Don't do that kinda stuff!" Kenny looked down the hall at the rapidly vanishing crowd of girls. He stared at Maggie for a second, but when Ashley happened to cross his eye-line, he changed subjects. "And by the way, what I just witnessed from you was truly pathetic."

"Hey, don't call me pathetic!" Trick snapped back. "You're the one sneaking around in the woods, wearing ski masks, saving people, and then not telling them. Also, I don't know what you're talking about."

Kenny rolled his eyes, amazed at his friend's inept ability to understand the opposite sex. "Oh, come on!" Kenny groaned. "Ashley! Did you just hear what she said?"

Trick blew it off. "So what? That doesn't mean anything."

"Dude," Kenny said putting a hand on Trick's shoulder, "she wants you."

Trick scoffed at the absurdity of such an idea. She was far too pretty for the likes of him. "Oh, she does not."

"Yes, she does."

"Come on, that didn't even count as flirting."

"Yes, it did; she said that she wanted you to go to the parties so the two of you could hang out more. Ask her out already."

Trick attempted to break away from the discussion, suddenly finding himself very uncomfortable with the way the conversation had turned. "You're reading too much into this." Trick started down the hall for class, knowing he was already late. Kenny quickly obstructed his path, not ready to let this idea die.

"What's wrong, man?" Kenny asked in astonishment. "Do you think she's ugly or spoiled or something?"

Trick quickly retorted. "Of course not, she's obviously gorgeous and a really nice girl, down to earth and stuff, but why should I get so excited over what she just said?"

"It's not what she said," Kenny attempted to explain. "It's how she said it."

"Oh, yeah, that makes perfect sense," Trick said mockingly. "Do you even hear what you're saying?"

Trick tried to escape again, but Kenny was unrelenting. Kenny knew that as smart as Trick was, he knew very little about this particular area. "Yes, I hear what I'm saying, and I know what I'm hearing from her which is that she wants to be with you."

"Well, apparently I'm not hearing what you're hearing."

"Well, apparently you're deaf."

Desperate to get off the subject and on with his life, Trick shook his head and asked. "Why are we even talking about this?"

"What are we supposed to be talking about?" Kenny asked.

"Well, it's obvious that Maggie doesn't know about the rumor. Doesn't that make you a little happy?"

Reluctantly, Kenny dropped the subject about Ashley since he knew there was nothing he could say at this point to make Trick come around. Focusing on the big picture, he was very relieved to know that Maggie was still out of the loop.

"I'm ecstatic," Kenny admitted.

Trick nodded in acknowledgment, and the two started to walk for class. Soon after they finished discussing their matters, the bells rang to signal that they were late for class. Echoing throughout the halls, the closing of doors further hastened Trick and Kenny to get to class. Resolved to let this rest for the time being, they parted ways, but not before Trick made one final request to Kenny.

"Promise me one thing?" Trick pleaded.

"Anything."

"Come up with a more believable alibi for those of us who know about the rumor. I mean anything…throw in a UFO or a werewolf…anything would be more believable than the story you're pitching now."

Kenny couldn't help but smile at the notion. Putting up a hand as his solemn vow he replied, "I'll come up with something."

Trick smiled and then hurried through the hall to his class. As he approached the closed door, he saw Mr. Hamblin lecturing at the front of the classroom. Slowly and quietly, Trick opened the door and crept in so as to not disturb anyone. As he shut the door, a slight squeak of its hinges alerted Mr. Hamblin to Trick's tardiness. Trick threw an apologetic look on his face, which Mr. Hamblin accepted. Without a word, he motioned for Trick to hurry up and find his seat. Trick weaved through the rows and took his seat in the back of the room. No sooner had he sat down than Katie, who sat in front of him, turned around to talk to him.

"I was beginning to worry about you," Katie said with a false sense of distress.

"Your concern is duly noted," Trick replied.

"Why did you tell Kenny we know?" Katie whispered in disappointment.

"He deserved to know," whispered Trick. "Besides, we don't know anything for sure, and everybody else seems to know about it."

Katie defended herself. "Hey, I couldn't keep it quiet."

"Yeah, I'm sure someone had to torture you to get it out of you."

"I'm sorry."

Trick grabbed his notebook and textbook from his bag, placing them on his desk. Katie kindly turned his book to the right page and gave him a sheet of notes to copy. As Trick caught up, he assessed the damage the rumor already caused.

"Maggie doesn't know, right?" Trick asked.

"Of course not," Katie replied callously.

Trick didn't appreciate the tone. "Well, maybe what she said in the hallway was just an act—what do I know?"

"She really doesn't know." Katie assured him.

"What about Eric?" Trick asked.

"He's clueless, too."

Mr. Hamblin heard the two of them talking and stopped his lecture momentarily. Unsure where the disturbance had been coming from, he took Katie's turning around as proof enough they were the culprits.

"Katie," Mr. Hamblin said. "Would you mind telling me what is so important that you have to interrupt the class?"

"Sorry, Mr. Hamblin," Katie said turning around. "I was just trying to get Trick caught up with us."

"Well, that's fine—maybe do it a little quieter?" Mr. Hamblin suggested.

Trick scribbled out the notes to appease their teacher. Katie was amazed Trick could make anything out of the chicken scratches he put on his paper. With Mr. Hamblin's comfort with the discipline of the room restored, the lecture recommenced. Katie, still needing the answers to certain questions, waited a minute or two to make sure no one was paying attention. Slowly, she turned around in her chair and leaned back as far as she comfortably could.

"So what did Kenny say?"

"He's sticking with the Miller's lake story." Trick replied.

"Do you believe him?" Katie asked.

Trick sighed. "I don't know. I don't think he'd lie to me but going to a lake to hang out...that doesn't make any sense, either."

"No kidding. He went to the lake to 'kill time.'" Katie said mocking the whole story. "Nobody does anything like that. He's definitely the guy."

"I don't know," Trick replied skeptically. "The whole situation is just too weird."

Katie agreed with that sentiment as Trick returned her notes. Now caught up with the rest of the class, Trick hoped Katie would let the subject go for the time being. Aside from the discomfort the subject brought, he had another train of thought rushing through his head. He doubted that Katie could be much help, mostly because he didn't believe what Kenny had told him, but if there was something to this, Katie might know.

"If I asked her, do you think Ashley would go out with me?" Trick whispered.

"Are you kidding? It would make her year," Katie admitted candidly.

"Really?" Trick said, blown away by this revelation.

Katie replied as if this information was a matter of public record. "Yeah, she's been waiting for you to get a clue for like a year now." Then the implausible thought dawned on her. "You haven't noticed, have you?"

"Not really," Trick confessed.

"Come on, I mean that explains a lot, but she flirts with you all the time."

"I didn't know it was anything serious," Trick said in his defense. "I figured it was just some harmless fun."

Katie chuckled. "Girls don't act like that around every single guy they know."

"Some do."

Katie conceded the point. "Well, not her." Trick was content with that information, but Katie's curiosity took over. "Why are you even asking me about this?"

"No reason…really," Trick stumbled to think of how to brush this off. "Kenny said something about it; I thought he was wrong and just wanted a second, more reliable, opinion."

Katie laid it out in plain English. "Well, he wasn't and me saying that she likes you is not an opinion; it's a fact."

Trick paused for a minute trying to take in all that Katie's told him.

"So are you gonna ask her out?" Katie asked with a smile.

Trick's discomfort was taking center stage. "I don't know."

"Just go to the game on Friday, maybe the party," Katie suggested. "She just wants to see more of you is all."

Trick mulled over everything that Kenny had told him which Katie augmented. He wasn't one-hundred percent assured of their expertise on the matter, but they wouldn't lie to him on a whim either. Nevertheless, for the time being, he had to let the thought go and focus on what was going on in class. He was already far behind and needed to catch up. That seemed to be a recurring theme for him lately.

Chapter Three

Gotta Find Him

When class let out, Trick parted ways with Katie after both vowed to keep the other apprised of any new occurrences. Trick would then stop off at his locker before heading home for the day. Quite a lot had happened considering it was only a Monday. Oddly, none of it was that good...or bad. True, it probably would have been better had the rumor not spread throughout the entire school, but Kenny now knew whereas Maggie and Eric did not. In addition, it was a delightful revelation to hear of Ashley's interest in him, but Trick did not know how he would or wanted to proceed.

All the thoughts rushing through his head about Kenny, Maggie, and now Ashley, made the ten minute drive home seem no longer than a blink on his eyes. Happy to be home and done with all the uncomfortable moments of the day, Trick grabbed the mail, seeing what had come as he sauntered up the driveway past the basketball goal. He knew his dad wouldn't be home, so he had the house all to himself.

Trick's dad, Roy, purchased the land they lived on and paid to have the house constructed months before Trick was born. Valuing his privacy, Roy moved his family outside of town and then fenced in their quaint two-acre property. The design of the house was the brainchild of Roy and Trick's departed mother, Lilly. Several other families would eventually purchase land and build around them, including Maggie's, but Roy fondly remembered the times when they were all alone out there. The house's cream paint made it stand out among the surrounding trees. It was a simple, unassuming home, vaguely reminiscent of an old farmhouse despite some modernized upgrades. The garage in which Trick spent so much time was detached from the main house with a consistent color scheme.

Inside the house, just beyond the front door, was a simple welcome area with a table that had a phone in the back corner. A winding staircase led to the second floor where all the bedrooms were. Underneath the staircase was a doorway to Roy's office, which also served as a den when the family entertained. For the most part, Trick stayed out of that room. On the other side was the living room with couches, chairs, and an entertainment center. Beyond it laid a formal dining room and the kitchen. When he walked into the house, he set the mail on the table and punched the play button on the answering machine. He hadn't seen the blinking light on the small screen but he knew there'd be a message.

"Hey, son." It was Roy. "Looks like I'm not gonna make it home tonight like I thought. The meetings are going longer than expected. That's a real downer because these things are boring like you wouldn't believe. Anyway, you're on your own for tonight and probably tomorrow if things keep up like this. But don't be too worried, I'll be home, at the latest, on Wednesday night, and it's not like you haven't had to spend a few days on your own before. I hope I can be home sooner. Love ya, kid."

Trick erased the message with a sigh. Picking up a small book of coupons, he began sifting through his dinner options as he uttered. "Well, I wonder what I should do for dinner tonight: leftovers, burgers, tacos possibly...."

With all of his attention on the message, Trick didn't realize that the front door was still open. He also didn't realize that Maggie had walked up the driveway and was standing in the doorway. "How about some pizza?" she asked while walking in.

Despite the surprise, Trick was unfazed, almost like he expected her to be there. "I don't know," he replied, "I had pizza for lunch, and don't you have a home cooked meal waiting for you at home?"

"In theory, yes," Maggie explained, "but I told my mom I'd be eating out tonight, so I don't think she's planning on me being there."

Trick had an idea what was about to happen, but he wanted to joke a little before the mood changed drastically. "Still, I don't know about this pizza idea."

Maggie, either, wasn't in the joking mood or was too distracted to notice Trick's subtle humor. "Well, whatever...just pick something and I'll be fine."

Quite uncharacteristically, Trick misjudged the current temperament of the room. Having hoped for some light-hearted banter, he soon realized things were going to get serious rather quickly. Since he was on a page of coupons for pizza, Trick set aside his disdain for the idea, ripped the page out of the book, and grabbed the phone.

"I take it this is more than a social call," Trick said.

Maggie shrugged her shoulders. "Maybe, if you're up for a little ranting."

Trick smiled. "I always am."

Maggie took a step in the living room and sat down on one of the chairs. Trick patiently waited on the phone for someone to pick up at the restaurant. Hoping to distract herself more than anything, Maggie gazed around the oh-so-familiar walls of Trick's house. A picture of Trick's family from the time his mom was alive hung above the marble fireplace at the back of the room. They were such a happy family; Maggie could remember them well. She had a plethora of memories about Lilly from the time she was younger. Lilly would always listen to her when she talked, sometimes more than Maggie's own mother could stand to. Maggie loved that about her and loved even more that that trait had passed on to her son.

"Delivery please...." Trick said on the phone. "I got a coupon for two mediums...let's make one pepperoni and the other beef...I'll hold..."

Maggie snapped out of her thoughts. "I thought you weren't sure about pizza."

Trick grunted. "Please, I went a whole week on pizza once...dad's idea, oddly enough."

"I just don't wanna be a bother."

Trick rolled his eyes. "You never have been before; you never will be. Go ahead and make yourself comfortable upstairs, I'll only be a minute."

Maggie smiled and then trotted up the staircase to his room. Trick got the total for the food and the ETA for the delivery. Before joining Maggie upstairs, he counted out the money and tip for the pizza.

On the way up the stairs, he reviewed all that had transpired that day between him, Kenny, and Katie. He had already decided he did not want to tell Maggie about Kenny, not because he felt pressure from everyone else to keep the secret from her, but because he didn't know how she'd react to such a notion. He needed to figure out more of the details before he made any moves.

Maggie had left the door to his room open. Not attempting to sneak in, he went unnoticed by Maggie as he entered and sprawled out on his bed next to the door. Across the room sitting at his desk was Maggie browsing the internet on his computer. Waiting for her to get the conversation started, Trick looked at the junk in his room. All his video game gear lay strewn about the floor by the TV. His movies and books sat slanted in their rows, some almost falling off the shelf. He dared not look at his closet, fearing the atrocity it held. Suddenly, he really regretted not cleaning up over the weekend. After a few minutes, Trick couldn't think about the room anymore and focused on Maggie.

"So, how shall we get started?" he asked.

Maggie jumped. "Oh, okay," she replied slightly startled. "Well, I'm sure that you've heard the stories about what happened on Friday night."

Trick was adamant about keeping things relaxed. "Yeah, nothing more than a typical Friday night life saving."

"Well, there's more to it than that," Maggie confessed.

"What do you mean?" Trick asked.

Maggie paused for a second and swung the chair around away from Trick. She stalled momentarily by pulling on a thread on her shirt and breaking it off. After a deep breath and sigh, she turned back towards Trick though she averted her eyes still. She was about to tell him what only she and the boy from Friday knew. All the things she had been too afraid to tell Eric or Katie were about to come out again. She wasn't sure how she'd react after she rustled up all those thoughts nor was she one-hundred percent certain she wanted to say anything. Of course, this was different; she could tell Trick anything.

For his part, Trick could feel the tension building like a dense fog as he sat hopelessly trying to think of a way to make this easier for her. But he knew he would have to wait until she was ready.

"It's just that...." Maggie's voice broke—a sign that this would be harder than imagined.

Trick tried to get her to continue. "What is it?"

Maggie forced the words out. "I told Eric that I didn't talk to the guy who pulled me out of the lake...."

Trick couldn't help himself from stating the obvious. "And you did?"

Maggie shuffled around in the chair before answering. "I did," she replied trying to fight her anxiety. "I did talk to him, and I'm certain that I know him."

Again, Maggie paused before she continued. She stared intently at the ground so that Trick couldn't see the distress on her face. Beginning to feel a pinch of anxiety himself, Trick sat up on the bed. It felt like this whole issue would blow up in a matter of moments. If she remembered his voice, Maggie probably had identified him already.

"He said that he might tell me someday who he is," Maggie finally blurted out. "That means that he's still around somewhere."

Trick's heart began to slow down as he realized that Maggie hadn't put a name to her suspicions. His concerns dropping, Trick kept her talking.

"Well, that's a good thing isn't it?"

Maggie shot up from the chair and paced around the room. She stopped at the window and looked out across the street at her house. She didn't want to be here anymore. There was more to tell, but it was the hardest part.

It was the part that made the least amount of sense. This guy, this self-proclaimed Guardian Angel, loved her? He loved her but hid behind a mask? He said what he said and then just disappeared? It was aggravating, infuriating in a way. There had to be some kind of logic to this, but she couldn't figure it out on her own. Hopefully, Trick could.

"There's more."

Trick perked his ears, the concern escalating again. "I'm listening."

Maggie opened her mouth to speak, but the words didn't come. She wasn't ready for this; she couldn't explain now. She still hadn't totally grasped the concept herself. If that was the case, then how could Trick possibly understand?

Trick tried to help her along. "Maggie, what is it?"

Rather than answer the question, Maggie ranted. "It's someone I know, but I don't get how they could do this to me. They saved my life on the one hand and created a world of confusion in the other."

At that point, Trick realized that if he was going to get to the point, he had to force the issue. "Normally, I hate to throw accusations around, but this feels like a good time for it. I'm getting a feeling that this mystery man said something else...something that's really gotten you spooked."

Maggie turned and faced Trick. He was zeroing in on the truth, but she still wanted this to be secret. She almost resented Trick at this point. "He said something, but it's not that big of a deal," Maggie assured him. "It wouldn't mean more than anything else that he said."

Trick sighed before continuing. "Maybe…why don't you tell me what it was and I'll give you a second opinion."

"Maybe I don't need your opinion about this."

"Hey, you came to me, you obviously need something."

Maggie glared at Trick momentarily. As animosity spewed from her eyes, she began to feel a swell of despair come over her. Slowly, the look in her eyes softened, and tears began to form. As her heart beat with a rapid pace, her breathing became heavier. She could see a look of terror quickly appearing on Trick's face. Her next words leaked out only to alleviate his concern.

"He told me he loved me."

Trick couldn't reply. Hearing the words only deepened Maggie's distress as she dropped down on the bed, tears hanging in her eyes. Trying to be the slightest of help, Trick sat down next to her and wrapped an arm around her.

"He told me he loved me," Maggie repeated. "He had his arms around me; I was shivering and freezing cold realizing how close I had been to dying. Then he left me—disappearing into the woods. I yelled for him, asking if I would ever see him again. That's when he said he might tell me who he is. I asked him what I was supposed to do until then. That's when he said it: 'Just know that I love you, that's all you need to know.'"

Maggie nestled her head on Trick's chest underneath his soothing arm. Trick was still too flustered to say anything that could be of help. At this point, he didn't know what to think regarding Maggie, the rumor, or Kenny. Luckily, he didn't need to say anything before Maggie got talking again.

"Ever since I heard him say that, I've been thinking about who it could be and I can't come up with anyone."

Trick just blurted out a simple question, "No one, huh?"

Maggie attempted to alleviate the tension. "Well, there's you."

Trick gave her a strange look that made Maggie laugh. She was delighted to be laughing at this point.

"I know, I know," Maggie replied as she sat up. "That doesn't make any sense because you never leave your garage on Friday nights."

Trick felt obligated to defend himself. "That's not entirely accurate."

Maggie chuckled again. "When I think of who might have done this, guys like David, Ricky, Jimmy, Jordan, and even Scott, none of them make any sense. Of course, all those guys were at the party. Then I think about someone like Kenny…." Trick tensed up when he heard Kenny's name. "…and he was with you all night so it's not like he could have done it."

Trick suddenly hated himself for going along with Kenny's story. He loathed lying like this, especially now that he grasped the gravity of the situation. Yet at the same time, he knew he couldn't throw Kenny under the bus while the guy was so vehemently denying the allegations.

"Why would someone be so afraid to tell me?" Maggie asked.

Trick had an answer for that. "Everybody's got secrets that they work hard to hide, Maggie. We can know someone for our entire lives, and they can still be hiding something from us. If they don't want us to know, they can usually keep it from us. The more precious they consider a secret, the harder they'll work to keep it hidden."

Trick paused for a moment, thinking about some of his own secrets. He, better than anyone, understood the concept. He looked at Maggie, who was mulling over what he had said. When she looked back at him, she saw a deep, almost frightened expression on his face. Unable to deal with the tension anymore, Maggie smiled and joked.

"So then it could be you?"

The smile broke Trick from his thought-filled trance. He smiled himself and winked. "Sure, it could be. What would you say to that?"

Maggie stood up from the bed. "I'd say you're crazier than I thought." Trick clutched his chest, joking that she had hurt his feelings. Maggie laughed some more before she continued. "It just doesn't make any sense...keeping it a secret."

Trick was surprised. "You really think so?"

"I take it you disagree."

"You could say that."

"Alright, convince me."

"Oh, okay, we got a guy who confesses that he loves you moments after saving your life. He does this with your boyfriend barely out of sight knowing that you are not going to leave this guy for him."

Maggie nodded almost as if she followed what Trick was saying and even agreed with him to an extent. However, it brought up another problem. "Then, why say anything at all?"

Trick shrugged his shoulders before admitting, "The male mind is a very odd place, Maggie. A guy realizes he's in love with someone else's girlfriend, he isn't about to step on someone else's toes just on a whim and a feeling. He's gonna need purpose, a solid reason for believing he's got a chance. At the same time, he doesn't want to go unnoticed entirely."

"So you're suggesting that maybe this guy said this to me so I'd remember him if Eric and I broke up?" Maggie asked. Trick nodded to which Maggie could only roll her eyes. "What's wrong with you, guys?"

"Whatever is 'wrong' with us," Trick replied, "you girls did it to us."

"That hardly seems fair."

"Fair or not, it's the truth."

Trick popped off the bed and sauntered over to his bookshelf. Having stared too long at the mess over there, he was determined to do something about it now. The atmosphere had returned to the lighter side, and Trick was content to keep it there. Dinner would arrive soon. They could finally relax after a stressful day. Maggie, however, had other things still rumbling around in her head.

"Should I tell Eric?" Maggie asked.

Trick eyed the books as he replied. "Some would say that he deserves to know."

"What do you say?"

"I say that it's up to you."

That was the one answer Maggie didn't want to hear. She was too uncertain about this situation and hoped Trick would be willing to provide some guidance. Honestly, though, his response did not exactly surprise her. Trick normally tried to keep a safe distance from any relationship questions Maggie posed. It was admirable really. For as much as Trick wanted to help her, he didn't want his bias to influence Maggie's actions. He wanted to stay the impartial observer, not for himself, but for her.

Still, Maggie needed to expand on her options. "I guess I could tell him and hope he doesn't see it as a threat."

Trick nodded. "Explain things properly and I'm sure he'll see it that way."

Maggie pressed on. "On the other hand, there's always a chance that he won't be able to let it go at that. He may want the answers like I do."

Trick wasn't sure where she was going with this. "And if that's the case?"

Maggie connected the dots. "It may actually be a good idea to just keep this under wraps and not tell him."

Trick sighed. "If that's your true intent then, yes…that may be the proper course of action."

"Why else would I do this?" Maggie asked.

Trick shrugged his shoulders, hoping to avoid venturing down that road.

A long period of silence followed. Maggie considered what Trick said, attempting to draw some sort of conclusion about all this. At the very minimum, she wanted to have a rational reason for all the mystery. For the time being, though, the most important thing seemed to be the fact that she could handle the situation as well as she was.

Trick tried to add everything up as well. As the only person who knew about the rumor and what happened out on the pier, he had several angles to consider. Most importantly, of course, was Maggie who seemed slightly obsessed with finding answers. On the surface, Kenny appeared to be an avenue to those answers, but Trick understood there were deeper issues at play. On the outside of all of this was Katie, who was sifting amongst the sand for any clues. All that didn't even take Eric into account. Whatever Trick would eventually say, he had to be careful to whomever he talked.

Normally, such silences would grow awkward and uncomfortable for two teens. However, Trick and Maggie were such good friends they enjoyed each other's company in any sense. To some degree, the silence was almost welcome. It gave them an opportunity to collect themselves after the soul bearing session they had just put themselves through. Eventually, Maggie joined Trick in reshelving the books. He had an odd collection for someone his age. On two of shelves, he had sports books, biographies, and memoirs from the past. Others were sports statistics which every boy that age memorized volumes of.

Another shelf held some light reading, novels for the younger generation, but not any great classics. Those were on another shelf. The top shelf was perhaps the most curious. Along with a copy of the King James Bible, Trick had an array of poetry anthologies including anything from Shakespeare to Frost. Maggie was about to ask him about them when the doorbell rang.

"That must be the pizza," Trick said, heading for the door.

Maggie grabbed at her pocket, but it was empty. Trick had listened to all her ranting, she wasn't about to just let him pay for this, too. "I'll pay ya back later."

"No, you won't," Trick said as he ran downstairs.

The doorbell rang again as Trick reached the door. With money in hand, Trick swapped with the delivery boy, leaving a generous tip. As Trick shut the door, Maggie came down the stairs to help. She took the boxes so Trick could run out to the garage and grab some drinks. By the time he returned, Maggie had plates on the table and the first slices were already served.

Trick went to the kitchen to get some glasses and ice since the pop was warm. He also grabbed some napkins, which was a surprise even to him. While they ate, the conversation was at a minimum. Eventually though, the silence was broken.

"So, what else is going on?" Trick asked.

"Not much," Maggie replied picking up a napkin. "Everyone's excited for the game on Friday."

Trick motioned for a napkin himself. "Who are we playing anyway?"

Maggie handed one over. "We got the Grizzles. It's the last game of the season before playoffs start, and it's a game that you should be at. But of course, you won't be there. Instead you'll be at home playing pool alone in your garage."

"Don't be so sure about that." Trick tried to subtly slip in before taking a bite.

But news of that nature had no chance of going unnoticed. Maggie stopped mid-bite and glanced over, greatly bewildered at Trick. For a minute, she could only stare at him, unable to comprehend this unfathomable change of heart. Trick, knowing his true intent would warrant some unwanted attention, tried to avoid Maggie's eyes by burying his face in his pop, taking one long sip. Suspicious of his suddenly guarded behavior, Maggie finally asked.

"Does that mean you're coming to a football game?"

Trick shifted nervously. "Well, nothing's for sure, but I might."

"Why the sudden one-eighty?" Maggie asked with vested interest.

Trick cleared his throat before answering, preparing himself for the barrage of questions about to come his way. "Well, Ashley said something about wanting to hang out together and...."

Before Trick could continue any further, Maggie's chuckling abruptly interrupted him. Her pizza had dropped to her plate, and she was covering her face with a napkin. Trick sighed at her reaction. As the laughing continued, Trick's annoyance at her reaction grew, forcing him to inquire.

"What is so funny?"

"You're coming to the game because Ashley asked you to," Maggie said.

"That's not true," Trick snapped.

Maggie teased, "Yes, it is."

"Maybe a little bit."

"Ohhhhh!"

"No, no, no," Trick stopped her. "Don't 'ohhhhh,' there's no call for that."

"Yes, there is. You two are finally going out. That's so sweet."

It was the 'finally' that caught Trick's attention. First Kenny, then Katie, and now, even Maggie knew that Ashley had been harboring feelings for Trick all this time. He began to wonder if he was that dense or just that stupid. Truly, it took something special to be that oblivious if everyone around him could figure it out.

"What do you mean finally?" Trick asked.

Maggie grunted. "You're serious? She's had a crush on you for a majority of her high school career. She's even passed on other guys hoping you'd come around."

"Now, that can't be true," protested Trick.

Maggie set him straight. "You better believe it's true. We tried to get her to move on and forget about you, but she was dead set."

Trick couldn't help but be a little insulted that Maggie would try to convince someone to not be interested in him. "Some friend you are."

"Don't get snippy with me," Maggie fired back. "Everything you had done to that point indicated that you weren't interested."

Trick rolled his eyes at the notion he had somehow scorned Ashley's advances. In his head, he could think of no such instance where Ashley had shown even the remotest interest in him. Now, to hear that he had deterred her in some fashion…he couldn't fathom it.

"What did I do?"

Maggie sort of clammed up after the question. She had the evidence to present but didn't want Trick to see it all after he admitted being ignorant to the facts. She considered just letting him off easy and tried to convince him the details weren't important.

"There have been…a few instances where you spurned her feelings."

Not getting the hint, Trick persisted. "Give me a 'for instance.'"

Maggie swallowed hard, not really wanting to proceed, but Trick had insisted. "Okay," Maggie began. "For instance, there was the time she asked you to go to the movies with her."

Trick thought it over. "She never asked me to go to the movies."

"Well, maybe not in so many words," Maggie clarified. "But you have to remember last April when she came up to you, me, and Katie asking if any of us had seen 'Death by Decapitation.'"

Trick remembered. "A horrible film—I felt bad I saw it in the theater."

"You're missing the point," Maggie continued. "It wasn't about watching a good movie; it was about being alone with you for once. But of course, you didn't pick up on that, and apparently her mentioning nine other films didn't clue you in, either."

Trick averted his eyes as he fidgeted in his chair. With everything spelled out for him, his own lack of awareness was embarrassing. He started getting a light feeling in his chest from all the blood storming his face. Grabbing his drink, he tried to settle himself. Maggie gave him a minute before she moved on to the next incident.

"Then, there was the time she said that she had an extra ticket to the Lifehouse concert."

"My favorite band," Trick replied.

"And what did you say?" Maggie asked.

Trick sighed, realizing his folly. "I had homework that night."

Maggie added, "Homework you had an entire week to finish."

Trick stood up from the table, already fed up with this assault on him. As he walked to the kitchen to get some more pop, he offered his futile defense. "I didn't know that I had that much time to get it done. As I recall, I was the only person to turn in the assignment so quickly." Maggie shook her head and called after him.

"Even so, you could've put it off for a few hours."

Trick said nothing more about that occasion and came back with a full glass. He sat down at the table, a defeated look stretching across his face. Maggie couldn't help but smile at the situation, knowing how much this was eating Trick up now that he couldn't avoid the truth. Though she never would have guessed that Trick was actually interested in Ashley, she was happy to see he was at least considering the idea.

"So, I've made some mistakes," Trick admitted.

"There's more," Maggie reluctantly confessed.

Trick put his hand on his head. "I don't know if I can stand all of this."

"Hey, we've all had to endure this," Maggie declared. "It's only fair that you should have to, too."

Trick dropped his head and moaned. "Fair enough."

Before she would continue, Maggie picked Trick up off the table. Even she would acknowledge that she was enjoying this far too much. She wasn't fighting her smile anymore though, a fact Trick was slowly coming to resent. It was bad enough for him to have to sit through all of this, but why did it have to make her day?

"How about the time you helped her rehearse for her play?"

Trick groaned in agony. That particular memory was resonant in his mind now. He wanted to stop the discussion right there, but he knew Maggie wouldn't let him off the hook so easily. Taking a deep breath, he prepared himself for the not-so-pleasant trip down memory lane.

"That's right," Maggie said satisfied with herself. "You remember. Even I was there for that one when you cowered away when the kissing scene came up."

"With all due respect," Trick interjected, "you weren't very helpful in that little scenario, and neither was Katie. Both of you snickering behind me, it was very unsettling."

Maggie conceded. "Okay, you got me there." Trick nodded, pleased to have one small victory. Unfortunately, Maggie was not finished. "However, you didn't help anything when you turned down her personal invitation to watch the play itself."

Trick tried to slip away to salvage what little dignity he had left, but Maggie stopped him in his tracks and backed him into his chair. Standing right over him, pointing a finger, she read him the riot act. "You said you didn't really like going to the plays and that you were just gonna play pool with Kenny, Jordan, and Scott. Do you have any idea what that can do to a girl? I mean, you really screwed up before, but that was probably the worst thing you could've done. She felt totally rejected, not just in romantic sense, but in a general friend-sense. That really hurt her when you said no."

"Alright, I've heard enough." Trick exclaimed standing up for himself. He backed Maggie off him and stood up tall. He straightened himself up for a moment and then said, "I get it; I've made a lot of mistakes. And looking back on everything, I must be blind as a bat. So if I've screwed up so much, then why is she still trying to get with me?"

Maggie shrugged. "To be honest, it's beyond me, too. She must really think you're really something underneath it all."

Trick walked into the living room and slumped down on the couch. What had seemed like an innocent encounter before had really escalated quickly. He realized if he was going to accept this invitation to the game, he would be walking into something that already had some build up to it. Maggie could tell he was feeling the stress of the situation and took a seat next to him. Throwing an arm around him, she tried to rationalize it all for him.

"All kidding aside, you are something special, Trick. We all know it, and that's why she wants to get to know you. So don't sweat all that old stuff," she said. "It's in the past, so leave it in the past."

"With all the fun you're having with this, why would I want to do that?" he said with a smile.

Maggie smiled, too. "Oh, come on, how often do I get to tease you like this? You're usually so unshakeable it's nice to see you're human."

Trick chuckled, which Maggie was happy to hear. Once it was all out there, she realized how harsh it might have sounded, but Trick needed to hear it all if he didn't believe that Ashley was interested in him. Furthermore, if he decided to pursue this, he needed to understand how she felt about it.

The silence had gone too long. "So," Maggie asked, "are you going to ask her out?"

"I'll go to the game, probably the party," he clarified. "Let's not get too far ahead of ourselves, though."

Maggie smiled and bear-hugged Trick, which caused him to roll his eyes. Though this was a cause for celebration for Maggie, Trick felt she was reading too much into this. He was going to a game, maybe with more intent towards spending time with Ashley, but it was still just one game. Maybe Maggie was just happy that he was finally breaking out of his shell and spending time with his friends outside of school and these small get-togethers, but also just as likely, she might have been expecting more from him that he planned to input.

Chapter Four

The Week's Work

The next day, Trick went to school earlier than usual. Derby High ran on a certain block scheduling system that made the normal forty-five minute class last ninety minutes. To accommodate this, students had eight classes split into a two-day schedule. Trick worked his schedule so that his core subjects—math, English, science, and social studies—were all on one day and his electives were on the other. The one elective that had been a constant throughout high school was his TV Journalism class.

Along with his classmates, Trick filmed and edited a ten-minute newscast that aired on the school's TV channel on a bi-weekly basis. After four years of running through the process, Trick had the whole thing down easily and even made a name for himself as one of the lead anchors for the newscasts. However, the process could be quite time consuming. As a result, Trick spent his time before school in the news studio perfecting his craft. Aside from that, the studio was a nice quiet place to be in.

The studio was very spacious with high ceilings. One side of the room housed the set: a news desk, cameras, and lighting set up for shooting. On the other side sat a string of digital editing bays for the news and other projects in the class. The real draw of the room for the students however, was an old couch next to the editors. It was a raggedy couch, most likely from the late 80s, but was more comfortable than anything else in the building.

The actual classroom was just outside the studio and served as the classroom for all the journalism classes, which included yearbook, newspaper, and photography. The news studio was just one subset of the room along with a dark room in the back and a computer lab in an adjacent room. Throughout his years, Trick had become accustomed with them all but spent most of his time in the studio.

Today, he worked right up to the bell before joining the others in the classroom. Though he was the only four-year student, there were several others who worked together as an "Advanced Team," including Maggie, Katie, Kenny, Jordan, and Scott. The day was a typical starting point for them: they watched a tape of their latest newscast. Once the tape had played, the instructor, Ms. Rutherford, who happened to be a male-student favorite, critiqued their performance.

"Not bad," she concluded. "I don't know if it's one of the best things you've put together…." She went on to point out a few particulars that jumped out at her. Trick scribbled down notes while the others were at full attention.

"I know you all worked very hard, but I really think you can do better. After all, with college around the corner, you seniors are going to want something you can show off. With that said, I want Trick, Maggie, Katie, and Kenny to go into the studio and see if you can work out these kinks. Scott and Jordan can stay out here and help me for today. I really want you to show all the beginners what thirteen years of experience can really do."

A small pocket of cheers rang out from the beginning group. Trick smiled as he sarcastically asked. "You really want us to disappoint them this early into the year?"

The class laughed and Ms. Rutherford quickly quieted them. Then she addressed Trick and let her own sarcasm shine. "Alright, you got your smart-mouth comment in for the day. Now how about you take your team and create something that won't make me regret keeping you around for four years." The class laughed again. Trick shook his head as he fought a smile, but he knew Ms. Rutherford had gotten the better of the exchange. Taking the others with him, Trick walked back to the studio and shut the door behind him.

As soon as the door closed, Trick and Katie each took a spot on the couch. Kenny grabbed a chair from an editing bay and rolled it over by the couch, putting his feet up on a table. Maggie sat down at one of the editing bays and turned it on. She had a paper bag at her feet; what she was doing with it no one knew. Katie and Kenny watched her, trying to get a glimpse at what was in the bag. Trick thumbed through his notes as everyone else occupied their time.

"Trick, can I get this video started?" Maggie asked.

"What is it?" Trick asked, not entirely paying attention.

"My parents want me to put together an anniversary tape for my grandparents," Maggie explained. "It's their fiftieth."

Katie moaned, "How sweet!"

Maggie echoed. "Yeah, it really is—unfortunately, I have about a bag of pictures and hours of home movies that they want included in this and about a month to get it done."

"Talk about pushing the issue," Kenny empathized.

"Yeah," Maggie said, "because I don't have enough to do."

Trick finally answered her original question. "Go ahead and do whatever you've got to do. The list of things Ms. Rutherford gave us should keep us plenty busy. To be honest, that's fine with me; I'd rather not help the beginners today."

Katie echoed the sentiment as she laid her head against the back of the sofa. "Amen to that."

Once everyone had settled, Trick jumped in. "First thing, we gotta keep the audio consistent throughout the show. I'm sure we all know what I'm talking about there so I'll move on. Second, Ms. Rutherford seems to think that our anchors aren't familiar enough with their scripts."

Katie objected. "Well, we never get it put together in time to practice."

Trick scribbled on his pad. "Well, I'll let you handle it this time then."

Katie frowned. "I shouldn't have said anything."

"What else?" Kenny asked with a smile.

Trick didn't want to take up too much time with this because the more time they had to actually fix the problems, the better off they'd be. He browsed the notes again, looking for some way to sum it up. "Oh, nothing else too major," he said. "It's just little stuff, some dead air coming out of a story, and no substance to the sports section."

"That one's beyond our control," Maggie called out.

"That's what I tell her," Trick replied. "She keeps saying we can do more with it."

Trick paused again as he glanced over his notes. There was something else he felt he needed to bring to everyone's attention, but he couldn't think of what it was for the time being. Kenny and Katie sat patiently waiting for him to find it while Maggie kept working on her project. Finally, Kenny's patience ran out.

"Is that it then?" he asked.

Trick gave up on his search, certain he'd remember whatever it was eventually. "I believe so, and that means we can go ahead with our next show." He ripped out a sheet of paper and wrote their names down on it. "Alright, who wants to do what?"

"I wanna do the movie review," Maggie claimed.

Trick rolled his eyes as he marked her down. "Don't take anything too strenuous. You're gonna have to take the music review, too, ya know?"

"Fine with me."

Katie pulled out her own notes. "I'm gonna profile two of the new teachers to the school. Maybe find one right out of college and one from another district."

Trick nodded. "Okay, that always goes over well."

Kenny had his idea, but he wasn't sure the others were going to be happy about it. He'd done a story very similar to this before and since Ms. Rutherford wanted nothing but the best, it may not fit the bill. Knowing that, Kenny bided his time before saying his story idea. When Trick finished writing Katie's story, he looked over to him.

"I'm gonna report on the dance team's fund raiser."

"They're doing another one?" Katie asked surprised.

"Yeah, they do two every year," replied Maggie, her eyes still on the screen.

"That's what it was!" Trick exclaimed. Everyone jumped as Trick dug through his notes before finding a sheet of paper and holding it up in the air. "I hold in my hand a warning from our beloved administration. They considered Kenny's last story about the dance team to be somewhat inappropriate due to what they deemed 'questionable attire'."

Kenny snatched the note out of Trick's hand. "It was a car wash," Kenny interceded. "What was I suppose to do? They were wearing swimsuits."

"Don't complain to me," Trick said. "Do you really think I had a problem with it?"

"Can we move on here, gentlemen?" Maggie asked. "What's your story, Trick?"

"Well, it's the beginning of the fundraising for Thanksgiving for the Poor," Trick responded. "I guess that's as good as anything."

"Why do you always have to be so professional about this?" Katie asked. "Your story sounds so much better than mine."

"Don't sell yourself short," Trick replied patting her on the back. "We all do our part around here. Besides, the guy running it is my fourth block teacher. He's got old tapes and everything just lined up for me. All I gotta do is put them together."

Katie dropped her jaw and shook her head. "Just shooting fish in a barrel for you, isn't it?"

"Don't even have to cock the gun," Trick added.

With the main stories assigned, the newscast needed some small pieces to fill up the time. After about five minutes of discussion, the team had a list of stories that the beginners could investigate. They also picked a date to film so that all that remained undecided was who would be anchoring this go around. Trick had been on camera the last two times, so he recused himself from the position.

"How about you, Maggie?"

Maggie accepted. "Gladly."

Trick wrote her name down for one of the anchors. Certain that Kenny wouldn't be keen with the idea of working alongside her, Trick cracked a smile. What would be even better was the reaction of the school seeing the two of them on camera together. Kenny was already making notes on his paper, clearly unaware of what was about to happen.

"Kenny, I'm gonna go ahead and pair you up with Maggie."

Kenny was jolted from his business. "What's that now?"

Maggie kept her focus on the project on the screen. Katie chuckled as Trick repeated himself. "I'm gonna have you be the anchor with Maggie for this go around."

"What about sports?" Kenny asked looking for a safety hatch.

"Uh...." Trick tried to think of a way to get a sports anchor without giving it to Kenny. He glanced out into the classroom and found inspiration. "Katie, get Jordan and Scott back here for a minute."

"Of course, my liege," Katie remarked with a sardonic curtsy.

Katie walked out of the studio while Trick smiled and Kenny frowned. Maggie was still oblivious to what was happening. Katie tapped Jordan and Scott on the shoulder, motioning for them to follow her. Quietly removing themselves from the room, they popped their heads in the doorway.

"What's up, Chief?" Jordan asked.

"Need a sports anchor," Trick said. Kenny folded his arms in disgust.

"I'll take it," Jordan said immediately.

"Okay, that means you'll have to be the field reporter, Scott," Trick added.

"Sounds good to me," Scott replied.

"Good, we're gonna tape on the fourteenth, so be prepared,"

"That it?" Jordan asked.

"That's all I got," Trick replied.

"Alright."

Jordan and Scott rejoined the class and Katie retook her seat. Trick wrote the boys' names down, sounding them out just to mock Kenny. When he finished, he looked up with that smile still beaming on his face. The only solace Kenny could take was that Maggie wasn't paying any attention to what was going on. As Trick continued to smile, Kenny shook his head in resentment.

"What?" Trick asked innocently.

Kenny had to be cryptic to hide his malice. "I just think that someone else deserves to take the lead on this one."

"Really? Huh! I honestly that this would be something you'd *dive* right into, ya know?" Katie choked up trying to hide her smile. Kenny started violently shaking his head, demanding that Trick stop, but Trick wasn't quite finished yet. "I mean, if you think about, this is really gonna give you a chance to step out of the shadows and really show your face."

Proving to be the final straw, Katie erupted in laughter. Realizing how much attention she was drawing to herself, she jumped off the couch and bolted for the door. Everyone else outside the studio stopped and watched her leave the room in a huff. The confusion plain on everyone's faces, Ms. Rutherford looked into the studio. Trick shrugged his shoulders as if he didn't understand. When Ms. Rutherford sat back down, Trick shook his head at Kenny as if he couldn't believe it. Maggie was lost in the whole mess as well.

"What's her problem?" she asked.

Trick shook his head while smiling at Kenny. "I have no idea."

When Katie returned, she explained her outburst with some story about something that had happened to her the day before. When no one understood her reaction, she assured them they had to be there to truly get it. The rest of the class went by without any incident.

Later on that day, after school, Trick was at his locker that, much to his dismay, was located on the bottom row in F-Hall, number 1006. Down on a knee, he rifled through his locker to find the books he required for his homework. While he was unloading his bag, Ashley came walking down the hall and stopped next to his locker. He didn't notice her at first, but as he closed his locker, he was pleasantly surprised to see a beautiful pair of legs standing next to him.

"Hey, Trick."

She smiled as she leaned against the lockers.

Trick could presume the main reason behind this little social call. No doubt Maggie spread word to Ashley that he was considering attending the game on Friday. The hope in Ashley's eyes was unmistakable. With a mixed feeling of uneasiness and anticipation, Trick stood up from his locker. He didn't want to tip his hand too much, nor did he want to spurn yet another advance.

"How's it going, Ashley?" Trick asked.

"Good. I was talking to Maggie earlier. She said that you were gonna go to the game on Friday."

"Well, I'm thinking about going to the game...maybe the party."

Not wanting to get too excited, Ashley fought off a smile before she continued.

"You don't normally go to the games. Why the change of heart?"

"Well, I guess playing pool for five hours every Friday isn't as appealing as it used to be." Trick replied with a chuckle. Ashley laughed, too, still uncomfortable and hoping there was more to it. "Aside from that," Trick continued, "it would be nice to hang out with people I don't see as much as I'd like to."

Ashley's discomfort dissipated in an instant and replaced itself with a warm smile. With a newfound resolve, she asked a question she almost gave up on. "Really? That's nice. Well, as long as you're going, do you think you could give me a ride...maybe take me home afterwards?"

Normally, Trick wouldn't have given a second thought to the request and would have agreed instantly. However, after everything Maggie had told him the night before, he couldn't help but be a little leery about the request. He could tell by her tone that this was something more than an ordinary ride. It was a feeler, a testing of the waters before going any further. He had a feeling that things could escalate quickly but also took this at face value: it was just a ride after all.

An uncertain smile broke across his face. "I'd love to."

Ashley's smile intensified. "Great," she exclaimed. "Pick me up at six-thirty?"

"Okay, see ya then," Trick said.

"Well, hopefully I'll see you before that."

Trick chuckled as Ashley started to walk away. Just before she vanished around the corner, she turned back to him, smiled, and waved. Trick forced a bigger smile and waved back. Then, she turned away and took off prancing down the hall. Once she was gone, Trick tumbled back against his locker and let out a deep sigh. All she did was ask for a ride to a football game, but he felt exhausted from the tension. Even though they had been alone, he felt as though a million eyes watched the encounter. Once he regained himself, he picked up his book bag. There was no misreading this signal; Ashley hadn't left any opportunity for that.

Ready to go home and take things easy, Trick sauntered on down the hallway towards the student parking lot. As he turned the corner, he saw Kenny talking to a beautiful girl. He couldn't tell who it was from behind, but she had her dark hair pulled back in a ponytail. She was wearing short green gym shorts, a grey T-shirt, and white running shoes. Only when he got closer did he realize it was Jessica, a friend of Maggie who happened to be on the dance team. He couldn't hear what they were saying but caught the tail end of the conversation.

"… so you can just meet me then," Kenny said.

"That's kind of late isn't it?" Jessica asked.

"Don't worry about it, it's plenty of time."

That was the last Trick heard before he was close enough to become part of the discussion. Sneaking up behind Kenny, Jessica could see him approach. She smiled as he slapped Kenny on the back.

"Plenty of time for what?" Trick asked

Kenny jumped back quickly which caused Jessica to laugh. Trick smiled as well as Kenny shook his head and rolled his eyes. Jessica covered her mouth, and Trick put his hands up in a non-threatening manner as an apology.

"Sorry Kenny, didn't mean to startle you."

"Don't worry about it," Kenny replied tapping his hand to his chest. "Just give my heart a minute to restart."

Jessica just laughed. "How's it going, Trick?"

"Eh…I'm doing alright," Trick replied. "How about you?"

"I'm doing pretty good," Jessica echoed. "I saw you talking to Ashley a little while ago. Are you finally gonna ask her out?"

Trick dropped his arms disheartened. "Am I seriously the only one who didn't know about that?"

Kenny ignored his whining and answered his previous question. "I needed someone to interview for my story. Jessica agreed to help out."

"Well, she's good people like that."

Jessica smiled at the compliment. "I like to help however I can, but right now, I've got to get back to practice so I'll see you two later.

Jessica turned and ran down the hallway. Trick and Kenny waved as she turned the corner. Once she was out of sight, Kenny whipped around and slugged Trick in the arm, which created a thud that echoed in the empty hallway. The cheap shot knocked Trick off balance, causing him to drop his bag.

"Hey, now, what was that for?"

Kenny's reply was stern. "For what you did in TV this morning."

Trick laughed to himself. "Yeah, that was pretty funny."

Kenny disagreed. "I can't believe you did all that."

"Well, believe it," Trick said. "I got witnesses."

"Man, just shut up."

Kenny rolled his eyes as he picked up his book bag and walked away. Trick grabbed his, still smiling, and ran after Kenny. Though Kenny appeared to be upset, Trick knew better. "Oh, come on," Trick said. "It's not like Maggie caught on to what I was doing."

"What makes you so sure about that?" Kenny asked.

"Believe me, after everything she told me last night, she would have said something."

"Do you think she's ever gonna know?"

"Well, I'm not gonna say anything, neither is Katie or anyone else for that matter. She'd have to overhear it or you'd have to tell her."

Kenny scoffed, "I'm not about to do that."

"I'll tell you something you should do…." Trick began.

"Yeah, what's that?" Kenny retorted

The two had reached the front doors and Trick stopped walking. Kenny partially opened the door then stopped when he realized that Trick wasn't following him. Kenny turned briefly and did a double take, wondering what was so important. Playing along, he shut the door and stepped back towards Trick. Kenny looked around the area for a second to make sure they were alone. Then he motioned for Trick to go on and once Trick had his undivided attention, he explained himself.

"You need to act normally around Maggie."

"What do you mean?" Kenny asked shocked.

"Well," Trick digressed, "if you hadn't flipped out about being an anchor, then those jokes wouldn't have been such a big deal."

"You could have just not told them."

"How long have you known me?"

Kenny smiled as Trick patted him on the back and then walked out the door. Trick had had his fun and Kenny wouldn't deny him of that. But now, the tables were set to turn and Kenny saw his opportunity to get back at him. Following Trick out the door, Kenny walked out in front of him and then turned around so he'd still be face to face with him. The big smile that had been on Trick's face transferred to Kenny.

"Ya know you really should be careful how hard you push the jokes on this."

Trick was intrigued. "Is that so? What, pray tell, makes you say such a thing?"

"Well, a little birdie tells me that you are thinking of going to the football game on Friday but don't really have that much interest in the game."

Trick rolled his eyes. "Okay, I get it, yeah, I'm going to the game so I can hang out with Ashley—stop the presses everyone!"

Kenny kept the ammo coming. "And what, pray tell, were the two of you talking about before you interrupted my meeting with Jessica?"

Trick was already anticipating the barrage of jokes and laughs that Kenny could have at his expense. Unfortunately, he wasn't in any position to keep this from Kenny. After all the fun Trick had had at Kenny's expense, he knew

Kenny was entitled to some fun at Trick's. Trick shifted the bag on his shoulder, tried to pop his neck for a second, and cleared his throat before unveiling his revelation.

"She asked for a ride to the game and I said yes."

Kenny stopped in the middle of the sidewalk and dropped his bag. He covered his mouth with a mocking shock-and-awed look on his face. Then he put a hand on his chest and looked to the sky. "Aw!" Kenny moaned. "Isn't that sweet!"

"Shut up," Trick replied playfully shoving him aside.

"So you mean to tell me...."

"Shut up."

"...that she just asked you...."

"Shut up."

"...and that's all you'd been waiting for?"

Trick didn't even bother to reply at this point. Walking on past Kenny, he didn't wait for him to run back and get his bag. Kenny hurriedly picked up the bag, not ready to let Trick get away.

"Come on, Trick; it's kinda funny."

"It's obviously hilarious for you," Trick said.

"Well, looking at it from my point-of-view it is," explained Kenny, stopping Trick from going any further. "There you were, completely oblivious to the fact that Ashley had a huge crush on you and as soon as you get a clue, you're *diving* right in. Seriously, who knew that you had a thing for her?"

Trick was quick to correct Kenny's logic. "Okay, stop right there. I'm not *diving* into anything. I'm giving her a ride to a football game, not going out on a date. I never said I had a 'thing' for her; I just said I wanted to spend some more time with her, that's all."

Kenny smiled and put an arm around his friend. "You know nothing about women, do you?" Trick brushed the arm away and went for his car.

"I'm telling you, man," Kenny assured him. "You think you're giving a ride, I guarantee you that more is going to happen with this than you're preparing for. Think of it, the two of you are going to be alone in your car before and after the game. You better believe she's gonna sit next to you at the game. She'll probably try to talk you into going to the party, if she hasn't done that already, of course...." Trick averted his eyes, he actually suggested he'd go, "...And after all her failed attempts in the past, she's gonna try to leave a lasting impression one way or another."

"That sounds diabolical."

"They're women," Kenny shrugged. "It's what they do."

After a moment of thoughtful silence, Trick and Kenny parted ways for the day. They were two of the last cars to leave the school that day. When Trick got home, he went through his normal routine of checking the mail and the messages. With all his core classes tomorrow, he had plenty to do. He fiddled around with some homework for ten or twenty minutes before deciding that it would not be best to get started on an empty stomach. He didn't feel like eating much at that point, so he did some laundry to help him work up an appetite. As he walked to the garage, he glanced across the street at Maggie's house. He saw her light on in her room and hoped she was doing okay. After all she had told him yesterday, he could only assume the incident from Friday still had her shaken.

Maggie, who had been home for an hour, wasted no time getting right to her room to do her homework. Her bag lay in a chair by her door. The radio on her nightstand by the bed provided some needed noise. She hadn't made the bed that day. She did put all her clothes away, though, neatly folded and placed in her walk-in closet opposite the door. Across from her bed, she had the piece from the mask sitting on her desk by her computer. She was lying in bed trying to concentrate on her homework, but she couldn't focus. Staring at the soft blue walls, all her thoughts were on Friday. The more she tried to put it out of her mind, the more stubbornly the thoughts remained. What the stranger said was stuck in her head, replaying over and over again. She just wanted to know who he was. Downstairs, the phone rang, providing a momentary break from her thoughts. She didn't bother to pick it up, but listened for her mom to answer. A few seconds later, she heard her mom call out.

"Maggie! Eric's on the phone!"

Maggie sighed. She didn't talk to him much today and was hoping the evening would be much of the same. She didn't necessarily want to keep him at a distance, but she had other things on her mind. "Okay," she yelled back, "I'll get it up here!"

She went to the nightstand, turned down the radio, and picked up the phone.

"Hi, Eric." Her greeting was lethargic.

"Hi, beautiful," Eric replied with unbridled enthusiasm. "I didn't see you a whole lot today."

"Yeah, I guess I was just kinda tired."

Eric paused for a second. The detached tone of Maggie's voice was robbing him of his own joy. "Are you alright?"

"Yeah, I'm fine." Maggie then reiterated, "I was just a little tired today."

Eric, disheartened with Maggie's response, paused again. He knew that something more was wrong with her and was certain it had something to do with what happened on Friday. He felt terrible that he wasn't there for her, but he was definitely trying to make up for that now. She was making it difficult though, being so distant. They had barely talked over the last few days, each day adding to his own concern.

"Are you still thinking about Friday?" he asked, trying to keep his cool.

Maggie was defensive. "So what if I am?"

"Babe, the guy pulled you out and disappeared. You said you didn't even talk to him or anything, so I don't get why you're obsessing over this. Please, explain it to me."

Maggie froze at the recanting of her lie. She had spoken to that man, even begged him to stay and tell her who he was. The best he could do was to say he loved her and leave. Even now, she was distracted with all her thoughts about why he did what he did. She was debating whether or not to let Eric in. She thought back to what Trick had told her and again resented him for staying so impartial on this issue.

With each passing moment of silence, Eric's suspicions about the night grew and grew. Not able to stand the silence, he said the first thing he could think to say.

"That's all that happened, right?"

"Yeah," Maggie replied breaking out of her thought, "of course."

"So then it's not that big of a deal?"

Maggie didn't respond to his question right away because she was still trying to justify lying to him. It was the best choice to make right now, but why did she feel so rotten for doing it? Whatever her reasoning was, she knew it was right...somehow. Maybe she didn't totally understand it now, but it would make sense eventually.

For his part, Eric was losing more of his patience with every silent second that ticked away. Something more was definitely going on here; he knew her well enough to understand that. What he couldn't comprehend was what would have happened that she would have to keep from him. The more scenarios he played out in his head, the more serious the idea became. Finally, he couldn't stand being in his own head anymore and needed to hear someone else's voice.

"Maggie," he said softly.

"It's just so aggravating."

"You're telling me," Eric replied callously.

Eric's tone was quite insulting. Maybe Maggie was a little off today and had been since Friday, but all things considered, she deserved a little slack with this. He should be more understanding of the way she was feeling.

"Well, it's not a common occurrence to have my life saved," Maggie explained with a twinge of irritation. "Especially by some masked man...."

Eric couldn't stand it anymore. "That's not what's going on here. That's not what the big deal is!"

Maggie gasped. "Well, then you tell me what it is."

"I don't know," Eric admitted. "But I get the feeling that you're hiding something from me. Like there's some part of this you're holding back. Something else happened on Friday, but you don't want to tell me and I don't get it."

This accusation, although completely accurate, propelled Maggie into a whirlwind of rage. First of all, there was no reason for Eric to be this snippy. Second of all, he had no right assuming that she was hiding anything important from him. After all, from her point of view, what she was hiding from him was for his own good. She knew what it would do to him if he knew this guy loved her. Besides, she didn't want to find him because she loved him, too; it just bothered her. And as much as she didn't need that mystery hanging over her head, she definitely didn't need these accusations.

"So now you don't trust me?" Maggie asked.

"I didn't say that and don't throw this back on me. I just want you to be able to get past this, and I don't understand why you can't."

"I just can't," emphasized Maggie. "I'm sure I'll be able to soon but for right now, I just can't."

Eric realized Maggie's quandary and began to empathize again. He did wish to help after all, and he was currently unsuccessful towards that goal. This wasn't a witch-hunt; there was no hidden agenda on Maggie's part. She was just curious. He hated the thought, but she was close to dying that night. It was only practical that she would want to thank her rescuer properly.

"I want to help you get through this," he finally said softly.

Maggie recognized the love in his voice and realized how quickly she'd flown off the handle. She remembered then that she didn't have to go through all this alone. She had those people around her willing to be at her side. She used one of them just yesterday, why did she fail to use this one today?

"I know you do."

"But I've got to know everything that happened Friday if I'm gonna be able to do that." Eric still couldn't fight the thought that Maggie was with-holding information. "You can't hide anything from me."

Maybe that's why it was so easy to misinterpret Eric's intensions. Every time he tried to be helpful and appeared genuine, he turned face and said something like that. Maggie was already struggling with the fact that she was holding back from him. His prodding wasn't helping anything. She needed him to trust her and believe that she would tell him everything he needed to know when he needed to know it.

"I've told you about everything that happened on that night," she stressed.

"Okay," Eric replied taking her word. "If you remember anything else, you'll tell me about it, right?"

"Of course," Maggie replied. "Look, I want to get back to my homework so I can relax the rest of the night. I'll talk to you later."

Eric understood that at least. "Okay…goodnight…I love you."

"I love you, too."

Maggie hung up the phone and looked gloomily at her homework. She knew that no matter what she did, she wouldn't be able to focus. As she sat in silence, she heard a bouncing sound reverberating from outside. Curious, she walked to the window and saw Trick playing an imaginary basketball game in his driveway. She looked down on him, contemplating going over and talking to him.

He paused momentarily on the driveway, as if he could feel her gaze. He turned around and looked up to her window. With a smile, he waved before going back to his game. Maggie smiled briefly and then sat down at her desk. She'd bothered him enough, she told herself, let him be for once.

Chapter Five

Game Night

Trick refused to believe Kenny when he first guaranteed that this ride situation would evolve into something more before Friday arrived. Over the course of the next three days, however, he would watch Kenny's foresight come to fruition.

It all started on Wednesday, when an overjoyed Katie approached Trick under the impression that Trick had asked Ashley out on a date. Trick worked quickly to correct the misunderstanding, but it didn't take away from Katie's excitement towards the situation. Instead, she began taunting Trick about waiting to make it official. He reminded Katie that this was just a football game after all and that her vested interest was unwarranted. If only it had been that easy to convince her.

Thursday, Katie and Maggie approached Trick with a proposition. Concerned that Trick would blow the evening in his usual fashion, they suggested making the evening a group event so Trick wouldn't be on his own. Trick wasn't too keen on the idea, considering the value he placed on his privacy. He also didn't believe he needed someone holding his hand through this like he was that inept with women. Sadly for him, Maggie and Katie had already discussed this with Ashley, and she was all about it. Painted into a corner, Trick agreed.

Hoping that Friday would bring him some sort of relief, Trick only found more of the frustration that had plagued him throughout the week. No other plans appeared for the evening ahead, but he did receive advice from everyone he knew and even a few he didn't. By the end of the day, he was searching for a place to hide.

Once school let out, he recoiled to the safety of his house and locked himself in his room. Some part of him wanted to call the whole thing off and just forget about it, but he knew the ramifications of such a move. As he lay on his bed agonizing over the situation, he heard a knock on the door. Roy had returned home the day before. Trick told him nothing of his plans for the evening but suddenly found himself in need of his father's guidance. After letting his dad in, Trick sat on the edge of the bed and Roy, sensing his son's need for fatherly advice, grabbed a chair and pulled up next to him.

"Alright kid, what's wrong?"

"Well, I decided to go to the game tonight," Trick informed him.

"Good for you," Roy encouraged. "I've been telling you that it would be good to get out of here and be a teenager for a change."

Trick nodded before explaining his real problem. "There's a little more to it than just the game." Roy straightened up, sensing the seriousness of Trick's tone. "I'm actually going so I can hang out with this girl, Ashley." Roy couldn't help but smile. For the time being, Trick couldn't match his enthusiasm. "And we're friends and everything and she's really cool, but I don't know if I like her or not."

"Is there any reason that your mind has to be made up so quickly?"

"Well, from what I've been told, she's had a crush on me for about a year or so."

Roy let out an understanding 'uh huh' which stopped Trick's explanation. Hoping his dad could make enough from his account, Trick waited for his father's reply. Roy sat back in his chair and rubbed his chin. He was excited that his boy was finally becoming a bit of a socialite, but he didn't want him to get discouraged after one night. Roy would never admit it to Trick, but he always had hoped that Trick would end up with Maggie. Having watched the two grow up, he knew how much he cared for her, but if this was where his son headed, he was happy about that, too.

After thinking it over, Roy looked at his son, who was anxiously twiddling his fingers. The anticipation was driving Trick crazy; Roy could see that. It worried him a little. He didn't want his son taking this too seriously. It was just a game after all.

"Let me ask you this son...."

Just hearing his dad's voice helped Trick calm down.

"If this girl really has the hots for you like you've been told, do you really think she's gonna go all soap opera on you if you don't ask her out tonight?"

Trick mulled it over before shaking his head.

"That's right. She understands that this is a process. It doesn't just happen. You'll go out tonight, have some fun, maybe even start to get a clear indication on how you feel about this girl. If that leads to a date inquiry, then it will. If it doesn't, it doesn't. She'll understand...better than you're thinking she will."

"But everyone is making it seem like it's such a big deal," Trick interrupted.

Roy nodded. "To them, it probably is. They've never seen you in a situation like this before. Seeing you take a step like this and actually open yourself up is something they want to see. They're not worried you'll mess up or hoping they see something; they just want to see you happy."

Hearing everything played out as his father was describing provided more comfort than any of his own thoughts. It made him feel silly realizing that he blew this so far out of proportion. After a minute, his frown curled into a smile, and his genuine excitement about the evening returned. Roy smiled as well and patted Trick on the knee.

"I know you're special, kid, but I don't think you're that special." He winked.

Trick laughed. "Thanks dad, that's the pick-me-up I needed."

A few minutes passed before Kenny arrived, ringing the doorbell. It was a small marvel that Trick had convinced Kenny to come with him. Kenny remained a little apprehensive being around Maggie in any case, but for Trick's sake, he agreed to put that apprehension aside.

Roy made sure Trick was comfortable with everything before Trick left the house ready to get his evening started. As he and Kenny got into Trick's car, Kenny reminded Trick that he owed him one for this. After a roll of his eyes, Trick got in the car and the two sped away.

Originally, Trick drove to Ashley's house to pick her up. Kenny was riding shotgun at the time but swore he'd move to the back when they arrived. Trick wasn't so sure he wanted that but understood it was going to happen anyway. About five minutes from her house, Trick received a call from Maggie on his cell. Apparently, Maggie and Katie were already at Ashley's house and the three of them were going to ride together. Maggie promised that Trick would get to take her home.

After a quick U-turn and an explanation to Kenny, Trick headed for the Wendy's up the street where the girls agreed to meet. Yet, when they arrived, the girls weren't there yet. They did look through the window to see Jordan and Scott waiting for them inside.

"We're the only ones here?" Kenny asked when he and Trick were indoors.

"For now," Scott nodded. "So, whose idea was this?"

"Guess," Trick replied sarcastically.

Jordan sighed. "Geez…this is pathetic. You're not even technically dating her yet and she's already bossing you around."

Trick snapped back. "Oh, shut up. It'll probably be this one night and then I'll be done with the whole thing."

"So, uh, you're not gonna ask her out?" Scott asked. Secretly, Scott had always been attracted to Ashley himself but knew she wanted to be with Trick.

"I don't know," Trick replied, regretting his rash statement. "I'm just gonna have to play it by ear."

"You'd be pretty lucky, man," Scott added. "She's really hot."

The four of them took a seat at a table as they waited for the rest of their party to show up. "I know, I know," Trick said tired of hearing the same old thing. "It's just kind of strange to think she's had a crush on me for so long."

Jordan interrupted. "A hot girl has a big crush on you and is waiting on pins and needles for you to ask her out...." Jordan looked at Kenny. "I'm not seeing the strange part."

"Hey, don't ask me," Kenny replied with a smile. "I think he's completely nuts."

"No kidding," Scott echoed. "The only strange part is that you're not jumping at the chance."

Once the conversation shifted away from him, Trick began to feel more comfortable about the whole thing. Hearing the barrage of questions knocked him off balance a bit, but he remembered what his dad told him earlier and let it all roll off his back.

The boys conversed for about ten minutes before Scott checked his watch. His hunger was getting the best of him, and the wait had been too long. He suggested ordering now. Trick felt inclined to wait for the girls, but Jordan and Kenny convinced him that would be foolish. There was no telling when they'd arrive, and they might not want to eat. Once convinced, Trick ordered, and the boys got their food.

Eating, they sat in respectful silence until the girls finally arrived. Disappointed, but not surprised, that the boys started without them, Katie strolled up to the table.

"I take it you didn't have the manners to order for us?"

Jordan scoffed. "Oh, yeah, because we know what you'd want."

"Did you at least save us seats?" Katie asked.

"There might be enough," Jordan said, making no promises.

Katie rolled her eyes and playfully shoved Jordan in the back of the head. He frowned at first then turned around to give Katie a glare. To his dismay, she was already walking away. For a moment, he stared longingly at her in her holey jeans and tight black sweater. Scott watched with a smile as Jordan stared.

"See something you like?" he asked.

Jordan shook it off. "Just eat your food."

Scott, Trick, and Kenny exchanged smiles as Jordan refocused his attention to the tray in front of him. Scott couldn't help but laugh when Jordan tried to sneak another look at Katie.

The girls were already critiquing the evening.

"Why didn't you say anything, Ashley?" Maggie asked.

"I don't know," Ashley replied uncomfortably. "What was I supposed to say?"

"Hello?" Maggie suggested.

Ashley explained herself. "I guess I'm still nervous."

Katie understood. "And let's not forget, you spook the deer, and he'll run."

Maggie was quick to defend. "He's not that timid."

Once the girls paid for their food, they stood around the drink fountain discussing matters beyond Ashley and Trick.

A few minutes passed; the girls' orders came up. They all took their seats with the guys. Kenny was at one end of the table. Trick sat next to him, and

Ashley next to Trick. Scott pulled up a chair and sat at the end of the table next to Jordan. Katie took the chair next to him and Maggie sat in the final spot. Unnoticed by everyone else, Kenny's nerves went on high alert when Maggie ended up sitting across from him.

It didn't take long for the guys to finish their food since they ate first. Scott was gentleman enough to clear their trays. When he came back, he patted Trick on the back.

"So Trick, your first game," he proclaimed triumphantly.

"So what?" Trick replied, not understanding the significance.

"Oh, the first game is the key game. It's the one that sticks with you, and you always remember." Scott explained.

Jordan couldn't help but smile as his eyes shifted between Ashley and Trick. "And you're really gonna remember this one."

Jordan laughed under his breath. Only Katie heard his remark, and she didn't find the same humor in it that Jordan did. Calmly and casually, she slid her arm under the table and jabbed it into Jordan's side. The smile quickly vanished from his face as he almost spilled his drink. Setting it down, he demanded an explanation.

"Be more careful," Katie suggested.

"But you bumped into me!" Jordan protested.

Scott was quick to get the topic back on more pleasant matters. "Ya know, I still remember my first game. We didn't move here until I was seven, and where I grew up, we didn't have much of a high school.

"Then I came here with that big stadium filled to the brim with fans; it was really something else. I was with my folks. We came in just about ten minutes before the game expecting to find a seat easily. It ended up taking so long that we almost missed kickoff, but we caught a spot on the grass next to our neighbors. I spent the whole game on a beach towel just talking football with my dad."

Everyone smiled and paused for a minute to remember their own first games. Katie brought her memories forward next. She reminisced about being carried in on her father's shoulders and falling asleep somewhere in the third quarter. Kenny told a story from the time he was a little older. During a terribly boring game, he and Darren ran out onto the field during a timeout, which almost resulted in security throwing them out of the stadium. Every one of them had a story to tell. Every one of them was bursting with enthusiasm while they recollected. For his part, Trick just soaked in the memories of all those around him.

"It sounds like you guys always manage to have fun," Trick said when they had finished. In a sense, he regretted having missed out on all of those memories and not being able to make any of his own.

Ashley put a hand on his thigh. With a playful smile, she seemed to be making a vow to him. "I'm sure you'll have fun tonight, Trick."

"I sure hope so," Trick replied flirtatiously.

The sheer brazen nature of Trick's suggestive remark took everyone by surprise. Once the shock wore off, they all had smiles as wide as the ocean on their faces. The girls went back to their meals, while the guys continued to talk. Ashley shared her memories of games past while she ate, and Trick hung on every word. Scott and Jordan discussed their own shenanigans at the game while Katie sat mortified by their juvenile behavior. Only Kenny tried to stay out of the conversation. Maggie felt some concern by his silence and tried to provoke him into some dialogue.

"So, what's going on with you?"

"Not a whole lot," Kenny replied his voice jittery.

Maggie waited for more, but Kenny wasn't about to say anything else. His guard was up and he wasn't about to implicate himself in any way. As he took a long drink, he remembered Trick's advice. He had to be normal around Maggie and not act like anything weird was going on. The more he strived to look innocent, the more he made himself stand out. On top of that, he realized he was being awfully rude to someone he considered a friend.

"How about you?" he finally asked. "How have you been this week after the whole lake rescue thing?"

Now it was Maggie's turn to be uncomfortable. Nervously massaging her cup with her hands, she took in a deep breath. Kenny swallowed hard when he saw he'd touched on a sensitive subject.

"I'm doing okay," Maggie said without any conviction. "It's been tough— a little weird. Actually, it's mostly been weird." She chuckled and Kenny reciprocated out of courtesy. "It had me shaken for a while, but I think I'm doing better. I just wanna know who it was really, but I kinda doubt I'll ever know."

The desire in her eyes almost saddened Kenny. All at once, his guard dropped and compassion replaced any uneasiness he felt. "You really want to see him again, don't you?" he asked.

Not intentionally eavesdropping, Trick and Katie both perked at the question proposed by Kenny. No one else seemed privy or they engrained themselves in their own conversations too deeply to notice. Careful not to appear obvious, Trick and Katie anxiously waited to see what would happen next.

"More than anything," Maggie replied.

Kenny smiled. "Well, if it's that important to you, I'm sure that you'll see him again eventually."

"Thanks, Kenny," Maggie said with a smile, touched by the sentiment.

Kenny raised his drink and nodded to say, "You're welcome." They both smiled for a while longer before Maggie got up to throw her trash away. A different kind of smile had broken across Katie's face. She looked like the detective that had just cracked a big case. She nodded contently while Trick sat with a frown. He was silently pleading with Katie to not go too far with this, but he was too late.

Trick's silence eventually caught Ashley's attention. She had been telling him about her trip to state with her friends, a story Trick would remember the basics of but would be sketchy on the details. Concerned she was boring him; she stopped and tapped him on the shoulder.

"Is something wrong, Trick?"

"No," Trick replied refocusing his attention, "I was just thinking that we should get going so we can be a little early."

"I like the way this guy thinks," Scott stated. "If we go now, I should be able to make a trip to the concession stand before the game starts."

Katie reminded him, "You just ate. What do you need more food for?"

"We all have our traditions," Scott retorted.

"What's yours…weight gain?" Trick asked.

Everyone laughed, with the exception of Scott who gave Trick a glare. He knew he could have made some offhand remark about Trick and Ashley but didn't want to be that cruel. Instead, he mocked their laughter and then encouraged them to leave.

As they left, Trick offered to take Ashley in his car. He had promised a ride to and from the game after all, and he intended to make good on that promise. Kenny made himself scarce and rode with Scott and Jordan. Katie and Maggie drove as well.

Once on the road, Ashley wanted stories from Trick. She had already told him about all her times at the games; she wanted to know more about how he spent his Friday nights. Warning her that they weren't nearly as impressive as the tales he heard at dinner, he relayed his typical evening routine of pool in the garage with music on and pop in the fridge. The more questions she asked about what he did, the more he remembered small things that happened along the way—times when friends had been over or he'd just really enjoyed having some time to himself—and suddenly he didn't feel so bad about missing all those other games. He just wished he'd had someone there in the garage with him.

A steady assortment of cars already had most of the parking lot to the stadium filled. Settling for spots in the back of the lot, they managed to park near each other. Once out in the cold, they felt the stiff breeze that promised another frigid night. Jordan quickly zipped up his jacket and shoved in his hands in his pockets.

"Man, its cold out here."

"Too much for ya?" Katie asked, nudging his arm.

Jordan sneered. "Please, I could be in a tank top, with shorts and flip-flops, and I could just stand out here for hours."

"Okay," Katie frowned, "I don't need that visual."

Jordan frowned as she walked away. She was so infuriatingly crude that it drove him nuts, and he loved it.

"I'm glad I brought a jacket," Maggie said.

"I don't think mine's gonna be enough," Ashley confessed.

Trick popped the truck of his car upon hearing Ashley's distress. Throwing the trunk open while garnering a certain amount of attention, he pulled a rather large green blanket from the trunk and held it majestically in the air. Just looking at that thick wool fur coat began to warm everyone.

Jordan stood next to him, not impressed.

"You keep a blanket in your car?" Jordan remarked.

"My dad makes me keep it in the car during the winter," Trick explained, "just in case I should ever have a use for a blanket.

"Well," Jordan said suggestively, "you'll have a good use for it tonight."

Katie frowned and hit Jordan upside the head.

"Would ya stop with the hitting!" Jordan pleaded.

"Oh, deal with it ya, baby," Katie replied.

"Alright, let's head in, folks," Kenny said, breaking them up.

"Yeah," Scott said, rubbing his hands in anticipation, "the hot dogs are getting cold, the pretzels are growing stale, and the nacho cheese is slowly hardening."

Maggie stopped and held her stomach. "What a disgusting thought."

They ran through the parking lot, weaving in and out of the small spaces between the parked cars. As they entered the main gate, the full magnitude of the stadium hit them. A magnificent stone structure, it was Derby's pride and joy. Looking straight up the beige backside of the stands, a white press box gleamed in the setting sunlight. A silver wolf adorned the brick above the entrance. Looking up the ramp, the distant view of that luscious green field pulled them in.

As they walked up the ramp, the field stretched out before them: dark green turf from one end to the other, perfectly painted field goal posts and a billboard displaying the team's storied history. To their left was a metal set of bleachers that seemed out of place. Added only a few years ago, they quickly became the student section. Walking that way, Trick took notice of the main section of the stadium. The rows crawled up a seemingly impossible distance before plateauing. A vibrant fan base had already claimed most of the prime seats. In contrast, the visitor's side across the field was mostly bare.

It didn't take long for the seven of them to find a row to stake claim to in the student section. Once they secured their seats, Scott grabbed Kenny and the two of them ventured to the concession stand. Since it was located on the other side of the stadium seating, they offered to get the others anything they wanted. Trick asked for a drink, as did Maggie and Ashley. Jordan told Scott to get him whatever Scott was getting himself.

Still about thirty minutes away from game time, Trick looked around at the sights. Some of the players were warming up on the field, but his interest lied in what was happening in the stands. He recognized a number of people, all of which would be surprised to see him at the stadium.

Not too long after they had arrived, the cold proved to be too much for everyone to bear. Trick promptly spread the blanket across them, which was also helpful in saving seats. Jordan was at one end. Katie sat next to Jordan and found a comfortable spot underneath the blanket. Ashley sat in the middle with Trick next to her and Maggie at the other end. As he worked the blanket around, Ashley couldn't help but wonder why Trick had never been to a game before.

Trick was reluctant to answer at first. He had a confession to make but wasn't sure he wanted to tell. With all his friends around, however, he had no reason to hide it anymore. "Actually, I've been to the games before. It's just been a while."

Ashley was intrigued. "How come you stopped coming?"

Suddenly, everyone's eyes were on him. He chuckled, trying to psyche himself out. "Whenever we came, it was mom's idea. She was a cheerleader in high school and missed the whole atmosphere but didn't like the crowds. Dad was against the whole idea. So whenever he was out of town, mom would bring me. To avoid the crowd, she'd park the car near the fence where we could still see the game.

"For the next couple of hours, it was just the two of us together. She'd bring snacks and keep the radio on so we could listen to the game. During half-time, she'd change the station and find some music we could sing to. Usually, I didn't make it to the fourth quarter without falling asleep. She'd want to leave as soon as I was tired, but I didn't want to leave. I was having too much fun.

"Then, when she died, I lost interest and couldn't bear the idea of going without her being there."

When he finished, there wasn't a dry eye around him. Jordan fought it off while Katie stared at the ground in deep reflection. It was just the kind of story that made all of them want to hear their mom's voice and maybe even feel her warm embrace.

"I didn't know that," Ashley said, breaking the tension.

Maggie wiped away a tear. "I didn't, either."

"I don't think anyone knew," Trick admitted. "That was one of the things that made it so special. It was just our little secret."

Such a show of sensitivity endeared Trick to Ashley even more. Unbeknownst to him, Ashley scooted a little closer. About the same time, Scott and Kenny returned from the snack bar. Holding Jordan's food along with his, Scott carefully negotiated his way past the others before sitting down next to Jordan. Kenny looked, hoping there was room for one more down that way but no such luck. He was stuck sitting next to Maggie, certain that would play over well.

Maggie offered him part of the blanket that Kenny was quick to refuse. He could already imagine what people were thinking with him just sitting next to her. He wasn't about to add fuel to the fire by getting under the blanket with her.

On the other end, Jordan removed himself from the blanket as Scott handed him his plate of nachos.

"You're just going to get cold again," Katie assured him.

"Shows what you know. This nacho cheese will keep us warm for hours."

Scott and Jordan chuckled to each other as they clinked chips before divulging in their warm treat. Scott took a quick glance down the row, hoping he hadn't missed anything.

"Anything happening?" he asked.

Trick hadn't seen Ashley move closer, but Jordan had. Staring over at the steadily decreasing space between them, Jordan whispered. "Ashley isn't exactly waiting for the kickoff to get started, if ya know what I mean."

"And Trick...?"

Jordan shook his head. "His defenses won't hold. I say Ashley's gonna go in for the kill somewhere towards the end of the first quarter, and I'm guessing that that's more action than Trick's ever gotten in his life."

Though they were trying to be inconspicuous, Katie couldn't help but overhear the two of them. Trick was doing so well to this point; she wasn't going to let these two morons ruin it for him.

"Will you two shut up," Katie warned. "In case you hadn't noticed, there isn't a whole lot of room between you and them."

"What?" Jordan chuckled. "They're not paying attention to us."

"Yeah, they're kinda busy," Scott winked.

"I swear I'll dip the two of you in nacho cheese if you don't knock it off."

Not about to test such an unsettling threat, Scott and Jordan went back to their plates. From that point on, the conversation became much more civil until the game started.

As the action commenced, the Wolves got the ball and began marching down the field. As the crowd quickly became engrossed in the game, a hush of anticipation quieted them.

Even in the student section, the noise held at a minimum. It was only when Ashley put her hands in her lap to warm them, that Maggie nudged Trick in the shoulder. Unresponsive at first, a harder jolt caught his attention. Keeping an eye on the game, he leaned closer.

"Did you see that?" Maggie asked.

"See what?"

"A simple 'no' will do," Maggie retorted. "Ashley put her hands under the blanket to keep them warm."

There was a suggestion hidden somewhere in that statement, but Trick couldn't put together what exactly it was. "That's for the update," he said. "What am I supposed to do?"

Maggie sighed and then spoke slowly so Trick could understand. "Put your hand under the blanket and hold her hand."

Trick looked down towards Ashley's lap where her hands currently resided. "That's a pretty dangerous area to just go grabbing," Trick said.

"No, you moron," Maggie replied. "Just put your hand under the blanket on the bleacher. Eventually, she'll put her hand there, and then you grab it."

Trick glanced under the blanket. He didn't remember there being that little space between them. "There's not much room down there."

"Just do it!" Maggie demanded.

"Okay," Trick said defensively.

Frightened, Trick snuck his hand under the blanket and cautiously set it on the space between Ashley and him. Maggie rolled her eyes and sighed at Kenny. He had witnessed the entire exchange and smiled sympathetically at Maggie. Even with his hand down there, Trick doubted that this would actually work. The bleacher was freezing, why would Ashley put her hand there? He illustrated his doubt by shaking his head at Maggie. She smiled and winked.

"It'll work."

"Just so I know," Trick asked, still skeptical, "how long do I have to keep my hand under here. If it doesn't work, I'm gonna feel like an idiot."

Maggie smiled. "There's not much that can help that."

As Trick scowled at Maggie who just smiled back, he felt the tips of two fingers rest gently on his hand. He jumped at first, surprised by the effectiveness of Maggie's suggestion. Ashley quickly withdrew her hand, fearing she had chanced too much. Staring earnestly at Trick, she waited for his response.

When he kindly smiled at her, she managed to relax. A smile briefly broke across her face though she was still unsure how to proceed. Taking the initiative, Trick grabbed her hand gently and set his down on the bleacher between them. The smile returned to Ashley's face as she turned to catch what had unfolded on the field.

Trick looked over at Maggie who was still smiling. Thankfully, she didn't feel the need to say 'I told you so.'

As the game pressed on, the Wolves started to build an insurmountable lead. Their first possession had generated a touchdown. After a quick defensive three and out, their offense took the field and again scored, this time on a long pass. Working fast, they managed to end the first quarter with a field goal to take a 17-0 lead.

Resolved to right their wrongs in the second quarter, the Grizzles came out and built their own scoring drive. The lead down to ten, the Wolves responded with another field goal.

The remainder of the second quarter saw a shift in play. The game grinded to a defensive halt as neither team was able to make headway. However, the Wolves were able to turn defense into offense in the last minute by intercepting a pass and returning it for a touchdown. The 27-7 lead brought the home crowd to their feet.

When they jumped up, the blanket dropped, revealing Trick and Ashley's hand holding to everyone around them. Kenny couldn't help but notice. For someone that was concerned about escalation, this seemed an odd move for Trick.

Maggie saw it another way.

"Well," she smiled, "this is going better than I expected."

"I wouldn't cry victory just yet," Kenny said.

"Why not?"

"The guy is worried about moving too fast. If he's not careful, things are gonna get out of hand."

Maggie glanced over at the two of them, smiling and still holding hands. "He looks pretty content to me," she said.

"For now."

Maggie looked at Kenny with concern, a sentiment he could only echo. After a few minutes, the crowd died down and the last few seconds of the half ticked away. Scott, Jordan, and Katie decided to go for a walk. Ashley was anxious to join them so she could assess things with Katie. Trick prepared to go when Ashley told him to stay and vowed to return quickly. Truthfully, Trick didn't mind the break.

As the four of them walked down the stone sidewalk, Scott headed for the concession stand again. Jordan was up for another round, but Katie couldn't believe they could take much more. Ashley was too excited to care.

"Well, I think this is going well," she said beaming with joy.

"I told you this was a good idea," Katie said.

"Do you think he's having a good time?" Ashley asked.

"Of course, he is." Katie replied and then tapped Jordan on the shoulder. "Isn't Trick having a good time?"

"A good time?" Jordan repeated. "This is quite possibly the greatest thing that has ever happened to him."

Ashley was very pleased to receive such an endorsement. But at the same time, she couldn't help but be concerned about the party.

"Has he said anything about the party?"

Scott didn't expect the question. "What…to us? No, but we haven't really talked to him about it. I'm sure he'll go, though…he is your ride after all."

Everything seemed to be playing out so well. He was having a good time; he was committed to going to the party afterwards. The last answer Ashley wanted was to the riskiest question of the night.

"Do you think he's gonna ask me out?"

"I don't see why he wouldn't," Katie replied to pick up her spirits. She glared at Jordan trying to get him to do the same.

He held up his hands, wanting no part of this one. "Hey, I'm just an innocent bystander, don't ask me."

Katie sighed, disappointed at his cowardice.

Scott, on the other hand, proved more helpful. "I don't see what's gonna stop him."

Ashley smiled at the thought and started almost bouncing with her every step. Katie shot Scott a grateful look. A little disappointed that Ashley would be taken, Scott was at least happy to see her happy. Jordan, suddenly getting confident, mulled over the evidence.

"You think so, Scott?" he asked.

"Yeah."

"Yeah," Jordan echoed. "Yeah, I think you're right." Jordan nodded at Ashley who was still smiling. He also looked at Katie, who gave him an appreciative smile. That made him smile as well as he turned to face the front of the line as they approached the counter. "I'd be surprised if he can go that long without doing something stupid, though."

Scott rolled his eyes as they both ordered.

As they waited patiently for their food to come, they conversed with friends that walked by. It would be a few more minutes before they made their way back over to their seats. That worked out for the best because Maggie and Kenny were questioning Trick about how he was doing through the first half.

"I'm doing fine," was Trick's only reply.

"Ya sure?" Kenny asked. "You're coming on stronger than I thought you would."

"What do you mean?"

"Well, for starters, you volunteered to drive her here so the two of you would be alone. From what you told me, I didn't think that was what you wanted to have happen. After that, you're holding hands during the game. If you had bought her dinner, this could be a date on its own."

Trick thought it over, but Maggie didn't want him to become dispirited. "You're just enjoying yourself," she assured him. "There's nothing wrong with that. This was the whole point of the evening. You wanted to see if you would enjoy being around her, and I'd say that you are."

Trick nodded. "I am, but Kenny's right, I don't want to rush things."

Maggie shook off the idea. "Look, unless you start making out with her in the middle of the game, you're not going to go too fast. The most that Ashley is expecting out of tonight is you asking her out. And not even on a real date, just out."

Trick began to mull things over. He still wasn't sure what he was going to do, but he currently leaned towards taking this further. But as Kenny said, he didn't want to get in over his head. Sensing the conflict, Kenny looked to calm Trick's nerves.

"Look, I'm not saying anything you're doing is wrong or misguided. I'm just saying you seem to be into this. It's a good thing."

Trick smiled and then put the idea out of his head. He was enjoying himself after all, that was quite enough for right now. If anything else progressed beyond this, then he'd roll with it. What he needed more than anything was to get out of his head and not allow all the possibilities to overwhelm him.

When Ashley and the others returned, food filled Ashley's hands so Trick wasn't able to hold hands any longer. He did watch the halftime festivities conclude and chatted with some of his friends in the crowd.

In the third quarter, the Wolves came out fired up. It showed on the field. Already holding a 20-point lead, they scored a touchdown and field goal within the first five minutes of the quarter.

By the beginning of the fourth quarter, the lead was in the thirties and the second string squad was already on the field. Most of the excitement was gone from the crowd with the victory assured. Some of the crowd had left to go home. The night had gotten progressively colder and staying wasn't worth it. Most of the remaining crowd's attention was elsewhere anyway. Just about all of the student section remained, holding the tradition of heading to the Smith's only after the game was over.

For his part, Kenny suddenly wished he hadn't promised Trick he'd stay with him through the whole night. He was freezing in the cold and just wanted to go somewhere warm. The blanket was always inviting, but he dared not partake. Throughout the game, he had noticed some wandering eyes looking his direction. No doubt, this was because he sat next to Maggie.

Maybe if more of the students had left, he might have gotten under the blanket but not under these circumstances.

Try as he might to hide his discomfort, Maggie couldn't help but see him shivering again. Getting some slack in the blanket, she held up a corner inviting him in.

"Are you sure you don't wanna get warm?"

"No, that's okay," said Kenny. "I'm used to the cold."

His refusal to warm up perplexed Maggie. She began to wonder if something else was amiss here, like maybe she was offending him somehow. Kenny knew he needed to change the subject quickly.

"So, where's Eric tonight?" he asked.

Maggie shied away from the question. "He's like Trick…doesn't like the whole football scene. He'll be at the party though."

"Well, that's good."

"Yeah," Maggie looked for something else to talk about now. "I was kind of surprised you were able to come to the game tonight. Don't you usually work Fridays?"

"I've had the last couple off," Kenny admitted.

Maggie remembered Kenny distinctly telling her that he was working last Friday. He worked and then went to Trick's house afterwards. Why would he lie about that?

Confused, she turned to Trick.

"Hey," she talked so Kenny couldn't hear them, "didn't Kenny come over to your house last Friday after he got off work?"

"Yeah," Trick replied, hoping he was staying consistent with the lie.

"He just told me that he didn't work last Friday."

Trick suddenly felt trapped. If he said anything more, he might blow Kenny's cover and reveal his lie to Maggie. On the other hand, he might end up digging himself a deeper hole by lying to Maggie more.

Trick's concern over Kenny's slip of the tongue was so great he didn't notice Katie asking him if he was going to drive Ashley to the party. After asking the question two different times, Katie shook Trick's shoulder to get his attention. He blinked a couple times, snapping out of his thought. The concern was still prevalent on his face, so Katie asked what was wrong.

"Kenny's slipping," he replied simply.

Katie knew something good had happened and wanted the details, but before she could get them, the game ended. Swearing to Trick that they'd discuss this later, they exited the stadium and prepared to party.

Chapter Six

The Party and the Aftermath

Upon arriving at the Smith's house, Ashley and Trick separated for a brief period. Ashley joined the other girls in the kitchen while Trick took a seat with the guys in the living room. Darren had started a discussion about a favored movie he had seen last week. Though Trick hadn't heard of the movie, he was happy to sit and listen. Every now and then Trick would get the feeling he was being watched. When it became too much for him, he glanced into the kitchen. He didn't see anyone looking at him, but he did see four or five girls turning their heads and giggling as if they had been looking at him a moment ago. Just what he needed—all eyes on him.

In the kitchen, Katie scorned the girls for making Trick so uncomfortable. She made her deer analogy again, but Maggie wasn't there to refute the comparison this time.

Sitting off to the side, Maggie had her eyes focused on the pier. Now that she was here again, her mind wandered back as well. It was a vain hope, she knew that, but she desperately wished he was out there somewhere. She just needed a sign, any sign, that would let her know, and she'd be out there in an instant.

Eric had just arrived at the party and immediately went to find his girl. He checked with Trick and said hi to everyone there. Kenny shied away from him, unsure if Eric knew about the rumor. When Trick told him Maggie was in the kitchen, Eric left without a word about it.

"It wouldn't kill you to relax a little more," Trick told Kenny.

"Yeah, well, I'd rather be prepared, thank you very much," replied Kenny.

Eric entered the kitchen and saw Maggie staring out the glass door. Frozen with concern, he watched for a moment, hoping she'd look away herself— no such luck.

A pie-faced friend of his named Luke walked up behind Eric and slapped him on the back. Luke informed him that the rest of Eric's friends were dancing in the living room. Eric promised to join them in a minute. Once he was sure Maggie wouldn't break her stare, he decided to do it for her.

"Hey, you alright?" he asked placing a hand on her shoulder.

Maggie was only half-attentive when she replied, "I'm fine."

Eric knew better and turned her towards him. "Hey, don't let this ruin your night. You came here to have fun, right?"

"Yeah," Maggie regretfully admitted.

"So let's have some."

Eric walked off, motioning for Maggie to follow him. Maggie started to slowly move away from the door. After a couple steps, she hesitated and peeked out at the pier one more time. Seeing nothing out there, she left the kitchen and joined Eric in the living room.

Kenny watched the scene play out from across the room. More concerned with Eric than Maggie, he felt a swell of pity in his gut for her. After everything she had told him, even he wanted her to see him again. He became so captivated by her that he didn't notice Katie walk up to him and take a seat on the armrest of his chair.

"Ya know," she said, "she'd feel a lot better if he showed up."

"Showed up," Kenny repeated. "What do you mean by that?"

Katie continued, "I'm just saying that if you were to disappear for a while and change into your personal 'Batman' costume, she'd be very happy to see you at the pier."

Kenny groaned and shook his head. "You got me all wrong."

"Really...cuz your armor is already starting to crack."

"What do you mean?" Kenny asked. Still annoyed by the accusation, he couldn't help but wonder what she had on him.

"Maggie knows you lied to her about work last Friday."

"No, I didn't."

Katie smiled at his incompetence. "Yeah, you did. According to your original story, you went to Trick's house after work. Tonight, as Trick told me, you told Maggie you didn't work last week." Katie feigned shock as she walked away from him, allowing him to wallow in his error.

Trick would've been more concerned, but he couldn't shake the discomfort of eyes watching him from afar. Jordan, realizing what was going, leaned in to talk to Trick.

"They know that you know, ya know?"

Trick, unsure at what he was getting at, gave him an okay sign with his hand. "Thanks Riddler," he replied.

"What I mean," Jordan explained, "is that the girls in the kitchen know that you know you're being watched. They're trying to bait you into making a move. And honestly, you look like you're about to break."

Trick looked around at the other faces, and they all nodded in agreement. Looking for an out, Trick appealed to more knowledgeable minds. "So what do I do?"

Jordan stood up and motioned for Trick to do the same. "Switch me spots," he said. "If you're more hidden from view, their eyes won't bother you. If you're lucky, they'll get frustrated and leave you be."

A cool wave of calmness swept through Trick as he took Jordan's seat. The watchful gaze that had followed him was suddenly gone. While he felt relief, Jordan knew that this was at best a stall. The only question became how long it would be before they felt the girls' retaliation.

The answer came quicker than they expected. It was Darren who first noticed a group of girls walk over to the stereo. Rummaging through a stack of CDs, they carefully selected one and played it over the surround sound. As the first song played, everyone but Trick perked their ears at the sound.

"Oh, no," Jordan groaned.

"What?" Trick asked, not understanding the situation.

Darren pointed to the source of the disturbance. He scorned himself for not saying anything sooner. Now, they were trapped with no possibility of escaping—just a pack of wide-eyed gazelles waiting for the lionesses to strike. Trick followed the eyes of his comrades, seeing the girls now squaring off on the other side of the room. He still couldn't figure out exactly what was going on.

"It's gonna happen," Darren said gravely.

Scott clutched Jordan's arm. "I'm scared."

Jordan patted Scott on the head. "I know, kid, I am, too."

Trick was growing tired of being out of the loop. Standing up in front of all of them, he tried to get their attention. But the events transpiring on the other side of the room kept the others occupied.

"Will someone tell me what is going on?" Trick demanded.

Kenny put an arm around Trick to brace him for what was about to happen. "They're getting prepared, and in a moment, they'll make us...dance."

The very word made all the boys shudder.

"What's the big deal?" Trick asked.

"This ain't your typical dance session where you're just happy to be close to a girl," Scott cautioned him. "This is serious. We're talking a solid hour of constant dancing with no hope of pause or escape."

Trick rolled his eyes and started to walk for the kitchen. Jordan jumped up and pulled him back to the couch. "Are you insane, stay with the pack! You don't stand a chance out there on your own!"

Trick rolled his eyes as the girls made their way across the floor. He didn't believe it was going to happen. The others pitied him for that. He would learn soon enough what they all could feel in the pit of their stomachs.

"Brace yourself, boys!" Scott yelled.

Linking arms, the boys closed their eyes and waited for the first selection. Trick looked around laughing at all of them for being so scared. What on earth could be so terrible about dancing anyway? As he shook his head in dismay, he felt a hand grab his arm. Looking at the hand and then at Ashley who the arm belonged to, he smiled, reluctant to leave his seat.

"Come on, Trick," Ashley smiled. "We're dancing."

"I don't really dance," Trick replied in a futile effort to save himself.

Ashley jerked him off the couch. "That's about to change."

Unraveling from their recoiled crouching positions, the guys peeked at the dance floor. Trick was still pleading with her to not do this. Unfortunately for him, Ashley already had her heart set. Picking up the rhythm of the tune, she started swaying her hips back and forth. Trick's complaints subsided as her movements soon entranced him. A few seconds later and he danced along with her.

Still out of harm's way and in their seats for the time being, the boys watched as Trick vanished in the shuffle. They suspected he would be the first to go, and now, they sat wondering who would be next.

"Poor guy," Jordan said. "At his first party, too."

"There are worse things that could happen," Scott said.

"Show some respects, boys," Kenny announced holding out a hand. "The first victim."

"Yeah," Jessica said, grabbing his hand, "and you're number two."

Before he could even attempt to defend himself, Kenny felt a pull as Jessica yanked him off the couch and onto the dance floor. It took only a few seconds before it was down to two, just Jordan and Scott. Katie stood in front of them, arms folded as if she was letting them choose who would stay and who would go.

"Well, old friend," Jordan said, "it's down to you and it's down me. One of us will go free and the other will be lost to the great dancing abyss out there."

"Yeah, and guess who's going to the abyss." Katie grabbed Jordan's hand.

"No!" Jordan howled. "Take the other one, he's very limber! Limber!"

Scott leaned back in the couch with a satisfied smile on his face. Sprawling out in all the extra room he suddenly had, he basked in the glory of surviving the onslaught. As he laughed at the unfortunate masses who failed to mount an escape, he felt a delicate tap on his shoulder. He cautiously turned to see his friend Sabrina standing over him with a smile on her face. Defeated, he stood up from the couch and joined the rest of his fallen brethren.

After a few minutes of dancing, Trick was enjoying himself quite thoroughly. This was nowhere near the atrocity the others made it out to be. After all, it was dancing for crying out loud. A handful of songs played before Trick started to feel a little winded. He tried to make a move towards the kitchen but the girls quickly blocked his path. In fact, the girls thwarted any attempt by Trick, or any other boy for that matter, to take any hiatus from the dancing. Wondering exactly what was happening, he appealed to Kenny and Jordan for help. They could only say over the roaring tunes that they had told him so.

Suddenly understanding their prior concern, Trick contemplated how long this would last.

Though it was unknown in the beginning that the CD had twenty-five tracks on it, the boys learned as much when the music stopped after the twenty-fifth song. Well more than an hour had passed since Trick last sat down, but the pain throbbing in his body told him it had been longer than that. His legs were wobbly as though he was standing on wet noodles. Part of his shirt had turned a darker color thanks to the sweat soaking into the fabric. He gave up on the idea of feeling anything below the waist.

The only positive was that the music had stopped temporarily, and they could rest if only for a moment. On the way back to the couches and chairs, Jordan assured Trick that the dancing was not finished.

"We gotta get that CD," Jordan suggested. "We get it, burn it, then find the people who made it, and kick them right in the shins."

"Good idea," Scott said. "Let's get started next week. I'll think I'll have recovered by then."

Trick didn't bother to sit in a chair, but collapsed on the floor and considered that close enough. Kenny was lying across the chair directly above him. Patting him on the back, Kenny complimented him for having survived round one.

"You didn't even look that bad out there," Jordan informed Trick.

"Yeah, like you were really bustin' a move," Scott scoffed.

"I didn't feel like showing off."

"Yeah, that's what it was," Kenny said patronizingly.

As they continued to argue about each other's dancing futility, they slowly made their way into the kitchen and grabbed anything cold. The cooling streams of nectar eased the pain of their sore muscles and helped them regain their breath. Jordan was still adamant in his defense of his dancing, while the others just played along. Tired of their scrutiny, he vowed to show them all up if he got the chance.

No sooner had he said it when the music started to play again. The boys whipped around to see their respective partners waiting for them. They didn't even bother to put up a fight this time.

"Looks like this is your chance to prove yourself," Scott said pushing Jordan over to Katie and then joining Sabrina himself.

"It never ends," sighed Darren, slowly walking towards the floor.

"Let's go," Jessica said, taking Kenny's hand.

"Every time I think I'm out," Kenny muttered, "they pull me back in."

"You're not getting out of this one, Trick." Ashley said with a smile.

Trick remarked, "That would suggest that I got out of some other one." Regardless, Ashley dragged him back to the floor.

With everyone gathered around, Jordan grabbed center stage on the floor to strut his stuff. Grabbing Katie by the hand, he took the lead of a style that would be closest to swing music. He pulled her in close, clasping her around the waist. Then he began moving their hips to the beat of the music only to spin her away and beckon her back to him. Katie was somewhat taken aback by Jordan's moves, but at the same time drawn in to his allure. Following his every move, Katie returned as Jordan raised his hands calling for applause.

After giving him his just due, Darren, Kenny, and Scott all took their time on the floor to show off their best moves. While each was entertaining in their own way, none were that impressive. People were more appreciative of the risk they had all taken by grabbing the spotlight. Kenny was the last to go and finished by pointing to Trick, who had simply been enjoying the performances to this point. Unwilling to answer the call at first, Kenny, Jordan, Scott, and others eventually shoved Trick into the limelight with everyone encouraging him to give it a go.

Realizing he wouldn't escape without a brief performance, Trick began to roll his hips and shoulders to the rhythm of the music. As he moved closer to Ashley, she mimicked his movements. Together, they began to dance a very basic salsa step that more than impressed the crowd around them. The dancing was not top-notch, but the fact that Trick was participating heighted its appeal. After a few seconds, he stopped and took her hand. Spinning her into him much like Jordan did to Katie, he slipped behind her placing his arm around her waist leading into some bumping and grinding. It was so sudden and fluid that the crowd burst into applause and cheering.

"Where did he learn to do that?" Jeff asked.

Eric smiled. "That kid is full of more surprises than you realize."

Matt, a freshman who was also Jessica's brother, had watched the whole exhibition from the kitchen. As he watched, he saw Kenny cheering everyone on. Kenny and Matt hadn't gotten along for a long time. Having recently heard of the rumor surrounding Kenny, Matt thought it his duty to inform Eric of these developments. "So, Eric, I saw Maggie come in with Kenny tonight."

"Yeah, Maggie and some other people got Trick to go to the game tonight, but I just didn't feel like going myself."

Matt smiled, knowing that Eric knew nothing about Kenny's theoretical involvement in last week's events. As he took a seat next to Eric, he saw Jeff, Brian, and Avery shaking their heads, warning him not to say anything. Matt was in no mood to comply.

"I just think it's kind of a risky move considering all the people that are saying Kenny is the one who pulled her out of the lake last week."

"Kenny!" Eric repeated in disbelief. "You've got to be kidding me; there's no way!"

"Afraid not, Chief," Matt restated. "According to what I heard, Kenny showed up at Trick's house only minutes after Maggie was rescued dripping wet from falling in a lake."

Eric looked around at his friends trying to decipher if Matt was telling the truth or just blowing smoke. They all knew about the rumor but also knew there wasn't much evidence to back it. Brian finally spoke out against it.

"It's just a dumb rumor some girls started spreading. No one thinks it's true, and Maggie doesn't even know about it."

"Besides," Avery added, "I heard that Kenny was over at Trick's all night after he got off work. Trick wouldn't lie about something like that."

Eric knew Avery was right but couldn't dismiss the idea immediately. After all, he had suspected something more than what he'd been told was going on. Even if this was just a rumor, it might be a clue to what was really bothering Maggie. But he didn't want to approach Kenny if it truly wasn't him. He had to bide his time and pick the opportune moment.

His buddies could tell this was bothering him. Matt sat with a sadistic smile on his face, but the others were genuinely concerned.

"Seriously, Eric," Jeff said, "don't put too much stock in it. I mean, it's not like it really matters, anyway, right? If anything, it'd be nice to be able to thank whoever did it."

Eric nodded in agreement, though he had other thoughts running through his mind. Right now, he just needed to find Maggie and talk to her. He didn't want to tell her about the rumor because he wasn't sure how she would react to such a revelation. After looking all over the house, he couldn't find her anywhere, not even with Katie and Ashley.

The truth was that Maggie wouldn't be found anywhere in the house. Instead, she had slipped outside and was standing out on the pier. Despite the cold, it was a beautiful, clear night with the moon out in its crescent form and the stars dancing in the night air. The stiff breeze that had been blowing all night had subsided temporarily, so Maggie didn't feel too cold, but she did feel silly. Certain that she wasn't going to find what she was looking for, she stubbornly stood her ground looking for any sight of him. Every now and then, she looked behind her, expecting Eric to find her and convince her to come inside. He hadn't come yet. She didn't know whether to be happy about that or disappointed.

Inside, Trick had just completed another dance set with Ashley. His initial moves had set the bar a little too high for him, but he managed to hold his own. The two of them stepped into the kitchen to grab a drink. Ashley repeatedly complimented him on his moves for which Trick humbly thanked her. He never thought of himself as much of a dancer, but apparently, he'd picked up a step or two.

As they talked, Trick glanced outside and saw someone on the pier. Positive it was Maggie, he wanted to check on her and make sure nothing was wrong, but he couldn't bring himself to leave Ashley. Luckily, the solution presented itself as Scott entered.

"I hate to break the two of you up," he said, "but Jordan won't leave me alone. I really want to show him up, but my partner bailed. Can I borrow Ashley for a dance?"

Trick turned to Ashley hoping she'd say yes. "Is it okay with you if I miss one?"

Ashley nodded. "Don't go too far, we're not done."

"I'm just gonna catch my breath," Trick assured her.

Once Scott and Ashley returned to the dance floor, Trick grabbed his jacket. Eric was still aimlessly wondering the dance floor. He asked Katie again, but she still didn't know where Maggie was. A little frustrated, Eric remained determined to find her.

Had Trick known Eric was looking for her, he would have let him talk to her. As it was, he was happy to lend her an ear. The icy sting of the outside air barely bothered him, thanks to all the heat he'd built up while dancing. As his feet clomped on the pier, Maggie turned to see who it was but said nothing. Trick sighed disappointedly when he noticed she didn't have a jacket and started to remove his.

"I expected you to be Eric," Maggie admitted.

"Sorry to disappoint," Trick said as he started to wrap the jacket over Maggie's shoulders. She knocked it away.

"I don't need it," Maggie stated.

Trick played along, "I know—you're only turning blue because you ate Willy Wonka's gum."

Maggie chuckled as she conceded. "Fine."

Trick draped the jacket over her shoulders as the cold night air introduced itself to Trick's chest. Taking a second to adjust, he stood arms folded with his hands digging into his arms. Maggie pulled the jacket together to warm up. She knew what he was going to ask but didn't want to answer.

"Aren't you gonna be cold?" Maggie stalled.

"I've survived worse."

That was the second time she'd heard that line that night. "You and Kenny both," she said with a roll of her eyes. The comment slightly startled Trick, but he didn't occupy much of his time with it. The silence rolled on as Trick patiently waited for Maggie to get to the point. The longer he remained exposed in the cold air, the more he wished she'd get on with it.

"Your dancing sure has gotten better," Maggie commented.

Trick laughed. "I hope it's okay. I didn't mention that you taught me my moves."

Maggie nodded and smiled. The memories of Trick's inept beginning dance moves swept through her mind. If only she had had a video camera.

Trick's patience was waning rapidly in the cold. "So, we gonna keep beating around the bush as I drift towards hypothermia, or are you gonna be merciful and be direct?"

Maggie sighed. "I guess we can go with the direct approach tonight."

Trick stood waiting for Maggie to begin. She collected her thoughts so she could properly explain herself. It was bad enough she felt so silly being out here, she didn't need Trick thinking she was losing it or anything. Letting out one last sigh, she disclosed her concern.

"I feel stupid standing out here."

"At least you've got a jacket now," Trick said trying to lighten the mood.

Maggie smiled but ignored him. "He's not gonna come tonight. I couldn't even get him to stay before, why would he come now?"

Trick sighed. "I don't know what to tell you."

Maggie turned towards him, and Trick saw the desperation in her eyes. "Tell me that I'm out here for a good reason. Tell me that I'm not wasting my time waiting for this guy to show himself again."

Trick took a step towards Maggie and spoke softly. "You're hoping. You can't go wrong with hoping; we all do it. We all have to do it if we expect to make it through life. Not everything can be logical. We can't always act rationally. Sometimes, we have to go with our heart. If that means you gotta stand out in the cold on a pier waiting for a man in black to show himself, then that's what you do."

The frustration was mounting for Maggie. "What are the odds of that happening?"

"Odds," Trick repeated, showing animosity towards the word. "Odds don't mean anything, especially when it comes to this. They're just numbers on a paper somewhere removed from the event. We use them to make us feel like we have some kind of control over a situation when it's actually out of our hands. When we have the odds in our favor, it gives us confidence. When we don't, we use it as justification so we can to cower away without feeling bad about ourselves.

"The fact is that one of two things is going to happen: either he's going to come or he isn't. If you want to believe he's going to come, then stay here and hope. If not, then go inside and hope he shows up some other time."

The words provided some comfort, but in other ways, they only added to the frustration. Maggie turned back to look over the lake.

"I hate that this is that far out of my control," Maggie confessed. "That nothing I do to try and find him may make any difference at all."

"It may end up that way," Trick admitted. "Or maybe, somehow, everything you're doing is playing a role...."

"You don't have to try to make me feel better," Maggie interrupted.

"I know," Trick acknowledged, "but I like to."

Maggie looked back at Trick; this time, her eyes were grateful. Wrapping her arms around Trick to show her appreciation, she smiled at her luck of having such a wonderful friend. Even tonight of all nights, when he's actually here for himself, he still had time to worry about someone else.

Their embrace broke up when they heard the faint sound of steps on the pier. They turned to see Eric standing behind them with a concerned smile painted on his face.

"Everything okay out here?" he asked.

Maggie joked. "Just feeling nostalgic, I guess."

"Good idea to bring someone with you," Eric said pointing at Trick.

The air was ripe with awkward silence. Three was definitely proving to be a crowd at this point. Eric had questions for Trick and Maggie both but didn't want the other around to hear what he had to say. As far as she was concerned,

Maggie had finished talking for now and she was ready to get warm inside the house.

"Well, I've got enough air for now," Maggie said, to remove herself from the situation. She hoped Eric would follow. "Are you coming, Eric?"

"In a minute," Eric replied. "I think I could use some air myself."

"Okay," Maggie replied.

She gave Trick a concerned look, a little leery about leaving the two of them alone out there. She trusted Trick without question but couldn't figure out why Eric would want to talk to him alone. In a vain attempt to rescue Trick from the impending onslaught of questions, Maggie stopped.

"Trick, what about your jacket?"

"Just leave it by the door," Trick replied to assure her he would be okay. He was still looking at Eric, understanding he wanted to have a word with him. "I'll be in soon."

The two boys watched Maggie walk all the way back to the house. Eric preserved the silence, not wanting to chance Maggie hearing anything he was about to say. Trick, nerves somewhat on edge and skin beginning to shiver in the cold air, waited patiently. As soon as the kitchen door closed, the two faced each other again. Eric sighed as he made a surprisingly candid confession to Trick.

"I remember when Maggie and I started dating." Eric stepped to the edge of the pier and looked to the sky as he digressed. "Everyone knew that you two were the best of friends, thick as thieves. You were neighbors, hung out at school, even had some of the same classes. A lot of people said you two were destined to be together. I didn't buy it at first—thought it was just a lot of talk to be honest.

"Then, I started listening to the way she talked about you. I saw how much time you two were together and how happy she was around you. It took me a few months to see all that, and I hated you for it."

Now Trick couldn't help but be uncomfortable. He wasn't sure where this was going, but he couldn't imagine it was anywhere good. Swallowing that discomfort, he listened carefully as Eric continued.

"I hated that she seemed to be happier with you than with me. I hated that she'd rather talk to you than anyone else, including me. And I hated that whenever we went out with my friends, she wanted to invite you along. It made me think I was losing her."

Trick had to interrupt at this point. "Come on, Eric. I'm like family to her. It would never be like that between us."

Eric nodded in agreement. "I know, Trick, I know. I figured that out eventually. After a while, I saw that you were important to her, but not like I was. It was just the history between you that made your friendship so strong, and once I had some history with her, all that concern subsided."

Trick was relieved to hear that.

"I'm telling you all this, Trick, because I know you'd be the one she would confide in. I may not like it, but you probably know her better than anyone else. I can't shake the feeling that she's hiding something about this whole rescue from me. And that's making me feel like I'm losing her again."

Trick sighed deeply for two reasons. One, he may not have been great friends with Eric, but the two of them were getting closer as he continued his relationship with Maggie. To have the kind of trust Eric spelled out to him was a sign of that, but Trick wished Eric didn't trust him so greatly. Because Trick's second reason was that despite the fact that Eric was right, he knew it wasn't his place to tell him something Maggie was trying so desperately to hide from him. He would have to lie to Eric for Maggie's sake.

"Something else happened with the guy that saved her," Eric theorized. "Something big. That's why she wants to find him. That's why I think I'm losing her again."

"Eric, she went through a pretty traumatic experience," Trick said, building a defense. "For that matter, you did, too. I mean, it's an especially unique situation, and I can't say I'd come out the same after it. She probably feels vulnerable right now, maybe a little isolated since she was the one in grave danger. Now she's just trying to come to terms with it, and she's gonna have to do that on her own."

Trick built a good case; Eric owed him that. However, he still couldn't shake the idea that there was something more to this whole thing. "So she hasn't told you about anything odd that happened that night."

Trick started shaking his head, but it took a second for his response to come out. He still didn't like having to lie, even if it was for a good reason. "No, nothing different from what she's told you."

Eric seemed satisfied with everything Trick had told him. He still wasn't one-hundred percent convinced that he had the whole story, but he was convinced Trick had told him everything he knew. There was just one more topic to cover.

"So Matt tells me that Kenny showed up at your house last Friday after falling into a lake."

Trick thought about jumping in the lake himself. His luck tonight had really taken a dramatic turn towards the unpleasant side. Suddenly, he had another situation he'd have to lie about.

"Yeah, but he wasn't anywhere near here," Trick assured him.

"Is that what he told you?" Eric asked. He didn't bother to explain the rest of the rumor since Trick seemed to know what he was talking about.

"Yeah."

"And you believe him?"

Trick shrugged his shoulders. "I've got no reason not to believe him."

Eric nodded his head as he put all the pieces in his head together. He trusted Trick even if he was more a friend-of-a-friend than an actual friend. If Trick believed Kenny was telling the truth, then Kenny must be telling the truth. Giving Trick an appreciative pat on the back, Eric left the pier without saying anything more. As he walked the path back to the house, he saw Maggie waiting for him at the door. When he got in, he said nothing about what Trick and he talked about and just went back to the festivities. Maggie remained suspicious and wondered why Trick remained at the pier.

Trick couldn't help but feel the screws beginning to tighten, suggesting that things were going to get much worse before they got any better. He was the only one who saw all the elements of this situation and knew they'd all collide eventually. What would happen then? Whose side would he be on? With all the lies he'd been telling, would he be on anyone's side? He suddenly reviled everyone who was putting him in this position but knew he could never act any other way.

As he stared out over the lake, he suddenly remembered Ashley. He had no idea how long he'd been gone but he was convinced it had been too long. Sprinting to the door, he flung it open, happy to be in the warmed air. He searched for Ashley but didn't find her anywhere. While pacing through the living room, he saw Kenny and Jessica sitting on the couch talking about who knew what. He asked where Ashley was, and Jessica told him she'd be right back.

The frustration Trick was feeling practically appeared on his face. Neither Kenny nor Jessica felt comfortable enough to ask Trick what was wrong. Eventually, Kenny dared ask what happened.

"Oh, nothing much," Trick replied. "I just got grilled on the pier by Eric who—by the way—knows about the rumor."

Kenny suddenly sat up and took notice. Jessica even seemed a little concerned by the revelation.

"He knows?" Kenny repeated.

Trick nodded. "Oh, yeah, he knows and he's concerned."

"But it's just a rumor," Jessica restated.

"I know that," Trick said, insulted she'd have to remind him. "That's why I called it 'the rumor.' But this is high school. Rumors become truths faster than the Royals lose baseball games."

"So what did you tell him?" Kenny asked, concerned.

"Oh, don't you worry," said Trick patting his knee. "After he told me how much he trusted me, I strung together an elaborate web of lies that should keep him off your trail."

Kenny smiled. "Good man."

Trick couldn't echo the sentiment. "Yeah, I'm a regular Good Samaritan."

Before they could go any further, Ashley returned and sat on the armrest of Trick's chair. "Hey, you," she said. "I thought maybe you'd flown the coop."

"I may want to flee, but it ain't because of you, Ashley." Trick said.

"What's wrong?"

Trick was still tense. "Oh, we're just discussing how Eric has moved into Rumorville, but it's okay because I lied to him about everything along the way."

Ashley gently rubbed Trick's shoulders to calm him. Her tender touch was extremely comforting. As Ashley worked her fingers into his muscles, Trick started to breathe easier. He sat back in the chair and closed his eyes. He wanted to drop the subject entirely, but there were just too many questions left unanswered.

"Who told him?" Jessica asked.

"Actually, your brother did apparently," Trick replied with his eyes still shut. "So, ya know, make sure you pat him on the back for that later...maybe, use a hammer when you do it."

Jessica and Kenny looked at each other and frowned. It wasn't a surprise to either of them that Matt would do something like this. Jessica got up from her chair, ready to have it out with Matt. Unfortunately, she couldn't find him anywhere.

For a few more minutes, Trick sat with Kenny, trying to make him feel better about Eric knowing about the rumor. One of the few calming facts Kenny had held onto regarding this whole situation was that neither Maggie nor Eric knew of Kenny's implication. Now that the finger was pointing at him, he was certain Eric would be watching him more carefully. All things considered, he didn't need that.

Trick repeated his same advice to Kenny: don't act any different and just play aloof to the whole thing. The more he tried to look innocent, the more attention he garnered. Kenny knew the advice was sage but didn't believe it would work anymore. He wanted to remove himself from any suspicion. If it took blatant actions, then so be it.

When Trick had finally had his fill of the conversation, he invited Ashley back to the dance floor. Pleasantly surprised, Ashley jumped at the chance. Happy to be in a more relaxed atmosphere, Trick allowed himself to focus solely on her. Even during this night, he hadn't really looked at Ashley as anything more than a friend. He had held her hand, danced with her, but that was more playing the part, not really putting himself in it. Now that he was actually considering it, he loved the idea of her being there for him and the two of them really giving this a shot.

As the party wound down and the hour grew even later, Ashley wanted to get home. Truthfully, she had probably been out too late as it was. She had things to do in the morning and knew she'd barely be awake for them now. Ready to go himself, Trick said his goodbyes before walking Ashley out to his car.

The drive home, they were mostly quiet—it had been a long night after all. Ashley was having trouble keeping her eyes open, and Trick was still reeling from the whole experience. As he watched her sitting in his car with her eyes closed, he felt comforted by her presence. Maybe, it was all the stress that the night had brought him or maybe he was genuinely happy to have her there with him. In any event, having her there seemed to alleviate some of his stress.

Ashley had dozed off during the ride. When he arrived at her house, he gently nudged her awake. She was embarrassed she'd fallen asleep.

"I'm sorry."

"No, I wish I could do the same."

Ashley laughed as she fumbled for her keys.

"Would you walk me to the door, I'm afraid I'll fall asleep along the way?"

Trick nodded as he unbuckled his seat belt and walked around to her door. Taking her hand, he gently guided her out of the car. After that, he stuck his hands in his pockets as she fumbled with her keys. When she got to the door, she unlocked the dead bolt and pushed the door open slightly.

"Well, this was fun," Ashley said.

"Yeah," Trick said. He paused briefly, thinking about all the fun he had truly had that night. It was definitely better than what he typically experienced on a Friday night. He didn't know exactly what the future held, but he knew he wanted to experience this again. "We need to do this again some time."

Ashley, shocked at his candor, smiled like a schoolgirl. "You mean it?"

"Absolutely," Trick replied sincerely. "Let's do something next week."

Ashley could barely reply, she was so ecstatic. "Okay, well there's a movie I wouldn't mind seeing, and I'm sure we could make it a group thing again."

"Sounds great," said Trick. "It's a date then."

"Yeah, it's a date," Ashley repeated, happy that Trick had said it first.

Ashley turned toward the door and pushed it wide open. She paused for a second before turning around and giving Trick a kiss on the check. He smiled and said goodnight as Ashley returned the sentiment and disappeared into the darkened house.

As he walked back to his car with a noticeable bounce in his step, Trick realized his dad had been absolutely correct. This whole thing with Ashley had been a process. He didn't have to have the answer right away, and at no point had anyone expected him to. It would and did come to him.

Chapter Seven

Feature Presentation

Though Trick felt exhausted by the time his head hit the pillow that night, he was amazed at how quickly the night had flown by. He opted to put aside all the drama that had developed with Eric and focused on the time spent with Ashley. The next day, he got a call from her while he was shooting pool in his garage. He got another on Sunday while doing his homework. At first, Roy didn't understand the attention his son was suddenly and unexpectedly receiving, but once Trick explained, Roy was delighted to hear it.

As a new school week started, everything seemed to be an extension of the party. Trick wasn't sure how, but Ashley managed to track him down in the TV studio before school. They also managed to find each other at lunch and in between a couple classes. The conversation never amounted to much and the handholding didn't persist. Trick already knew there were whispers about them; he didn't want to fuel the gossip.

Outside of school, Ashley called Trick on the phone habitually. The idea that Ashley's fantasy was coming to fruition brought a chronic smile to her face whenever she heard Trick's voice. Trick still felt swept away by the initial rush that Friday had given him.

It wasn't until Wednesday that they began to tie up the loose ends for the movie on Saturday. Trick regretted his inability to make the game Friday, but he had to be home because Roy was getting ready to leave again and wanted to spend some time with Trick.

It was easy to get Maggie to agree to come along. Surprisingly, she convinced Eric to come along with them as well. Kenny declined the invitation, even before he heard that Maggie and Eric were coming. Once they were on board, Trick knew better than to ask Kenny again. Still, Trick wanted to expand the crowd to help him alleviate his reservations. As he worked in the studio during class, he had the idea of asking Katie and Jordan. They seemed to be developing a little thing of their own, so Trick assumed they'd go for the idea. Katie agreed, but Jordan was more reluctant.

"What are we gonna see?" Jordan asked, fearing a chick flick.

"I think it was called 'City of Demons' or something like that," Trick replied. "I don't know…Ashley picked it out."

Jordan was confused. "But that's a horror film."

"Really," Katie said sarcastically, "I thought it was a Disney animated classic."

Jordan scowled at her for her remark. "I really don't see how that's necessary." He then turned back to Trick and nodded. "Alright, I'm in."

Trick extended an invitation to Scott as well who had been eavesdropping on the conversation.

"I don't know," Scott said. "I don't wanna be the seventh wheel or anything."

Jordan clarified his position. "Excuse you, if you're a seventh wheel then that means that Ms. Thing over there and I are a couple."

Katie scoffed. "In your dreams, Poindexter."

As the two stared each other down, the dynamic of Katie and Jordan's hostile relationship sparked Scott's interest. Maybe, he would be the only one on his own in a way, but watching the two of them go after each other could also prove to be more entertainment than he'd get elsewhere.

"Alright, I'll go," said Scott.

Trick gave the thumbs up all around and told everyone to meet in the lobby of the theater around six-thirty. As he walked out of the studio, Maggie rushed by him with a thick folder stuffed to the brim with paper scraps. Written in black magic marker on the front was 'Grandparents' Anniversary.' While she had finished part of the tape, she was still behind schedule and needed to make some solid progress if she hoped to get it finished.

She was so concentrated on the project that she didn't even bother to say hi to everyone in the room. Instead, she grabbed a seat at one of the editing bays and threw herself into the work.

"Well, Maggie, we're up to seven for Saturday," Trick informed her.

"The more the merrier," Maggie replied her attention elsewhere.

"How's the project going?" Trick asked.

"Very slow, unfortunately," Maggie replied as she rummaged through the folder. "I don't know how I'm gonna get this done. I'm not gonna have time after school for a few weeks, but I gotta have it finished by then. And every other day I'm busy before school with STUCO. I don't think working just an hour a day will do it."

Trick and the others decided it would be best to give Maggie the room so she could work quietly. Just as he shut the door, Trick offered some encouragement. "Don't worry about it too much; I'm sure you'll find a way."

Maggie didn't reply but nodded her head to indicate she had heard him. Trick shut the door and continued his work in the classroom. In a small stroke of bad luck, Ms. Rutherford approached Trick with a project request from the building's administration. Though he had a full plate already, the project was important enough to warrant special attention. And there was no one else she would trust with the project.

Trick accepted the assignment, but it ate up much of his free time for the rest of the week. He still managed to see Ashley every now and then, but for the most part his schedule was booked. It was alright though—they still had Saturday. No school project could get in the way of that.

Come Saturday, Trick was elated to have a distraction from all his work. With Roy still out of town, he had the house to himself. He sort of wished his dad were there to remind him not to blow things out of proportion and just take it all in stride. Unfortunately, he wouldn't be back until Monday. And after a short week's stay at home, he'd take off for nearly a month. Leaving the day after Thanksgiving, he wouldn't return until a few days before Christmas. Trick wasn't happy that his dad was gone so much lately but knew there wasn't anything he or Roy could do about it.

After giving himself a pep talk over the things he was sure his dad would have said to him, Trick threw on his jeans, pulled on a baseball jersey over a white-T, and slung a ball cap on his head. The weather had been consistently cold, so he wanted as many layers as he could. He arrived at Ashley's house about six. He rang the doorbell, hoping she was ready to go. Instead, a middle-aged man in an argyle sweater vest with khakis, reading glasses, and a news-paper tucked underneath his arm answered the door.

"Can I help you, young man?" he asked.

"I'm here to pick up Ashley," Trick replied.

Ashley's father welcomed Trick in and informed him Ashley would be ready to go momentarily. Leading Trick into the living room, he offered him a seat while he waited. Trick gladly accepted as he looked around the house.

"Trick is a rather odd name," Ashley's dad said. "No offense, but I do find it peculiar."

Trick nodded. "I understand, Sir. It's a nickname really, but I haven't gone by anything else in years.

"I see." Ashley's dad smiled and then got a little more serious as he leaned closer to Trick and whispered. "I was hoping you could help me out a little, son. My daughter has been telling me over and over again that this is not a date. But with the way she's been talking about you to my wife, I'm finding that hard to believe."

The word 'not' echoed in Trick's ears. His immediate response was to think that Ashley didn't want her parents too invested in this. He was certain that this was a date, but apparently, it was important for her parents not to know that. At the same time, he didn't want the first thing he told Ashley's father to be a lie. He'd done quite enough of that for a while. Luckily, he didn't get a chance to answer.

"Dad," Ashley said, running down the stairs, "what are you doing?"

Ashley's dad stood up trying to thwart her suspicions. "Just being polite, dear. Someone has to keep the boy company while he waits for you."

"I already told you this isn't a date. He just agreed to pick me up."

"Who said anything about a date? I was just making pleasant conversation with the boy."

Ashley grabbed Trick's hand and hurried him out the door. Ashley's dad made her promise to be home at a decent hour and shook Trick's hand, telling him it was nice to meet him. Ashley seemed slightly upset by all the attention and finally shut the door so her dad couldn't follow them any longer.

They were quiet all the way to the car. Once they were safe from any listening ears, Ashley sighed.

"I'm sorry about that," she said. "If I had told him that this was an actual date, we never would've gotten out of there so easily." Trick chuckled as he started the car. "It's just that this is my first real date, and he's pretty protective since I'm his only daughter."

"Well, I'm just glad you got there when you did," Trick admitted. "I'd hate to have to lie to the guy just after I met him.

Ashley smiled as Trick took off towards the movie theater. Derby's Movie Plaza was a six-screen theater built a few years ago. From the outside, the building looked like a big white warehouse. There was a marquee on the edge of the parking lot showing the movies that were playing. Inside, the lobby was fairly small but housed a concession stand and three arcade games. Movie posters from old classics and popular new releases adorned the walls around the ticket office.

After Trick bought the tickets, he found Katie, Jordan, and Scott waiting by the concession stand. Scott had already gone through and was holding a tub of popcorn and a rather large soda.

"It's about time you showed up. This was your idea after all," reminded Jordan.

Katie jabbed him in the ribs with an elbow. "You're fine. We're still waiting on Maggie and Eric, anyway."

With time to spare, Ashley decided to journey to the concession stand herself. "Do you want anything?" she asked Trick.

"No, thanks, I'll be fine."

Ashley smiled and then walked away. Jordan and Scott watched her get in line, confused as to why Trick was still standing there like an idiot.

"What is wrong with you?" Jordan asked.

"What do you mean?" Trick asked.

Scott supplied the explanation. "You don't let her go the concession stand, you ask her if she wants anything and then get it for her. Or, if you're not that comfortable with the relationship yet, you at least go with her."

Trick glanced at the line and saw Ashley still standing in it.

"Should I just go over there then?"

Jordan shook his head. "No, it's too late. You've already blown it. Just think next time before you speak."

Trick looked over to Katie, trying to gage if he had really screwed up that bad. Apparently, he had because she could only nod in agreement with Jordan and Scott. It wouldn't take much longer for Maggie and Eric to arrive. However, they seemed at odds when they did show up, bickering from the moment they entered.

"I just don't wanna talk about it right now," Maggie whispered grabbing her ticket.

"Why not, because I'm getting close to whatever it is that you're hiding from me?" Eric asked.

Maggie sighed and begged him to drop the matter while they were in public. Eric wasn't exactly willing to comply but did clam up as they joined everyone else. No one was overly anxious to ask how Maggie and Eric were doing; they could just as easily imply such a thing from their demeanor. Still, something needed to break the tension.

"Alright, looks like we're all here," Jordan said. "Let's head in."

Trick held back a bit, waiting for Ashley to pay for her snacks. Maggie broke away to talk to Trick while Eric was talking to Scott and Jordan. The three of them had gone off on a tangent about the Kansas City Chiefs. She knew he wouldn't notice her slip away. As she approached Trick, she couldn't believe she was about to ask this of him, especially on his first date, but she needed the favor.

"I know you'll hate me for this," she said, "but can I get a ride home from you?"

Trick didn't see the problem. "Yeah, whatever. Is something wrong?"

"I'll tell you later," Maggie groaned. "I'm sure you want to get back to Ashley. Where is she anyway?"

"Over at the concession stand," Trick replied.

"You didn't go with her?"

Trick sighed. "That's just scary."

Once Ashley was ready, the three of them caught up with the others at their theater, which was the last room in the building. No one really expected the movie to be a big hit and thus, showings only played on the smallest screen they had. Most of the one hundred seats in the theater were empty for the time being. Jordan picked out a row maybe a third of way back from the screen. Letting Scott sit next to the aisle, Jordan sat next to him. Katie reluctantly sat next to Jordan. Ashley, Trick, Maggie, and Eric all filed in after her.

As the lights dropped in the theater, Ashley moved to the edge of her seat closest to Trick. Having learned from his mistakes, Trick noticed her slide over and set his arm on the armrest palm up. Ashley gladly took it and set her head on his shoulder. It was going to be a good movie.

The movie opened on a group of college students making a return road trip home from spring break. Unbeknownst to them, they stopped in a city haunted by mythic monsters. When their car broke down, it forced them to try to find another way out by exploring the city. Shortly afterwards, they discovered one of their friends torn to shreds by what everyone believed was an escaped animal of some sort. As the suspense mounted, Maggie became un-nerved.

"Scared?" Eric asked.

"Maybe," Maggie whispered.

He wrapped an arm around her and scooted closer to her. Maggie was unwilling at first to accept his 'protection' but eventually moved in closer to him and took a hold of his other hand.

On the opposite side, Scott was gobbling down the popcorn, loving every second of was happening on the screen. Jordan envied him in that be-cause Katie was currently tainting his movie-going experience by fiercely clutching his arm. Not bothered at first, it became too much for him when she started digging her nails into his forearm. He tried to break her hold but would need the Jaws of Life to do so. Once out of options, he demanded an expla-nation.

"Could you ease up, please?"

"I'm scared," Katie admitted.

"Yeah, and I'm bleeding."

In an effort to salvage his arm, Jordan grabbed Katie's hand with his free hand and once she relinquished her hold, wrapped his other arm around her.

As the movie carried on, the level of suspense decreased. Maggie had been satisfied sitting close Eric for a while, but eventually she got uncomfortable and shifted to a more pleasant position. Still clutching Eric's hand, she went to put her other hand on the armrest, apparently unaware that Trick had had his hand there the entire movie.

When their hands first touched, Trick glanced down but looked away, fully expecting Maggie to move her hand. Instead, a few seconds later, Maggie started softly massaging the back of Trick's hand. Trick still said nothing, as-suming Maggie would soon realize her folly. When she failed to do so, Trick slipped his hand off the armrest and gave Maggie a confused look.

Embarrassed and confused by her own actions, Maggie recoiled her hand. Eric and Ashley were both concerned when they felt Trick and Maggie pull away from each other. With so many eyes on her suddenly, Maggie was very apologetic.

"I am so sorry, Trick," she whispered.

"It's okay," he assured her.

Trick thought it best to keep his hands to himself from that point on. Resting it comfortably on his knee, he shook his head and refocused on the screen. Ashley, who had seen a small part of the incident, was perplexed.

"What was that about?" Ashley asked.

Trick shrugged. "Beats me."

Not exactly satisfied with the explanation, Ashley knew she couldn't get any more answers presently. Before dropping the issue, she glanced over at Maggie who was still trying to make sense of what she had done.

Eric was chuckling. "I think you freaked him out."

Maggie sighed. "Did Ashley see?"

Eric nodded, which only made Maggie feel worse. He assured her that it was no big deal, and Ashley would see it that way, too.

For the duration of the movie, Trick stayed close to Ashley. There remained a small amount of discomfort between Trick and Maggie, as both were cautious about even looking at each other. Luckily, they could let the moment pass them by since movie etiquette demanded their silence. Actually, the time proved beneficial as it allowed everyone to put the minor lapse in perspective. Ashley would have been embarrassed to admit it, but at the time, she was a little upset by Maggie's actions. However, once it was all behind them, she just blew it off as nothing big.

As the credits rolled, everyone stretched out in their seats. While there wasn't much of a crowd in attendance, they still waited for everyone else to clear out before they headed for the exit.

"That was a good movie," Eric said.

"Yeah," Scott said, still munching on his popcorn, "top notch."

"Was it?" Jordan asked, rubbing his ear and fixing his shirt. "I couldn't really tell. I only caught about half of the movie because someone kept screaming in my ear and for some reason the circulation in my left arm was getting cut off."

"Don't complain to me," Katie said walking past him.

Jordan sighed, wanting to say more, but knowing it would be better for him if he let it go. While Katie annoyed him in more ways than one, he was also very attracted to her. Of course, he would never admit such a thing. Trick walked up from behind Jordan and patted him on the shoulder. Ashley was following closely behind him, holding his other hand.

"Don't worry about it, man," Trick said. "On some level, I'm sure she really appreciated your sacrifice."

"It is nice to have someone to latch on to," Ashley admitted with a smile.

They walked through the lobby together, rehashing their own personal favorite moments from the movie. As they left the theater, they began to part ways for the evening. Jordan and Scott had driven together and not long after Katie said goodbye as well. As Maggie and Ashley continued to discuss the movie, Eric checked his watch.

"Hey, we'd better be on our way, Maggie," he said. "I have to be at work early tomorrow so I want to turn in."

Maggie hadn't told him yet that she had another ride. She thought about accepting for a moment, wanting to avoid infringing on Trick's evening any further. But if the ride to the theater was any indication, she knew the ride home wouldn't be pleasant.

"Actually," she replied, still unsure if she wanted to impose on Ashley and Trick, "you can go on ahead; Trick said he'd take me home."

This was the first time Ashley had heard of the idea, too. A pinch of jealously crept up her spine as she had had an understanding that the rest of the night would be a two-person affair, not three. This was their first date after all. Why would he bring someone else along when they were having their first date? Pulling Trick off to side, she made sure Maggie and Eric weren't paying attention.

"She's coming with us?" Ashley asked.

"We're just gonna drop her off," Trick assured her. "After that we can do whatever we want. I just get the feeling that things aren't that great between them right now."

Ashley nodded to give her consent to the plan, but she still wasn't thrilled with the idea. All in all, it didn't matter anyway. It was still a wonderful evening.

Eric gave Maggie a kiss on the cheek just as Trick and Ashley finished their chat. He shook Trick's hand as he said goodbye and gave Ashley a hug. As he made his way through the parking lot, he pulled his keys from his pockets and checked his phone. Once he was out of sight, Maggie turned to Ashley to offer an explanation. She knew that this needed one.

"Ashley, I'm sorry about this. It's just that we really had it out before the movie, and I knew we'd just argue more if I went with him. I don't want to ruin your date or anything."

Ashley put a hand on Maggie's shoulder. "It's okay," she sympathized. "It's no big deal. I don't think anything's going to ruin this evening."

Trick echoed the sentiment. "Yeah, it's no big deal. I'll just drop you off at your house and then it'll be just me and Ashley again."

It was a nice idea, but Ashley remembered something that would interfere with those plans. She wished she had remembered it sooner because it seemed like a really bad time to be bringing it up. Her shoulders slumped as she spoke.

"Actually, Trick, I have to cut the evening short. My dad is taking the family out of town for the day, so I really do need to be home early."

Though this sudden turn of events dashed his hopes, Trick didn't want to seem too disappointed. He rethought his plans before he responded. Maggie felt even worse than before, afraid she had done something that made Ashley uncomfortable and that was why she was going home. As much as Ashley assured them she really needed to go home, it didn't seem to alleviate the despair the two had.

Most of the car ride home was silent, the air filled with uneasy tension. Trick couldn't help but feel he had been mistaken in agreeing to take Maggie home. He should have known better that that, especially after their little moment during the film. To him, it wasn't anything, but he shouldn't have assumed Ashley would see it the same way. Maggie was mad at herself, too. She had championed this idea from the beginning and was one of the reasons Trick agreed to go along with this. Now, she had thrust herself between them during their first date. She should have asked Katie for a ride, but they were never alone so she could ask. Ashley knew the mood had swung in a bad way. It was no one's fault necessarily, just the timing in the way the chips fell. If she could calm the situation somehow, she would, but there didn't seem to be anything to say.

Since Ashley lived closer to the theater, Trick dropped her off first. He parked on the side of the road and walked Ashley to the door. As they walked up the driveway, there was still some uneasiness.

"So you had a good time?" Trick asked.

"Yeah, it was awesome," replied Ashley.

Trick was watching her carefully, attempting to decipher her mood. She had a smile on her face, but it seemed forced. Normally, her smile beamed elegantly and naturally, almost like she couldn't control it; it just happened. Now, she seemed to be putting on a show more than really feeling it. To Trick, it further cemented the fact that he had done something wrong.

"I probably should have told you I was gonna take Maggie home."

Ashley could see his thought process here and wanted to put a stop to it right away. Halting in the middle of the driveway, she took his hand in hers.

"Look, it's no big deal, honestly. I understand why you did it and if it were me, I probably would have done the same thing."

He wanted to believe her more than anything at this point but couldn't accept that as the truth. She hadn't told him before that she needed to be home right after the movie. Her dad didn't say anything before they had left. It all seemed too coincidental to have just happened the way it did. Still, he nodded to her that he believed her. As they finished the walk to the door, Trick began to plan ahead.

"So, you'll be out of town all day tomorrow."

His tone seemed to be more of a question than a statement, almost like he wasn't totally convinced Ashley would actually be gone. She realized then that he still didn't believe what she had told him.

"Yes, we'll probably get back fairly late, too."

Trick nodded again but didn't say anything else. In his head, he was thinking the trip was her wanting some space. He was happy to oblige in this instance since he was still thinking he screwed up already.

"I'll give you a call Monday then."

"Good."

Once at the door, Ashley took Trick's other hand, and the two stood face to face. To Trick, it felt like he was following a script of some sort rather than following the flow of the evening. He desperately wanted to go back and rewrite the last couple hours. He could live with making mistakes he didn't realize he was making, but to be conscious of those errors was distressing. All he could hope was that Ashley was being truthful, even if that seemed doubtful at the time.

"Are you okay?" Ashley asked.

"Yeah, I'm doing great," replied Trick in a vain attempt to cover up his concern. "I just wish the night didn't have to end so soon."

"I know what you mean."

Something was different. Not just some little thing that could be overlooked, either, but something dramatically different. They had been in this same situation not but a week ago: standing in front of Ashley's door having spent a wonderful night together. Both of them could feel it, they just refused to acknowledge it. It was one night after all. They couldn't expect too much at this point.

"Well then, goodnight," Trick said.

"Goodnight."

Ashley leaned forward and rose up to the tips of her toes. Trick leaned in as well. As their eyes closed, their lips met. In a moment that Trick and Ashley had been anticipating since they started down this path, they finally locked in a kiss. Trick felt the soft, warm feel of her lips against his but felt nothing else. The distant memory of the butterflies in his stomach from a week ago was just that, a memory. The dizzying rush of anticipation that created a joy in his heart he had never experienced before wasn't there anymore. Something was different.

As he pulled away, he noticed the smile on Ashley's face. It still wasn't that natural smile that struck him so compellingly before. Maybe, she experienced the same thing that he had. Maybe, she felt the change as well. In any event, the moment seemed to have failed to live up to the hype.

"You'll call Monday?" Ashley reiterated.

"Yeah, definitely," Trick replied.

Ashley said goodbye as she opened the door and went inside. After a final wave, she shut the door and disappeared. Trick stood staring at the closed door for a moment. He was blaming himself, trying to rationalize what went wrong that night, but no explanation could provide him any relief. He walked back down the driveway, head down. What was supposed to be one of the most memorable moments of his life only left him hounded by regrets.

As he reached for his car door handle, the smile that was on his face just hours ago seemed to be a dream. Everything accomplished that night, seemed as quickly undone during that short walk to the door. He opened the door and slumped into his seat. Maggie had moved up to the front seat. She was still gazing at Ashley's house as Trick sat with both arms on the wheel. He wasn't ready to start the car.

"That was sweet," Maggie said with a hand over her heart. "I couldn't hear what you were saying or anything but I'm sure it was sweet, too."

When Trick didn't respond, Maggie looked at him. His head was down, eyes staring blankly forward. The gloom lingering about him was unmistakable. What Maggie witnessed at the door lifted responsibility for ruining the night off Maggie's shoulder, but his look brought it all back down on her. She couldn't let him down like this.

"What is it?" she asked.

"Something's not right," Trick struggled to admit.

"No, I saw the whole thing," Maggie said. "Everything looked right."

"It didn't feel right," Trick snapped. Then he hesitated for a moment before throwing his head back and smacking against the seat. He began rubbing his eyes with his hands. "What did I do?"

Maggie knew it wasn't his fault. If she hadn't asked him to take her home, then they could have avoided this entire mishap. He needed to know that, too.

"It's me," Maggie said. "I should have left you alone. I should have asked Katie for a ride home or sucked it up and gone with Eric. I never should have asked you."

Trick dropped his hands from his face. He was vehemently shaking his head. It wasn't that.

"That's not it," he said. "There's something else. Maybe it's something I'm not getting or maybe something I overlooked, but this just isn't right. I should have known better than to add a third wheel to a date, but I didn't care. It didn't matter if it was you or Jordan or Katie, I would have said yes either way. And when she said she was going out of town tomorrow, I didn't believe her. I didn't believe her for a second, when I had no reason not to believe her. There's no trust. It doesn't feel like a give and take. I feel like I'm walking a tight rope or something. I'm afraid to lean the wrong way or say the wrong thing. I'm afraid I'll upset the balance, and then the whole thing will crash. She can tell I'm not comfortable, too, and that I don't believe her."

Trick jammed the key in the ignition and turned fiercely. The car roared to life. Maggie wanted to say more, to calm him and comfort him and let him know that everything would be okay. She wanted to apologize more because whether he wanted to admit it or not, she did play a role in the sour turn the evening had taken. He was too upset to listen however. He needed to calm himself down like he always did. It was easier for him to take on all the blame himself, and he wouldn't allow anyone else to take a small part of it.

As he drove, he remained silent. Maggie was troubled. She wanted him to talk it out the way she always did with him, but he didn't function that way. Instead, he kept it all inside and worked it out for himself. His eyes focused intently on the road and darted out the side window every now and then. She watched him, looking for the proper time to insert her comfort. It was nearly impossible to judge what the right time was. After a while, he started to relax, the noticeable tension in his muscles released. His breathing was calm, not erratic as it had been previously. When he finally let out a big sigh, she knew he was feeling better, but before she could ask anything, he spoke.

"So...you said you'd tell me what happened with Eric."

Maggie wasn't about to get into her problems. Having openly admitted that there were already problems between him and Ashley, he needed to talk this out. By the way he was talking, things sounded fairly dire. Then, at the flip of a switch, he wanted to forget about that and put the spotlight on Maggie. Not gonna happen.

"You can't be serious," she said upset with him. "After all of that that you just told me, you think I'm gonna pester you with my problems when you so obviously need to talk?"

Trick knew she wouldn't go down without a fight, but he'd hoped he wouldn't have to defend himself on this one. He shifted uncomfortably in his seat as Maggie insisted that he talk about his problems for a change.

"Look, I really don't want to think about this anymore," confessed Trick. "I know that if I do, I'll just end up blaming myself more and driving myself crazy. What I really need right now is to get out of my own head for a while. If you really want to help me, then give me something to distract me."

Maggie refused to consent to this request. "Maybe I don't wanna talk and would rather go home."

"Fine, I'll take you home. I'll find something else to distract me."

Maggie looked hard at Trick's face, trying to find a crack in his armor, but there wasn't one there. She felt utterly selfish talking about herself when her concerns lay with Trick. But she knew him well enough to know that he couldn't find anything to distract him if he was alone. If she went home, he'd go back to thinking about Ashley and would come out much worse than what he was right now. Her only hope was that she could eventually get something out of him after she had said her peace.

Unpleased with the situation, she told him not to take her home. He was happy to hear it but didn't admit it.

Trick pulled into his driveway and shut off the car. Maggie followed him to the garage. Once inside, she grabbed a bar stool and sat it next to the pool table. Trick went to the fridge.

"What do you want?" Trick asked.

"I'm fine, thanks," Maggie replied.

Trick grabbed two cans of Dr. Pepper anyway and set one down in front of Maggie. She rolled her eyes as she took the can and opened it. Still preoccupied, Trick grabbed the pool rack and flung it on the table. Working quickly to align the balls in the black frame, he set the rack and grabbed a cue. After the break, he sized up the table, waiting for Maggie to get started.

She was still holding out on the hope that he would change his mind and talk about his problems, but he wasn't about to crack. She took a few sips from her drink, watching him play. Finally, the silence had gone on too long for Trick as he felt his mind wandering.

"We gonna talk or what?"

"I was hoping maybe you'd take the lead," Maggie admitted.

Trick shook his head. "Keep dreaming."

The crack of the cue ball against the five-ball echoed in the room. The noise prevented Maggie from arguing the point any further, just as Trick hoped it would. When the echoes disappeared, Maggie reluctantly aired her grievances.

"Eric has been on a weird kick lately. Ever since last Friday, he's been asking more and more questions about what I remember after that guy pulled me out of the lake. I think something spooked him after he found us on the pier."

If Trick needed something to distract himself from Ashley, he certainly found it. He was sure something had spooked Eric on Friday because Trick was the one who had spooked him. Despite all his promises, Trick knew Eric didn't totally believe him after he heard the rumor about Kenny. Who knew what had happened during the week that provoked Eric further.

Regardless, Trick had another lie approaching him. He couldn't say anything to Maggie about what had Eric spooked because then he'd have to explain the rumor to her. He had already promised too many people that he wouldn't reveal the rumor. At the same time, it would help her immensely to understand the situation if she knew what he knew.

"Has Eric said anything to you, Trick?" Maggie asked.

Trick sighed, knowing he had to be careful. "He's concerned that he may be losing you."

"Why would he think that?"

"Mostly, he doesn't buy your story about nothing else happening that night," Trick said as he lined up a shot. "I'd think that was weird myself, but I know that you are hiding something from him."

Maggie didn't appreciate the sarcasm. "Well what else am I supposed to do?"

Trick set the cue down on the table for a minute so Maggie could tell he was serious. "Tell the man the truth. Let him know what's bothering you so he knows he's got nothing to worry about. That's all he wants."

Maggie shook her head. "Knowing is not gonna make him feel better."

"Well, in the meantime, not knowing is making him feel worse," said Trick. "You can't assume how he's gonna take this…you just can't."

Maggie paused for a second, not entirely sure what to do next. Trick's logic made a lot of sense in theory, but he didn't know Eric like she knew him. He was concerned at this point, but if he knew the truth, he would become obsessed like her. Only his motives wouldn't be so innocent. Trick could not assume that; she could.

"It's just better this way," Maggie said.

"Is it now?" Trick asked grabbing his pop. "You couldn't stand two small car trips with him tonight. How long until you can't be in the same room with him?"

It was a realistic possibility but not a thought Maggie wanted to dwell on. It wouldn't come to that. She wouldn't let it.

"It'll all get swept away soon enough," she promised.

"How so?"

"Eventually, I'll see that he isn't coming back. Once I see that, I won't give him another thought and things will go back to normal. Then, that'll be the end of it."

Trick wasn't convinced. "It's been pretty hard for you to focus on anything else lately. You told me that."

Trick lined up a jump shot on the table. The cue ball was resting behind the nine-ball, but Trick needed to pocket the four on the other side. If he hit the cue ball right, he could bounce it over the nine and hit the four.

"It's barely been two weeks," Maggie said in her defense. She knew Trick wasn't going to change his stance on this. He wanted her to tell Eric for all the right reasons, and he as far as he was concerned, he was right. She could only hope to prove him wrong in time. "Honestly, I think about him less and less every day."

"Liar," Trick replied.

Before Maggie could respond, he struck the cue ball. Maggie watched as it soared over the nine, collided with the four as it landed on the table, and propelled the four into the corner pocket. Trick knew he was right; Maggie couldn't argue that.

Chapter Eight

Missed Opportunity

Maggie stayed over for a couple hours before going home. Trick would say nothing more in regards to Ashley in the time Maggie was there. Sunday passed without incident. Come Monday, Trick was anxious to call Ashley and feel out the situation. His plans met a slight interruption when he had to run to the airport in Wichita to pick up his dad. Not wanting to be in a situation where he would have to end the call as soon as his dad arrived, Trick refrained from calling Ashley while at the airport. Roy's flight was due to arrive at five, which would get them home plenty early; however, a series of delays kept Roy's plane from taking off for three hours. He would not arrive in Wichita until ten-thirty that night. When he got home, Trick thought better than to call Ashley so late. It would be the first in a series of events that drove a wedge between the two.

That Tuesday, Trick worked in the TV studio before school, during lunch, and after school. He failed to see Ashley all day and only talked to her briefly that night when he called her. As time rolled on, they saw less and less of each other, and their calls got shorter and shorter. Prior engagements kept them from getting together over the weekend. Come Sunday, Trick didn't even bother to call.

The following Tuesday was the last day on the schedule before Thanksgiving break. In the TV studio, Trick was lying on the couch. Since it was before school, Ms. Rutherford didn't mind him relaxing on it. He even got to the point where he could leave the lights off. He liked to think in there. It was quiet, solitary. Something about lying with his legs hanging off the arm-rest at his knees while staring up at the ceiling pattern really got his brain churning.

He didn't know what to do. This thing with Ashley seemed to have lost all its momentum. He figured it was just a matter of time before she moved on and called the whole thing off. If it were to happen, he wasn't even sure how he'd react. He'd be disappointed definitely, because he knew how special she was. Yet, he had made such a mess of things, it might be the smart call to pull the plug.

About twenty minutes before class started, a sudden flash from the lights blinded Trick momentarily. He jerked his head to the side, almost falling off the couch. Squinting, he looked to the door and saw Maggie there with an apologetic look in her eyes and a hand over her mouth.

"I didn't wake you up, did I?" she asked.

"No," Trick said with a smile. "Ms. Rutherford makes sure I don't sleep in here."

Maggie seemed relieved as she trotted over to the editing bay. She seemed frantic with the thick folder shaking in her arms. Trick wondered why she would be here so early. Normally, she didn't show up until the five-minute bell rang.

"So, what brings you here?" he asked.

"I've got to get this anniversary video finished," Maggie replied. "My parents told me the party got moved up to this Sunday which means this is the last day I have to work on it. Not helping matters is the fact that I'm nowhere near being done with it."

"How much do you have left?" Trick asked, getting comfy on the couch again.

"I'd say about seventy-five percent."

"Ouch!" Trick exclaimed. "No way you can finish today."

"I've got to try or at least get something presentable done."

Maggie plugged the project disk into the editor. As the computer uploaded the data, she sorted through the papers required to complete the video. Trick had just closed his eyes when he heard her get up and dash out of the room. He sat up again, waiting for her to come back in. When she did, she was holding a piece of paper. In a huff, she sat at the monitor, her eyes darting back and forth between the paper and the screen.

"This isn't possible," said Maggie reviewing the paper.

"What is it?" Trick asked.

Rather than answer, Maggie ran to her cubbyhole in the classroom. She grabbed a different folder, whipped out a piece of paper, and ran back into the studio. Trick was still looking for an answer but did not get one. Finally taking matters into his own hands, he got off the couch and walked over to the monitor. As Maggie scrolled through the clips on the monitor, she compared them to the paper. Remembering Trick's question, she answered.

"It's done."

"What's done?"

"The video," Maggie replied. "It's done, the trimming, the sequencing, the music, the titling, it's all done!"

Trick shook his head. "Twenty-five percent isn't done, Maggie."

"I know that. I didn't do this." Maggie confessed.

"So, who did?"

"It would have to be someone that was in here just about every day last week."

Trick thought for a minute. Ever since Ms. Rutherford assigned him that project for the administration, he had spent most of his time after school in the studio. He could only remember one other person being there with any consistency, and he wasn't about to bring up his name.

"I don't really remember anyone else being here," Trick said.

Maggie left the studio. Trick followed. Ms. Rutherford was sitting in the computer lab helping a yearbook student with one of the pages. Maggie didn't bother to wait to ask her question.

"Ms. Rutherford, you're here until about five every night right?"

"Except on Fridays," Ms. Rutherford corrected. "Why, did you need to stay after?"

"No, I was curious if anyone was in the studio last week after school."

Ms. Rutherford stood up and looked at Trick. She never really paid a whole lot of attention to the studio but knew he had been back there.

"You'd be better off asking Trick...." she began.

"I didn't remember," he interrupted.

Ms. Rutherford apologized for not being able to help. Disheartened, Maggie started walking for the studio. Trick felt relieved that Ms. Rutherford didn't remember Kenny being back there with him. He really dodged a bullet on that one. Or so he thought. Not long after he had let out a satisfied sigh, Ms. Rutherford stepped out of the computer lab.

"You know, Maggie, now that I think about it, Kenny was back there quite a bit. Never got a look at what he was working on, but it must have been quite a project. Trick, I'm surprised you forgot that."

Trick knew he had to cover his tracks carefully. "Oh, yeah, he was so quiet I forgot he was back there."

"Actually, I remember you two making quite a ruckus...." Ms. Rutherford said.

"Thank you," Trick interrupted.

"I almost had to kick you out of here...."

"Thank you!" Trick said a little more forcefully.

Maggie and Trick went back into the studio. Maggie's excitement for the finished tape made her completely overlook the fact that Trick remembered Kenny being there. As they walked through the studio doors, Katie was standing over the editor looking at the completed project.

"Hey, you finished," she said. "Congrats."

"Actually, I didn't finish it," Maggie cheerfully admitted. "I had a secret elf finish it for me. And you are not going to guess who it was...."

Katie had one guess. Actually, she thought it was more of a joke than an actual guess. She couldn't stop smiling as she said his name. "Kenny?"

Maggie was shocked. Trick was horrified.

"That's right! How did you know?"

Katie quickly saw the error of her ways. She really wasn't being serious when she said it was Kenny, but now that the thought was out there, Maggie couldn't ignore it. What she needed was an excuse that would make her think of Kenny, and luckily, she had one.

"Oh, I wasn't being serious," she replied. "He just happened to be in here a couple mornings when I was in here."

Trick covered his face with both hands as it all blew up in front of him. It was bad enough that Katie had implicated Kenny right off the bat, but now to add to the evidence by saying he was in the room before school was too much. The smile that broke across Maggie's face only made Katie regret what she had said.

"You saw him in the morning?" Maggie repeated, gaining interest. "Ms. Rutherford said he was here after school with Trick."

"Oh," Katie moaned, "really?"

"Look, I'll be right back," Maggie said, walking for the door. "I've got to go get my blank tape out of my locker so I can record this project."

Maggie ran out of the studio and fumbled through a cabinet for a new blank tape. Once she was out of earshot, Trick lowered his hand. Walking inconspicuously over to Katie, he could almost hear the dirt piling on Kenny's grave. Katie still had a remorseful look on her face, but it wasn't enough to mend the wound.

"What is wrong with you?" Trick asked.

"I'm sorry." Katie replied.

Trick reminded her. "We are trying to keep a rumor under wraps here."

"One has nothing to do with the other."

For the time being, Katie was right, but Trick knew that could change. "Okay, I'll agree to that. Now, let's just say that Maggie starts to question why Kenny would do all this work. And if he did all of this work, he might have pulled her from a lake as well. In fact, this whole project thing might be a signal to her that he's still around."

Before Katie could answer, Trick presented another scenario.

"Or how about this: If Kenny's name is attached to that tape in any way, whether he actually did it or not, how is Eric going to respond when he hears that Kenny did all that work for Maggie just for the heck of it?

"Lastly, what if Kenny didn't do it? When Maggie goes to thank him, he'll get defensive. She'll think that's weird and start asking questions. These questions will inevitably bring her to rumor, which brings us back to scenario one, which makes scenario two all the more likely. So do you see how much more there is to this?"

Katie thought about arguing the point, but the thought Trick put into his little Doomsday picture impressed her too much.

"How did you do all that?" she finally asked.

"Panic," Trick replied. "You can do a lot when you're fueled by panic."

They nodded as Kenny ambled into the room. He slung his backpack onto the couch and fired up one of the other editing bays. Trick and Katie stood in terror of what was about to happen. Even if Kenny did all that work, they doubted he'd admit to doing it. As calmly as he could, Trick strolled over to Kenny. Kenny greeted him as he got started on his work. Trick wasn't sure what to say, so he went directly to the point.

"You're so gonna wanna leave like now."

Kenny chuckled. "What do you mean?"

Before Trick could explain anything further, Maggie walked into the room with a blank tape in hand. He turned in fear when he heard her. Katie jumped, startled by the situation. Kenny, confused by their actions, looked to see what was going on. When he saw Maggie, he didn't know the specifics, but he knew it wasn't good.

"I hate the plastic wrap on these things," Maggie was saying, holding the tape. "It takes five minutes to get it all off…." She paused as she saw Kenny sitting next to Trick. A big smile formed on her face as she pushed the tape into the VCR. "Well there he is…my own personal hero!"

The accusation was quite unsettling to Kenny. As he looked to Trick for some kind of reassurance, the worst possibility ran through his head that Maggie knew the rumor. Trick looked away, slowly walking over to the couch and sat down to watch the fireworks. After a few tense filled seconds of silence, Katie joined him.

"This is gonna be bad, isn't it?" Katie asked.

"Oh, yes." Trick nodded violently.

Kenny was still on edge, thinking about running but knowing that wouldn't help anything. A bead of sweat formed on his forehead even though the room was cold. Maggie hit record on the VCR before explaining her praise.

"I came in today to find that my grandparents' anniversary tape was completely finished," Maggie announced.

Kenny felt relief that it wasn't the rumor, but he also felt confusion.

"What does that have to do with me?" he asked.

Maggie laughed. "Oh, don't be modest," she said. "Trick and Katie told me you've been in here before and after school. I just don't get why you'd do it for me."

Kenny glared at Trick and Katie, who were both looking up at the ceiling to avoid his gaze. Luckily, Maggie wasn't paying any attention to them at this point as she kept her eyes on the screen. Kenny felt it necessary to clear his name.

"Sorry to disappoint, but I didn't do it."

"Really?" Maggie asked. "What were you working on, then?"

Kenny didn't want to answer that question. "I can't say."

Maggie smiled, thinking he was just being shy. "I get it."

Kenny wasn't pleased with her coyness. He was already irritated that two of his friends had sold him out. He didn't need this on top of it. He could already see Eric finding out about this and putting two and two together.

"I'm serious here," Kenny said. "I had nothing to do with it."

Maggie laughed it off. "Alright Kenny, whatever you say."

That was the final straw. Standing up from his chair, Kenny lost his cool.

"I didn't do it, alright! What, do you think I'm joking? I had nothing to do with it! I got better things to do than fix your problems!"

The outburst drew the attention of Ms. Rutherford, who suggested Kenny come out of the studio and calm down. Everyone else in the studio was aghast at the turn the situation had taken. It was one thing for Kenny to be upset about the accusation, but to yell at Maggie for it seemed a little much.

Quite insulted, Maggie went back to the monitor, embarrassed that Kenny had yelled at her in such a manner. Katie couldn't do anything but stare at the spot Kenny had been standing in. Ms. Rutherford asked Katie to come to the classroom since the bell was about to ring, but she let Trick stayed back in the studio in case Maggie needed help.

They sat in complete silence for a few minutes. Trick wanted to apologize to her for leading her down the path that suggested Kenny had done the work. He wanted to apologize for more than that, but he knew it wouldn't help right now. Instead, Maggie broke the silence.

"I just had a crazy thought," she said her voice a little shaky.

"Lay it on me," Trick replied.

"For a second, I thought maybe this had something to do with the guy who saved me," Maggie admitted. "It's kind of hard to think that now, huh."

"Yeah, I guess so."

After that, the silence really settled in. Trick stayed on the couch for a while longer, but once Maggie finished recording the tape, she said he could go on to the classroom and she'd be out momentarily. Trick took his seat with that look of disbelief still prevalent on his face. Katie said nothing to him because she was still in shock herself. Kenny, sitting arms folded with an angered looked on his face, didn't feel bad at all for his outburst. Even when Maggie came out and took her seat, he showed no remorse. The upcoming break was more than welcome now.

For Thanksgiving, Trick and his dad went through the normal holiday routine. In the morning, they got up early to visit Trick's grandparents on his mother's side. This was the tenth Thanksgiving they'd spent without Lilly, but Roy and Trick kept a close relationship with her parents. After a morning of stories about Trick's school year and Roy's work, they enjoyed lunch together. Soon after that, Roy and Trick left to go back home. Roy's family would be coming to their house for dinner.

It was around four in the afternoon when the first of Roy's family showed up. His brother, sister-in-law, and four of Trick's cousins arrived first. Trick was older than the rest of his cousins but loved having them around. He only saw them a handful of times per year, and they always seemed so different. A few minutes later, another of Trick's uncles with his family of five arrived as well. When Trick's other uncle pulled into the driveway with Roy's parents, it meant their family football game could begin.

Every year, the family played a game of touch football in the yard while they waited for the meal to be set. Trick always accepted the annual challenge of guarding Uncle Pat, who had played football at a junior college. Even though Pat had lost a step, he could still take Trick whenever he wanted, though he usually went easy on him. The game was more for the smaller kids anyway. But as Trick watched his cousins go, he realized it wouldn't be long before the game grew much more competitive.

The game ended with Trick catching a touchdown pass over Uncle Pat, which thrilled him to no end. As his grandma called everyone in for dinner, Trick lobbed the football towards the garage, and his eyes wandered across the street to Maggie's house. He could see her watching him from the living room window. Though she couldn't see the entire back yard from her house, Maggie was able to catch most of the action. Trick hadn't talked to her since the incident Tuesday in the TV studio. He hoped she had gotten over the unpleasantness. He waved at her; she waved back. He stood still for a few seconds before one of his cousins ran over, grabbed his hand, and pulled him towards the house.

Putting everything else out of his head, Trick spent the rest of the evening listening to everything he could about his family. One of his cousins was going to start basketball this winter. Another just finished her volleyball season. The others were excited about the things they had done in school, which Trick could never hear enough about. His uncle was getting a promotion at work. His aunt and other uncle were planning a family trip to Florida over Christmas break. His grandparents were going on a cruise as well. Everything with him seemed to be small by comparison, but everyone wanted to hear about Trick's impending graduation and college selection. He didn't have all the answers yet but could admit he was eager to start college. It wasn't until ten at night that his family started to clear out. He wished they didn't have to go. He loved seeing them and being worry-free for a change.

The next day, Roy shipped out early in the morning. Apparently, too early in the morning to wake Trick because when he awoke, Roy was already long gone. He stumbled down the stairs and found a note tacked on the fridge.

Didn't wanna wake you up that early, kid. I figured that if I did, you wouldn't be in the best of moods. So, you're on your own again for a while, but don't worry, I'll check in on you every once and a while. If you get in any trouble, you better be able to cover it up before I get back. Anyway, leftovers are in the fridge, call if you need anything. Have fun!

Trick smiled as he tossed the note aside. Foraging through the fridge, he found the makings of a small lunch buffet. Taking his picnic for two up to his room, he set up everything nicely on his desk before turning on his TV and putting a movie on.

About three in the afternoon, he heard someone at the door; the handle turned a few times, then went silent. A minute later, a key when into the lock, rattled it loose, and the door opened. Trick didn't bother to leave his room, knowing it was Maggie. Hearing the TV in his room, she trotted up the stairs to see Trick sitting on his bed with a plate of food on his chest. He had also pulled up a chair next to the bed for her but kept his eyes on the TV.

"You know, it could've been someone else," Maggie said.

"Sure it could have," Trick said. "And something besides the sun is gonna rise in the east tomorrow."

"I'm not that predictable," Maggie said.

"There's a plate and can of pop on the chair for you."

Maggie had almost sat on it before Trick said anything. She scowled at him, trying to let him know he wasn't right about everything. To prove her point, she set the plate on the floor but opened the pop. They sat in silence for a few minutes while Trick ate. When he finished with his meal, he put the plate on his desk, covered all the food, and shut off the TV. He brushed some crumbs off his shirt before facing Maggie.

"So, to what do I owe the pleasure?"

He was assuming that something had happened to her that she needed to talk about. For that reason, Maggie could take solace in the fact that he was wrong. She may have had something happen to her over the past few days, but she was much more concerned with his predicament. It had been some time since he had said anything about Ashley, but she knew him well enough to know she was still on his mind. Maggie had let him off the hook before. She wasn't about to let him do it again.

"This isn't about me," she proudly proclaimed.

Trick asked, taken aback, "So, this is purely a social visit?"

"No, this is about you," Maggie said definitively.

Trick sighed, trying to think of a way to weasel out of this one. He didn't want to chat about Ashley…not now; he wanted to keep things positive. When he looked in Maggie's eyes, he understood there would be no dodging the issue this time. She came to discuss this, and discussed it would be. Trick shook his head a few times before he began, and Maggie sat coolly, patiently waiting for him to open up.

"I haven't even talked to her this week," Trick confessed.

"Why not?"

Trick shrugged.

"Pick up the phone and call her then," Maggie ordered.

"I can't," Trick replied. "Things have really soured over the past couple weeks. I really don't think that she wants to talk to me."

"Of course, she does, she cares for you," Maggie corrected him. "She's wanted this thing with you for so long. Don't you remember how excited she was when you finally asked her out?"

"Yeah, I remember. I also remember the look on her face when we first kissed, and the way she looked all last week when we were together. Whatever I had going for me before, I've lost it now."

Trick seemed upset, but he was still trying to hold most of his feelings inside. He wouldn't make eye contact with Maggie while she was there. His tone was plain, his answers blunt. He was on the verge of giving up if he had not done so already. Maggie needed to get him thinking positively again. She needed to find a way to right something she had wronged.

"It's just a rough patch. Everyone has them. If you just give it time and try to work through it, you'll be fine. But you can't give up on this."

"A rough patch," Trick repeated. "Is that what this is? Something tells me that a rough patch to start a relationship isn't the best sign."

Maggie was getting frustrated that Trick didn't seem to be fighting at all to keep this going. She had assumed that he did feel something for Ashley, but maybe she was wrong about that.

"Do you even care if she doesn't want to date you anymore?"

The question made Trick pause mid-breath. He couldn't think about anything else with that question lingering over his head. It was the one he hated; that he refused to give any thought to because either answer presented a dilemma. If he said no, that he didn't care, then he risked straining his friendship with Ashley if she did want to pursue this more. If he said yes, but Ashley wanted out, then he'd be open for a world of hurt if she rejected him. In the end, he had to be true to what he felt.

"Yeah, I care," he replied. "I don't know what I feel for her, but I do know that something special was there."

Maggie smiled, touched by the honesty and vulnerability his answer displayed. To her, his course of action was set—he had to call her now. He had already wasted so much time contemplating. It was time to act.

"So pick up the phone," she reiterated. "Call her and tell her the truth."

Trick wasn't convinced. "What am I supposed to say?"

"Tell her what you just told me. Tell her that you think she's special and that you don't wanna give up on this so quickly. Let her know that she means something to you and that you'll try to make things right again."

Trick gathered his thoughts for a quick second, regaining his resolve. Reaching for his phone, he knew Maggie was right about everything. As he dialed the numbers, he began to feel silly for having acted the way he did. If she really was going to be someone special to him, he couldn't hide the truth from her. And he couldn't remain so guarded. The phone rang, intensifying Trick's determination. When he heard someone pick up, he could barely hold in his exhilaration.

"Is Ashley home?" Trick asked.

Ashley's mom had answered the phone. "I'm sorry, she's not. She had a date tonight."

Thrown for a loop by what he heard, Trick could barely muster a reply. "She had a date," he repeated. Maggie's jaw dropped. She attempted to hide her expression, fearing it would rattle Trick. He was too stunned to notice. Ashley hadn't even called their date a date to her parents, but her mom knew about this one. It said everything all too clearly.

Ashley's mom broke the silence. "Yes, she left about five minutes ago. It was quite a surprise to us when she told us about it. We really didn't know that she was seeing anyone like that."

Trick fought to hold his composure through this awkward turns of events. "Do you know when she'll be back or who she was with?"

Ashley's mom strained to come out with an answer. "Well, I'm not sure when she was going to be back, but the young man that came to the house was named Scott."

Just hearing his name almost knocked Trick to the floor. "Oh…well…thank you."

"Would you like to leave a message?" Ashley's mom asked out of courtesy. "I can make sure she calls you when she gets home."

Trick quickly declined the offer. "Oh no, it's nothing that important. I'll just see her at school."

He slowly hung up the phone and stared down at the ground. Unable to lift his eyes any higher at this point, he seemed to be a shadow in a fog. Maggie, knowing only what she had heard Trick say, could only sit in silence, her own heart breaking a bit. It wasn't fair. It wasn't right for things to go down like this. Trick deserved better than what he got.

"It may not be what it seems," Maggie said holding out a last sting of hope.

Trick was more pessimistic. "Her mom knew it was a date. When we went to the movies, she didn't even use the word date because she was too concerned about her parents knowing. If they know now, then it's definitely what it seems to be."

Trick rose up from the bed and slowly paced across the room a few times. He was searching for something to do, something that would alleviate this pain and anger he was suddenly drowning in. This twist of fate had revved him up like a car engine. All this negative energy was surging through his body trying to find an escape but nothing was available. He had an urge to punch the wall but couldn't bring himself to do it. He thought about running out of the house and going until he couldn't run anymore. Under the circumstances, he felt like he'd be running forever.

When nothing would calm him, he took a long, deep breath and plopped down in a chair. He did whatever he could think of to calm himself down. He covered his face with his hands and rubbed his eyelids with his fingers. He rested his elbows on his knees, told himself not to worry, that things were happening this way because it was for the best. At the same time, the knowledge that his own mistakes led to this result fueled his rage. His pulse quickened. His breaths grew short and hurried.

Maggie could tell he was spinning out of control. It was a rare sight for him, but one she had seen before. There was nothing she could say that would make him feel better, nothing that would bring him serenity. Instead, she knelt down next to him and placed a hand on his shoulder. Instantly, he began to calm; his breathing slowed. Maggie felt a tear forming in her eyes. She couldn't bear to see him like this. A moment later, Trick dropped his hands and wrapped his arms around her. She was more than willing to wrap hers around him. As she held him, she felt more tears, all hers, none of them his.

"She was wrong to do this to you," Maggie said, her voice shaken and angered. "You didn't deserve this."

"I can't exactly blame her," Trick replied bluntly. "I pushed her away, even if I didn't want to."

"No," Maggie exclaimed. She pulled away from Trick a little. Taking his face in her hands, she looked painfully into his eyes. "She knew you weren't perfect. She knew you were gonna make mistakes. If she couldn't deal with that, then she should have at least told you to your face. Instead, she sneaks out on you, and you have to find out from her mom. She knew better than that."

Trick placed his hands on Maggie's, and they held on to each other tightly. At that point, it didn't matter who was to blame for the way things ended. It only mattered that things had ended.

Maggie would stay with Trick a while longer. She didn't say much to him; she just didn't want him to be alone at the moment. In the back of her mind, she had anticipated this possibility. She considered that maybe he had missed the boat and let the opportunity bypass him. She considered it, but never in her wildest dreams would she have expected it. Ashley didn't seem the type of person to abandon something so quickly, especially something she wanted so dearly. The more she thought about Ashley, the more Maggie grew irate at her. All this time, she waited on pins and needles for Trick to come around. Now that he had, she wanted to pull the plug at the first sign of trouble. It just didn't seem right.

Chapter Nine

Things Change

Trick confined himself to his room for the next several days. Only coming out for the necessities, he switched off his cell phone as well. If his dad needed him, he'd call the house phone, and he'd rather not talk to anyone else. Luckily, those who knew about the affairs that had transpired were limited to him, Maggie, Ashley, and Scott. Neither Ashley nor Scott would be stupid enough to try to contact him given the situation, and though it frustrated her to no end, Maggie knew better than to try. He would be okay, in time, but until then he sought solitude. It tore Maggie up inside to be so useless to her best friend, but she had no recourse.

By Sunday, Trick was too stir crazy to keep himself locked up inside. Venturing out to the garage, he played pool for a few hours. He also went ahead and turned on his cell phone. He didn't expect anyone to call, but he figured he could stand to talk to someone if they did. Unfortunately, the one call he had was from Ashley. While he wasn't about to call her back, he did listen to the message she left for him. She asked him to call her back because they really needed to talk. Unlikely.

Trick ignored the message and went outside. Even pool failed to lighten his anxieties. Outside, he grabbed a basketball and started shooting. As he got into it, he started making cuts, drove to the basket, and lost himself in an imaginary game. He noticed that Maggie's house had a mess of cars surrounding it, but he didn't concern himself with why. A little bit of thought and he would have remembered that her grandparents' anniversary celebration was today. The video proved to be a huge hit. There were tears in people's eyes and requests for copies. Maggie couldn't help but smile at all the compliments despite the fact that she didn't put it together.

As her relatives were leaving, she spotted Trick out in the driveway. She smiled, happy that he was finally out in the real world. Once it was down to just her and her parents, she crossed the street to check up on him.

"You finally came out," she said thrilled at the prospect.

"I guess even I can't stay inside forever," Trick replied.

Maggie waited, hoping he'd say something more, but when he didn't, she decided to fill the silence.

"The video went over well," she informed him.

Trick suddenly remembered why all the cars were there. "Of course it did, people love that mushy stuff."

Trick took a shot and ran after the ball. Maggie watched him for a minute, trying to figure out if she should pry any further. In the end, her curiosity was too high.

"Are you okay?"

"Fine," Trick replied unconvincingly.

Maggie grabbed the ball and glared at him for lying to her. Out of breath, Trick bent down, putting his hands on his knees for a minute. He motioned for her to throw him the ball, but she stubbornly refused to do so. Trick sighed.

"If you're not gonna give me the ball, I'll just go get another one."

Maggie sympathetically responded. "Trick…."

Before she could say anything more, Trick cut her off.

"Don't go there…not right now."

Maggie softly bounced him the ball but didn't have anything else to say. She didn't want to leave him so quickly even if that's what he preferred. Instead, she stood silently by the goal as the game went on around her. When the silence became too much for her, she went for broke.

"There's nothing wrong with talking about this."

"I don't talk about these things," Trick said. "So, if you're just waiting for me to open up, you might as well leave me alone."

"Maybe I don't think you should be alone right now," Maggie confessed.

Trick picked up the ball and held it underneath his arm. He was getting a little agitated by her stubbornness. "Maybe that isn't your call to make."

"Trick," Maggie said in her defense, "I'm just trying to help you."

"Did it ever occur to you that maybe you can't?" Trick snapped.

Mostly likely, Trick didn't mean for his remark to sound like it did, but regardless, it was offensive to Maggie. "No, that thought never for a single second occurred to me because you have always been there for me. You have always been able to help me because you're my best friend, and I thought that I meant the same thing to you." Maggie paused for a minute to see if Trick was going to react in any way, but he only took another shot. Dispirited, Maggie threw up her arms. "What do you want from me, Trick?"

"Nothing…okay? I don't want anything from anyone!" Trick barked. "Can't you understand? I just want to be left alone for a while."

Maggie looked into his eyes, still slighted by what he had said. She understood Trick wasn't mad at her. That wasn't anger in his tone; it was sorrow.

He was aching and needed time to recover. Why she couldn't assist in the process, Maggie didn't understand. While she was willing to concede for the time being, it still seemed wrong to imply that she couldn't help him feel better about this.

"Fine," Maggie said bluntly. "You want to be alone, then I'll leave you alone. But don't ever criticize me for trying to be a friend to you."

As she stormed off, a twinge of regret flickered in Trick's eyes. He suddenly hated himself even more for pushing someone else away.

"It's got nothing to do with you," he admitted. Maggie hesitated and turned to listen. "I know that you'd be there for me if I ever needed you to be, but I just don't work that way. I listen to you because you need to talk it out, but I try to keep things to myself and work it out my own way."

Maggie sighed and shook her head. "It can't always work that way, Trick. You can't always wear this mask to hide yourself from everyone. You can't bear the weight of the world on your shoulders because you're trying to be self-sufficient or whatever reason you're doing this for. Everyone has to have someone that they can turn to, no matter what. For me, that's you, it's been you, and I really hope it'll always be you. Why can't you do that with me?"

Trick held the ball, knowing he had no good answer for that question. As Maggie walked away, he tossed the ball aside and marched indoors. Heading straight up to his room, he slumped down on his bed and, despite the early hour, tried to get some sleep. He wasn't tired; he wanted the day to be over.

School went relatively well on Monday. Trick got a few sad looks from some people as he walked the halls. Some others gave their sympathy, which seemed unnecessary to Trick. To his pleasure, he didn't see Ashley all day. Whether it was luck or she was trying to avoid him, he didn't really care. It worked for him either way.

The next day in class, however, he knew he'd have to see Scott. While he wasn't overly upset at Scott, there were definitely other people he'd rather see. Everything went well for a majority of the class. It was only towards the end of the hour that Trick walked right by Scott who stumbled out of the way in a fright.

"What is your problem?" Jordan asked as he helped Scott up.

"He startled me is all," Scott replied.

That ridiculous notion proved to be enough to set Trick off. Fed up with the whole blasted thing, he got in Scott's face. "Oh, shut up ya moron! I didn't do anything to you when you put a dent in my car with a baseball bat or when you set fire to the couch in my living room with a match. I'm not gonna do anything to you now!"

Confused, Scott cautiously asked. "You mean, you're not mad at me?"

"No," Trick said convincingly, "I not mad at you. It isn't your fault; it's mine. I broke what I had going; you picked up the pieces. I don't begrudge you one bit."

Still nervous, Scott backed away; even Jordan felt a little startled. Trick glanced around the room and noticed all eyes looking at the three of them. Ms.

Rutherford was thankfully out of the room, otherwise the treatment of the situation would have gone quite differently.

Instead, Trick stormed into the studio and slammed the door. He worked it out with his teachers to stay in the studio all day so he could finish his project for the administration. They needed it finished soon, and he desperately wanted to get it out of the way. Maggie stood at the door, watching him as he labored over the project when his attention was truly elsewhere. Kenny and Katie soon joined her. Jordan and Scott kept their distance.

"I hate it when he gets like this," Maggie said.

"Like what?" Jordan asked.

"Every time something happens that really gets to him, he finds all these little chores to keep himself busy. Then he just shuts out the rest of the world and works like a maniac."

No one else really seemed to know what she was talking about except Kenny. While there had been smaller incidents in the past, one stood out among them all. The time when Trick really seemed to be in a downward spiral and no one could be sure if he'd pull out of it.

"I remember when his mom died," Kenny said.

Maggie nodded. "I was thinking about the same thing."

"What happened to her again?" Katie asked.

"A drunk driver hit her, going fifty-five on a country road. By the time the paramedics arrived, it was too late." Everyone held a respective moment of silence before Maggie continued. "After the funeral, he spent days in the garage just doing little things that didn't need to be done. They had just finished constructing it then, and his dad had all these plans drawn up for it. He was going to put them on hold for a while, but Trick took on the chores himself. He cleaned it out, started painting it, and turned it into the place that it is today. That pool table was the nastiest thing out there, and now it almost looks like it's brand new."

"But he was only eight," Katie remarked, astounded by the work.

"Yeah," Kenny said with a smile. "It was a pretty remarkable feat for someone so young. He probably spent a month in that garage cleaning it up. His dad tried to get him out and about, but everything he tried failed. I never saw him outside the garage or the house for that month out of the summer."

Maggie concurred. "I only saw him a few times and he was always sitting in the grass next to the garage staring into the back yard. When I'd ask him what he was doing, he just said he was thinking about the tree."

"The tree?" Kenny repeated. "He never said anything about a tree to me."

"I'm not surprised," Maggie said. "I was astounded he told me about it."

A few seconds ticked by as the others waited for Maggie to tell the story. She hadn't considered telling it, however. She knew it was personal to Trick and that he wouldn't necessarily want everyone to know about it.

"Well?" Jordan finally asked.

"What?" Maggie replied.

"What's the tree thing?" Katie asked.

"I couldn't...." Maggie started to say.

"Come on, we're his friends," Kenny said. "We just wanna know; we're not gonna say anything about it to him."

Maggie thought about it for a minute. She watched Trick as he clicked away on the editor, oblivious to everything else around him. Maybe it would help them understand what he was going through. Maybe it would provide some sort of explanation.

"Okay," Maggie agreed. "Trick told me once that when he was about six he was sleeping in his room when he woke up to his parents arguing. They never fought, so he was curious about what was going on. As he eavesdropped on them, he heard his mother say something about him. He couldn't remember exactly what it was, but it upset him pretty bad. He started crying and ran from the house.

"After running for a while, he climbed up a tree and tried to hide in the branches. I guess he did a good job because it took his mom a while to find him. When she did, she tried to convince him that she didn't mean what she said and that she loved him with all her heart. When he didn't believe her, Lilly climbed up there with him and held him in her arms. She talked and talked until she finally convinced him that he was the greatest thing that had ever happened to her.

"Once she said that, Trick came down from the tree and wanted to go back inside the house. But before they turned in for the night, Lilly went to the tree and carved a heart in the bark and 4EVER inside it. She told him about how trees can live on forever. And because she put that mark in the tree, he'd always know that her love for him was endless, just like the tree.

"After that day, Trick and his mom were closer than they had ever been. When she passed away, he had to latch onto the things that he remembered about her. One thing she wanted was to finish that garage for the family. So he finished it and whenever he needed it, he could go to that tree in his yard."

Katie had a tear in her eye. "Wow! That must have made it really hard for him when she died. That must be why he spends so much time in that garage now."

"Well, that's not gonna work now," Kenny admitted. "We've gotta snap him out of this somehow. But what could do that?"

"I think I have an idea." Maggie said.

Class came to an end and the students moved on to their next class with the exception of Trick. Maggie checked on him one last time, but he didn't even move when the bell rang. She sighed deeply and then grabbed her book bag. Kenny joined her as they left the classroom and headed down the hallway. The only thing they currently had on their minds was Trick.

"This really has gotten to him, hasn't it?" Kenny asked.

"Afraid so," Maggie replied. "It hurts to see him like this."

"I know what you mean. He's never all smiles or anything like that, but he still seems like a completely different person."

Maggie's face slumped to a frown. Kenny decided it would be best to drop the subject for the time being and get on a happier note. Unbeknownst to him, Eric was walking behind them listening to what the two of them were talking about.

"Hey, your grandparents' anniversary was Sunday, wasn't it?" Kenny asked.

"Actually the anniversary wasn't Sunday. We just had the party for them on Sunday." Maggie corrected. "Why?"

"Oh, I was just curious to know how they liked the video," Kenny said.

"It went really well," Maggie said with a smile.

"That's good to hear."

Once Eric heard mention of the tape, he felt he had a good time to inter-ject. Picking up his pace, he stepped in between Maggie and Kenny.

"Kinda funny isn't it?" Eric asked.

Surprised and disappointed, Kenny could only utter. "What's that?"

"Oh, just the fact that the first chance you get, you're checking to see how your work did." Eric explained.

Kenny knew what this was about but didn't want any part of it. He thought he had made himself unconditionally clear before when he said he had no role in the making of that tape. Apparently, some people needed to hear that more than once.

"My work," Kenny repeated with a smirk. "What are you talking about?"

"Eric, I told you he didn't do it." Maggie said.

"Oh, I know what you said," Eric said. "I also know that you don't really believe what he said to you. That you actually do believe that he did it, and he just won't admit it." Maggie shook her head, embarrassed that he'd admit something she told him in private. Eric then turned to Kenny. "It's kind of strange to me, Kenny. I mean, all you did was a good deed. Why would you wanna hide that? What possible reason could you have for hiding from some-thing like this?"

Eric's subtle hints to the rumor weren't cute to Kenny. Eric's coy smile was out of sight to Maggie, but it was staring Kenny right in the face. He knew if Eric went much further, suspicions would shoot every which way. He couldn't stop it either; it all depended on Eric.

"Eric, just drop it," Maggie said.

"I'm just saying it seems a little weird, doesn't it?"

Maggie walked away in a huff, leaving Eric and Kenny alone in the middle of the hallway. As a crowd of people passed them, Eric kept his eyes focused on Kenny. Kenny watched everyone go by, trying to recompose himself. After the crowd had thinned out, Eric stepped closer to him.

"Ya know, I didn't have a problem with you pulling her out of the lake," Eric said. "I would have thanked you for that alone, but this, doing the tape for her. It feels like you're taking it a bit too far."

"Eric, you've got this all wrong. I had nothing to do with the tape or what happened at the Smith's," Kenny tried to be as sincere as possible, but appar-ently it didn't help.

"I got sources that say otherwise," Eric retorted. "And to be honest, I've got no problem blowing the lid on this whole thing. So watch yourself because I ain't about to go down without a fight."

Just then, Jessica came strolling around the corner. She searched up and down the hallway seeing only Eric and Kenny standing there. Unnerved by the two of them being alone, she called out to Kenny.

"Hey, you're gonna be late for class, come on."

"I'm coming, Jessica." Kenny called back as he gradually backed away from Eric. Their eyes didn't break from each other. They were still one wrong move away from taking this to the next level. As Kenny slowly walked away, Eric's frown morphed into a devious smirk. Once he was a few feet away, Kenny turned his back to him. Eric walked away in a fury as Kenny shook his head. Jessica put a hand on his shoulder to try to calm him down.

"What was that about?" she asked.

Kenny took a deep breath. "It looks like Eric has bought into the rumor hook, line, and sinker."

Kenny stomped off to class with Jessica trailing behind him. She tried to tell him not to worry, but he was already a few steps ahead of her. He needed something to take the heat off him. He contemplated talking to Trick but knew he wouldn't be much help at this point. Instead, the whole situation festered in his head as the day went on.

After school, Kenny went home immediately. He had enough of school for that day and wished to wash his hands of it. He knew that sooner or later, he'd have to do something about it, but he wasn't sure what he could do. His search for answers caused him to call Trick, and as Kenny expected, Trick didn't pick up. It wasn't that Trick ignored the call or refused to talk to him, Trick was still at school working in the studio. After the TV class, no one had bothered him, save Ms. Rutherford checking on his progress. He worked right past the final bell and on into the afternoon.

It was close to four o'clock when he heard the door creak open. He turned to see Ashley standing at the door. Her hand fiddled with the door handle as the discomfort of the moment overwhelmed her. After a deep sigh, he refocused on the screen and continued working. Ashley expected that kind of welcome but wasn't going to leave until he had heard her out. After a few seconds, Trick figured that out, too.

"Did you need something?" Trick asked.

"I just wanted to talk to you for a minute," Ashley replied.

Trick tried to duck the opportunity. "I really should get going. I've kept Ms. Rutherford here long enough. She doesn't mind staying when she's got work to do, but once she's finished she likes to get out of here...."

Ashley interrupted him. "I already talked to her, and she left. She just said that we needed to close the door and shut off the lights when we leave."

Trick had shut off the equipment and had his bag slung over his shoulder.

"Good to know," he said as he walked for the door.

Ashley quickly stepped in his way and held out a hand to stop him. He paused momentarily but didn't seem pleased.

"Trick, please," said Ashley.

Trick reluctantly agreed to hear her out. Dropping his bag on the floor, he took a seat on the couch. After a second, Ashley took a seat next to him. There was an awkward silence between them as Ashley prepared her explanation. It was going to be tough to get through, but after Maggie talked to her, she knew it was imperative. Ideally, she would have waited for Trick to come looking for the answers but that didn't seem likely to happen.

"I guess I should start, shouldn't I?" Ashley finally asked, trying to lighten the mood a bit.

"Makes the most sense at this point," Trick replied. He wasn't going to make it easy for her.

Ashley tried to sympathize with him. "I hear you're not doing so well."

"You certainly wouldn't know that for yourself," Trick lashed back.

Ashley nervously smiled. "I deserve that."

Ashley paused and looked down. Trick glanced at her and regretted his rash remark. He recognized this was difficult for her. It may not have appeared that way before, but now that she was here in front of him, he could see it. In an attempt to resolve some of the tension and make it easier for Ashley, he re-stated himself.

"I've been better, that's for sure."

"I'm not really sure how to explain this," Ashley admitted.

Trick shrugged his shoulders. "Just give me whatever you're got. There's no point in pulling any punches at this point."

Ashley thought about tiptoeing around the truth. It would be easier that way. Even if Trick said he wanted the truth, the truth could be harsh. Then again, lies weren't going to help anything at this stage.

"I'm sure you've heard all the stories about me having a crush on you," Ashley said.

She paused for an answer. Trick just nodded.

"So, I was pretty excited when you said you were going to the game. When you agreed to go to the party, drove me, and danced with me all night, it all seemed…I don't know…magical. You were funny, charming, and real. It was a side of you that I hadn't seen before. Few of us had ever seen that side of you before. It was like you took off a mask or something…."

As much as Trick appreciated the compliments, he wished Ashley would get to the point. Hearing all this stuff about how wonderful he was wasn't helping her argument.

"That night when you asked me out, it sealed the deal. All the pieces seemed to be falling into place just perfectly. It stayed that way all week, through the movie, and then it all seemed to come apart."

Trick shifted uncomfortably in his seat. Ashley wished he'd say something, but he wasn't going to say a word until she was finished.

"I don't think it was anything you did or said. It just didn't work after that. We had that incident with Maggie. I told you I would be gone, but you didn't seem to believe me. When we kissed, something seemed off. I couldn't tell if you were trying to force the issue or if I was. There wasn't the natural flow there had been up to that point. When that happened, I got scared. I figured that it was over.

"You didn't call that Monday like you said you would. I understood when you explained the next day, but for that night, I was on the edge. Even after you told me what happened, you seemed distant. I'm sure I did to you...."

She paused, but Trick didn't react.

"But I kept hoping that we could move past it because you kept calling. Even when I didn't really wanna talk or didn't have anything to say, you called. Then that day came when you didn't call. I lost it; I cried for hours that night. You didn't call the next day or the next day. It got to the point where I couldn't sit and wait any more. I couldn't spend another night clutching the phone in my hand, waiting for it to ring. Then, to my surprise, the phone rang. I hoped that it was you, but it wasn't. It was Scott.

"He just wanted to wish me a Happy Thanksgiving a day late. He asked how you were, and I couldn't answer. Instead, I asked him if he was free. He was leery about saying yes, but he eventually agreed. I told my parents it was a date because that kept you out of my head for a while. After that night, things just took off."

Ashley was finished. She cautiously looked over at Trick who had a solemn look on his face.

"Well, that's fantastic for the two of you," he said cynically.

"I wanted to say something to you. I wanted to call you and explain everything, but I didn't know what to say. I hated myself when I got home, and my mom said someone called asking for me. Immediately, I knew it was you, but I didn't dare call you. Because there was nothing you could do, it was just the way things happened."

It was hard to see, but Trick seemed to be feeling better about the situation. He wasn't about to let a smile go, but he seemed more at ease.

"Well, I don't entirely buy it," Trick admitted, "but thank you."

"It just wasn't meant to be," Ashley said.

"So the fact that I agreed to take Maggie home during our date didn't bother you?" Trick asked, trying to poke holes in her story.

"That by itself...no," Ashley said. "When I added in the hand thing in the theater and the fact that you disappeared at the party to talk to her, I was a little bothered by it, but I wasn't about to obsess over that. That had nothing to do with the way everything else played out."

Trick nodded, tentative about believing her or not. At that point, though, she had no reason to lie to him. Perhaps he could believe that things broke down as she said they did. He felt it himself after all. He told Maggie that something had changed. It was just depressing to think they had changed so quickly.

Now that matters were on the right path, Ashley got up to leave. Trick walked over to the lights and shut them off. As they walked through the sunlit room, Ashley still had some lingering concerns.

"So, where do we go from here?"

"I don't know," Trick replied. "I'm sure it'll be awkward for a while. It may be difficult to see you and Scott together, but eventually I'll get over it. Then one day, it'll kinda pass. We'll always have those questions, but we won't stress over the answers."

Ashley smiled. "So you think we'll still be friends?"

"All in all, I'm a pretty laid back guy. I try not to hold grudges."

Ashley stopped as Trick reached for the door. He was about to pull the handle, when he noticed her pause. Alarmed, he let go of the door.

"What is it?"

"You sound like yourself again," Ashley admitted.

"I guess I do," Trick realized. "Thanks, again."

Trick walked out the door, holding it open for Ashley. Once she was out, he shut it and checked to make sure Ms. Rutherford locked it. After saying goodbye, he started down the hallway. Ashley took off in the opposite direction.

Scott had been waiting in the wings with Jordan. When Ashley joined them, she had a smile on her face. Scott took it as a good sign.

"What took so long?" Jordan asked. "We've been waiting here for like an hour already."

Scott jumped to Ashley's defense. "Come on, man, it's been ten minutes."

Jordan shook his head in dismay. "Whipped already...can we go now?"

"Absolutely," Ashley replied with a sense of closure about her.

The three of them headed for the door. Along the way, Ashley relayed the meat of the conversation between her and Trick. Scott was relieved to hear Trick wasn't mad. Jordan was just happy the story had a relatively happy ending.

When they were outside, Ashley returned to a thought that kept popping up in her head. She had considered bringing it up to Trick but couldn't find the proper instance to do so. Considering his demeanor most of the time they were talking, he might have taken it the wrong way. Still, she needed to quell her concerns. Luckily, Jordan was the person who could do so.

"Can I ask you something, Jordan?"

"Knock yourself out, kid." Jordan replied.

"On the night Maggie fell in the lake, you were on the phone with Trick, right?"

Jordan pondered it for a minute. He remembered he was on the phone before Maggie and Eric had come in. He had called multiple people that night, but Trick was the one he was really trying to get to come.

"Yeah, that's right," confirmed Jordan. "I called him."

"Did he say he was at home or did you just assume."

"No, he said he was playing a game of pool. Didn't surprise me, either, because he was playing when we stopped by earlier."

"That's right," Scott remembered. "We stopped by his house after the game, thinking that if we were already there, he'd be more willing to go. Nothing we said could convince him to leave that room, though...why are you asking about Trick?"

Ashley was almost ashamed to admit it. "I thought maybe he was the one who pulled her out of the lake."

Jordan and Scott were flabbergasted. "That guy?" Jordan asked. "Please, he may be different, but he wouldn't be stalking around the woods in all black."

After that, Ashley quickly dismissed the idea. She had only had the thought in passing anyway.

Getting in their cars, they pulled out of the parking lot to head home. On the other side of the parking lot, Trick was exiting as well. What Ashley said was true; he pretty much felt back to his old self. Suddenly, everything that he had been putting himself through seemed so small and insignificant. There was too much other stuff going on for him to be dwelling on this. He had taken a chance, given it a solid try, but nothing came of it. It was time to move on.

When he got home, he checked the machine. There was one message from his dad. Nothing out of the ordinary, just a typical check up. Trick called him back and managed to catch him at his hotel. Spending the next hour or so catching up, Trick told his dad everything he had been through with Ashley. While Roy wasn't happy to hear things didn't turn out well, he was happy to hear Trick was handling it well now. The talk with his dad only heightened Trick's spirits. Not long after he got off the phone, Trick heard a knock at the door. To his surprise, Kenny was waiting for him.

"What's up?" Trick asked.

Kenny was frantic. "Look, I know you're kind of in a bad mood because of this whole Ashley thing, but some things happened with Eric today and I need your help."

"Okay," Trick replied.

"Really?" Kenny said, shocked.

"Yeah, really, come on in."

Kenny wasn't entirely convinced Trick was okay, so he gingerly entered the house. Once inside, he followed Trick to the kitchen. Trick didn't say anything more, waiting for Kenny to explain his problems. He was far too distracted, however, by Trick's sudden mood change.

"Are you sure you wanna do this?" Kenny asked.

"Yeah, I'm fine," Trick assured him.

"Really? Earlier today you snapped like an uncooked noodle."

Trick laughed. "I know. I was on edge, but Ashley came and talked to me. I'm feeling better about the whole thing."

While that explanation didn't alleviate all of Kenny's concerns, it did help him feel better about being in the house. Once he was certain that Trick was calm and ready to help, Kenny explained everything that happened that day. Trick listened intently as he made himself a sandwich. He offered to make one for Kenny, but he was too distracted to be hungry. Kenny did take something to drink, though.

As Kenny continued his story, Trick walked out to the garage. Setting up the table, he handed Kenny a cue. Kenny disagreed with the timing of the game and voiced his preference that they stay on topic. Trick assured him that the game would help him think. Though Kenny didn't really focus on it, he played along.

"So, you see my problem," Kenny said when he had finished.

"Yeah, I get it," Trick said, lining up a shot.

"What should I do?"

"I'd say relax for one."

Frustrated, Kenny lined up a shot quickly, shot too hard, and missed badly. The ball popped off the table and rolled onto the floor. It made it all the way over to Trick, who stopped it with his foot. Bending down to pick up the ball, he smiled.

"Very good…just for future reference, the ball goes in the pocket." Trick said.

"Are you gonna help me or be sarcastic?" Kenny asked.

Trick shrugged. "A little from column A, a little from column B…."

Trick tossed Kenny the ball and Kenny shot again. Taking a long relaxed breath before shooting, he knocked the six-ball into the side pocket. As he sauntered around the table to find his next shot, Trick offered his opinion.

"I really don't think there's much you can do about this," Trick admitted as he took a bite of his sandwich.

"Well, there's gotta be something I can do." Kenny said.

"Look, Eric may be talking a big game about telling Maggie the rumor, but he told me he's scared of losing her. The last thing he wants is her finding out about it."

Kenny slammed in the three-ball. He was intrigued at the idea that Eric was losing Maggie.

"You really think he's losing her?"

"I didn't say he was losing her," Trick corrected. "I said he thinks he's losing her."

Trick took a shot but missed his mark. Kenny smiled. He was beating Trick, which was always special. Kenny believed Trick was good enough to go on ESPN tours or something of that nature. After he knocked in the seven-ball, he focused in on the eight-ball. Still looking for answers, Kenny appealed to Trick again.

"So, you really don't think there's anything I can do?"

Whatever answer he had wouldn't satisfy Kenny's concerns. After all, Kenny was trying to force an issue Trick believed wasn't there. If he wanted to change someone's state of mind drastically, he had to suggest something drastic.

"If you're really that concerned, I guess you could distance yourself from Maggie for a while," Trick finally suggested.

Kenny was taking his shot when he heard Trick's proposal. Losing his focus for a second, the pool cue shot out of his hand. The tip of the cue almost speared Trick in the side. As he watched it fly off the table and land on the floor, Trick felt as if he had touched on a nerve. With an eyebrow raised, he shifted his gaze to Kenny.

"Problem?"

"Are you suggesting that I go out of my way to avoid Maggie?" Kenny found the notion absurd.

"That would be what I said, yes."

"Well, that all sounds wonderful," Kenny said with a scowl.

Trick couldn't help but find Kenny's resentment of the idea intriguing. He believed Kenny when he said he had nothing to do with the tape or what happened at the lake but to get this worked up was curious. It didn't make Trick suspicious at all, but he could understand that it would make other people suspicious.

"You're getting a little defensive about all this, aren't you?" Trick asked.

"I think I have the right to," Kenny replied. "I haven't done anything wrong, but I gotta change my life."

"Hey, if you want to stop people from watching you, you can't give them anything to look at. This is merely an avenue to accomplish that."

The idea was ludicrous to Kenny, but it was also the only idea either of them had. He knew it would help remove the cloud dangling over his head. At the same time, he loathed the idea that he had to spurn a friend to prove a point. Tired of the subject, Kenny moved on. Trick wasn't sure if he had been any help but did what he could.

Kenny stayed at Trick's house until ten or so playing pool. On the trip home, Kenny thought over the notion of ignoring Maggie for a while. It might be easier than he thought it would be. He still wasn't thrilled about the idea. It was ultimately insulting to him that he had to lower himself to alleviate the unfounded fears of a paranoid moron. Despite his reservations, he was going to follow through with the plan.

The next day, Kenny kept his distance. It proved easier than expected, due in part to the fact that he didn't have any classes with her that day. He knew it would be more difficult in their TV class, but he was committed to do anything that helped solidify his innocence.

As he walked into English class, his teacher needed a favor. In a cruel twist of irony, Maggie had left her notebook in class. Kenny, chosen by his teacher to return it to her, tried to get out of it by claiming he didn't know where her next class was. Luckily, in a manner of speaking, someone else knew and told him where he needed to go. Fed up with his rotten luck, Kenny left the classroom and stomped down the hall.

When he arrived at his destination, he glanced in before entering. He saw Maggie sitting in the front of the room, listening intently to the ongoing lecture. Kenny felt fortunate that Eric wasn't in the room with her. He did spot some of Eric's friends, though, which was enough to convince him to play the role he'd settled on.

Kenny walked into the room. Scratching right above his eye so he didn't make eye contact with anyone in the room, he set the notebook on the teacher's podium.

"This is Maggie's," he said.

Not even waiting for a response, he turned his back to the room and headed for the door. Maggie got up to retrieve her notebook despite the confusion she felt towards Kenny's actions. She didn't know why he acted the way he did, but she knew who to blame.

Kenny went back to class. Though not comfortable with what he did, he understood he'd have to get accustomed to it. If Eric was going to get off his case, Kenny had to be more than convincing. Later that day, as he opened his locker, Kenny was happy to see a friendly face. Jessica was at her locker just a few feet away.

"Hey," Jessica said.

"Hey, yourself," Kenny replied with a frown.

"You sound like you're having a good day," Jessica said sarcastically.

"Nothing like being on eggshells all day," Kenny groaned.

"I don't think this is gonna help."

Kenny sighed in frustration even though he didn't know what Jessica was talking about. With his luck, he could assume the particulars of what was happening. As he turned, he saw Eric approaching with a smile on his face.

"What do you want now, Eric?" Kenny demanded.

Eric threw up his hands, trying to appear innocent. "Hey, calm down big guy. Sounds like someone had a rough day." Eric continued to smile having heard what Kenny did when he returned Maggie's notebook. He couldn't help but gloat a little. "I was gonna thank you for returning Maggie's notebook, but if you're gonna jump all over me for it, then forget it. I also wanted to tell Jessica that Matt was looking for her."

Like most people that knew Kenny, Eric knew there was tension between Matt and Kenny. It centered around Jessica's parents. Matt liked to lie about Jessica and Kenny dating which her parents didn't like. Jessica's parents even grounded her solely based on Matt's word that the two were a couple in the eyes of the student body.

Even now, when Kenny was trying to make Eric happy, Eric pushed his buttons. It was a lose-lose situation from just about every angle.

Chapter Ten

Party Time

The next day, Kenny arrived at school a little earlier than usual. After going to his locker, he wandered around the commons area for a few minutes. He saw Maggie, Katie, Ashley, and Jessica at a table talking with a bunch of friends. For a moment, Kenny contemplated sitting with them for a while. Matt thwarted his idea when Kenny caught him sitting a few tables back with a group of his friends. Knowing that sitting at the table with the girls would only bring him unwanted attention, he headed for the TV studio.

When he walked into the room, Ms. Rutherford greeted him. She was slightly confused to see him there so early but had an idea of what he wanted. Motioning him to go into the studio, she knew Trick was already in there. Thanking her for the heads up, Kenny opened the studio door. Trick was sitting with his feet kicked up on the news desk. He had a newspaper out with a bottle of orange juice and a cereal bar next to him.

"Why don't you just get a fridge, a microwave, a bed, and move into this place already?" Kenny asked.

"I can't afford the rent," Trick replied, not looking up from the paper.

Kenny walked over to the couch, plopped down, and groaned. The sheer irritation in his voice was enough to attract Trick's attention. Setting the paper aside, Trick saw Kenny sitting on the couch with head cocked back and hands over his eyes. Understanding that his services were required, he got up from the news desk and grabbed a chair closer to Kenny.

"Alright, let's have it."

"Do you know someone that just annoys you to no end?" Kenny asked.

"Oh, I know what you're talking about," Trick replied. "I got this cousin, Kasey. Kid used to eat grass clippings when he was younger. It had the entire family freaked out until he stopped. But anyway, this kid has an unhealthy obsession with French toast...."

Trick's zealous answer was all but lost on Kenny. Normally, he would have been willing to listen to anything Trick wanted to say. Under these circumstances, however, he wanted to be the one venting. As soon as Trick looked at him, he realized that, and stopped his story.

"Do you know Jessica's younger brother?" Kenny asked.

Trick replied. "Oh, sure, Mike or Mark or...."

Kenny corrected him. "Matt."

"Matt, of course, what do you have against him?"

"Jessica's parents are kinda strange about dating," Kenny began.

"Strange, how?" Trick interrupted. "They don't like it."

"They don't allow it."

"That is strange."

"Tell me about it," Kenny said. "One day, I was over at Jessica's house. We were working on a class project. A few hours after I had gotten there, her dad bursts into the room demanding that I leave. According to him, Matt said he saw the two of us making out earlier. So he reads me the riot act about how his daughter can't date and if I'm not gonna respect the rules of his house, then I can leave.

"The next day, Jessica tells me that she was grounded for two months because of what Matt said. I didn't help matters when I confronted him about it. He laughed at the whole thing, which only upset me. I lost my cool and started wailing on the kid. Ever since then, we've always been leery of him catching us hanging out too much."

As the two of them sat in awkward silence, the door opened up. Maggie and Katie walked in talking to each other. Kenny shifted on the couch clearly uncomfortable by Maggie's unanticipated appearance. Trick seemed to notice but didn't say anything. Katie pulled up a chair, taking a seat next to Trick. Exhausted, she rested her head against Trick's shoulder.

"What's up?" Trick asked, a little surprised by the personal contact.

Katie said. "I was up late doing homework last night."

"I'm sure you'll survive," Trick said, patting her on the back.

Maggie took a seat on the couch next to Kenny, who quickly scooted as far away from her as he could. Maggie hadn't noticed the move, and she smiled at him when she sat down. Kenny nervously smiled back. Maggie felt he was a little unnerved but didn't really think much of it. Besides, she had other matters on her mind.

"Hey, thanks, for bringing my notebook to me yesterday."

"No problem," Kenny said with a half smile.

"You must have been in a hurry," Maggie commented. "You didn't even say hello to me."

"I had a lot of work to do in class, so I didn't want to waste any time."

"Ouch!" Katie exclaimed. "Maggie, Kenny just suggested that saying hi to you is a waste of time compared to doing homework."

Maggie laughed. "That's pretty harsh, Kenny."

Katie and Trick both chuckled as Kenny's discomfort grew. His throat suddenly went dry, and he felt like he was having a hard time breathing. There was too much to reveal if he was going to explain why he acted the way he did, and the longer he stayed there, the more questions would hound him. Before he said anything else, he stood up from the couch and walked out of the studio. The others were a little confused and somewhat insulted.

"What's his problem?" Katie asked.

Trick knew, but wouldn't say." Beats me," he replied.

"He was like that yesterday, too," Maggie said. "When he brought me the notebook during class...."

Trick interrupted at this point. He had heard part of the story but still didn't know exactly what was going on.

"Kenny had your notebook?" Trick asked.

"Yeah, I must have left it in class or something. When my teacher found it, I guess she asked Kenny to bring it to me. When he did, he didn't say anything to me or even give the notebook to me. He just left it with my teacher."

"That is weird," Trick agreed.

"I know," Maggie said. "And I can't help but think that Eric is involved in all this somehow."

Maggie's suspicions suddenly made Trick and Katie uncomfortable, too. They were certain she knew nothing about the rumor, but if Eric was suddenly becoming suspicious of Kenny, it couldn't be helpful. Katie had to say something to keep from looking too concerned over the matter.

"Why would you think Eric is involved in this?" Katie asked.

"Just the way he's been acting lately," Maggie explained. "He got in Kenny's face the other day about helping with the video. I keep telling him that Kenny may not have been the one who did it, even though I thought he did, to begin with. For whatever reason, he doesn't believe me when I tell him that."

Trick got up from his chair, walked over to the news desk, and grabbed his juice. Gulping the rest of it down, he knew he could explain what was going on. The only question was whether or not it was worth it to do so. Katie and Maggie had watched him carefully, trying to gage if he knew anything or not. They could tell he did, and it had to be important.

"What do you know?" Maggie asked.

"It's nothing," Trick assured her.

"Even I don't believe that," Katie said.

Trick glared at her. He didn't need her convincing Maggie to take this any further. What he had to say, Maggie might misconstrue to an extreme extent. Rather than play it dumb and try to sweep the issue under the rug, Trick tried to sidestep the severity of the situation.

"Eric thinks Kenny's plotting against him with the whole tape thing," Trick explained. "He finds it odd that someone would do all that without an ulterior motive. He's already on edge about the lake. This just isn't helping anything."

"So what did he do, threaten Kenny or something?" Maggie asked.

"He didn't threaten him," Trick quickly refuted. "He just made it clear that he didn't appreciate someone trying to make a move on his girl. To avoid suspicion, Kenny decided to put some distance between him and you."

Maggie shook her head, shocked that Eric would do such a thing. She wanted to have it out with him right then and there. Fortunately for everyone else involved, the bell rang and it was time for class. There was more Trick needed to say because he knew that if he left things as they currently were, Maggie would assume the worst. It was just fear; it wasn't mistrust or anger, Eric was doing the only thing he could think to do.

The rest of the day, Kenny continued with his ignoring Maggie plan. Now that the idea was in her head, she could see how he was distancing himself from her. She didn't like it one bit. Every now and then, she made an extra effort to go up to Kenny and say something to him or ask him to come give her a hand with something. With every conversation, Kenny backed away and every inquiry he turned over to someone else, usually Trick. Every time Kenny blew her off, Maggie's resentment towards Eric grew.

When school ended, Maggie went straight home. Trick tried to catch up with her so he could set the record straight, but she didn't want to talk. She already knew what he was going to say, and whatever Trick wanted to tell her wouldn't change the way she felt. Eric had no right to do this to Kenny or to distrust her like this. Like it or not, Trick understood that this was one of those instances that she didn't need to talk—at least not to him.

Maggie gave herself time to calm down and cool off before she got on the phone. She had chosen not to see Eric during the day but felt it necessary to talk to him now. She needed an answer; she needed to know what she had done that made him so scared that he felt it necessary to intimidate Kenny like he did.

"I know what you're doing with Kenny," she said when he picked up.

Blindsided by the accusation, Eric could only respond, "What?"

"Don't play dumb with me," Maggie demanded. "I've seen how you've been watching him lately and how he's been acting around me."

Eric took a minute to regain himself before saying anything. He thought he had been subtle in his actions. Apparently, he hadn't been subtle enough. Not that it mattered; he still had good reason for what he had done. He could see the writing on the wall and that she was hiding something from him.

"You're overreacting," Eric finally said.

Brian happened to be in the room with Eric. He had grown concerned when Eric answered and then paused for so long. Once Eric spoke, Brian knew Eric was talking to Maggie. While he suddenly wanted to be elsewhere, he also recognized how quickly this situation could get out of hand.

"Oh, sure, someone does a nice thing for me doing that tape, and you blow up at him," Maggie said. "Clearly, *I'm* the one overreacting."

Eric worked quickly to defend himself. "I am so sorry that I find it odd that this guy would do all that work for you. Don't you?"

"No, I don't care why he did it. I'm just happy he did."

"Don't you see how naive that is?" Eric fired back. "No one would do something like that out of the kindness of their heart. There's always a reason."

Maggie couldn't believe how stubborn he was being about this. "You're ridiculous. I can't believe you can't understand someone being selfless. What other reason would Kenny have for doing this?"

Eric had an answer for that. Previously, he had been reluctant to share the rumor with Maggie because he feared it would peak her interest. At this point, however, he didn't care. If she really thought Kenny had purely innocent intentions, then she needed to know what he was really after. Once she knew the truth, she'd see things his way.

"Oh, I can tell you what reason he'd have…." Eric began.

As confused as Brian had been through their conversation, he was able to pick up on what Eric intended to do. Eric may think that was the best route to take, but Brian greatly disagreed. Eric wasn't thinking this through properly. Maggie was mad at him now because he was picking on Kenny. If he continued to do so by implicating Kenny in the events that happened at the lake, it would only anger her more.

"Don't you dare tell her about the rumor," Brian warned.

Eric paused for a moment. When he saw the desperation on Brian's face to stop him, he put a hand over the phone so Maggie couldn't hear.

"What is it?" Eric asked.

"If you tell her, she's only gonna obsess about it," Brian explained. "She's mad because of what you've said about Kenny. If you point your finger at him, it's only going to provoke her further."

"But I'm right," Eric said.

"That is so far from the point right now," Brian informed him. "If you want her to get back on your side, you have to show her you're on hers."

Eric thought it over. It may be the right call, but he didn't want to make it. The accusation of doing something wrong when he just knew the truth that Maggie wouldn't accept was frustrating him to no end. He did see the bigger picture, though. As he continued to pause to calm himself down, Maggie had grown tired of the silence.

"What about Kenny?"

Eric stumbled through his response. "It doesn't matter what the reason is…."

"You mean you don't have one," Maggie replied.

He thought about saying it right there. He had a reason, a good one, too, and for her to suggest he didn't really hit a nerve. Maybe he wasn't gonna say anything about the rumor, but he would air his grievances.

"Oh, I got one," Eric snapped back. "You better believe I got one. And I'm sure it's all tied to whatever secret you're keeping from me!"

Maggie didn't want to go there. She thought they had settled all of this. "Eric, there is no secret."

Eric had finally had enough of the lies. He had given her every opportunity to tell him exactly what happened that night, and she had scoffed at every single one of them. Waiting for her to come around wasn't working and wasn't going to work. He couldn't stand back and be patient about this anymore.

"Oh, sure there isn't," he replied sarcastically, now saying whatever came to mind. "You've been saying that ever since it happened, and you know something…I don't believe you. I've never believed you. Something happened that night that you don't want me to know about. And the way I'm thinking, there's only one reason that you wouldn't want me to know this secret. You love this guy, don't you?"

Maggie was speechless. She didn't even know who had done this. He had said he loved her, but how could she know how she felt for someone who hid his identity from her? She could see where this was going. They were at a crossroads.

"Yeah, that's what I figured," Eric said. "Go ahead, admit it. Say that you love this guy because it's clear you've already given up on us."

"No, I haven't, Eric. I don't even know who this guy was. It wouldn't matter who he was, I love you," Maggie said forcefully.

"You got a funny way of showing it."

"I don't wanna talk about this anymore."

"Hey, you're the one that called."

Almost in tears, Maggie hung up the phone. She couldn't have said anything else without completely breaking down. It was then she realized that she should have told him everything from the beginning. Trick had attempted to get her to see that, but she refused to listen. Now, there was no telling how things would end up.

Eric hung up the phone and slammed it down on his desk. Still fuming, he stalked around the room for a minute. Brian had sat down on the floor and had a hand on his face. He was slumped against Eric's bed, shaking his head. When Eric saw him, it angered him even more that his friend wasn't in synch with him on this one.

"What's with you?"

"Nothing," Brian said calmly, "I just witnessed a train wreck."

That night, Maggie had trouble sleeping. She paced around her room for a while holding her phone. In her heart, she desperately wanted to clear up all the chaos with Eric. In her head, she feared things would just get worse. She would eventually fall asleep trying to make a decision. When she did, she dreamed of being at the Smith's. She imagined herself out in the woods with Trick in the dead of night. He led her to a spot where the man in black was sitting around a campfire, waiting for her to arrive. Finally able to end it all, she reached to see who was behind the mask. As her fingers touched the frayed edges of the fabric, she awoke.

Rattled, she snuck out of the house and ventured across the street to Trick. Though it was two in the morning, he still answered the door. Once her eyes saw him standing in the doorway, she began to cry. As she unloaded every detail of what had happened that night, she really lost it. He did what he could to comfort her and make her feel better, but he realized this was far beyond his scope. If she was going to right the ship, she'd really have to work at it.

Unfortunately, whatever Maggie did over the next few weeks proved fruitless. Things between her and Eric deteriorated to an even greater extent. Nothing Maggie did would make Eric waver from his point that she was hiding something from him. He would not change his stance that he had to know what it was. They were both on the brink of calling it quits, but neither truly wanted that to happen. As much as they felt the wheels falling off, neither wanted to be the one who ended it. Somewhere underneath all the anger, bitterness, and animosity, they still loved each other dearly. There was just no telling if that would be enough to keep them going.

The last day before Christmas break brought news of a party at the Smith's to celebrate the seniors only having one more semester of high school before graduation. Billed as the party of the year, most of the senior class expected to be there in some capacity. Trick kept with tradition and declined the invitation. Maggie refused to go if Eric was going to be there, a sentiment that Eric reciprocated. Despite numerous attempts to convince Maggie to go, she had decided on spending the evening with Trick so he'd have some company. While he appreciated the thought, he knew she'd rather be at the party. After some convincing, she agreed to go. What sealed the deal were some inaccurate reports that Eric wouldn't be attending.

That night, Maggie and Eric remained unaware of each other's presence for a good part of the evening. Still, it was only a matter of time before they ran into each other. Everyone knew; they just hoped to prolong their ignorance for as long as possible. When they did finally run into each other, they were in the kitchen. Everyone else in the room promptly cleared out. Left alone, they didn't say much. They only counted the seconds before they finally managed to escape each other.

"I thought Eric wasn't going to be here." Maggie said when she got back to her crowd.

"I didn't think he was gonna be here, either," Katie admitted. "Where did you see him?"

"In the kitchen getting a drink." Maggie moaned.

Katie tried to keep her spirits up, "Don't let it get to you."

They met up with Ashley and Jessica so Maggie could regain the party spirit. Going on to another side of the house, they wanted as much distance between Eric and them as possible. After a few minutes, Maggie put Eric out of her mind. She could feel something more was going to happen, but she wasn't concerned about it. Back by the kitchen, Eric was just as upset that his friends misled him.

"I thought Maggie wasn't gonna be here," he said slapping Brian on the arm.

Brian hadn't seen Maggie since he got to the party, so he assumed that he'd heard the truth before. "She's not," he replied with a shrug.

"Well, I saw her here."

"Who cares," Brian sighed, "It's no big deal?"

"Yes it is, we're fighting, and I'm getting tired of it," Eric explained. "I came to this party to forget about this whole thing, but it's following me wherever I go."

Not really paying attention but wanting to get out of the conversation, Brian suggested a drastic course of action. He knew Eric wouldn't like it, but maybe if he explained it just right, Eric would go with it.

"Tell her to tell you it's over."

Eric shook at the idea. "I don't want to end things between us. I just want her to stop with this whole thing...."

"Trust me, you won't have to," Brian interrupted. "When she hears you say that you want to end it or hear the truth, she'll freak out because she doesn't want to end things between you two either. Then she'll tell you everything."

Eric thought it over for a second. It didn't sound like a good plan, but maybe if things got worse he could use it as a last resort.

As the party went on, Maggie and Eric maintained their distance. However, while Maggie was losing herself in the party atmosphere, Eric resorted to spying on her from across the room. Brian and his friends tried to get Eric to join them, but he refused. He was determined to make sure Maggie didn't spend any time alone with Kenny.

After a while, Maggie noticed that he was watching her. She tried to ignore him and not let him interfere with her good time, but the longer he stared, the harder it got. As the party began to sour, someone put some music on to get people dancing. Maggie grabbed a partner to dance with, but Eric refused to partake. Sitting on a couch across the room from Maggie, he struggled to keep an eye on her.

Eric's buddies came over to him every now and then, trying to get him off the couch and onto the dance floor. He remained content with where he was and even convinced a few guys to stay with him so he could have a network of eyes working for him. He knew where Maggie was; he wanted to know where Kenny was, too. He knew he had seen him earlier, but Kenny slipped away before Eric could say anything to him. Kenny was lucky in that way.

After all, it was Kenny's fault that this was happening. He jumped in the lake, saved Maggie's life, did that video for her, and he was trying to steal her away from Eric. The longer he sat there doing nothing, the more it festered in his mind. In his frustration, he went to the kitchen and grabbed a beer. He'd had a beer every now and then at these parties—his parents didn't mind—but this time, he was drinking for different reasons all together.

The longer he watched Maggie dance, the more ideas began to take flight in his head. Were he rational at this point, he'd see right away how silly they were. Instead, they were making perfect sense to him. He was seeing a picture that really wasn't there, but it was real to him. Maggie was making a fool out of him. Everyone knew about this rumor regarding Kenny; she must have known, too. She only played along to keep him in the dark. Maybe she didn't know who did it, but she was trying to find out. That's why she purposely left that project unfinished. She wanted to see if someone would finish it for her, and what do ya know, someone did. She had all her answers and now just needed to drop some dead weight.

As the drinks kept coming and his mind kept racing, everything came to Eric with crystal clarity. He knew what he had to do; Brian had given him the idea earlier. There was no way Maggie was going to end this relationship. He was too good to let go. If he told her it was either the secret or the relationship, she'd jump at the chance to tell him. It wouldn't take any prodding then. He'd know everything.

Getting up from the couch, he stumbled a bit but quickly collected himself. Brian tried to stop him, but Eric assured him he knew what he was doing. He almost fell several times while making his way across the dance floor. As he tripped over people's feet, he kept his determination to get to Maggie.

When he reached her, she had her back to him, as she hadn't seen him coming. He gently tapped her on the shoulder, and she turned around. Disappointed, she frowned at first, but then forced a smile across her face.

"We need to talk," he informed her.

The smile vanished, but Maggie agreed to settle things. If it was going to happen eventually, it might as well happen now. The only thing that bothered her was the audience. "Let's not do this here," she said as she started to walk for the door.

"No!" Eric yelled.

Eric yelled loud enough to make most of the people around them stop and take notice. Maggie looked around and saw all the eyes of the partygoers on them like they all knew something big was going to happen. There was a level of tension and anticipation in the air like the calm before a storm. The music shut off and suddenly, they were center stage with the spotlight on them. Maggie was embarrassed, but Eric was too inebriated to know to stop.

"I've let you get by with way too much and I'm tired of it!" Eric yelled. "I'm sick and tired of you having this big secret about what happened to you at the lake that I just can't know about."

Like moths to a candle, people began to crowd around them. It was demented in a way, but everyone knew some bad stuff was going down that they weren't going to miss it. Feeling more humiliated by the second, Maggie desperately desired to be out of the public eye. She walked up to Eric and placed a hand on his arm. She whispered in his ear, hoping to talk some sense into him.

"Please," she pleaded, "let's go somewhere quiet."

"No!" Eric refused and pulled away. "No, we're gonna talk about this right here and right now. I tried to do this just the two of us, but you didn't wanna do it that way. You had to keep it to yourself. Well congratulations! Cuz we're gonna do this out in the open and if you don't tell me what happened, we're through!"

"What?" Maggie asked.

A veil of silence cloaked the room. Brian was standing in the back of the crowd, but he heard Eric distinctly. He wanted to kick himself for suggesting this course of action. It wasn't the right time, and Eric wasn't in the right frame of mind.

"That's right," Eric continued. "You're gonna tell me the truth or I am going to break up with you."

The words were torturous in Maggie's ears. She looked into Eric's eyes, desperate to find some sympathy, but there was none lurking there. He'd gone utterly dead inside. He wanted his answer, and he was going to get it or walk away. Maggie was beyond the point of hiding this any further. She scanned the crowd looking for help from anyone. She saw Katie…Ashley…Jordan…Scott. They all wanted to help her, but there was nothing any of them could do. She closed her eyes, futilely calling Trick's name in her head. She wanted him there, but he wasn't coming.

"Alright," she said her voice trembling. "You want to know what happened. I'll tell you what happened. When I came to, he was holding me in his arms. Once he knew I was okay, he tried to leave. I stopped him, wanting to know who he was. We talked for a few minutes, but I couldn't get him to tell me who he was. But he did tell me one thing."

"He told you something," mocked Eric. "This is what you've had to hide from me?" Eric started laughing, "Oh, please, tell me what he told you."

"He told me that he loved me."

That revelation promptly stopped Eric's laughing. The silence in the room deepened. The confusion swarming through everyone in the crowd rendered them speechless. Eric's face turned beet red with anger as his biggest fear materialized in front of him. This guy, whoever he was, was trying to move in on his girlfriend. As his eyes took on a crazed look, he stepped dauntingly towards Maggie. Jordan and Scott prepared themselves. They weren't sure what he was going to do, and they weren't going to risk Eric catching them off guard.

"That's what he told you, huh? He loves you." Eric stepped back. He could feel the anger boiling over. Clinching his fists and grabbing his hair, he burst out in anger. "I'll kill him! Nobody tries to steal my girlfriend from me."

Eric scanned the room looking for Kenny. It was time for Kenny to pay for everything that he had done. He thought he could just sit back and get away with all of this. Well, he was dead wrong. He'd understand that soon enough. As Eric stalked around her, Maggie came to a decision. She thought telling him the truth would save things. It hadn't.

"What girlfriend, Eric?" Maggie asked.

Eric stopped and turned to her. "You of course," he replied, thinking her stupid for having to ask such a question.

Maggie shook her head. Eric grabbed her arm. Jordan and Scott tried to step forward, but Katie and Ashley quickly stopped them. Eric wasn't going to hurt her. There was no reason to push him any further.

"What do you mean by that?" he asked.

Maggie yanked her arm free and took a step away from him. "Take a guess, Eric. It means that we're through!"

Eric lost it. His anger had already blown his top. Now he was volcanic. He had gotten the answer he sought but lost more than he bargained for. For a minute, he thought about apologizing, about trying to make amends. But he had nothing to apologize for. He was right. He had been right from the beginning. No way was he going to put his tail between his legs and come crawling back.

"You cannot break up with me!" Eric yelled.

"I just did." Maggie replied, keeping her emotions inside her.

Maggie started to walk away, forcing her way through the crowd. Katie tried to reach her, but Maggie was long gone. Rather than follow her, Katie let her go. The last she saw of her, Maggie was in the kitchen walking out the back door. She'd be on the pier; Katie knew it.

Meanwhile, Eric had shifted his focus back to Kenny. If he was determined to find Kenny before, his resolve was unshakable now. If his relationship with Maggie was over, someone was going to pay dearly for it.

"Come on out, Kenny! Quit hiding! Your secret's out already!"

No one moved in the crowd. The silence only provoked Eric further.

"Get out here and take what's coming to you! Don't make me find you. I'll only get even madder and beat you even more!"

Eric waited for a few seconds. As the crowd dispersed, he went searching for Kenny within the multitude. He barged into every room of the house but couldn't find Kenny anywhere. The longer his search persisted, the more his anger intensified.

On the pier, Maggie finally let her pain out. Crying almost uncontrollably, she could scarcely stand. She didn't dare go back in the house after what occurred. Everyone would be feeling sorry for her, giving her piteous looks. She had to leave. Unfortunately, she hadn't driven herself tonight. She had only one option.

Trick, as usual, was out in the poolroom, and he'd worked himself into a corner. Lying in front of him was possibly the most awkward shot he'd ever attempted on this table. He had one knee setting on the edge of the rail while the cue ball was resting about an inch in front of the one-ball. Had he been aiming for the one-ball, the shot would not have been so troublesome. However, the ball he was aiming for was the fourteen at the other end of the table. He would have to jump the cue ball over the one while angling the ball to the corner to pocket the fourteen-ball. The proximity of the cue ball to the rail forced him to hold the cue as high as he could with the stick wrapped behind his back.

With some clever balancing, he inched himself into the proper position. Once he finally got himself situated, he lightly pushed the tip of the cue towards the ball. He had invested all this time into the shot, he wasn't about to rush it. Once he had the perfect spot picked out and the right speed with the cue, he took the shot. Just as he brought the cue down, his phone rang in his pocket. The surprise call caused him to lose his balance. The cue hit the ball, but not nearly like Trick wanted to. As he crashed down to the ground, the balls went flying around the table. Scrambling to see if anything went in, Trick was disappointed to see the mess he had left on the table. Shaking his head, he answered the phone.

"Hello?"

"Trick, it's Maggie," she said while crying.

Trick could barely understand her. "Hey, what's wrong?"

"I need you to come get me," Maggie said, ignoring the question.

"Okay, where are you?"

"I'm at the Smith's."

Trick promised her he'd be there shortly. She thanked him repeatedly as he bolted out of the garage. Trick's immediate thought was that the debacle with Eric had taken a devastatingly grave turn. Despite his hope that they would resolve their conflict amicably, he had seen the signs on the wall foreshadowing a more dire result. He had to run inside the house to grab his keys, and once he had them, it was back out the door and into the car.

Maggie waited out on the pier for a few more minutes. She was looking out to the spot where Trick had been standing in her dream, hoping that sooner or later she would see someone out there—that maybe her dream would actually come true so this nightmare would end. For a moment, it did. While she was gazing out over the lake, a mysterious figure broke out of the woods. She peered closely, thinking it might be a deer or coyote, but it was actually a person. It was too dark to see him or her clearly, but she knew someone was out there. Whoever was there paused for a minute in the clearing then sprinted back into the trees. Maggie thought about going after him or her for a quick second, but realized that she could never catch up.

Aside from that, she heard the faint sounds of a car pulling up to the house and shutting off. She assumed Trick had arrived. After one last look over the lake, she walked back from the pier into the house. She made her way through the crowd, not stopping for anyone. A few people tried to ask if she was all right, and while it may have seemed rude to ignore them, Maggie didn't really care right now. Her eyes were still red from all the crying, which she thankfully wasn't doing right now. That could quickly change, however, and the longer she lingered in the house, the more likely a breakdown became. When she was a few feet from the door, Eric, still aimlessly searching for Kenny in the house, spotted her.

"Maggie!" he yelled.

She stopped reluctantly and turned around to face him, hopefully for the last time that night. "What do you want?" she asked.

"Well, I figured you were out at the pier waiting for your big hero, am I right?" Eric paused and laughed at himself, but Maggie refused to acknowledge the question. Eric had lost everything that mattered to him; he figured he might as well go for broke. "Of course, you were. Well, I thought I could save you the trouble of wondering who it was. See, everyone in here knows that it was Kenny. Everyone knows that he showed up at Trick's house soaking wet mere minutes after you were miraculously rescued."

Everyone in the room was shocked that Eric revealed the rumor to her. They knew he was angry about the situation, but they didn't know he'd be dumb about it, too. It didn't matter in any event because Maggie wasn't inclined to believe him anyway. She just shook him off.

"Why should I believe that?" Maggie asked. "You're obviously drunk."

At that time, Trick walked in the door. When he saw the crowd around Maggie and Eric, he assumed the worse. Katie had made her way to the door, too, hoping to catch Maggie before she left. She was thankful that Trick had arrived. Eric was, too.

"Don't believe me," Eric said. "That's fine, I can understand that. So why don't you ask your good friend, Trick." He pointed to Trick still standing by the door. Everyone looked over at him. "He knows all about it."

Trick sighed and turned to Katie.

"He's dumber than I thought." Trick stated.

"Be thankful you just got here." Katie replied.

"Oh, they all knew!" Eric continued. "And they all kept it from you, too. They lied to you. Even your best friend lied to you. Kenny showed up at his door only minutes after the whole thing went down, and he still didn't bother to tell you."

Even though the accusations seemed ludicrous, Maggie couldn't help but wonder if they were true. She began doubting all those times that Trick seemed to be hiding something and she just blew off. For his part, Trick had heard all he needed. The longer the two of them stayed there, the deeper Eric dragged Maggie into this mess. Trick walked up to Maggie and took her hand.

"Let's get out of here."

"Is it true, Trick?" Maggie asked.

Trick paused and gulped. He had to tell her but not here. "We can talk later."

Maggie nodded, and they walked for the door. Eric pursued them, unwilling to let them get away just yet.

"In fact, Trick lied to me, too." Eric said. He forced his way between them and got in Trick's face. Trick worked to avoid his gaze. "You told me that I wasn't losing her. You told me that you didn't believe that Kenny did it. You said he was nowhere near here. It was all a lie, wasn't it, Trick? You were trying to help Kenny, weren't you, Trick?"

Trick didn't answer him and instead tried to slip past Eric so he could escape the insanity. Tired of people ignoring him, Eric grabbed Trick by his shirt and punched him in the jaw. Trick stumbled back a little bit but stayed on his feet. Jeff and Brian instantly grabbed hold of Eric. He fought to break away from them, wanting more than a piece of Trick. Luckily, Jeff and Brian managed to keep him wrangled. Trick rubbed his jaw for a minute, as Maggie stood horrified at Eric's brash actions. Jordan and Scott came over to check on him. He waved them away.

"You ready to go?" Trick asked Maggie.

"Yeah, let's get out of here," Maggie pleaded.

As Trick opened the door, Eric called after them one last time. "Fine…go!" he yelled still held back by Jeff and Brian. "But we are through! Just like you said!"

Trick slammed the door behind him, beginning to feel a fit of anger festering in his gut. He balled up his fists and kicked the ground. He was mad: mad at Eric for punching him, mad at Kenny for not being able to clear up this mess, mad at Maggie for making him lie to everyone, mad at himself for letting him trap himself in the middle of this fiasco. But all that anger seemed trivial once he turned to Maggie. She placed a hand on his face where Eric had punched him. She started to caress it, wishing she could've prevented it somehow.

"Do you want to go home?" Trick asked.

Maggie shook her head. A second later, the tears started again. Trick threw his arms around her, and she buried herself in his chest. She cried and cried feeling the nightmare coming full circle. Everything she had seemed to be disappearing right in front of her. Even now in Trick's arms, she felt completely isolated.

Once she managed to compose herself, Trick walked her to his car. He kept an arm around her, and she kept both of hers around him. As he drove back to his house, Maggie stared at the dark bruise slowly forming on his face. The guilt she felt was overwhelming. She dragged him into this. He may not be showing it, but he had gotten hurt in the process.

"I'm sorry about your jaw," she said.

"It'll be fine," he assured her.

"I guess I really made a mess of things, huh?"

"This is not your fault," Trick corrected her. "No one could have foreseen this. It's just an unfortunate turn of events."

The rest of the way to Trick's house, it was quiet. Trick was trying to fit everything inside his head. Everything that happened left him stunned. Whether she knew it or not, everything Eric said about him was true. When she eventually called him on it, he couldn't hide anymore.

Maggie sat looking out the window. She knew she couldn't escape all this madness, though she desperately wanted to. If she could just wind back the clock, everything would be different. She could fix everything so that this would never happen. If only it were that easy.

When they arrived at Trick's house, he went to the kitchen. Maggie flopped down on the couch, sinking into the onslaught of thoughts now enveloping her. When Trick came back, he had an ice pack on his jaw.

"Anything I can do?" Trick asked.

Maggie smiled and replied. "You're doing plenty."

Taking a seat next to her, Trick was content with her reply, and for the next few moments, they sat in silence. Maggie kept her eyes on the floor, lost in her own thought. What was she going to do now? Eric was irate. All her friends had seen the public spectacle that was their break-up. At least she had Christmas Break to let it all smooth over. Trick held the ice to his jaw a while longer. Once it was feeling better, he set it off to the side. Eric had popped him good; Trick had to admit that, but there were other matters taking precedence in his mind.

"What happened?" Trick asked.

"I guess he'd had enough," Maggie said. "He said he wanted the 'secret' or else."

"Did you tell him?"

"Yeah, I told him, he laughed, and then I ended it."

"You ended things?" Trick asked surprised.

Maggie started to cry again. "It was already over. He was gonna beat up Kenny as soon as he got the chance. After that, nothing would have been right."

Trick put his arms around Maggie again. She rested up against him. "Good thing Kenny wasn't there." Trick said.

"He was."

Trick looked at Maggie rather confused. He didn't see Kenny there. In fact, no one had said anything about Kenny being around.

"I saw him there earlier," Maggie admitted. "I think I saw him after I called you, too."

"You think you did?" Trick repeated.

"Yeah, I went out to the pier after I broke up with Eric," Maggie explained. "While I was waiting for you, I saw someone out around the lake. I couldn't see who it was or anything, but it makes sense that it would be him."

That was enough to prove to Trick that Maggie believed what Eric said about the rumor. She had put all the pieces together that everyone else tried to keep from her. He was shocked that she'd think it but was more concerned with how she was going to react to his lies. He shifted uncomfortably on the sofa.

Maggie felt his discomfort. She sat up on the couch and looked into his eyes. Like Eric said, Trick was her best friend. He was the one person she'd never expect to lie to her. He was always there for her, even tonight. He always put her ahead of himself. That made what she had to ask so difficult.

"Is it true?" Maggie asked. "Was what Eric said about Kenny true?"

And just like that, the cat was primed to jump out of the bag. He knew it. Maggie finally pinned him down, and he had to reveal every little detail that he knew, whether he believed them to be true or not. All the lies ended tonight. He doubted that she'd be able to forgive him for it.

"It is true," Trick confessed. "There is a rumor about Kenny being the guy that pulled you out. Just about everyone, including me, knows about it. That night, not long after you were saved, Kenny showed up at my garage door soaking wet."

The betrayal stung worse than anything Eric said to her. Maggie had always been able to rely on Trick, and now she couldn't even do that. She jumped off the couch and paced around feeling her sorrow and despair turn to anger and resentment. Everyone knew? They all knew about Kenny only to sit back and watch her relationship die? How could they? How could they make such a fool of her? Now livid with Trick, she had to know everything.

"How long?"

"Maggie," Trick said trying to keep things calm.

It was too late for that. "How long after I was saved?"

Disappointed in himself, Trick sighed. "More than long enough for him to run from the Smith's house to here."

Maggie wanted to slap him. Standing next to him while he sat on the couch, she had to restrain herself. "Why didn't you tell me about this?" Maggie asked.

"Because it was just a rumor," Trick explained.

Maggie didn't buy into this explanation and demanded something better. "And you don't think I'd have taken it like a rumor?"

Trick would have liked to keep things civil between them, but the chances of that happening were growing smaller by the second. "No, I didn't think you would."

"Don't you think I'm smarter than that?"

Trick stood up from the couch and took Maggie by the shoulders. He looked straight into her eyes, trying everything he could think of to illustrate his unwavering sincerity. He understood that lying to her was wrong, but it was more important that she understand he was telling the truth now.

"I know you're smarter than that, and I should have told you. I'll admit that now and every day for the rest of my life, but you gotta trust me, it's not true."

"Why should I?" Maggie asked. Then she broke his hold on her. "Why should I trust you anymore? You've lied to me before, why wouldn't you do it again?"

Now that Maggie was questioning his motives, Trick couldn't help but get a little agitated himself. He tried to be the nice guy for everyone involved in all this. How did they thank him? A punch in the jaw and now this.

"This isn't fair," Trick said. "You can't do this to me. I have to lie to Eric for you, I have to lie to Kenny for you, I have to lie to you for Kenny, and I have to lie to Eric for Kenny. When does it stop, huh? How am I supposed to know who's secrets to keep and who's to tell? You tell me, why am I supposed to tell you everything I know?"

"Because I came to you and I told you how scared I was," Maggie replied. "I came needing to know the truth, and you purposefully kept it from me. I've never kept anything from you because we're best friends. We don't have any secrets. It's been that way ever since we were kids. You can pretend that you owe Kenny something or that you should treat us all equally, but you know I don't do that with you."

He may not have believed he had done wrong keeping this from Maggie, but he hated that he had hurt her so acutely. His defense broken and torn to shreds, he knew she was right about everything she said. They were supposed to be best friends, closer to each other than anyone else. They knew things about each other that no one else knew. There weren't supposed to be secrets, but there were.

As the silence grew, Maggie had had enough. She turned her back on him and headed for the door.

"Where are you going?" Trick asked.

"Home," Maggie replied.

"Maggie, you know I'd never do anything to hurt you."

Maggie paused at the door for a minute.

"Doesn't look like it on this one, Trick."

Slamming the door behind her, Maggie was gone. Trick started to go after her, but then thought better of it. He held his hand at the door handle for just a second then slammed his head into the door. How could he have done this? He was supposed to be there for her. He was supposed to look out for her to protect her like she protected him. As he walked the stairs to his room and flopped down in bed, he realized a harsh truth. He let her down. She had every right to be mad at him. He was mad at himself.

Chapter Eleven

An Escape

It would end up being a short night for Trick. As he squirmed in bed trying to forget everything that had happened that night, he couldn't get what Maggie said out of his head. He was still angry. Angry at Maggie, angry at Kenny, angry at Eric and now, he was angry at himself. All he wanted to do was remedy this situation, but he had no idea how to do that. Once he was able to fall asleep, it felt like he had barely shut his eyes when he heard a loud screeching noise blare through his ears.

Jolting from his slumber, he frantically scrambled in his bed trying to figure out what was going on. He was terrified beyond rational thought. His eyes were darting everywhere unable to focus on anything. When his heart finally started beating at an acceptable level again, he looked above him to see his dad standing over him with an air horn.

"Rise and shine, sleepy head!" Roy yelled.

Trick glanced over to the clock on his nightstand. There was no light shining through the windows, so he assumed it was early. He was correct. A red five and two red zeros shown on his clock's face. He sighed in disbelief. Whatever his dad was excited about, it definitely wasn't worth this, and his wake-up service was far from necessary.

"Dad, it's five in the morning," Trick whined.

"Yes, it is," Roy proclaimed exuberantly, "but that is not the point. Now, get up you've only an hour to pack."

Trick was still rubbing the sleep out of his eyes as Roy opened his closet and pulled out a few bags. Trick refused to budge from his bed until his dad told him exactly what was going on.

"Pack for what?"

"We're going on a ski trip!"

"What?" Trick shouted. "I can't just up and go!"

"I think you've got to kid," Roy said with a smile. "Pack for three weeks and if you wanna catch up on your sleeping, it's an eight hour car ride, sleep then."

Trick couldn't fathom this unprecedented impromptu getaway. They had gone on trips in the past but never so spontaneously. He always knew plenty of time before hand so he could properly prepare. Maybe this was Roy's way of making up for all the time he'd been away, but this was a peculiar way of doing it. Even though it sounded like a fantastic idea, Trick couldn't buy into it wholeheartedly.

"What about our family? We'll miss Christmas. Won't the neighbors worry that we just disappeared?" Trick asked.

Roy smirked. "Our family isn't going to be around because they have their own trips planned. If you're that worried about the neighbors leave a note on the door."

Trick sat up in bed, still thinking his dad had gone off the deep end a bit. It was then that it hit him—Roy said they'd be gone three weeks. Christmas Break was only two weeks.

"So I'm gonna miss the first week back from school?" Trick asked.

"I believe that would be true, yes," Roy said with a smile.

Trick popped off the bed. "I'm in!" he exclaimed.

"I had a feeling that would get you going," Roy said.

Trick grabbed all the essentials for the trip and anything else he could fit in his bags for the vacation. Getting a sudden burst of energy from the excitement of the situation, he bounded down the stairs with bags in hand. Roy was fixing a quick breakfast in the kitchen as Trick ran out the door towards the car. He threw his bags in the trunk next to Roy's and slammed it shut. As he headed back to the house, he glanced over at Maggie's house. The house sat in the darkened night, not a single light on, which wasn't surprising since the sun had yet to rise. It may not have been the best situation, but he felt good about getting away from it all for a while. It was clear from last night that Maggie wanted her space anyway. Still, he couldn't leave just like that, so after a quick bite, he grabbed a piece of paper, a sharpie, and scribbled a simple note.

BE GONE FOR THREE WEEKS

He taped the note to the door as they embarked on their journey. With a blanket and pillow in hand, he settled into the back seat. Roy fired up the car, pulled out of the driveway, and they were on their way. Trick didn't want to leave his dad without someone to talk to, but he was too tired from the combination of last night's events and a short night's sleep. Besides, Roy understood that his son would need a little shut-eye. Managing to sneak in a four-hour nap, Trick awoke around nine-thirty in the morning. Once he was up, he climbed into the front seat to keep Roy company. For a good part of the trip, they discussed how Trick's last days of the semester went. Trick went on about classes, finals, but chose to leave out what had happened with

Maggie. When the discussion petered out, Trick took in the magnificent scenery.

The mountains loomed on the horizon as they trekked towards the Colorado landscape. The more they drove, the more the gargantuan landmasses began to take shape and become the glorious structures that skied over the ground and dominated the clouds. Between them, cavernous valleys provided homes to droves of trees and forests that hid a world of wildlife rarely seen by the human eye. As they drove through it all, the weather turned the world into the winter wonderland Christmas time was supposed to bring. Kissing the rows of treetops and blanketing the ground with white snow, it created a picture perfect scene.

It all seemed vaguely familiar in a way. Trick had resided in Kansas his entire life but knew the Colorado winter well. As they went deeper into the state, all the memories of those past trips with his dad and the few with his mom came gushing back to him. It was truly a getaway, a hiatus from whatever was happening back home. They never called to check up on anything. When they were away, they were just that. He needed that more than anything right now. A few weeks on the slopes with his dad, just the two of them, would be much more than a vacation. Since this used to be a frequent event, he knew he had restaurant hopping, movie marathons, and countless other carefree activities to look forward to.

They arrived in the same town they always went to and drove to the same hotel they would always stay at, The Rocky Slopes. It was, bar none, the best hotel to lodge at for skiing and snowboarding because it provided easy access to the slopes and was one of the largest and most luxurious hotels in the state. It stood thirty stories high, each floor holding one hundred rooms. While the hotel featured many luxuries such as: an Olympic sized pool, Jacuzzis, a five-star restaurant, exercise room, and day spa, the big draw for Trick and his dad was the rooms. A two-bedroom suite, the room had a living room with a fifty-five inch flat screen TV, DVD player, VCR, two couches, one love seat, two chairs, and a full kitchen. Each bedroom had a king sized bed, a closet, a dresser, and a bathroom with a walk-in shower. Since they were up on the twenty-ninth floor this go around, they also had a balcony with a view of the mountains and slopes. Once they were unpacked in their rooms, Trick stood out on the balcony so he could fully appreciate what he was about to experience.

Being experienced skiers and snowboarders, Roy and Trick didn't have to secure much gear before they were ready to hit the slopes. Going easy the first day just to get their legs underneath them, they only stayed out on the mountain for a few hours. That night, they went out to a favored steakhouse before turning in so they could be out early the next day.

At seven in the morning, they both awoke and prepared for their first full day out on the mountains. They ate a quick, light breakfast so as not to waste any time, then headed out together. For the first few days of the trip, Roy and Trick always stuck together. At some point during the second week, they would break apart for a while to give each other some space before reconnecting the final week. It was much easier to stick together during the first week because the slopes closed a few days for Christmas. On Christmas day, Trick thought about calling home but remembered what this trip was all about. Besides, he was having too much fun with his dad.

Once the slopes reopened, they were out on them. They weren't in peak form quite yet, but they were more willing to take bigger chances. They were also more prone to wearing themselves out to the point that they preferred to stay in for dinner. Those conditions made for the perfect occasion to hold a movie marathon with a buffet of pizza and pop to sustain them. Six movies played that night, starting at five in the evening and lasting till five in the morning. Pizza boxes lay strewn about the floor, and pop cans were stacked high on the coffee tables. Roy could barely keep his eyes open as the last movie ended.

"What is it, five or something?"

"I think that's what it says," Trick replied, straining to see the clock.

"Perfect...you think we oughta clean up?" Roy asked looking at the damage.

"Not today," Trick replied, nuzzling up on an armrest of the sofa.

"Good idea...what are your thoughts on skiing?"

Trick paused to consider the question. Roy thought he had fallen asleep when he finally blurted out. "Let's shoot for two or three in the afternoon. Anything before that would just be irresponsible."

It sounded good to Roy. "I'm with you, kid."

They slept the rest of the morning and into the afternoon. Trick woke up somewhere around three but saw Roy still sleeping and didn't have the heart to wake him. It was the first day that they missed out on skiing when the slopes were open. It was also the last day of the first week. It felt as though it had gone by so quickly, but that was partly because of the days around Christmas. Trick knew the second week would last a little longer.

When he finally woke up a few hours later, Trick found a glass of orange juice sitting on the table by his head. Roy was in the kitchen. Having been up a few hours already, he had cleaned up the mess and prepared the leftover pizza for dinner. Trick slowly rose from the couch, grabbed the juice, and took a seat at the dinner table.

"What's with the juice?"

Roy laughed. "I figured I better slip something healthy in there in between all the pizza and steak."

Roy tossed Trick a paper plate, which he caught. Getting up from the table, he sifted through the leftovers to find his desired selections. As he carefully decided on his choices, Roy tossed the empty boxes.

"So, you ready to go out on your own, tomorrow?" Roy asked to remind Trick that it was time to split up for a while.

"Yeah," Trick said with a mischievous grin, "it'll be nice not having anyone holding me back."

Roy smiled as well and pretended to take offense. "The nerve of kids these days. Actually, I didn't want to tell you this, but you were holding me back."

"Well, of course, you wouldn't want to say that dad—you're not a liar."

Their joking argument quickly turned into a friendly bet. Each vowed to take on the most challenging peak the following day. Holding to a code of honor, whoever won the challenge would have the loser treat him to dinner. Sealing the deal with a toast of orange juice, they finished the pizza and retired to their respective rooms.

There they remained all evening, spending some private time alone before turning in for the night. When Trick came out of his room the next morning, his dad's door was already wide open. He glanced in to see he was already gone and had left a note on the front door that read:

CATCH ME IF YOU CAN, KID!

Trick just chuckled under his breath and fixed some breakfast. When he finished eating, he changed into his gear, grabbed his board, and headed for the slopes. In the morning, Trick constantly kept an eye out for his dad, and though he never saw him, he knew he was out there somewhere. Around noon or so, he found a small place to eat lunch. He checked his phone to find his dad had texted him a picture of Roy on the highest slope with a big thumbs up. Trick cautioned the old man 'to be careful and not hurt himself' before heading back onto the slopes himself.

A few hours into the afternoon, as Trick ventured up a trail few frequented, his thoughts wandered back home. He wondered if anyone had noticed he was gone. He wondered how Maggie was doing. Had she visited his house wanting to talk only to find he had vanished? Had she confronted Kenny about the rumor now that she knew? Or had Kenny kept himself hidden as he had so successfully done at that fateful party? As much as he thought about it all, Trick didn't want to know the answers yet. It would all be waiting for him when he got home, so that's where he would leave it.

As Trick climbed to the top of a peak, he locked himself into his board and dropped his goggles over his eyes. Primed to make his run, he stopped at the last moment, spotting something out of the corner of his eye. Down along of the path about thirty yards near the trees appeared to be someone lying in the snow. Trick could spot the jacket and saw enough to make out a slight amount of movement. Wasting no time, Trick rushed down to help assuming someone was injured.

"Are you alright?" Trick asked.

"It's my ankle," she replied.

Her voice was soft and calm despite the fact that she was in some pain. She seemed disappointed in herself for doing this in such a remote area. As Trick looked at her thin body, he realized how easily he could've missed her and flown right past her. Her straight blonde hair was flowing out of her ski cap. Her goggles hid stunning green eyes but her overall beauty was evident enough to make Trick pause. Shaking it off, he reminded himself what was going on here.

"I hate to tell ya this, but the course doesn't cut through here."

She appreciated his candor. It lightened the situation and assured her that it was nothing serious, even though Trick knew nothing about what had happened. Her hard expression broke into a smile.

"I decided to make my own path," she said. As Trick examined her ankle, she added. "It's sprained pretty bad."

"Have you been here long?"

"No, just a couple minutes," she replied.

Trick was at an impasse. He'd hurt himself in the same fashion several times and knew exactly what to do: wrap it, maybe ice it for a while, and stay off of it for a few days. But something about that plan didn't really seem to be taking shape up on the mountain. He had to get her down but wasn't sure how. It was too reclusive to expect any help to come wandering by. He could leave her, go get help, and bring them back, but it would be just as fast to get her off the mountain himself.

"Do you think you can stand?" Trick asked.

She shook her head. "I've tried, it hurts too much."

"Okay, well...." Trick paused and looked down the mountain towards the hotel. It would be quite a trek, but he could manage it. "Where are you staying?" he finally asked.

"At the Rocky Slopes...why?"

"Well, it's not that far away, I should be able to get you there quickly," Trick explained. "I'm staying there myself."

He offered a hand to her, but she was hesitant to accept it. For one, she didn't even know his name. Secondly, this seemed like too much of an imposition.

"You don't have to do that," she assured him. "I can wait here while you go and get help."

Trick understood her reluctance though he couldn't abide it. "It would take me about an hour to get someone up here. And for where we are, we'd still have to carry you down the mountain a ways. I can get you back to the hotel faster than that."

Reluctantly, the girl took Trick's hand, and he hoisted her up to her feet. With the injured ankle dangling off the ground, she stepped firmly on her good foot leaning against Trick to find her balance. Once she was stable, Trick wrapped her arm around his shoulders, put one of his around her waist to bear some of her weight, and the two started down the mountain. Even with board and skis in hand, it wasn't that difficult of a journey.

"My name is Amy by the way. And my hero today is...?"

Trick chuckled at the idea of being a hero. "Trick," he replied.

She repeated the name in her head since it was rather unusual. She assumed it was a nickname but didn't feel like inquiring at the time. As they slowly hiked down the mountain, her intrigue towards a young man willing to forfeit his day to assist a complete stranger peeked. She didn't think she could feel so at ease in the arms of someone she just met, but she did.

"So, what room are you in at the Slopes?" Amy asked.

"Tweny-nine twenty-two," Trick replied.

"Really! I'm just down the hall from you in twenty-nine eighteen."

Had he not been concerned about falling down the mountain, Trick would have shown his true astonishment at the coincidence. As it was, he could only vaguely echo her surprise.

"See," he said, "this isn't even going to be an inconvenience. Once I drop you off, I can go straight to my room with no hassle."

Amy was not going to let Trick play this off as no big deal. "Oh, don't try to downplay this. You didn't even know my name thirty seconds ago, and now you're practically carrying me down a mountain. It'll take up your whole afternoon."

Trick glanced around at the sky and the trees around them. The sun was gleaming through a small section of the clouds, illuminating the crystals of snow on the ground. The entire world around him seemed to be alive with the full vitality of nature.

After examining the scenery, he shrugged it off. "Giving up a pretty day to meet a pretty girl seems like a fair trade."

Amy smiled. "You're already rescuing me; you don't need to flatter me, too."

Trick was a little embarrassed that he had been so frank, but he couldn't deny the truth. "I just call it how I see it."

Trick kept focused on the path ahead. Normally keeping those thoughts in his head, he couldn't believe he had spoken so brashly. Hopefully, Amy wasn't too uncomfortable because of his remark. If only he knew what Amy was really thinking, then he'd be relieved. She felt quite flattered by him and found him charming, which proved to be the reason for the smile breaking across her face.

Suddenly self-conscious of his thoughts, Trick turned quite shy the rest of the way down the mountain. Amy thought it was sweet. He was so captivating to her that when other people offered to help, she sent them away. It took longer that way, but, as long as Trick was willing to go along with it, she was perfectly willing to accept that if it meant more time with him. When they reached the hotel lobby about an hour later, Trick stashed their gear by the door.

"Can we rest for a minute?" Amy asked.

"Yeah," Trick replied.

He found a chair in the lobby and gently eased her into it. She asked him to join her, but he refused to rest until he procured an ice pack. Try as she might, she couldn't convince him that it could wait. Away and back in a flash, he had the bag ready to go. Amy removed her jacket and the snow paints she had been wearing, revealing more of her amazing figure. Again, Trick was temporarily distracted and felt the ice warming in his hands. Once he recomposed himself, he gingerly removed her boot and wrapped the pack against her foot. Exhausted, he fell down in a chair across from her and removed his own coat.

"Is it any better?" Trick asked.

"A little bit," Amy replied. "I should be able to walk on it in a day or so."

"That's good."

Trick sat up in his chair and rechecked the wrap. On the one hand, he wanted to make sure the wrap wasn't too tight. On the other hand, he was becoming more nervous being around Amy with these feelings he was so rapidly developing. Amy smiled and laughed to herself as he checked his handy work.

"You do too much," Amy informed him.

Trick shrugged. "Come on, this was nothing."

"Oh, really," Amy replied. "So what else are you gonna do tonight more strenuous than rescuing an injured girl and carrying her down a mountain?"

"Oh, you didn't hear?" Trick asked jokingly. "I was gonna go liberate some baby seals from poachers. They were supposed to put up flyers."

Amy laughed which forced Trick to smile. They continued their small talk as Trick explained his small vacation with his father. Amy was part of a church group from Ohio that made the trip annually during the winter break. It was a large group, well over one hundred kids, that made the journey this year.

As they sat in the lobby, Amy noticed her two roommates from the trip walk in. She hadn't seen Jill or Kayla since lunch when the three of them went their separate ways. Amy wanted to try the more difficult trails, but the girls weren't as interested. Now, the way things looked, she was sure they would overreact. She was right. As soon as they saw her, they mobbed her with questions about what happened, if she was alright, and how on earth she made it all the way back to the hotel by herself.

It was at that point that Amy introduced them to Trick who was trying to be inconspicuous for the time being.

"You helped her down the mountain?" Kayla asked.

Trick nodded. "Not the whole mountain, but most of it."

"That is so sweet," Jill said.

Trick blushed so quickly that Amy could see that he wanted the spotlight off him. With all he had done for her, she was sure she could do this small thing for him.

"Alright, before this goes too much further, I think we better go upstairs."

Kayla and Jill let Trick off the hook and returned their focus to Amy. Their hands were still full of equipment, so they weren't sure how this was going to work. Luckily, there was a simple solution.

"I can take her," Trick offered. "I'm on the same floor anyway."

As Trick got up from the chair, Jill leaned in and whispered to Amy, "Is he for real?"

"I hope so." Amy replied.

Trick helped Amy to the elevator as the four of them rode to the ninth floor. As the elevator doors opened, Kayla sprinted ahead to open the room. Trick still shouldered a majority of Amy's weight, although she was able to use the wall to help steady herself. Once she was at the door, Jill and Kayla were able to take over, and Trick retired to his room.

After a quick shower, Trick threw on some jeans and a T-shirt before taking a seat on the couch. With nothing else to do, he switched the TV on and watched for a while. He didn't know when his dad would be back but hoped he had selected a place for dinner. Even with dinner pending, Trick opened a bag of chips and enjoyed a small snack. Not more than an hour later, he heard a knock on the door. When he answered it, Amy was standing there. They stood in awkward silence for a while as Amy nervously rubbed her arms before Trick finally broke the silence.

"I'm just guessing that there's more to this visit, but I'm not entirely sure what."

"Well," Amy replied, "I was just out for a walk testing the ankle and I wanted to say thank you again."

"Glad to help," Trick replied with a smile.

His smiled seemed to unnerve Amy as she seemed ready to say something but abruptly paused. A second later, she laughed nervously and looked down the hall. Jill and Kayla were watching everything from their door.

"Just ask him," Jill called down to Amy.

Surprised by the voice, Trick stuck his head out the door and looked for the source of the intrusion. He saw Jill and Kayla both with their heads poking out the door. He waved at them, and they politely waved back. When Amy said nothing in reply, Trick imagined the possibility of this taking a while. Feeling she should spend as little time as possible on that foot, Trick decided to speed up the process.

"Ask me what?"

Amy staggered a while longer before answering. "Well, on New Year's Eve my group is having a party in the ballroom downstairs. I was supposed to go with this guy I was seeing, but he broke things off and skipped the trip. And I was just wondering if...if you would like to go with me?"

"Yeah," Trick replied instantly.

"Really?" Amy said. Apparently, she didn't expect him to say yes. "Well, it's not formal or anything like that; you can dress totally casual. And you can just stop by my room and we'll go down together."

Trick smiled. "Sounds perfect."

A big smile beaming across her face, Amy jumped towards Trick to hug him. She stumbled a bit as she landed but luckily, Trick was there to catch her. She swore to him that he had no idea what this meant to her and thanked him repeatedly for saying yes. He couldn't help but smile at the idea that someone was excited to be going anywhere with him. She staggered back down the hall refusing help from anyone. As she approached their room door, Kayla and Jill hounded her with 'I told you so's.'

As Amy disappeared into her room, Roy stepped off the elevator. There in his arm was a pretty brunette. Both were smiling and giggling still dressed in full skiing attire. Roy looked up and saw Trick standing at the door with a coy smile on his face.

"Oh, Jessi," Roy said to his companion, "there's my boy right there. Trick! There's someone I want you to meet."

Trick stood by the door as they approached. Jessi reached to shake his hand, which he gladly accepted. Years ago, this would have made Trick outrageously uncomfortable. Now, he was greatly delighted to see his father happy.

"Trick, this is Jessi," Roy said making the introductions. "And Jessi, this is Trick."

"Oh, he's adorable," said Jessi. "You're father has told me a lot about you."

"Oh, that can't be good," replied Trick.

Jessi laughed. "He is funny."

"He is that," Roy said proudly rubbing his son's head. "Jessi and I ran into each other out on the ski lifts. We were both on our own so we agreed to share the ride. We talked the whole way up and things just went from there."

Trick began to get the feeling that he'd be on his own for dinner tonight. He didn't mind either. It was exciting to see his dad like this.

"So anyway, I told her maybe the three of us could go out and grab a bite to eat. You know, get to know each other a little better."

The offer was sincere, there was no doubt about that, but Trick knew better than to accept. While his dad honestly would enjoy having Trick with them, Trick preferred not being the third wheel for the evening.

"No, dad, that's okay," said Trick. "You two go out and have a great time. I'll just run across the street and grab something quick."

"Trick, I'd love for you to come," Jessi insisted.

Trick was persistent. "And it's not like I don't want to come, but honestly I'm feeling kind of tired. I'd rather stay in tonight. I had a pretty grueling day."

His explanation was good enough. Roy smiled at him, appreciating what Trick was doing for him. Jessi smiled, touched by the relationship the two shared.

"Well, then I must insist that you come to my New Year's Eve party," Jessi said. "Your father already agreed to come. There will be some people your age...."

Trick pursed his lips, feeling bad about having to decline this one as well, but he wasn't about to renege on his promise to Amy.

"Actually, I've already got plans," Trick sheepishly admitted. "It's kind of tied to the day I had. I was up on the slopes and saw this girl by the trees. She had injured her ankle so I helped her back to her room, which is right down the hall actually. Anyway, she invited me to a dance on New Year's Eve, and I'd really like to go with her. Sorry."

Jessi choked up and placed a hand over her heart. Clutching Roy's arm, she could barely speak. Roy held a proud smile on his face. That was his boy.

"That is the sweetest thing I've ever heard," Jessi finally said. "Don't you feel bad for a second; you just have a wonderful time with that girl. She's very lucky to have met you."

Jessi said goodbye for now and then went back to the elevator. Roy threw his arm around his son after she had gone, happy for himself but happier for his son.

Trick returned to couch and watched some more TV. Roy retreated to his room to prepare for his dinner date. When he reappeared from his room, he was dressed in slacks with a button-up shirt and tie and completed the ensemble with a nice sports coat. Clean, shaven, and all dressed up, Trick had to admit that his dad looked smooth. Leaving Trick some money for dinner on the table, he was out the door and on with his evening.

Trick stayed on the couch for a while longer. Eventually, his stomach began to growl, and he knew it was time for dinner. Grabbing the money and slipping a key into his back pocket, he began thinking of where he wanted to eat. He wasn't two steps out the door when he almost ran into Amy who was walking towards his door. They both jumped when they saw each other coming and narrowly missed a collision.

"Oh, hey," Amy said having to gather herself quickly.

"What's up?" Trick asked.

"Nothing much," Amy replied. "What are you doing?"

"Well, my dad had a date tonight so I'm on my own for dinner. Thought I'd head out to get something to eat," Trick explained.

"You don't mind if I tag along, do you?" Amy asked. "My roommates are watching a movie that I'm not a big fan of, and I thought maybe we could hang out."

"That would be awesome," Trick said with a smile.

Amy was still limping a little so she took Trick's arm to help stabilize herself. They walked to the elevator, and Trick pushed the button. As they waited for the doors to open, Amy couldn't help but wonder.

"So, is this a date?" Amy asked with a smile.

"What?" Trick replied.

"Well, we are going out to dinner together," explained Amy.

"I guess it would be then."

Amy smiled as the elevator doors opened, and they went to get their food. Trick wasn't comfortable with Amy being out on her ankle all night, so once they got their order they went back to Trick's room. It just so happened that one of the movies Roy and Trick had rented was her personal favorite. Sitting next to each other on the couch, they watched the movie while they ate. They spent that entire evening together.

Then came New Year's Eve. Roy was gone by seven, leaving Trick a good hour to get ready, pick up Amy, and get downstairs to the dance. Unfortunately for Trick, it didn't take him that long to get ready. He went slow, took his time, but was ready to go in thirty minutes. He attempted to distract himself by sitting down on the couch and watching TV, but it didn't work the slightest bit. Constantly checking the time and fidgeting on the couch trying to get the time to go by faster, he finally gave up trying with fifteen minutes left to wait. Early or not, he was going to pick her up now. When she finally answered the door, she literally took his breath away.

"Wow!" he could only say.

She was wearing a leopard print tank top that practically molded to her body and exposed her mid-drift. Her tight dark navy jeans were hugging her hips like a second skin. Completing her outfit was a pair of black spiked heels probably two inches high. She pulled her hair back in a tight ponytail giving a clear view of her face, which was only sporting the slightest bit of make-up to complement her natural beauty. And when Amy heard Trick's wow and saw his reaction, she blushed.

"Come on, I don't look that good," she said.

"I take it you haven't looked in a mirror?" Trick asked.

She smiled. "Let's go."

They took the elevator down to the lobby and walked the hallway to the ballroom. Amy ran into a few of her friends along the way but kept Trick close to her. They were all excited for the night and thrilled to finally meet Trick. He had become a bit of a legend with all the stories Amy, Jill, and Kayla had been telling about him.

When they entered the ballroom, most of the room was already full. The severely dimmed lights in the room complemented the numerous strobe lights flashing above them. Streamers, balloons, and Christmas lights lined the walls of the room. To one side set a buffet table of snacks and drinks with small round tables surrounding it. New Year's confetti and balloons decorated each table. On the other side in one corner was a DJ booth with speakers. It took a minute for Trick to take in everything since he had never been to something like this before, but with Amy's hand in his, he couldn't be uncomfortable. Even when he heard the music start to play, he was fine with it.

"I suppose it's asking too much of you to like to dance," Amy said.

"Hey, it's your party. I'm with you the whole way."

"Good, because we're gonna be out there a lot," Amy warned him.

"That sounds oddly familiar."

Amy pulled Trick out on the dance floor and immediately started dancing. She was better than Trick had ever seen which normally would have been intimidating to him. At this point, however, he could care less and threw himself into the music. He didn't do anything to show off, just kept with the rhythm. As he watched his partner's hips sway to the music, he suddenly felt as if they were the only two people in the room. He hadn't realized how tired he had gotten until after the first break. As Amy led him back to the dance floor, she noticed he was sluggish.

"Are you alright?" Amy asked.

Trick hesitated for a minute and looked around the room. Then, he gazed deeply into Amy's eyes and felt an odd calming sensation overwhelm him. It was unexplainable and beyond anything he could understand. Though he felt tired a moment earlier, that feeling was quickly gone. He smiled and placed a hand on her cheek.

"I don't think I've ever been better."

Amy smiled, taking his hand in hers, and they started dancing again. As the music played on into the night, Trick found the determination to keep going. When he was partying with Ashley at the Smith's, he felt obligated to keep going. Here, he desperately desired to keep going. He would be introduced to a multitude of people he had no chance of remembering even if he wasn't about to drop to the floor in exhaustion. He wasn't paying attention to anything outside of Amy, and she wasn't paying attention to anything outside him. When the music finally stopped, Amy had pity on Trick and took him over to a side table. He sat down in the chair and grabbed a water bottle.

"We don't have to dance to every song," Amy said, hoping he wouldn't take her up on that.

"You said you wanted to; trust me, I'm good for it," Trick promised.

Amy put a hand on top of Trick's, and he, in turn, gently squeezed her hand back. They gazed into each other's eyes for a moment and smiled. Then Amy heard the music playing overhead and signaled for Trick to get back onto the dance floor.

"You're gonna regret saying that," Amy vowed.

"It's a safe bet."

This time the music refused to stop as each song seemed to go on for hours and hours. Time seemed to slow as Trick held Amy in his arms and felt her body pressed up against his. It was so simple here. Nothing like it had been before. This was all so real.

About thirty minutes till midnight, the music stopped. Trick took refuge at one of the tables where Amy sat next to him, rubbing his back as he rested his head on the table. Jill, Kayla, and a few others found them.

"Geez, Amy," Kayla said, looking at Trick. "Did ya kill him?"

"No, I just wounded him," Amy replied.

Jill smiled. "Well, give him a minute to recover. We need to talk to you...alone."

Kayla and Jill took Amy away. Trick stayed face down at the table. A few of the guys Trick had met earlier took the seats next to him. One of them, Daniel, set a bottle of Gatorade by Trick's head. Finally raising his head up from the table, Trick stared at the bottle for a minute.

"I think that it's real, but I don't want to take a chance and be wrong."

"Trust me, it's real." Daniel assured him.

Trick reached out and grasped the ice-cold bottle. The initial chill worked quickly to alleviate some of his fatigue. He took a long drink from the bottle and then shook Daniel's hand.

"Good man."

Daniel laughed. "It was the least I could do. After seeing you out on the floor ninety percent of the evening, I was afraid you'd drop dead. I'm Daniel remember?"

Trick had to give it some thought. "Did we meet on the dance floor?"

"That's right," Daniel said. "And that's Todd, Tom, and Josh."

Trick looked around the table and then raised a hand as high as he could in his condition. "How's it going, guys?" Trick asked.

"Well, I think we're doing better than you are, man," Todd said.

"No kidding," Tom added. "We got the marathon man over here putting in more time on the floor than the four of us combined."

"It's pretty impressive when you think about it." Josh said.

Trick took a minute to catch his breath. He had about half of the bottle left, probably enough for a couple more drinks. His legs were tingling, almost like they were asleep, only less sensation, but the longer he sat, the more feeling came back to them. He knew he couldn't fully recover, he just hoped he had enough in the tank.

"I don't get how you do it, man," Daniel admitted.

"What do you mean?" Trick asked.

"Well, you met Amy, what, a couple days ago. Ever since then, it's like the two of you fit together so perfectly. How does that happen to two people that just met?"

It was an intriguing question, and everyone was anxious to hear Trick's answer. As he thought it over, they leaned in to hear him better. It was something he couldn't help thinking about. There were people back home he'd been around his whole life, and he'd never acted this way with them before. He had always guarded himself so closely, been so careful to protect himself. Here, he was out in the open, vulnerable, and he didn't care anymore.

"I wish I had an answer for you, guys," Trick admitted. "I think it all just boils down to luck, and I am the luckiest guy in the world right now."

They all raised a glass to that. Trick spent a few more minutes talking with the guys while Amy and the other girls were talking in private. Trick looked over to where they were a few times and saw her looking back at him.

"You two have been getting pretty close," Jill said.

"I know," Amy agreed. "It's just been an unbelievable night. I hope it goes as well for the rest of the time."

"I'm guessing you're not gonna have to worry about anything," Kayla said confidently. "This one seems to be the real deal for you."

"You think so?" Amy asked. "I can't believe how well we're clicking. Everything is so far beyond what I thought it was going to be. It's made me forget about everything that's happened."

They continued to converse while Trick talked with the guys. After a while, Amy and the girls joined them and they talked until about ten minutes before midnight. The music started up again, and everyone walked out onto the dance floor. The music was very slow this time.

"One last go around, huh?" Trick asked.

"You're the one that promised." Amy reminded him.

"A mistake I'll make over and over again."

Trick tightly wrapped his arms around Amy's waist, and she nestled hers on his shoulders. As the time before midnight dwindled away, the two moved closer and closer to each other. By the time the last minute of the year began to tick away, no light shown between them. As they slowly moved in perfect rhythm with the music and each other, Amy closed her eyes and rested her head on Trick's chest. He tucked his head down, resting it gently against hers.

As the countdown started at ten, Amy lifted her head. Looking longingly into Trick's eyes, she caressed his check with her hand. For a few more seconds, they stared at each other losing themselves in space. It was only when she heard 'one' that Amy reached for Trick. Before she could reach him, he pulled her to him, and she felt his lips on hers.

After a few seconds, they slowly removed their lips and again looked into each other's eyes. This was what Trick hadn't felt when he kissed Ashley so many weeks ago, the excitement of it all and the sensation emanating from his heart. That lightheartedness he experienced so briefly once before now felt amplified ten-fold. He still couldn't believe his unfounded luck.

"Happy New Year, Trick," Amy said.

"Looks like the best one yet."

For the next few hours, Trick and Amy danced and talked with Amy's friends. It wasn't until the clock struck three that they finally decided to call it a night. There weren't many people left in the room, but a few couples pressed on. Trick walked Amy back to her room, kissed her one more time, and said goodnight. As he sauntered down the hall, he felt like he could burst from all the happiness he felt. Even when he felt the soft comfort of his bed, he couldn't sleep.

The following afternoon, Trick woke up to his dad cooking a late lunch. They swapped stories about their New Year's parties and stayed in the room most of the afternoon. It was only after dinner that Roy got ready to head out again.

"You're gonna see her again?" Trick asked.

"Well, we have a good time with each other," Roy admitted. "Why, you think something is wrong with that?"

Trick shook his head. "No, I think it's great. I'm just not used to seeing it."

Roy smiled and gave his son a hug. Trick didn't necessarily like it, but Roy also kissed him on the forehead. Once Roy left, Trick threw in a movie. He thought about going to see Amy but vaguely recalled something about them going on a one-day retreat. Around ten, Trick left his room and headed for the Jacuzzi. He was just out the door when he saw Kayla and Jill going into their room.

"Still recovering from last night?" Kayla asked.

"Something like that," Trick replied. "What are you guys up to?"

"We just got done eating," Jill said. "Amy should be up in a few minutes."

"Tell her I said hi."

"Will do."

Trick went downstairs and smiled when he saw an available tub. Wasting no time, he rushed into an empty room, shut the door behind him, and eased into the water. Resting his head against the back of the tub, he closed his eyes and let the jets work their magic. His mind wandered back to the previous night, reliving everything that had happened like the dreams they seemed to be, but the memories were too real. He couldn't explain why this was happening and didn't go searching for an explanation. In the past, he'd thought up plans and attempted to figure everything out, but he dared not risk losing what he now had.

When the door creaked behind him, it jolted him from his thoughts. He turned quickly to see who it was. As he had hoped, it was Amy standing in the doorway wearing a turquoise bikini with a white towel wrapped around her waist. In this ultimately simple world, she was a glimpse of heavenly things.

"How's it going?" she asked.

"It's getting better all the time," Trick replied.

Amy dropped the towel and slowly slipped into the water. Taking a seat on Trick's lap, Amy wrapped her arms around his shoulders just like the previous night.

"Why is it that I always smile when I'm around you?" she asked.

"I don't know," Trick replied. "I don't give it much thought; I'm just thankful I get to see something so perfect."

Amy laughed. "That may be the best thing about you; you always know exactly what to say. You know what I want to hear even if it's not always true."

Trick shook his head. "I could never lie to you."

Amy smiled for a minute, but then rather oddly, she backed away. Swimming to the other side of the tub, she turned her back to him and rested her head on her folded hands. Trick could sense what the problem was; it was the same problem that he refused to give any thought to until he absolutely had to. Apparently that time had come. Moving over to her, he placed a hand on her back. She turned to him.

"I'm sorry," she said. "It's just that sometimes, I realize that I'll be going back to Ohio soon and you'll be going back to Kansas. I hate to think that I'm gonna be without you."

"It's not a pleasant thought for me, either," Trick assured her.

"Then let's not think about it," Amy suggested. "We've only got a short time left. Who knows what'll happen after that. If we just spend this time worried about what'll happen later, then we'll just end up wasting it. I don't care that this is going to end—at least not right now."

Trick wrapped his arms around her. "I feel the same way."

Amy started caressing his face. "So if we're gonna make the most of this...."

"...then there's no time to waste." Trick said.

The two then started kissing each other. They would spend the next hour in that hot tub together. When someone finally came to close it for the night, they left. Still kissing each other up the elevator to Amy's door, they resolved then and there to enjoy every last moment they had until the trip came to an end.

The next day, they went skiing with Roy, Jill, Kayla, and a few of Amy's other friends. They had such a great time they ended up going out to dinner together. Roy proved to be just as big of a hit as Trick. Jessi came along some days; others Roy and Jessi went off on their own.

Every day that Amy and Trick spent together, they grew closer. They talked; they laughed; they enjoyed each other's company. The entire time Trick was with Amy, his thoughts never once wandered back home. Maggie, Kenny, Eric, what had happened at the lake, it all seemed to be a lifetime away.

Then, somewhere during that third week, it all started to come back to him. He began wondering what he was missing in school and what was happening with all of them. When he left, things were in a bad way, not just on their end, but his end, too. Being with Amy had wiped all that bitterness and animosity away. He was genuinely concerned about them again, and he knew he had to be there for them.

Despite his wandering thoughts, Trick had an unforgettable week with Amy. Any time that he wasn't with his father, he was with her. Both held to their word and never once mentioned anything about leaving. Not until the day they had to leave.

Fittingly, Amy and Trick left on the same day. Roy agreed to wait to leave until Amy had gone. Once everyone packed their gear and was ready to depart; only the final goodbyes remained. As he stood by the church buses, Trick dealt with it the best he could. First, he said goodbye to Kayla, Jill, and everyone else he had met from the church group. They made their goodbyes quick because they knew Amy's couldn't be so quick. As they stared into each other's eyes for the last time, for a while at least, Amy started to tear up. Trick took her hands in his and smiled for her.

"I've got your number and we'll call each other," Trick said as more of a vow than anything.

"I know," Amy replied, "but I am still going to miss you."

"I know, I'm gonna miss you, too."

Amy threw her arms around Trick. It was getting harder and harder to control the tears. What they had felt in such a short period of time was so intense it hurt to know it was concluding. What they experienced had been so real, and it was about to be relegated to memory.

"I won't be able to touch you and feel your arms around me anymore."

Trick consoled her. "It'll all work out in the end. I swear."

"What if it doesn't?"

Trick pulled away and looked Amy in the eyes. Placing a hand on her cheek, he brushed away a tear. "It will. Even if it's not me, you'll find someone. You're such an amazing person."

"But I want that person to be you."

"It still could be."

Amy chuckled under her tears. "There you go again…saying the right thing."

"You know I'm right. Just remember what we had, and what's yet to come. And I will always be there for you, even if I'm hundreds of miles away."

Amy hugged Trick again and held him tightly. They needed to have every second they could have because each one could be the last. When they finally said goodbye to each other, they knew the moment had come.

They let go of each other and then looked into each other's eyes. After a brief second, they kissed one last time as if it were their only time, and then Amy got on the bus. Trick stayed and watched the bus pull away. Amy stuck her head out the window, her smile shining bright in the daylight and waved at Trick. Trick waved back and a few seconds later, five more people stuck their heads out the window and waved at him as well.

Once Amy was out of sight, Trick headed for his ride home. Roy was packing the rest of his luggage in the car when Trick walked up.

"You alright, son?" Roy asked.

"I'm ready to go home," Trick replied.

Roy put an arm around Trick and hugged him. They piled in the car and drove out of the hotel parking lot. As the mountains disappeared and transformed into the grassy plains of Kansas, Trick found his thoughts returning to Derby. He wanted to be back, he needed to be back, but he didn't know how he'd be welcomed back.

Chapter Twelve

Catching Up

It wasn't long after they got back before Roy had to run to the office to check in since he had taken a three-week hiatus. Once his dad was gone, Trick lugged his bags up to his room to unpack. When he packed it all weeks ago, he didn't feel like he had brought so much stuff, but he certainly didn't feel that way now. Everything that he had taken took him two hours to unload. To help pass the time, he put some music on which became the reason he didn't hear the door open downstairs. As he tossed some things in his closet, he turned to grab something from his bed and standing in his doorway was Maggie.

Seeing her stopped him in his tracks. The last time they spoke, it didn't end pleasantly to say the least. She looked well, happier than she had been weeks ago. She stood with a straight, emotionless face, arms folded casually across her body. Trick couldn't decipher if she was happy to see him or not. In any event, he wasn't going to be the first to say anything. Trying to be difficult to read himself, he blankly stared back at her. Finally, Maggie took a deep breath, dropped her arms, and walked towards him.

"Aren't you gonna say hi?" she asked, giving him a hug.

Trick paused before responding. "Wasn't sure if I should."

Trick's arms hung loosely around her because he still wasn't sure if she was mad at him or not. Everything seemed okay, but it might just be the initial shock of him being back. Honestly, Maggie truly had forgiven him; she just wasn't sure how to say it. She was also nervous because she had realized something big while he'd been gone. Once she realized it, she knew she had to tell him, but also knew it would be difficult. As she grabbed him tightly, she mentally prepared herself, and when she released him, she smiled. Trick said nothing and his face was still stone.

Maggie took a seat on his bed tensely clasping her hands in her lap. Trick cautiously took a seat at his desk, placing a fair amount of distance between them.

"I came by your house the day after the party, but all I found was a note on the door." Maggie said.

"Yeah, we left in a rush," Trick replied.

"Oh...I thought maybe you didn't want me to know where you had gone after everything I said to you," Maggie admitted.

Trick shrugged his shoulders, insinuating that that wasn't the real reason, but it was awfully close. "All things considered, I didn't think you'd care to know where I was."

Maggie frowned at Trick as she interrupted him. "You should know better than that."

Trick looked at her for a minute as she sat with a slightly irritated expression. He was too worried that she was mad at him to notice her uneasiness. On some level, she probably was still furious at him. Apparently, she was mad about his implication, too. After a few seconds, the tension dissipated when Maggie smiled again.

"I can barely go a day without talking to you," Maggie said. "Do you know how crazy it made me knowing you'd be gone for three weeks?"

Trick nodded as he sighed in relief. "Sorry," he said. "I thought you needed some space and figured that would be the best way for you to get it."

Maggie looked at him for a minute. As they sat there, her nerves began to waver. The only thing that seemed to help was talking. "Maybe, but three weeks is just too long. I mean, what am I supposed to do without you?"

Trick smiled. "Live a happier life?"

Maggie's demeanor turned dreadfully serious. "There's no chance of that."

Trick's smile vanished, surprised she was being so serious about this. Her sincerity was not only touching, it choked both of them up for a minute. During that poignant moment of reconciliation, they did more than absolve the animosity from weeks ago, they eradicated it. The relief pouring over him, Trick rose from his chair and warmly held out his arms. More than happy to accept, Maggie bounded off the bed and leapt into his waiting embrace. As they tightly held onto each other, order restored itself. Emotions were riding so high that Maggie became flustered. As she sat back on the bed and wiped a single tear from her eye, she was no longer confident she could say what she wanted to say. She lowered her head trying to hide it from Trick. It had caught Trick's attention, however, as he began to notice that she was nervous.

Every time she looked up at him, her lips began to tremble uncontrollably once she made eye contact with him. The more this problem persisted, the more she convinced herself she couldn't tell him now. This was definitely going to be harder than she expected. If she was going to say anything, she had to calm down first. She laughed nervously to try to release some tension, but it only compounded matters. The ensuing silence only escalated Trick's concerns, which unsettled her more. Maybe if she heard his voice for a while, it would help.

Finally, Maggie broke her silence. "Actually, I wanted to say something to you about your being gone, but uh…I think I'd rather hear about the trip first."

Maggie's demeanor still caused Trick a great deal of confusion. He was clueless about what she wanted to tell him, but it was obviously important. He considered trying to coax it out of her right away, but he felt that might be pressing his luck since she had forgiven him so easily.

In telling the story about everything that happened, Trick broke the tale into two parts: the part before Amy and the part with Amy. The first part was standard stuff as everything Roy and Trick did they had done before in years past.

Then, he came to Amy. He spared no detail of how they met and all of the time they spent together. He described Amy to Maggie to the best of his memory. His eyes lit up when he told her about New Year's Eve and everything else that happened after that. At first, Maggie was totally dazzled by the whole story. As she listened, her curious smile faded to a dejected frown. She couldn't help but think this was suddenly the wrong time to say what she had originally planned to say. Her resolve was fading by the moment as she watched Trick go on and on about Amy with a smile on his face he rarely displayed.

"It sounds like you had the ultimate fantasy trip," Maggie commented when he finally finished.

"Yeah, it just seems like it all ended so quickly, too," Trick said with the smile fading from his face. Maggie could see how much he missed her. She knew then it would be ultimately foolish to say what she wished to tell him.

"There was something you wanted to tell me?" Trick asked.

There was something that she wanted to say, but she didn't want to anymore. Still, she had to think of something. Trick would find it oddly suspicious if she didn't. For a moment, she considered saying it anyway, but it would have been crazy to do so.

"Oh, I was gonna tell you what happened around here while you were gone," Maggie said. Trick frowned a bit noticing a dramatic change in Maggie's tone. She sounded like someone had sucked the wind from her sails. Trick assumed it was frustration from the events she endured during his vacation, but she almost seemed disappointed by his story somehow. He quickly shook the thought.

"Well, the day after the party, I actually got a call from Eric," Maggie began. "He wasn't apologetic at all, just wanted to make sure that I understood this was really the end…."

Trick rolled his eyes. "As if you needed that cleared up."

Maggie nodded. "Yeah, I was really confused with the way we left things. Anyway, I made the mistake of telling Katie about it. She grabbed Ashley and Jessica, and the three of them were over at my house in a flash. I guess they thought I needed some sort of motivational group session to make me feel better. They talked, all saying the same things: I had done the right thing, there was nothing for me to regret, and that things would turn for the best soon. It was excruciating."

Trick laughed to himself as Maggie continued.

"The weekend after Christmas, I got a call from Katie. Jordan and her made it official over the break, and they were doubling with Ashley and Scott. She wanted to see if I'd be willing to go even if I'd be a fifth wheel. After she gave me this long speech about how I couldn't spend my entire break sitting around my room, I agreed to go.

"When I arrived, however, I learned I wasn't going to be the fifth wheel. They had invited Anthony to join us so 'I wouldn't feel awkward.' Talk about a plan that backfired." Maggie rolled her eyes as Trick tried to keep from laughing out loud. "So before the movie started, he tried to talk to me about Eric and said he was genuinely concerned about how I was doing. He told me how sorry he felt and how he wanted to make things 'better.' I tried to be polite, but eventually I just had to blow him off.

"And as if the night wasn't uncomfortable enough already, Eric showed up with a date." Maggie paused to let Trick fully visualize the situation. He shook his head in disbelief, relieved he was a state away when this all happened. "He took a seat a few rows in front of us with Angela, and the two of them put on a little show. You can imagine the affect that had on the rest of the night."

Trick had been silently listening up to this point, but his curiosity got the better of him. "How did Anthony react to the whole night?"

Maggie groaned angrily. "Not like I wanted him, too." Trick hid his smile, which Maggie didn't appreciate. "A couple days later, Ashley invites me over to her house for a small get together. Suspecting a trap, I told her that if Anthony was there or showed up, I'd go home. She assured me he wouldn't be." Trick knew it was a lie before Maggie told him. "When I arrived, the only available seat was next to Anthony, of course. To show everyone that I didn't appreciate what they were doing, I sat on the floor."

Trick couldn't hold in his amusement anymore. Bursting out in a roar of laughter, Trick tried to compose himself as quickly as possible. As he bottled the laughter back inside of him, Maggie glared at him. Trick was still smiling as he motioned for her to continue.

"I'm sorry, but it was too much," Trick explained. "I take it they all got the hint after that little display."

"Oh, yes they did," confirmed Maggie. "In fact, Anthony left earlier than I did. He was clearly upset at everyone who had talked him into doing this.

"The rest of the week, I didn't do much. There was a party at the Smith's on New Year's. Eric wasn't there thankfully. I didn't see him again until school started up. When I did, he made sure I took notice. All week, he had Angela on his hip and sat just in view of me while eating lunch together. They hugged, they kissed, they sweet-talked to each other…it was revolting."

Maggie shuddered as the memories replayed in her head. There really wasn't much more to tell, nothing of importance anyway. For his part, Trick noticed someone Maggie had failed to mention during her summary of the last few weeks. He wasn't excited to bring up the subject but had to know if anything had happened.

"What about Kenny? Anything new on that front?"

Maggie smiled a little hesitantly. She had chosen not to say anything about Kenny because she thought it would detract from what she planned to tell Trick. Since she changed her mind about that, she figured Kenny was fair game.

"Actually, I was hoping you could help me out with that," Maggie confessed.

Trick kicked himself for bringing it up. This conversation would most likely have taken place anyway, but he didn't need to make it happen. He spun around in his chair for a second, hoping to sidestep the whole issue. Sighing, he knew it was too late to avoid it, so he turned back to her. Biting his fingernail as he forced his next question, he was nervous about what Maggie was going to say.

"What did you have in mind?"

Maggie's smile grew. "Well, I haven't gotten a chance to really be alone with him. He's done a pretty good job of staying covertly hidden. I guess if the rumors are true, he's already had some experience with that."

Maggie chuckled. Trick did not.

"Anyway, I thought that you could work out an encounter during class in the TV studio. Maybe if you talked to Ms. Rutherford, she could keep everyone out of there for a while?"

Trick knew Kenny wouldn't accept this idea with open arms. If it was going to work, though, it would have to have Trick's name attached to it. Kenny would immediately come to him and demand an explanation for why Trick trapped him like he did. Of course, he didn't have a good reason to say no to this. As he debated the topic in his head, Maggie watched earnestly. She could see the struggle on his face. He didn't want to do it, but would he do it anyway?

"Alright," Trick conceded in frustration, "I'll work something out for Wednesday."

Maggie was about to argue when Trick cut her off.

"I am sure that you would like a more immediate turnaround, but with all due respect, I did miss an entire week of school. I need to catch up. I also have some stories that need to be told."

Trick smirked coyly as Maggie tried to frown at him.

"You're pretty proud of yourself, aren't you?" Maggie asked.

"What guy wouldn't be?"

Maggie laughed at bit to herself. It was the only way that she could mask the discomfort she felt regarding this topic. Trick smiled, too, as the two of them reveled in each other's company again. It had truly been a long three weeks.

"I am glad to be back, though," Trick admitted.

"Oh, why's that?" Maggie asked. In her mind, he preferred being on that mountain with Amy still.

"I missed this place," Trick replied as he looked around his room. "I missed my home, missed my room, missed my friends…missed you."

Maggie smiled and gazed into his eyes. She could hear a voice in her head, trying to convince her to say what she had thought of saying earlier. Unfortunately, she had louder voices telling her not to. Instead, she sighed softly.

"I've missed you, too."

Maggie stayed a while longer before heading home. Trick had one more day before going back to school, and she knew he needed to readjust to waking up in the morning. When he finished unpacking, Trick resigned to the garage for a few games of pool. Roy was still at the office, most likely would be there most of the night. He had told Trick he'd probably have to go out on the road again soon, so he left the car packed with Roy's bags.

All the excitement of being back and the long car ride earlier in the day left Trick pretty tired in the evening. He turned in early hoping to get back on schedule. Unfortunately, someone interrupted his peaceful slumber after a few hours.

When he heard the doorbell ringing, he tried to ignore it. He didn't know who it was, but he was certain he didn't need to talk to them that direly. Roy had a key, Maggie knew where the spare was, and Kenny would've called first. Wrapping a pillow around his ears, he attempted to drown out the bell. That's when the banging started, which proved impossible to ignore. As he stomped down the stairs, he heard someone yelling his name like a banshee. He flung open the door to see Katie repeatedly ringing the bell. He grabbed her hand, ending the nuisance.

"Thank you," Trick barked. "It works fine."

"Welcome back," Katie said nonchalantly as she came into the house.

"Come on in," Trick uttered, shutting the door.

"I just found out some interesting information regarding our good friend, Kenny," Katie said proudly.

Trick sighed as he trudged into the living room and flopped down on the couch. With his eyes closed and a hand over his forehead, he sighed. "I'm on pins and needles," he said apathetically.

"It happened when I was at the QuikTrip a few minutes ago…."

"QuikTrip the hot spot for info on high schoolers nowadays?" Trick asked sarcastically. "You got an informant there that deals the hot dish for slurpee syrup?"

"No, Kenny works there," said Katie, unappreciative of the attitude.

"Sorry, I was sleeping a few minutes ago," explained Trick. "I'm not quite awake yet."

"It's not even midnight."

Trick shrugged. "I've been in a different time zone for three weeks."

Katie ignored his self-pity. "Whatever. So I was talking to Kenny's manager and mentioned Kenny was a friend of mine. He starts telling me about how Kenny is the model employee: always on time, works an extra shift every now and then, and runs the place like clockwork. For a moment, he even went as far to say that Kenny had never asked for a favor the entire time he worked there. Then he backed up.

"He remembered that there was a Friday in October when Kenny asked to get off early. He said it was weird because Kenny was going to get the next few Fridays off, but he really needed this one off. After prodding him for a reason, Kenny said he needed to get to the Smith's party."

Katie hesitated and looked intently at Trick. Having laid out all the pieces out, she assumed it was obvious how they all fit together. He blankly stared back at her, saddened that he got him up for this. He started to stand up from the couch, ready to wash his hands of this whole ordeal.

"Do yourself a favor, Nancy Drew," Trick said. "Watch a few more episodes of Colombo before you try anymore detective work."

As Trick turned to walk away, Katie jumped up and blocked his path.

"Don't you see how big this is?" Katie asked. "Kenny told Maggie he didn't work that Friday. He told you that he went to Miller's lake after work. Now, he told his boss he went to the party. Which one is the truth?"

Trick put a hand on Katie's shoulder to show his sincerity. "I don't know, and furthermore, I don't care...goodnight," Trick replied.

"You don't find all this the least bit suspicious?" Katie asked, surprised at his apathy.

Trick groaned. "Look, in the first place, we can't prove beyond a shadow of doubt where he was that night because he was alone. Secondly, it really doesn't matter what he told his boss, he probably just wanted to get off work early. Lastly, you don't even know if we're talking about the same Friday...."

Katie was ready for that. "Oh, we are. The manager remembered listening to the game with Kenny, and it was only after the game ended that Kenny wanted to go."

Trick's interest began to rise. He knew how that would look if Kenny left just as the party was getting started. Katie could manufacture the timeline to support whatever theory she developed. He was also certain Katie was gonna tell Maggie all this soon.

"So, you think this cinches the deal, huh?" Trick asked as he tried to think of a way out of this.

"Well, I was already convinced before," Katie confessed. "I mean, I think I'd believe in E.T. before I believe the Miller's lake story. But this puts him at work, then at a party where no one saw him, and finally, at your place, soaking wet, shortly after the rescue took place. Maybe it's not proof, but he'll have a hard time explaining all that."

Katie was right about that. Trick stood with a curled finger under his lip. Since it wasn't airtight, he just needed to find the right hole to poke. He needed to find it quickly, too, because he also promised Maggie time alone with Kenny on Wednesday.

"What is it?" Katie asked concerned by the silence.

Trick looked at her for a minute. Having been so deep in thought, he had forgotten she was there. Knowing she'd get defensive if he tried to say anything negative about this, he shook his head and changed the subject.

"It's nothing really. I was just thinking about Wednesday. Maggie wants some time alone to talk to Kenny in the studio. Once she hears all this, he'll be walking into an ambush. Last time he was cornered, he bit back pretty hard."

Katie remembered when Maggie accused Kenny of making her tape. Still, she was steadfast in her resolve to bring this information to the light.

"He did all this to himself," Katie said. "He had to know that something like this was coming sooner or later."

She was right again, which Trick hated to admit. Eventually, Kenny would have to clear the air and reveal the truth, whatever that happened to be. Katie didn't stay much longer since Trick wanted to get to sleep, and that would be much harder to do now. He couldn't worry about it though. All his thoughts were just that. Nothing had happened...maybe nothing would.

Before classes started on Monday, Trick visited all his teachers to get his make-up work. He gave his explanation for his absence to all of them, which he was more than happy to do. All the work would take him a few days to finish before he could catch up, especially with the work he still had to do for Ms. Rutherford. He worked nonstop for all of first hour. Luckily, he was so refreshed from his three-week hiatus that he was breezing through everything. When there was about ten minutes of class left, Katie came back to check on him. He didn't even acknowledge her when she came in the door.

"Ms. Rutherford says you can stop for today," Katie informed him.

"Tell her I'm working through next block," Trick replied. "I talked to my seminar teacher and he's cool with it."

"Whatever you say," Katie said walking back out the door. Katie relayed the message then looked for Maggie. She hadn't mentioned what she had learned about Kenny to her yet. They had a little bit of time now, so she should be able to explain everything. Katie had to make sure Kenny wouldn't hear, so she pulled Maggie into the studio. Trick wasn't sure what was going on, but at first mention of Kenny, he pieced it together and wanted no part in it.

"Really, do you have to do this in here?" Trick asked.

"We need a private place," Katie explained.

"But it's not private, people are in here," Trick pointed out.

Katie stepped towards him. "You know all this. You don't count as people."

Trick turned around and went back to work. "Fantastic, I'm an 'it' now," he griped.

Maggie had become concerned as they argued. She had heard mention of Kenny, which she assumed meant Katie's information related to the rumor. But Trick had broken in before Katie could say anything else and time was running out.

"What's all of this about?" Maggie asked.

"Apparently Wilma fired up the Mystery Van over the weekend and did some hardcore investigating," Trick remarked sarcastically.

Katie had grown tired of Trick's remarks. She could tell that he was trying to downplay what she was about to reveal to Maggie. Now that they were beyond the point of keeping secrets from Maggie, she would be privy to everything. The only matter of concern was how she would react to the news. More than anything, Katie wanted Kenny exposed so they could put this matter to rest. Trick appeared to have other intentions.

"Shut up, Trick," Katie said. "We don't have much time." Then she turned to Maggie, "I got a clue as to where he was that Friday night."

Maggie interest peaked. "Well, don't keep me in suspense, what do you know?" she asked.

"I talked to his manager over the weekend," Katie explained. "According to him, Kenny asked to be let off work early. When he asked why, Kenny said he was going to the Smith's party that night."

It was the first part of the story that had captured Maggie's attention. "He worked that night?" Maggie repeated. "He told me he didn't work that night."

"Well, he did."

Maggie thought it all over for a moment as Katie laid out the timeline of work, party, and finally Trick's house. It was all fitting together so perfectly now. Wednesday was becoming more and more important by the second. Even Trick could tell that. His only hope was that he could poke a hole in the story.

"Okay," Trick said pretending to play along, "so you're saying that he was at the party that night. If he left work shortly after the game ended and no one else saw him there, then you're looking at a two-hour window where he's just outside the house in the woods. What is he doing out there? He couldn't have known you and Eric would come out there. There's got to be a reason for him hiding."

Trick had a valid point; Katie would concede that. The focus of all of this had been who the person was, but the 'why' never came under consideration. Perhaps the hope was that once the 'who' was established, they could ascertain the 'why.' It was an important point to consider, but not the one Maggie or Katie focused on.

"Maybe there is a reason," Maggie conceded, "but if we're having this much trouble establishing who did it, it would be just as hard to find out why. The only way we're going to get to one answer is to find the other first."

Trick said nothing more, knowing what Maggie was after. She didn't care why Kenny had done this; she wanted to find the person who admitted he loved her. That was her focus now. It was the one aspect that maintained her attention. That was the one riddle she desperately needed answered. She was close to getting it now.

The rest of the day, Trick worked in the studio. Despite the mound of homework he had to lug home that afternoon, he wouldn't be able to crack open the books that night. No sooner had Trick arrived at home when Roy informed him he was going on the road. The car was already packed, and his flight was leaving in a few hours. They grabbed dinner together, ate some-where near the airport, and afterwards, Trick went to the airport so he could drive the car back home.

Trick hadn't been paying attention to his phone for the past few hours. He missed a call from Kenny, but there was no message. It probably wasn't vital that he call back, but Trick hadn't talked to Kenny much since returning from Colorado.

"Hey, what's going on?" Kenny asked when he picked up.

"Nothing, I just thought I'd see if you needed anything," Trick replied.

"No, nothing really," Kenny said. "I didn't get to talk to you much today. Now, I know you just got back, but I've been on edge lately. Ever since Maggie found out about the rumor, I've been trying to keep my distance...."

Trick finished the thought. "And you want me to be an inside source."

"If you could, that would be fantastic," Kenny said.

Trick couldn't believe it. He said he missed all this and was ready to be a part of it again. Now he had his opportunity. After a few days of catching up, his invitation to get back in the game arrived. He shook his head at Kenny's audacity and smiled.

"Well, I can tell you that Katie went to your place of work and talked to your manager," Trick said.

"Why would she do that?" Kenny asked.

"From what she told me, she initially had purely innocent intentions," Trick replied. "She was just there and mentioned that she knew you, at which point your boss began to tell her what a wonderful employee you were. He also revealed that you asked to leave work early the night Maggie fell in the lake. Now that by itself may not seem like a big deal, but he also mentioned that you were gonna be at the Smith's party."

Kenny could see where this was going. "So Katie now believes that I was at the Smith's house that night."

It was worse than that. "Not just Katie," Trick reluctantly informed him.

"She told Maggie didn't she?" Kenny asked rhetorically.

Trick didn't bother answering. Kenny paused for a second. When Trick didn't reply, he assumed he was right and went on.

"Well, this isn't going to be easy is it? I guess I'm just going to have to be more careful about not being alone with Maggie...."

As much as he wanted to avoid revealing the truth, Trick knew he had to interrupt Kenny right there. Kenny wasn't going to be able to duck Maggie like he'd been doing in the past. She was bringing the fight to him, and he de-served a notice of caution.

"About that," Trick said. "You're going to be working with Maggie alone in the TV studio Wednesday during class...."

Before Trick could say anything more, Kenny screamed over the phone, "What!"

Having anticipated such a reaction, Trick had moved the receiver from his ear though he heard Kenny clearly. The scream sent a shiver down Trick's spine.

When he put the phone back to his ear, Kenny was quietly, though impatiently, awaiting an explanation.

"Maggie was looking for a time when the two of you could talk. Wednesday in class became an option. She asked me; I set it up. I didn't necessarily want to, but after I kept all those secrets from her I felt I owed her one."

Kenny took a minute to plan his course of action.

"Okay, okay, no problem," he said. "I just won't come to school Wednesday. I'll fake an illness or break a finger if I have to."

"That sounds like a little much," Trick said. "Besides, if I were you, I wouldn't miss this for the world. Maggie already suspects you based solely on what she's heard from other people. If you completely bail on this, it'll only make her suspect you more."

Kenny didn't believe Trick's motives were so pure. "Are you just trying to make sure you don't get in trouble for telling me about this?"

Trick didn't appreciate the doubt. "Hey, watch it. I'm one of the few people that believed you when you claimed you didn't do this. Now that's not going to change, but if you want to change Maggie's mind, talking is the only way to do it."

"I really don't think I'm gonna be able to convince her," Kenny admitted.

"Well, you're gonna have to try," Trick told him. "Maybe if you had a more solid alibi you'd be better off, but you don't seem to."

"No, I don't."

Kenny thought for a minute. He couldn't say anything more than he was at Miller's lake. He had to stick with that. Anything else, any deviation from his story would open the door to the truth he wasn't ready to reveal. But if he was in that room with Maggie for the duration of class, he wasn't sure he could make the story stick. She would ask a question that he didn't have an answer for at the time. Some lie would come back and bite him. Then what was he to do?

In his frustration, he muttered. "This is just great, now they know I did it!"

And there it was. In plain English, Trick heard it clear as a bell. It wasn't forced or provoked in any way; Kenny just admitted that he did it. He confirmed the rumor that he had so adamantly denied since he first heard about it. Trick wasn't sure what to say.

"You did it?" Trick repeated as a question.

Kenny quickly retracted his statement. "No."

"You just said you did it," Trick reminded him.

Kenny continued to back track. "Well, that's not what I meant."

"Then how come that's what you said?" Trick asked, very concerned about the sudden turn this conversation had taken.

Shaken momentarily, Kenny quickly restored his resolve. Calming himself down for a minute, he coolly defended himself. "It was just a slip of the tongue."

Trick was still uneasy "Was it?"

"Yes, that's all it was," Kenny firmly stated.

Trick tried to let it pass and just pretend that it didn't happen, but the fact remained that Kenny admitted it. It was another secret Trick assumed he would have to keep. Kenny wasn't about to let Trick alone until he agreed to say nothing. Fearing this wouldn't be his only mistake, Trick wasn't entirely confident in Kenny anymore but still believed him.

"What happens if you do that when you're talking to Maggie?" Trick asked.

"It won't happen," Kenny assured him.

"Maybe I'm just a sucker for saying this, but if you tell me it was just a slip of the tongue then I guess I'll believe you," Trick said. "But you do something like that within earshot of anyone else and you won't have that luxury."

"I know that, Trick," Kenny said, just relieved he still had one believer. "It was just...I was a little rattled. Okay? I was flustered when you told me everything, but it doesn't change the fact that I wasn't there."

"Maybe it doesn't, but it does change how you'd be looked at. You open that door just an inch and it's gonna create a lot of problems."

Kenny appreciated the concern but wasn't that worried himself. For a moment, he wondered what had Trick so worried. Perhaps it was just the fact that he was the one that heard this little slip up. Maggie had been very upset at him for concealing the rumor from her as long as he did. If there was one friendship he wouldn't risk losing, it was hers.

"I understand everything you're telling me," Kenny said. "And I can assure you that there will not be a repeat mistake. I didn't mean it like I said it. I just wasn't thinking that clearly. My mind was in fifty different places at once. I give you my word; I didn't do this. I was at Miller's lake that night, not Smith's."

Trick sighed. "Okay then. You didn't do it. You were at Miller's lake."

"And you really believe that?"

"Yeah...yeah, I believe it."

"You're a good friend, Trick."

Kenny hung up the phone after that. Trick set his cell aside and flopped down on his bed. Guilt settled in. Was he really being a good friend? Maybe to Kenny he was, but what about Maggie? They weren't going to keep secrets from each other—not anymore. Well, here he was holding on to the secret of all secrets. He had, in a sense, the true identity of her hero, but he wasn't going to say a word.

Trick knew he wouldn't get to sleep anytime soon, not with everything taking on a whole new light right in front of him. There was so much more at stake now, more than there had been even just a few minutes ago. What had started as a simple conversation between two friends quickly became an inquisition that had the potential of getting out of hand in an instant. If that happened, all bets were off.

Chapter Thirteen

Back Into the Mix

Trick's nerves were running high come Wednesday. He had convinced Ms. Rutherford to give Maggie her time alone with Kenny. As he sat in the TV studio before class, he knew this situation had a volatile component that no one was paying attention to. If Maggie attempted to force a confession from Kenny, he'd deny it vehemently. Trick believed Kenny when he said he didn't rescue her but also believed that Kenny was hiding a secret of his own. If he was at Miller's lake as he claimed, he wasn't there for the reason he was alleging.

Kenny was hiding something that Maggie was desperately trying to find out about. His unwavering denial made him defensive of accusations. On the surface, he appeared annoyed by the incessant implications, but on another level, it really seemed to upset him. Then again, maybe Trick had misread the situation.

When Maggie came into the studio, she was giddy with excitement. She could hardly sit still as she took a seat on the couch. "So, everything is set, right?" she asked. "We're gonna be alone back here?"

Trick was reluctant to get involved any more than he already was. "Yeah, it's all set."

Maggie noticed that Trick seemed distracted by something. His thoughts were scattered elsewhere, and she feared something was askew with the plan for today. She didn't dare risk anything being out of place.

"What's wrong?" she asked.

There was plenty wrong, but where was Trick to start? He knew it wouldn't be wise to say anything about his talk with Kenny from the other day. Trying to explain his theory about Kenny wouldn't be received well either. Then again, if this situation got out of hand like he thought it might, then he'd regret not at least trying to set the record straight. He would have to be precise with his explanation, but there was a possibility he could do it.

"Look, I don't want to keep secrets from you anymore," Trick explained. "You need to promise me that what I'm about to say will be taken with a grain of salt. It's something that happened that I know wasn't supposed to happen. It doesn't mean what you think it means, and I can explain why...."

Maggie could barely pay attention—her mind was racing so fast. Whatever he was about to say truly was important. She couldn't begin to imagine what it entailed and was adamant about finding out soon.

"Okay," she promised, "whatever you say, I'll believe you. Just tell me what it is; I'm getting kind of scared over here."

Trick contemplated backing out, but he was already in too deep. "Monday after school I was talking to Kenny. I told him that Katie told you about his work request back in October. When I finished telling him, he said 'great, they're gonna know I did it,' but when I pressed the issue, he retracted."

That last part didn't matter to Maggie. Her eyes had grown wide, and she was just relieved that it was over.

"He admitted it?" she asked.

"He was flustered," corrected Trick. "You said you would take this as I meant it. I can explain everything."

Maggie jumped up from her seat. Trick tried to keep her thoughts grounded, but they were already sky high.

"What is there to explain?" Maggie asked. "That solves everything!"

"No, it doesn't," Trick retorted. "You gotta trust me. He didn't mean what he said."

"Well, of course, he'd tell you that," Maggie said. "He'd say that to anyone if he made that mistake."

Trick tried to capture her attention again, but his efforts were futile. Already lost in the idea that she had Kenny pinned down, Maggie began to plan what would happen next. Over the next few minutes, Trick tried to force a word in, but Maggie wouldn't hear it. He did manage to get a less than genuine promise that she wouldn't bring it up no matter what. When it finally came time for class to start, Trick had to yield and let things play out. He hated himself for telling her any of this.

With about a minute left before class, Kenny entered the studio and took a seat near Maggie. He kept his eyes on a different monitor and was content to let the silence last as long as it could. Maggie had a smile creeping across her face that she was trying to contain. She had to remember that this wasn't going to be easy. Even though she had the evidence, Kenny was going to stick to his guns. It would be an uphill battle all the way. Once she succeeded in tucking her smile and hope away, she began.

"Kenny, I know we've talked about this before...."

"More than once," Kenny groaned. He was fed up with all this nonsense and wasn't about to be cordial anymore.

His tone snapped Maggie from any lingering fantasy that this would be easy. "I guess I better get to the point then."

Kenny kept his eyes averted and said nothing.

"You lied to me about working the night I fell in the lake," Maggie continued.

Kenny admitted, "Yes, I did."

"Why?"

"I knew about the rumor long before you did, Maggie. I knew eventually someone would point a finger at me, and I wanted a viable alibi. I thought Trick could give me that, but I can't expect him to lie for me."

Maggie hesitated for a minute. She had to take this slowly and not get ahead of herself. It was going well so far—maybe not how she imagined it would, but he was at least talking openly about this.

"You also told your manager you'd be at the Smith's party," Maggie said.

"I needed a real reason to get off work," Kenny explained. "The truth is that I went to Miller's lake. I told Trick that, too."

"I know you did," Maggie quickly replied. "It just seems kind of odd that you would go to a lake by yourself at night."

It was something Kenny was used to hearing by now. "I know," he said with his patience beginning to wane. "It isn't a very common occurrence, but it doesn't change the fact that that's what happened."

Maggie could tell that if this was going to go anywhere, she would have to mention that he confessed to Trick. She was reluctant to do so since she had promised him that she wouldn't say anything. Surely he understood how important this was and would forgive her just as she had forgiven him.

"Kenny, I heard you admitted it to Trick," she said.

Stopping dead in his tracks, Kenny felt an initial reaction of disgust towards Trick and his untimely betrayal. He was under the impression that that little blunder was going to stay between them. He couldn't dwell on it long, however; he still had to stay focused on convincing Maggie he was innocent. That would be harder now, but he could still do it.

"Did he also mention that it was just a slip of the tongue?"

"He mentioned that, yes," admitted Maggie.

Kenny was relieved at that. At least Trick had helped him out in that small way. It would do little, he realized, but it was something on his side.

"Good, he should have said so because that's really the most important part of the whole thing," Kenny said. "I was just nervous when he said I'd be trapped in here with you all hour."

Maggie didn't appreciate the 'trapped' comment. Just because she was trying to get to the truth was no reason to imply this was some kind of torture. Her tone took on a slight change when she got back on topic.

"Well, I'm so sorry that you're 'trapped' in here with me. I didn't know that was such a painful prospect for you. I just wanted the chance to talk to you about all this, and since you've been hiding from me since Christmas, I didn't have many other options."

Kenny picked up on her annoyance. "I didn't mean it like that, okay? And I have not been hiding. I've just been busy."

"Yeah, you've been busy hiding," Maggie muttered under her breath.

"Okay," Kenny said rolling his eyes, "and why would I be hiding?"

"Obviously you have something to hide!" Maggie accused.

"No, I don't!" Kenny barked back.

Kenny and Maggie both went silent as the door opened behind them. They didn't realize it then, but their voices had gotten quite loud and carried through the glass panes into the classroom. Trick poked his head in the door as the rest of the class looked curiously into the studio. Most of them had an idea of what was going on.

"Kids, can we keep our voices down so other people don't start to get suspicious about what's happening back here, please?" Trick asked patronizingly.

"Sorry," Maggie said.

"Yeah, my bad." Kenny echoed.

Trick shut the door and gave the class the good old thumbs up to alleviate their concerns. With the situation resolved, he returned to his seat at the front of the room. Letting out a deep sigh as he sat down, he dropped his head down on the desk. Katie came over after she heard the thud and kindly patted him on the back.

"This isn't your fault," she assured him.

"No," Trick replied sarcastically, "I only led the lamb to slaughter and handed the butcher the knife. My conscience is totally clean."

Katie tried to make him feel better as class rolled on. In the studio, Maggie and Kenny continued working. Maggie tried to return the conversation to a civil level.

"So are you gonna tell me that wasn't you out at the lake at the Christmas party?" Maggie asked.

Kenny couldn't even be sure he knew what she was talking about. "What?"

"The party at Smith's when Eric and I broke up," Maggie clarified. "I went out to the pier while I was waiting for Trick to come get me. While I was out there, I saw a person down along the bank of the lake. Was that you?"

Kenny turned to face Maggie when he knocked something off his workstation. With his eyes widening and his pulse quickening, Maggie could see that she had rattled his confidence. Though he should have expected she would be on that pier, he couldn't believe it was her standing there and that she had seen him. He had hoped he was in the shadows enough to stay hidden, but apparently, he wasn't. Maggie took his silence as admission.

"It was you, wasn't it?"

Kenny didn't answer. He was searching for an excuse that would get him in the clear and out of the spotlight even if just for the moment. Whatever he was going to say, he needed to say it quickly. His silence only proved to Maggie that she was on to something. If she suspected something fishy was happening, she wasn't going to let it go. Right on cue, she threw another accusation at him.

"You saw me out there. You saw me and then ran back into the woods."

"Alright fine...it was me. I was down there, but that doesn't mean anything." Kenny said trying to shrug it off.

"No, it does," Maggie said. "Why would you be out there? You must have hoped that I'd come out there myself. That's why you were down there."

"No, it wasn't. I heard Eric getting upset at you and I bailed...."

It was a poor excuse, and Maggie recognized that. "Oh, whatever! You could have just left. Why would you go down by the lake? That doesn't make sense even for you!"

"Do you really think that I care whether or not this makes sense for you?" Kenny replied. "The only thing that matters here is that I'm not going to say it was me because it wasn't me. You have to realize that and move on with your life!"

A few seconds later, Trick and Katie unwillingly walked in. The conversation between Maggie and Kenny died off as Trick and Katie stood awkwardly at the door for a minute. Ms. Rutherford had been okay with one outburst, but it was clear to her that things were getting out of hand for whatever reason.

"Do you guys need something?" Maggie asked trying to cover up the tension.

Katie shook her head. "No, Ms. Rutherford just wanted us to come back here. She was concerned, and rightfully so I must say, that you two were having problems. So she sent us back to try and work things out."

"Good luck, this problem isn't going to be easily resolved," Kenny said.

"Well, I'm not the one being difficult," added Maggie.

Trick and Katie somberly took a seat on the couch believing they could do little more than try to keep things civil at this point. They didn't know the specific details about what had happened, but they could piece it together easy enough. Kenny and Maggie weren't looking at each other. There was a wall of tension forming between them. Both of them were nearing the breaking point. It was just a matter of who would break first. Kenny took some of his frustration out on Trick.

"Just want to take this opportunity to thank you, Trick. It's not every day one of your friends throws you to the wolves."

"You leave him out of this," Katie retaliated. "It's not his fault that you blew your own cover. He shouldn't have to lie for you all the time."

"Oh, my gosh, he's not lying for me," Kenny replied. "Even he will tell you that he believes my story of being at Miller's lake. He knows as well as I do that what I said the other night was a slip of the tongue and nothing else."

"I did say as much," Trick admitted.

"See," Kenny said turning to Maggie. "He admits it. He doesn't believe the rumor. He doesn't believe that I did it. Is that good enough for you?"

"No, no it isn't," Maggie replied. "He may be my best friend, but I have a mind of my own. I can form my own opinions, and my opinion right now is that you're not telling us the truth about all of this."

"Well, then, there's really nothing I can do is there?" Kenny asked.

"You can admit the truth," Maggie suggested.

"How long is this going to go on? I didn't do it. I won't admit it. I really wish you would just leave me alone!"

Silence enveloped the room. Maggie had tried to be diplomatic about this, but she couldn't be so accommodating anymore. This was supposedly the guardian angel that rescued her from drowning in the lake? The angel who swore to her that he truly loved her and would never abandon her if she needed him? Well, here she was, needing him to admit what he did and he was treating her like she was viciously attacking him. All she wanted was the truth and, up to and including now, all she was hearing was lies, and it was finally too much.

"Fine," she yelled as she stood up. A tear was forming in her eye. "If you're not gonna be honest about this, then I will leave you alone. In fact, I'll stop talking to you altogether."

Everyone was shocked as Maggie stormed off towards the door.

"Maggie," Kenny said going after her, "that's not what I meant."

Kenny tried to apologize, but Maggie refused to yield and sprinted out of the studio. The rest of the class watched in stunned silence as Maggie ran out of the room. Ms. Rutherford slowly made her way towards the studio. Kenny had his head in his hands while Katie and Trick sat with stunned expressions on their faces.

"Is everything okay back here?" Ms. Rutherford asked. "I think Maggie was crying when she left."

"She'll be fine," Trick replied out of reflex. "She just needs a minute."

Ms. Rutherford could only accept Trick's answer. As much as she would like to get involved, there was other business at hand. "If you say so. Kenny, you need to go to the office. Apparently, you have a doctor's appointment."

Kenny glumly left the studio without saying a word. Trick could tell that he was beating himself up for reacting so defensively. Maybe he deserved to feel that way right now. Katie certainly believed as much. It was one thing for him to keep his guard up about all of this before, but things had changed drastically. There was no need for secrecy anymore, the story simply needed to end.

While Maggie was out, Trick and Katie worked on the project Maggie and Kenny had started. When Maggie came back, she asked them to leave. It wasn't the time to argue the point, so they left.

"Somebody's gonna have to talk to her," Katie said once they were outside the studio.

"I'll do it," Trick volunteered. "I'm pretty much caught up on my homework. I'll go over to her house and try to talk to her."

"Do you think she'll want to talk?"

"No."

After school, Trick went straight home. Knowing better than to go over to see Maggie first thing, he went into his house to give her time to cool off. There was a message from Roy on the answering machine saying that he'd be home in a few weeks, get to stay until the beginning of March, but then would be gone until Trick's graduation. Trick made a note of it and then went to work on his homework. When he finished, he cooked up a quick meal. He didn't eat much. He wasn't that hungry.

After dinner, he decided the time had come to have his talk with Maggie. In the back of his head, he had hoped she'd come to see him. Unfortunately, it was not going to be easily. After bursting out of the classroom, Maggie hadn't spoken a word to him or Katie all day. He could only imagine the mood she was in now. Still, he couldn't just give up because it was going to be difficult. He strolled up to Maggie's door and rang the bell. Maggie's mother answered with a sympathetic look for Trick.

"She said she wants to be alone."

"Given the circumstances, I'm not surprised, Ma'am," Trick replied. "It was a pretty taxing day. Even so, I came all of this way."

Maggie's mom chuckled then rested her head against the door and stared at Trick. "Why are you always here for her, Trick? For so many years you've always been willing to come over here and talk with her no matter what."

Slightly embarrassed by the question, Trick mulled it over for a moment. "It's not everyone that gets to have a friendship like we have. I guess I'm just protective of that in my own way just like she is."

Maggie's mom smiled. "You're a sweet kid, Trick."

"Thank you Ma'am," Trick said. "I attribute it all to my father and mother."

She laughed a bit, but there was still the problem of Maggie wanting to be alone. She hoped that Trick would take the hint but didn't expect him to. "You're not gonna go away are you?"

"I'm as stubborn as I am sweet, I'm afraid." Trick replied.

"Well, she'll be pretty mad if I let you in."

Trick pointed to his left. "Should I climb up the side of the house and sneak in through her window like I've done in the past?"

The sincerity of this young man overwhelmed Maggie's mother. It was what every mother hoped for her child in a friend. Much like Roy, she had hoped Maggie would at least try going out with Trick. She put an arm around him and ushered him into the house. "I'll just take the heat for letting you in."

Trick thanked her and headed for Maggie's room. Bounding up the stairs two at a time, he was actually nervous about talking to her. He gently knocked as he gradually opened her door. Maggie lay sprawled out on her bed, her face buried deeply in her pillow. She didn't bother to look to see who it was.

"I don't wanna talk," Maggie replied. The pillow muffled her voice.

"That's fine," said Trick taking a seat on her desk chair. "We both know how much of a talker I can be."

Maggie groaned when she recognized the voice. "Oh, it's you."

Trick wasn't expecting a warm greeting but still felt a little put off. "It's nice to see you, too."

Maggie picked her head up off the bed. "It's not that. I just didn't like the way things went today. I feel bad about it, and now you're gonna try to make it all better again."

Trick attempted to lighten the mood. "I know—I'm a horrible human being."

Maggie shook her head. "Don't do this," she begged.

"What am I doing?" Trick asked playing dumb.

Maggie stared at him, slightly aggravated by this innocent routine. He knew what he was doing, but she was convinced it wouldn't work this time. Unfortunately, he wouldn't leave until they at least gave it a try.

"I just don't get it," Maggie began. "This whole fiasco has cost me my relationship with Eric, and I'm still nowhere closer to the answer. It persistently strains my friendship with Kenny to where we can't stand each other. I can't even control my own emotions when it comes to this anymore. Why would he still be hiding? He's got nothing to worry about."

"In your eyes he doesn't," Trick responded.

"Come on, what would Kenny have to hide?"

Trick shrugged his shoulders. "I can't answer that. I'm still under the impression that Kenny is innocent in this whole matter."

Maggie rolled her eyes. "No, it's him. It has to be."

"It has to be or you want it to be?" Trick asked.

Maggie didn't have an answer for that question. She had never really given it much thought. It wasn't that she wanted it to Kenny; he was just the closest thing to an answer she had. It made her reconsider telling Trick what she had wanted to tell him when he returned from Colorado. As she thought about it, she remembered the look in his eyes when he told her about Amy. Everything that had happened between the two of them was proof enough that it wouldn't do any good to say it. She was already having enough difficulties with her friends. She didn't want to risk anything with him. Still, having the thought prevalent in her mind made her a little nervous.

"I wouldn't care one way or another who it was," Maggie replied. "I just want to know who it was."

Trick wasn't convinced.

"With everything that's pointing to Kenny, it's hard to ignore it just because he says it's not true," Maggie continued. "Everyone else that I know can vouch for where they were. Even you were on the phone with Jordan when it happened. The longer I think about it, the more everything points at Kenny, the harder it all gets."

Maggie put her head down on the bed again, feeling the weight of it all crashing down on her. Her eyes started watering, but she didn't want Trick to see her cry again. It felt like she'd be doing too much of that lately. As much as she wanted an end and an answer, she was starting to believe that she'd never have either. The longer this dragged on, the more she needed an end and an answer. If those things never came, what was she going to do then?

"I can't handle it anymore, Trick," Maggie admitted through her tears. "I can't handle him lying to me, not telling me for whatever asinine reason he's got. I can't stand thinking about it. Every time I see him, I can't concentrate on anything else. It's too much. I don't know how I'm going to be able to keep going if Kenny doesn't admit he did it. It'll just drive me crazier than I am right now."

Trick got up from the desk and knelt down by Maggie's bed. Now that he knew it was happening, Maggie didn't care if he saw her cry. As she turned her face towards him, he placed a hand on her face and gently wiped away a tear.

Trick promised her, "It's not going to go like that. You just got swept back up in this because of the rumor and Katie and me. After a while, a week, two weeks, you'll stop worrying about it so much. Until then, you can't force yourself to carry all that fear, anger, and whatever else you're feeling by yourself. You gotta talk to someone, anyone who'll listen."

Maggie grunted. "So I'm just supposed to dump my problems on Katie, Ashley, and you?"

"You're not dumping when people genuinely care."

"No one cares that much."

"I think I know one guy that might."

Maggie laughed. He would single himself out like that. She often felt as though she was alone with this problem. It was nice every now and then to hear someone remind her that she wasn't. It may not be the ideal situation for anyone involved, but it's what friends did.

The thought began to cheer her up. "I am lucky to have someone like that."

She smiled at him, and Trick smiled back. He chuckled at bit to himself and then joked. "Yeah, you're lucky. What about that poor guy?"

"I think he's fine with it."

They both smiled. For the moment, Maggie's problem didn't seem so daunting. She was actually feeling like she might be able to put all this behind her. As she collected herself in silence, Trick tried to read how she was doing. He was concerned that everything he said would only provide a band-aid affect. That they might have covered up a small problem for now but hadn't resolved the deeper issue. He wasn't sure what the next step would be, and it made him uneasy.

Maggie dabbed her eye with a tissue. Out of the corner of her eye, she could see Trick watching her. The concern on his face was unmistakable, touching, and it reminded her how she felt about him. As quickly as the thought entered her mind, it unnerved her to have that notion replaying in her head. Now that she had convinced herself to say nothing, it was imperative that she stick to that plan. On the other hand, he was here wasn't he? He braved her angered temperament and stuck by her anyway. Why would he do that unless he felt the same way?

"Why are you always here for me, Trick?" Maggie asked, finally breaking the silence.

Trick hesitated at hearing the same question Maggie's mom asked mere minutes ago. He had never considered it odd that he did all this for Maggie, it was just something he always remembered doing.

"You'd be there for me," Trick replied. "It's just the kind of friends we are."

Maggie smiled, but it seemed forced to Trick. Almost like she didn't get the answer that she was hoping for. He was about to question it when she moved on.

"It's gonna be kind of awkward for a while isn't it?"

She was right about that. After the way she reacted to Kenny, he wouldn't exactly be anxious to try and mend fences. Luckily, they had time to allow all of this to just blow over.

"It won't be as bad as your anticipating," Trick said.

"It just stinks that all of this is happening in our last year together."

Trick concurred with that as well. He, Maggie, Kenny, Katie, Jordan, Scott, and Ashley had been close throughout high school. They stuck by each other, could count on each other, and loved each other. In their hearts they knew that was still true, but it didn't always appear that way—especially not after something like this.

Trick hung around a while longer but not much else happened. He went home that night and called Katie who had talked to Kenny a few minutes earlier. He was apologetic about what he had done and didn't like the way things ended though he understood that for the time being there wasn't much he could do to make things better. It would have to heal itself over time.

Katie admitted that she tried to force a confession from him but to no avail. Kenny was sticking to his story rather stubbornly. Trick laughed when Katie informed him she threatened Kenny's health if he was lying about all this.

She argued with Trick a little more about his belief in Kenny's story. She couldn't understand why he believed Kenny as adamantly as he did. Trick admitted having no good reason other than the fact that Kenny was so steadfast in his denial. Katie could accept that for Trick's sake but not her own.

The initial discomfort felt by Maggie and Kenny didn't last long. The first few days, they kept their distance even if in the same room. In class, if Kenny was in the studio, Maggie retreated to the computer lab. They moved farther away from each other in other classes they shared. At lunch, they sat at different tables. They didn't like to do it but accepted that it had to happen for a while.

That would last a week or so, but eventually, they got tired of the self-imposed restraining order. Surprisingly, it was Kenny who first broke ground as one day he sat with Maggie during lunch. They kept the conversation simple, discussing some schoolwork matters. After a few awkward conversations, things became natural again. The tension had resigned, and they were friends again.

By the end of February, everything was back to normal again. That not only applied to Kenny and Maggie, but Maggie as well. She hadn't completely put the events of that fateful October night behind her, but it wasn't dominating her life anymore. Trick couldn't even remember the last time they talked about it. Instead, all of Maggie's focus was on her upcoming birthday party. Though it was still a couple weeks away, she was already stressing over it. It was times like this that she was happy to have a class where she could get away with doing something other than schoolwork. She was at the news desk with papers spread out. Katie was helping while Trick worked on the editor providing an alibi.

"So, how many people are coming?" Katie asked.

"Right now, I've got thirty RSVPs," Maggie replied.

"Do you think you'll get any more?"

Maggie turned to Trick. "No, but there are some people I know will be there who haven't said anything yet."

Trick hadn't been paying attention to their conversation since he had no stock in it. When Maggie realized he didn't hear what she was saying, she picked up a pen off the desk and chucked it at his head. Striking him square on his temple, he snapped from his trance.

"I'm talking to you." Maggie said.

"Well, that's all well and good, but there's no call for gratuitous violence," Trick replied as he tossed the pen back.

"You'd just better show up," Maggie warned. "You are my date, you know."

Trick groaned. "Can't you find a real date?"

"No," Maggie quickly snapped back, "I can't believe you're making such a big deal about this. I bet things would be different if it were Amy."

As they were talking, Kenny sauntered into the studio and took a seat next to Trick. The project he was working on was for the two of them. They discussed some specifics of the tape for a while. When they finished, Katie was waiting with a question.

"Kenny, are you gonna be at Maggie's party?"

"Yeah, I put in my RSVP, didn't I?"

Maggie checked her list. "Yes, you did."

"I'm gonna spare you the suspense and admit I haven't gotten you anything," Kenny said.

Maggie chuckled. "That's okay; you don't have to get me anything."

"Sounds pretty cheap to me," Trick remarked with a wink.

"Oh, really," Kenny replied. "And what have you gotten for her?"

"I'm her date," Trick retorted. "That's my gift."

Katie scoffed. "Hold on to that receipt," she said to Maggie.

Everyone got a good laugh out of the joke with the exception of Trick. He merely nodded his head slowly with a frown on his face as he eyed the monitor. "Hilarious," Trick mockingly remarked. "We'll see who's laughing when I don't show up."

Maggie didn't take kindly to this insinuation. "It's either my party or the Emergency Room."

Trick smiled and turned to Kenny. "It's the threats that let me know I'm loved."

Kenny smiled and patted Trick on the back. Maggie and Katie both rolled their eyes as they went back to work.

"Just be there, lover," Maggie said.

They worked in silence for a few minutes longer. After a while, Katie got curious about Amy. She had heard the story when he came back in January, but that was the last time she had heard her mentioned. Considering Trick indicated they were going to keep in touch, she wondered if he had followed through.

"You know Trick, you haven't mentioned Amy lately," Katie said. "How are things going with that?"

"They're fine," Trick said looking away from the monitor momentarily. "We talked last weekend for a few hours. She said all was well up in Ohio. She said she missed me, but we have no idea how soon we'll be able to see each other again."

"It's kind of a rotten deal that you meet someone like that and end up being separated by five states," Kenny said sympathetically.

Trick shrugged his shoulders. "Yeah, it could've worked out a little better, but that's just the way it goes."

There was a slight anguish in Trick's tone. Everyone was aware of it and didn't want to say anything more about the subject. Trick had never stated it, but everyone knew how upset he felt now separated from someone he felt a genuine connection with. After the fiasco with Ashley, it seemed like salt on the wound. He had a girl that things didn't work out with dating a friend of his and another girl it did work out with living in a different time zone. Fortunately, Kenny would change the subject.

"Maggie, I'm surprised you got Trick to agree to be your date."

"Oh, he was happy to do it," Maggie said. "He knows it's not a big deal. I just wanted a friend around in case anything came up."

"I think she could do better," Katie said with a wink.

Maggie pushed Katie playfully as Kenny held back a smile. All eyes were on Trick as he worked. He looked around at all the stares.

"What? I totally agree with that."

Katie shook her head and rolled her eyes. "You're unbelievable, Trick."

After a small giggle, Maggie went back to work. She felt so relieved being able to do this again. The four of them, in a room together, joking, laughing, not walking on eggshells worried about upsetting each other. It proved to her that she had begun moving past the mess the last few months had brought. Perhaps she would never get an answer to her questions, and for once, she could tolerate that possibility.

Chapter Fourteen

Birthday Surprise

Life seemed to settle into a dull lull as the days counted down to Maggie's birthday. It worked out perfectly in that the party coincided with the beginning of Spring Break. Everyone would still be around before taking a week off from school and traveling wherever. Maggie was excited and nervous for the party all at the same time. Despite the fact that she no longer obsessed over the lake incident, she had been having some odd dreams as of late. She tried to write them off as nothing, but when the dreams became more repetitive, she couldn't ignore them. When it became too much, she had Trick talk her through them to alleviate her worries.

The biggest problem these dreams posed was the common thread of her at the impending party. In one, Kenny broke in, opened up, and confessed. In another, Kenny came face-to-face with the real the mystery man, proving once and for all that it wasn't Kenny. There was even one that saw Eric storm into the house and get in a fight with Kenny.

With the dreams making Maggie nervous about the party and being around Kenny, she grew more dependent on having Trick at her side. He may not be able to prevent anything from happening, but he could give her a shoulder to lean on.

As far as the party went, the house looked amazing. All of the furniture in the living room sat pushed against the wall opening up the floor. Blue, pink, and yellow streamers were encircling the room, and a giant birthday banner hung above the front door. The kitchen held a full spread of pizza, party subs, chips, dip, and a variety of pop. Outside were several tables with white table-cloths and confetti so not everyone would be crammed in the house. As a final touch, several fixtures along the wall had string with brightly colored balloons tied to them. Maggie couldn't thank her parents enough. Once everything was set, they took their leave so Maggie and her guests could have the house to themselves.

Everything was set up; she just had to wait for her friends to arrive. She hoped that Trick realized what the night had in store for him. She wanted him with her most of the evening especially when Kenny was around. Fairly confident she could control her nerves, she got a real boost from having a backup plan. The doorbell rang. Maggie hoped it was Trick; it was Jordan and Katie.

"Happy birthday!" they yelled.

"Thanks," Maggie replied with a smile. "Come on in."

Maggie showed them in and closed the door behind them. "Scott and Ashley will be in shortly," Katie said. "They're just parking the car."

Jordan made a B-line for the kitchen, leaving Katie to talk with Maggie. When Katie turned to talk to her, Maggie was looking out the window. Katie frowned as she watched her friend blankly stare at nothing in particular. Maggie couldn't figure why Trick wasn't here yet—there were only a few minutes before the party started.

"Something wrong?" Katie asked.

Maggie fidgeted with her hands for a minute before moving away from the window. "I just thought that he would be here by now."

"Who? Trick?" Katie asked.

"Yeah," Maggie replied hurriedly, "he's just right across the street or at least I thought that's where he was. So what's keeping him?"

Katie knew everything about Maggie's dreams and put a hand on her shoulder to comfort her. "He'll be here soon enough. He'd never let you down."

Maggie smiled, took a deep breath, and then stepped away from the window. Scott and Ashley entered the house shortly afterwards. They talked a little and started to play some music. A few more minutes ticked away, some other people showed up but not Trick. Maggie started to ask around and see if anyone knew where Trick was, but no one knew. He wasn't atrociously late, but later than was usual for him. Every now and then, she tried to catch a glimpse of his house to see if anything was going on but no such luck. She couldn't stare for too long or people might have noticed and gotten concerned. After a while, she gave up and engrossed herself in the party as much as she could. A few minutes later, Trick came bursting into the house, totally out of breath.

"I'm sorry," he proclaimed as he looked for Maggie. "I'm sorry, I'm sorry."

Maggie walked up to him with folded arms. "Where have you been?" she asked.

"I was practically out the door so I could get here early. Then my phone rang and it was Amy. We started talking, I said I had to go, but it turned out that she had a lot to say. Before I realized it, it was after seven. I got off the phone as quickly as I could and sprinted over here."

He was too cute to stay mad at. "It's alright," Maggie replied with a warm assuring smile. "You just worried me is all."

"I know," Trick said. "There were some things we just had to clear up."

"Anything you need to talk about?" Maggie asked.

Trick shook his head. "Now is definitely not the time."

Maggie smiled as she took Trick's hand. Leading him through the party, she was determined not to let him stray too far away. The more he was around, the more she could forget about the dreams and get comfortable. Once her comfort reached an acceptable level, she was more willing to go it on her own.

Not too long after he had arrived, Trick and Maggie had gone their separate ways. Trick was hanging out with Scott and Jordan as the two of them assaulted the buffet. Maggie was dancing in the living room with a bunch of her friends. Kenny stayed unnoticeably absent for the first hour of the party, but when Maggie saw him walk through the front door, she immediately stopped dancing. Apparently, he agreed to bring Jessica because the two walked in together. Once Kenny spotted her, he waved and started to walk over to her. Maggie swallowed nervously as Kenny approached her. Before she could take a step forward, Trick came out of nowhere and grabbed her hand. His touch immediately calmed her.

"I'm here," he said.

"Good," Maggie sighed.

Kenny said hi, happy birthday, and gave Maggie a hug. Jessica said hi to Trick and gave him a hug as well.

"Hey," Kenny said, "great party."

"Oh, thanks," Maggie said. "We haven't really gotten started yet."

"Then it's only gonna get better."

As Kenny and Maggie continued to talk, Maggie was surprised to find that she was much more comfortable than she thought she would be. She gave Trick a quick smile to let him know that everything was okay. Trick smiled back and looked at Jessica.

"How are you doing, Trick?" Jessica asked.

"I'm good, how about you?" Trick replied.

"Ready to graduate," Jessica said with a deep sigh.

Trick smiled sympathetically. "Tired of school, huh?"

Jessica shrugged her shoulders ashamed to admit the truth. "Actually, I'm tired of being at home. Matt has been a real pest lately. I love him, but I wouldn't mind some time away from him."

The music started to take over the room, a sign that the party was about to kick up a notch. The floor began to fill as more and more people started dancing. Trick quickly got the feeling Maggie had already filled his dance card. As Maggie started to get a feel for the music, he nonchalantly tried to step away. He hadn't even taken a step when Maggie grabbed his arm.

"Going somewhere?" she asked.

Trick had to lie. "No, I was just doing a little stretching."

Maggie poked Trick in the chest. "You're gonna have to do better than that if you're wanting to escape. You danced with Amy; you can dance with me."

Maggie yanked Trick out on the dance floor and started dancing. Fearing the repercussions for attempting to flee, Trick danced along with her. The first interlude came about twenty minutes later. Maggie hadn't allowed Trick to leave the floor, but now that the music had stopped, she graciously let him go. He immediately went to the kitchen for something cold to drink. Taking a seat on the counter, he slowly drank a Dr. Pepper. While he rested, Ashley came over to him.

"Do you mind?" she asked.

"Not at all." Trick replied giving her a little more room.

Ashley got nice and comfortable before pausing for a minute. A question had been on her mind ever since she heard about Trick's trip. She hadn't had the opportunity to discuss it with him until now but wasn't sure how to start that conversation with him. "So, what have you been up to?" she asked innocently.

"Not much really...you?" Trick hadn't picked up on her discomfort.

"Same," Ashley replied with a smile. She wanted to just jump into the topic, but was too nervous to do it. She couldn't let the silence last, though. "Ya know, it wasn't the smartest thing for you to show up late."

"Don't I know it!" Trick said with a chuckle. "I guess I lost track of time on the phone."

Ashley cleared her throat to help alleviate some of the tension. "Maggie said you were talking to that Amy girl you met in Colorado."

Trick nodded.

"You two must have really had something special up there," Ashley commented.

Trick nodded again. A nostalgic smile crept across his face.

Ashley shifted on the counter. This was harder than she thought it would be. "I was surprised when I heard how fast the two of you moved."

Now, with the path laid before him, Trick could infer where this was going. It had been months since the two of them had really been alone like this, and it was only natural for the question to come. Things hadn't worked out between them when it looked like they could have. While a multitude of factors contributed to their misconnection, Trick's guarded nature was definitely one of them. Barely a month later, he thrust himself into the torrid affair. What was so different?

"Yeah, well it was one of those things that just happened, ya know?" Trick tried his best to explain.

Ashley nodded. "It's just that you sounded like a completely different person from the guy that took me out a couple times."

"I don't know about different...maybe just wiser."

The notion caught Ashley's intrigue.

"After everything that I went through with you, I realized I couldn't agonize over every little thing. I had to go with what was happening and trust that everything would turn for the best. With you, I was trying so hard to control things so I wouldn't screw up. With Amy, I was still concerned that I would screw up, but I didn't let that dictate what I did. I just did whatever felt right, and it worked out."

Ashley thought about it for a moment. She wondered if that would have made a significant difference for them. The thought crossed her mind every now and then, but being with Scott had made her so happy that she didn't dwell on the subject much.

"I see what you mean," Ashley said. "I guess in a way, everything worked out for the two of us. I ended up with Scott. You were free to have your little romantic encounter on your trip." They both smiled. "Still, I wonder every now and then…about what would have happened if we had both played that situation right."

"It crosses my mind, too," Trick confessed.

Before they could say anything more, the music started up again. Ashley quickly said goodbye to Trick and then went to find Scott. As Trick watched her disappear into the crowd, Maggie ran in and grabbed him. She pulled him back onto the dance floor before he had a chance to defend himself.

"I didn't even get to eat," Trick complained.

"You can eat when you're dead," Maggie joked.

"I'll be reaching that threshold sooner than you think!"

As Trick begrudgingly took his place on the dance floor, Maggie tried to lighten him up. He was fairly unresponsive at first, but after a while, he got into the spirit. He would even be surprised when an hour passed before the next break in music. He was relieved, however. He hadn't eaten in a while and wasn't going to miss out on the opportunity. As he walked to the kitchen, he noticed that Maggie wasn't far behind.

"Are you gonna follow me everywhere I go?" Trick asked.

"Would that be so bad?" Maggie replied.

"No, I would never complain about such a thing," Trick said slightly sarcastically. "I do believe that some people would like to see a little more of the birthday girl, though. Up to this point, you've only been around me, and I wouldn't want to monopolize your time with all these people here to see you. So go ahead, I'll be fine on my own for a while."

Maggie frowned a little, upset that Trick was trying to get rid of her. She did see his point, however. "Well, okay, but don't go too far. The music is gonna start again soon, and I'd hate to have to go a round on my own."

Trick put an arm on her shoulder. His voice turned melodramatic. "If we're meant to dance, I'm sure we'll find each other…somehow."

Maggie rolled her eyes as she headed in to the living room to mingle. Trick stepped outside for a while and hung out with a group. As the party rolled on, Maggie became more and more used to not having Trick's company. She talked to all of her guests, answering the same questions about her birthday, the gifts, and how things had been going lately. After a while, she could answer all three questions with one answer, and before she knew it, she was having a marvelously good time.

Eventually, Trick did return and the two of them ended up sitting down talking with Kenny, Katie, Jordan, Scott, Ashley, and Jessica. The crowd had thinned slightly, but the party was still rolling. As they talked about several random topics, Kenny checked his watch.

"Hey, Trick, is it okay if I go use the phone at your house?" Kenny asked. "I need to call my folks, and I forgot my cell."

Trick pulled out his own cell. "Actually, my dad doesn't want people using the house phone. Just take this. You can go in the house if you want."

Kenny took the phone. "No, I'll just step outside. Thanks."

As Kenny walked away, Trick caught up with the topic at hand. It was a subject that every high school girl was enamored with, and every guy more tolerated than enjoyed. Luckily, it was one that Trick had absolutely no stock in—prom.

"It's only one month away," Ashley said.

"Can you believe it?" Katie asked.

"I've already got my dress." Maggie added.

"I bet just about every girl that's going does."Jessica said.

As the girls took off on a tangent that would undoubtedly result in a description of each other's dresses, the guys inconspicuously removed themselves from the conversation. This wasn't going to be the type of talk that required their input, so Jordan sank back into the couch, Scott sprawled out in his chair, and Trick kicked up his feet. They listened half-heartedly for a while. Eventually, they broke off on their own conversation.

"Prom, yeesh," Jordan said with a roll of the eyes. "I'm sure glad that my wallet's ready to take a hit."

"I've put in some extra hours at work," Scott admitted.

"Yeah, me, too," Jordan said with a sigh. "How about you, Trick?"

"Not going," Trick proudly proclaimed as he raised his glass in celebration.

Maggie already knew of Trick's plot to skip prom. Every time she heard him talk about it, she got upset. Senior prom was more than a regular dance; it signified the end of an era. Everyone should be appreciative of that and take advantage of the opportunity given to them. It was one of the last nights they could spend with their friends as high schoolers. He was the only one out of the ones seated there that wouldn't be going. She tried to set him up with someone, but he wasn't interested. Now, as he sat there with his glass raised, she could only shake her head disappointed at his pride in not going to prom.

"So, Jessica, who are you going with?" Maggie asked.

"Well, I had to get approval from my parents about my date, "Jessica explained. "They settled on Darren being the right escort for the night. Which is fine with me, we've been friends for years. What about you?"

"Actually, Scott, Ashley, Jordan, Katie, and I are going as one big group because I didn't want to bother with a date," Maggie replied.

"How come you didn't want to ask someone?" Jessica asked.

Maggie glanced over at Trick as she struggled to come up with an excuse. "Oh, it's just too much of a bother this late."

Ashley leaned over and whispered into Jessica's ear. "Trick won't go."

Jessica was appalled that Trick would dare leave Maggie dateless on prom night. They were best friends after all. He had to know what it meant to her. Even if he cared nothing for the dance himself, it shouldn't be too much of a burden to endure the night for her sake.

"Trick, how could you say no to your best friend?" Jessica demanded.

"I never said no," replied Trick quick to defend himself. "In fact, I was never asked."

"Only because you made it clear that you wouldn't go under any circumstances," Maggie reminded him.

"I said no to the other girls you mentioned," Trick corrected. "You never said that you wanted to go with me."

"And that would make a difference?" Maggie asked.

"No guarantees. As far as I'm concerned, my prom night still involves a twelve-pack of pop and my pool table. But if you really want someone to go with you that badly, then I suppose I'd be willing to stand in."

Maggie could tell that his offer was less than sincere. She knew he'd go if she bugged him enough, but she didn't want to force him into anything.

"Relax, Trick," Maggie said. "I'm not going to force you to go."

Trick sighed. The other girls shook their heads at him.

As the conversation reverted back to everyone's prom plans, Trick began to feel a twinge of regret that he wouldn't be a part of the festivities. There was a small part of him that wanted to go along for a change. He had always passed on the chances to go, then listened to all the stories later and on some level wished he had been a part of it. Fortunately, that part of him didn't override the part that didn't want to go. He wasn't the type to get dressed up nor was he the type that liked the big crowd. He preferred the quiet night at home where he did nothing but relax and take it easy. Of course, this was the last chance he really had to see what the dance scene was all about. He was about to say something when his phone hit him in the chest, and Kenny took a seat next to him.

"Thanks, Trick," he said.

"No problem."

Trick gave it another moment of thought and realized he'd rather not go. Whatever he missed, he was certain it wouldn't matter that much. Still, if Maggie asked him, he'd concede and take her. He agreed to that stipulation knowing how miniscule the chance was that she'd actually ask.

Now that Kenny was back, he wanted in on the conversation.

"So, what are we talking about?" he asked.

Trick summed everything up. "Well, there's been a little bit about prom dresses, little bit about prom dates, and a little bit about how cruel I am for making Maggie dateless at prom."

"I'm sensing a theme here," Kenny said.

"Speaking of prom, who are you going with, Kenny?" Jessica asked.

"Oh, I don't think I'll be going," Kenny admitted.

Trick threw an arm around him. "Cheers!" he yelled raising his glass again. "You can come play pool with me!"

"Save me a seat," Kenny agreed, patting Trick in the chest.

"Trick, I bet your tune would change if Amy was here," Katie said.

The idea peaked everyone's interest.

"You wanna fly her down here? You be my guest," Trick said.

"To be honest, I wouldn't mind meeting her," Maggie said.

"Heck, I just want to see her," Jordan said.

Katie smacked Jordan upside the head. "I'm sure that she doesn't compare to you." Jordan said to calm Katie's aggravation. "That said, she has become somewhat of a legend around here. I think we can all admit we would welcome the chance to see if she lives up to the hype."

Katie looked around at all the other faces, and they nodded in agreement. Grudgingly, she conceded the point.

"I suppose that's an acceptable reason," Katie said.

"It would be very romantic wouldn't it?" Jessica asked, swooning over the idea.

"Well, don't get too attached to it," Trick warned them. "As much as I would love to see her, I don't think dad would go along with the idea."

Just like that, the notion was gone.

"We tried," Ashley said.

"Let's get some music going again," Maggie suggested.

Maggie grabbed Jessica, and the two of them raced over to the CD player to make their selection. As soon as the music started, Jessica grabbed a partner and started dancing. Maggie took a moment to go into the kitchen and grab a drink. Katie followed her, an idea dancing in her thoughts that had her brimming with joy.

"Do you know what you should do?" Katie asked.

Maggie shook her head. "Not a clue."

Katie slowly guided Maggie into the idea. "Well, you heard Kenny say that he didn't have a date for prom, right?"

Maggie followed along, not too thrilled where Katie was going. "Right."

"So, I'm thinking that you might as well ask him to go with you. Especially since Trick is so dead set on not going."

"I don't know, Katie…."

"Trust me, this is a fantastic idea. I mean, you still believe that Kenny is the guy that pulled you from the lake, right?"

This was exactly the situation that Maggie wanted to avoid tonight. She had been doing a good job of keeping those thoughts out of her head. Now, Katie was forcing one on her. Maggie struggled with the idea, tracing her hand along the edge of her glass. She was nervous to say anything because she knew how easily she could start to obsess, but if she was ever going to be entirely past this, she had to be able to talk about it openly.

"Yeah, I think he did it…so what?" Maggie finally admitted.

"Well, think about it. This may be the event he's looking for to tell you the truth. He made this grand gesture so many months ago, maybe he's thinking big again. Plus, if he needed to smooth over everything that had happened between you, when better to do that then at prom?"

"Then why say he didn't want to go?"

Katie sighed. "How little you pay attention. He didn't say that he didn't want to go; he said he didn't think he was going. It was an open-ended statement. It wasn't definite, just a current status. Maybe he said that hoping a certain someone would change that."

"I think you're reading too much into this."

"Just think about it. Do you really think he hasn't had the opportunity to ask someone to go with him? And unlike Trick, Kenny usually doesn't miss out on these things. Why would he be so suddenly anxious to miss this one? It doesn't add up."

Maggie lowered her eyes as she thought it over. Katie was making some good points. Kenny wasn't the type to miss out on something like prom. He would definitely be willing to go with someone, but would he be willing to go with her? He had to know how that would look and what people would imply.

Maggie stepped outside the kitchen and looked over to where they had all been talking. Only Trick remained now. She scanned the dance floor looking for Kenny but couldn't find him anywhere. It almost seemed as if he had sensed the conversation taking place and fled.

After a second, Katie joined Maggie.

"Where is Kenny anyway?" Maggie asked.

"Isn't he out on the dance floor?" Katie replied.

"I don't see him."

Almost happy for the distance from the idea, Maggie shrugged it off. Coaxing Trick onto the dance floor, she distracted herself for a while. Every few minutes or so, her eyes would stray across the room trying to find Kenny. She never saw him. It didn't take Trick too long to notice that something was going on.

"What's wrong?"

"Nothing, I was just looking for Kenny."

Trick took a quick scan of the room.

"Don't see him."

"Do you think he left?"

"I don't think so."

There was a short intermission in the music while the disc was changed. During that time, Ashley came over wanting to switch partners briefly. Maggie was barely paying attention as she looked for Kenny so she agreed without argument. She had to remind herself what was happening when she turned back around and saw Scott in front of her. He didn't notice her surprised smile, which she quickly replaced with a more natural one.

As they danced, she still kept an eye out. It was about an hour now since she had last seen Kenny. She wasn't really giving much thought to the idea of asking him to prom, but his absence was stirring up her concerns from her dreams. A small voice in her head kept warning her of them. As hard as she tried, she couldn't shake those thoughts.

After a few dances, Ashley decided to switch back. Trick and she was laughing when they came back to Maggie and Scott. Scott politely thanked Maggie for the dances to which Maggie gave a reactionary response. She still couldn't spot Kenny.

"Still haven't seen him, I take it," Trick said when he saw the concern on her face.

Maggie shook her head. Trick knew she needed resolution on the issue.

"Don't worry about it," Trick said taking Maggie's hands in his. "I'll make a quick sweep of the house and find him."

Maggie looked thankful for the thought. "Are you sure you don't mind?" She only asked because she knew he'd look anyway.

"Just wait here," Trick instructed.

Maggie let her hands fall against her sides as Trick disappeared into the crowd. Moving out of the way, she did what she could to look for Kenny, too. After a few minutes, she saw Trick coming towards her. She was a little disappointed it was him and not Kenny.

"Did you find him?" Maggie asked.

Trick shook his head. "I asked around and no one has seen him for a while."

Maggie's eyes dropped and she placed a hand over her forehead. Trick wrapped an arm around her.

"I'm sure he's fine."

"That's not why I'm worried."

"I know."

Maggie looked around the living room for a few more seconds. After a while, she shook her head, frustrated with the ridiculous situation she was now in. Once she forced the idea out of her head, she invited Trick back to the dance floor. He was happy to provide a distraction. After a few songs played, Maggie took a break. She wanted to run upstairs for a minute to get something from her room.

On the way up the stairs, Maggie heard steps on the floor above her. The surprise stopped her. She almost tripped when she realized someone else was upstairs. There really wasn't any reason for someone to be up there.

"Hey," she called out. "Who's up here?"

There was no response, but she suddenly heard frantic running. Immediately taking off herself, she tried to follow the sounds she heard, but it was hard to hear with the music playing below. As she stalked the hallway, she feared she had lost the intruder. Putting her ear to each door, she tried to flush out the culprit. When she heard the creaking of a window, she knew it was coming from her room. Bursting through the door, she was shocked to see Kenny standing at the window.

He looked at her briefly, kicking himself for letting someone catch him, especially Maggie. Maggie froze at the door, eyes wide and agape. Kenny had one leg out the window; he was preparing to jump. Seeing Maggie suddenly made him feel like he needed to explain. He opened his mouth as if he had something to say and raised a hand illustrating that he could explain. A second later, he clinched his hand to a fist and looked away. Maggie took a step towards him, and he jumped.

Sprinting to the window, Maggie caught a glimpse of Kenny as he crashed to the ground and took off into the darkness. Maggie could only watch mystified by the possibilities that this presented. As she stared out the window, Jessica walked in behind her. She had heard Maggie calling on the stairs, and she was confused when she saw Maggie staring out the open window.

Maggie didn't even notice her there. Her mind had been tracing over the details of what had just taken place. What would have caused Kenny to jump from her second story window? Did she catch him doing something he didn't want her to see? If so, what could it have been? He was alone up here, wasn't he? Had he been in her room? Why would he be...suddenly an idea hit her.

Ignoring Jessica's presence, Maggie went to her closet. She started rifling through it. Jessica dodged the flying objects that Maggie threw over her shoulder. Jessica still didn't know what was going on. All she heard from Maggie was the quiet remarks she was making to herself. "He must have been looking for it." She repeated it over and over again without offering any explanation as to what she meant. Finally, Maggie emerged holding a small piece of black cloth.

"He must have been trying to take it," Maggie informed Jessica as if she should know what that meant.

"Who?" Jessica asked.

"Kenny," Maggie replied. She went back to the window, pointing as she went. "He was just here," she explained. "I was coming up the stairs, and I heard someone up here. When I got to my room, he had the window open. I tried to stop him, but he jumped out and took off." Jessica looked shocked when Maggie said he jumped but Maggie went on. "He had to be doing something secret, otherwise he wouldn't have left like he did. No one had seen him in an hour. This must be why!"

Maggie's enthusiasm was causing Jessica some concern. Maggie kept referencing the small cloth she had stretched out in her hands, but Jessica didn't understand what the big deal was and was almost afraid to ask.

"Maggie, why is that so important?" Jessica asked calmly.

"This is a piece of the mask," Maggie replied. "I accidentally ripped it off the guy who pulled me out of the lake back in October. Kenny must have been trying to get it back."

Jessica started to question Maggie's theory when Maggie bolted from the room. She flew down the stairs with the fragment in hand. Frantically looking for Trick, she saw him talking to Katie by the kitchen. She almost ran into them she was so excited.

"Kenny tried to take the ski mask!" she exclaimed.

All eyes turned to Maggie. Trick was speechless. Katie almost fainted when she heard the news. It was such a shocking move for him to make.

"How can you be sure?" Trick finally forced out.

"He was in my room," Maggie replied. "That's where he had been the last hour. He must have been looking for it. When I came up, he freaked out and jumped out the window."

Trick and Katie had the same response Jessica had. Maggie waited for them to say something. This was the final piece of the puzzle as far as she was concerned. He tried to take the mask back, and only one person would do that.

"There's your nail in the coffin," Katie said.

The two burst out in laughter and screams. They jumped up and down, hugging each other tightly. Trick just stood unable to comprehend the logic behind Kenny's actions. He hadn't done anything in weeks to provoke the situation. Why did he risk it now?

"Why would he want a piece of cloth back?" Trick asked.

Katie wasn't about to let him spoil this. "Oh, no, you don't," she said waving a finger in his face. "You can't defend what he did this time! Maggie caught him in the act. There's no other explanation for why he'd run like he did. It's finally over."

Once the initial shock of the moment wore off, Katie and Maggie turned their attention to what would happen next. Leaving the party behind them, they took a seat in the kitchen and talked for hours. Maggie was all but convinced that she would ask Kenny to prom now. And with what had happened, she couldn't imagine why he wouldn't go. Katie was concerned they were getting ahead of themselves, but there was nothing wrong with being prepared.

They were so preoccupied with the situation that they hardly noticed that the party had died. They had bigger fish to fry now.

Spring Break put a temporary hold on Maggie's plans. She went out of town with her parents to visit family though she was noticeably distracted the entire trip. When she returned home, she focused all of her attention on seeing Kenny at school come Monday.

Unfortunately, Kenny was gone Monday.

By the time Tuesday came around, Maggie was about ready to burst. She felt guaranteed to see him in TV class. Arriving early, she wasn't going to let any opportunity pass her by. Trick was already in the studio fully expecting that Maggie would show up. He didn't even look up from his monitor when she came skipping in.

"It's a great day, isn't it?" Maggie asked as she threw her arms around him.

"I've seen better," Trick replied, clearly not as excited as Maggie was. "I'll feel a whole lot better when this thing is finished."

Maggie couldn't concern herself with what he was doing. "Do you think he'll say anything today?"

"If he's here. I heard he had gotten sick over break."

"You don't think he's trying to avoid me, do you?" It pained Maggie to ask the question, but given Kenny's track record, it might be something he would try.

Trick preferred not to be honest but couldn't lie about this. "He might."

"Why would he do that?"

"Maybe he's not ready to admit it."

It was a hard thought to swallow despite its accuracy. Kenny hadn't been willing to even discuss the issue before. There was no reason to expect that to change. Even when she had caught him red-handed, he jumped out a window rather than talk it out.

Her spirits dampened even more when Kenny didn't show up at the bell. She spent the first part of class watching the door waiting for him to walk in. The anxiety and anticipation was too much to bear. She tapped her pen against her desk and her foot against the floor. Each second that ticked away dashed her hopes a little more. Still, she couldn't bring herself to stop looking.

As the minutes of the hour passed away, Maggie became more and more concerned that there had been no sign of Kenny. Trick had told her that Kenny was sick; perhaps, he hadn't recovered yet. It seemed more likely, however, that Kenny would be skipping class to avoid a confrontation. She couldn't ignore his history of adamant denial regarding this issue. Even now, at the end of the line, Maggie shouldn't be surprised at how difficult Kenny would be.

The day seemed to drag on. Firstly, because Maggie spent every opportunity she had looking for Kenny. Secondly, because she saw no sign of him no matter what she tried.

Trick tried to be whatever help he could. He kept an eye out for Kenny himself but never had anything positive to report. It was the same for Katie.

When the day ended, Maggie just wanted to go home. Unfortunately, she had a meeting with her counselor after school. She owned up to her obligation to appear but wasn't truly there. As the trivial words of the counselor bounced off her ears, Maggie kept wondering why Kenny continued to hide from this.

She had caught him in the act. He had to realize that she wasn't mad at him for hiding the truth for so long. Things between them were as they always had been. It would only be helpful to have this information out in the open for a change. So why wouldn't he want to get this all over with?

Maggie was paying so little attention to her current surroundings that the counselor had to cue her twice that the meeting had ended. She left barely having a clue what the counselor had said. It was after three-thirty and though most of the school was empty, Maggie still needed to stop by her locker on the lower level. She shoved her books in and yanked some others out. Her frustration at the subject was beginning to grow again.

As she stomped down the hallway, she almost didn't hear the voices talking around the corner. She couldn't be sure who it was, but she thought one of the voices was Kenny. Stopping short of the corner, she slowly poked her head out to see who it was. Trying to be as unnoticeable as possible, she saw Kenny standing in the middle of the hall with Jessica at his side.

"You're gonna have to face her sometime," Jessica told him.

"I know that," Kenny said.

"And you're gonna have to tell her the truth."

"No, I won't."

"Kenny, please, this has gone too far as it is."

While Maggie was listening in, Trick came walking out of the library and frowned as he watched her leering around the corner. Confused as to what was going on, Trick slowly sauntered up behind her, trying not to blow her cover, leaned in, and whispered in her ear.

"What are we doing?"

Maggie jumped back and then pulled Trick away from the scene. "They're talking about it." Maggie said.

"About what? Who's talking?" Trick asked.

Maggie put a finger to her lips to quiet him. She peered back around the corner to make sure they were still there. They were.

"Kenny and Jessica, they're talking about my party."

Trick now understood the reason for subtlety.

"What are they saying?" Trick asked in a whisper.

"Jessica's trying to get him to tell me the truth."

"About October?"

"I don't know what else they could mean."

Once he understood the situation, Trick and Maggie went back to spying. Carefully and cautiously, they leaned their heads into the hall. As they did, they saw no one standing in the hallway. Kenny and Jessica had vanished. Maggie smacked the wall, upset that she had let them get away. She was about to reveal herself to force the issue. Angered, she picked up her bag and stormed off.

Trick followed her but said nothing, knowing that Maggie was in no mood to listen to anything at this point. All this meant was that she would have to wait even longer to get the answers she was looking for. Kenny was trying to avoid her, and she didn't know when she'd get another chance to corner him.

Luck, however, finally proved to be on her side. As Maggie started trotting up the stairs with Trick right behind her, they both heard elevated voices down a separate hall. Maggie stopped and hurried back down the stairs. She ran over to the hallway to catch whoever it was. Sure enough, Kenny and Jessica were walking down the hallway arguing. Kenny was out in front with Jessica chasing after him. Kenny had his head turned towards her and didn't see Maggie standing in front of him.

"I don't care; I'm gonna tell Maggie as soon as I see her," Kenny said.

"What are you gonna tell her?" Jessica asked.

"That it was me!"

Kenny then looked up and crashed to a halt like he had hit a wall. He gasped for air, shocked that Maggie was standing there in front of him. Jessica stayed back, her eyes wide open in anticipation. Trick pursed his lips and put his hands on top of his head. It was really happening.

Maggie wasn't sure what to do. A smile had formed on her face without her realizing. Her eye produced a single tear that trickled down her face. She watched Kenny stumble in front of her as he struggled to find the words to say.

"What did you say?" Maggie asked, her voice trembling at the possibility of what was about to happen.

Kenny didn't reply at first. His hands were shaking as the enormity of the scope of the moment hit him. He smiled, slightly on edge, as he glanced down at the ground and let out a deep sigh. He covered his mouth for a second and looked back at Jessica. She couldn't get him out of this.

"Tell her," she said.

Kenny turned back to face Maggie. The smile was still shining on her face. The moment she had agonized over was finally here. Never before had it been so tangible. She always imagined having to jump through hoops or pry the information out of him. Now, here he was, about to admit it on his own volition. The anticipation was horrendous. As stressful as the last few months had been, these last seconds of denial seemed worse.

"It was me, Maggie," said Kenny finally as he looked her in the eyes. "I was the one that pulled you out of the lake that night."

The flood of emotion that poured out of Maggie was indescribable. As more tears fell from her eyes, she laughed in between gasps of breaths. She ran at Kenny and jumped into his arms. He caught her and held her tightly.

"I'm sorry I waited so long to tell you," Kenny admitted.

"I'm just glad you finally did," Maggie said.

Jessica smiled as she walked past them and headed up the stairs. Trick stayed a while longer, still unable to process what had occurred. Eventually, he realized he was in the way and left. As he hiked up the stairs, he glanced back at Kenny and Maggie one last time. They were still holding each other. They weren't saying anything; they were just savoring the moment.

Maggie had waited for long for this; she couldn't have anything spoil it.

Chapter Fifteen

The Date is Set

Kenny couldn't stick around for long to talk to Maggie because he was supposed to be at work, but he promised that he'd talk to her soon. It didn't dampen Maggie's spirits in the slightest bit; she was already on cloud nine because of the confession. The entire drive home, she couldn't wait to get to her house, race over to Trick's, and discuss everything that happened. He had left so abruptly, she didn't get to share her excitement. After parking on the street, Maggie opened his front door, which was unlocked despite the fact that Trick's car wasn't in the driveway. She made a sweep of the house, checking his room, the kitchen, the den, the garage, and even the backyard, but she couldn't find him anywhere.

Maggie stood in the doorway of the house trying to decide where Trick could be. Since the search uncovered nothing, she pulled out her cell phone and dialed Trick's number. As she looked up and down the road for Trick's car, she heard the faint ringing of Trick's phone. Confused, she followed the sound up the stairs and into his room to find his phone sitting on his bed. Trick must have been home a few minutes ago, but then he left and for whatever reason didn't bring his phone with him.

Taking a seat on his bed, Maggie was content to wait for him to come back home. She wouldn't be able to talk to Kenny for a while, so she had no other priorities. However, the more she waited and the longer Trick remained missing, the more Maggie grew anxious with anticipation. After bouncing off up the bed and pacing around the room, she picked up a random book off his shelf and started thumbing through it. After a few minutes passed, she heard the door open downstairs. Dropping the book on the floor, she bolted out of Trick's room.

"Trick, is that you?" she asked.

"No! It's Katie!"

Maggie bounded down the stairs into Katie's waiting embrace. They jumped up and down, screaming for joy. The sound emanating from them could make a dog howl, but somehow, they were both immune to it because the pure joy of the moment dulled their senses.

"I just heard, and I had to see you," Katie said.

"It's so exciting!"

"I wish I could have been there!"

"I still can't believe it happened!"

Wanting to make up for not being there, Katie pulled Maggie over to the couch to get the whole story. They had to restrain their emotions for the moment so they could have a rational conversation. The rush from the day still had them swept away.

"Tell me all about it," Katie demanded. "I want to know everything!"

Katie sat patiently, listening to every word that Maggie had to say. She started with the spying on Kenny and Jessica while he debated telling Maggie the truth. When she moved on to Trick's interruption, Katie almost lost her cool. She couldn't believe that Trick almost blew the whole thing. Of course, it all worked out in the end as the two of them caught up with Kenny only moments later. Then came the big moment. After what felt like an eternity wrapped in a few seconds, Kenny admitted the truth.

Once all the details were out, Katie and Maggie moved on to what would happen next. She was going to give Kenny the chance to ask her to prom to hold with tradition, but she wouldn't wait forever.

As they talked and talked, Maggie became more and more concerned that Trick hadn't returned. The story had Katie so captivated that she couldn't care that Trick wasn't around even though they were in his house. When an hour passed and he hadn't returned, Maggie started to worry a bit. If Katie hadn't been pestering her with questions, Maggie would've attempted to locate him somehow.

After the girls exhausted the conversation, Katie reluctantly went home. She wanted to hear more and talk about prom, now that they had that element to consider. Luckily, they still had time. Kenny wasn't hiding anymore so they didn't have to worry about that.

Maggie went to her room to do her homework. With her focus diverted elsewhere, she was just going through the motions with her history assignment. Answers were appearing on the paper, but she didn't know what the questions were. Her mind was racing back to the moment when Kenny told her. His admission still seemed like a dream ready for the world to prove untrue at any moment. Luckily, she had all the memories to disprove this theory.

The smile that had been on her face when Kenny told her still hadn't left. Only one thing could complete the greatness of this day, but Trick would have to come home for that. When she heard the faint sound of a bouncing ball, she knew the day really had come full circle.

As she ran from her house, she saw Trick in his driveway. The sun was beginning to set, but Maggie felt as bright as ever. Jumping on his back when she got close enough, she almost knocked him over.

"It's a great day, isn't it?" she asked.

"Interesting, to say the least," Trick replied with a half smile.

Maggie dropped off Trick's back and stood beside him, waiting for him to say something about what had happened. Trick kept smiling as he retrieved his ball. Maggie stood quietly, knowing that if someone was going to be happy for her, it would be him. He knew everything that she had been through, and now, it was finally over.

"So, where were you?" Maggie asked, hoping to break the seal on his mouth.

"When?" Trick asked.

"After school. I came over to your house and you weren't here. I even called your cell, but you left it in your room. I guess you were in a hurry."

Trick shook his head. "Not really, I just forgot it."

"I see."

"So, I take it the news has really brightened your year."

Maggie was ready to burst but didn't want to dominate the entire conversation. Besides, she thought it was odd the way Trick just left. She was a little concerned that something wasn't quite right with him.

"Well, before I get started, anything going on with you?" she asked.

Maggie grabbed the ball and fired up a shot of her own. She surprised herself when it went in, but it was just that kind of day for her. Trick grabbed the ball and bounced it back to her.

"Nothing that compares to this."

Maggie was prepared to shoot but dropped her arms in disappointment at Trick's answer. "Oh, come on, you always do this," Maggie criticized. "You always put off whatever is going on with you for my sake. You never even told me what happened with Amy. What did she have to say?" Maggie asked.

"That was like a week ago," Trick said.

"That doesn't mean it's not important."

Maggie shot and Trick grabbed the ball as it dropped through the net. He slowly walked out from the goal and then turned towards the basket rubbing the ball in his hands as a pained look crossed his face. Maggie wished she hadn't broached the subject but wanted to know what was wrong. Trick gazed at the rim for a while, ball raised in a shooting position, and then fired away. The shot rattled in, but Trick didn't bother to chase after it. Letting out a sigh, he watched it bounce off the driveway and settle gently into the grass. Thrusting his hands into his back pockets, he was debating what to say.

"It didn't go so well," he said finally, meeting Maggie's eyes again.

This was the only thing that could put a cloud in Maggie's sunny sky. "What happened?"

"It was just something we both knew was coming," Trick explained. "The distance was gonna catch us sooner or later, and it did. She settled on a college on the east coast, and I know I'm not leaving the state. We're just going in different directions."

Maggie put a hand on Trick's arm to comfort him. "I'm really sorry."

Trick shook it off. "Let's not think about that right now. I'm sure you could think of something happier to talk about."

Trick walked after the ball as Maggie stood in silence.

Maggie could think of something, all right, but with Amy suddenly out of the picture, she had a familiar thought run through her head. It seemed cruelly ironic that Trick would tell her this the same day Kenny admitted he was the guy who saved and loved her. The thought still rang true; Maggie believed that more than anything. She just didn't know how he would react. Was he too hurt from Amy to even consider it? Had he considered it and decided he wanted no part of it? There was none of that uncertainty with Kenny.

Kenny told her that night that he loved her. While she had never considered the possibility of being in a relationship with him, she was willing to give it a try. Someone that risked life and limb to save her certainly deserved a chance.

At the same time, she couldn't ignore what she wanted to tell Trick. If only this had happened a few weeks ago, it wouldn't be at issue. The news about Kenny wouldn't even mean as much depending on Trick's response, but now she didn't know what to do.

A smile finally broke across her face. "That was really something, wasn't it?" Maggie asked.

"It sure was," Trick replied. "Talk about being in the right place at the right time." Trick shot and made the bucket. As he was running after the ball, Maggie marveled at the way everything came together.

"I still can't believe it happened," Maggie admitted.

"I know what you mean," Trick said. "It was all so surreal."

"I'm glad you're okay with it because when you just walked away I thought maybe something was wrong."

Trick picked up the ball and held it against his hip for a minute. Maggie's comment had sparked an idea in his head just as Maggie suspected it would. She knew he wouldn't have just walked off without saying anything. He thought something was wrong but didn't want to say what it was.

Trick shook his head and tried to appear innocent. "I didn't think anything was wrong," he said unconvincingly. "It just felt like the two of you would like to be alone, all things considered."

"I don't buy that," Maggie said frankly. "I can see it on your face now that you've thought of something that's making you suspicious of all this."

She could read him like a book. Trick had to give Maggie that. He knew something was wrong with Kenny's admission, but he wasn't sure he wanted to explain. Moreover, he didn't want to do anything to disrupt Maggie's mood. He was standing there when Kenny said it and saw the expression on her face, and he didn't want to take that away from her.

"It's nothing," Trick said. "I'm just over-thinking things."

As long as it was nothing, Trick could say what it was.

"No," Maggie said, taking the ball from him. "I want to know what it is."

Trick rubbed the back of his neck with a hand, swallowed hard, and stared at the ground. What he was about to say would be tough to hear and even harder to defend, but Maggie wanted to hear it.

"I didn't buy his admission," Trick confessed.

Maggie rolled her eyes. Why on earth would he of all people do this to her?

"What does that mean?"

"Before I got there, you said Jessica was trying to convince him to tell the truth. That would mean that he didn't want to tell you in the first place. Then, for whatever reason, when we saw him again just minutes later, he was all gung-ho about telling you, and it didn't look like Jessica agreed with him saying it. It just struck me as odd that he'd be on opposite sides at that time."

Maggie's blood was boiling under her skin at that point. She couldn't fathom why Trick couldn't just accept this. Why did he always have to find these excuses? Why was there always something he picked up on that no one else did?

Since he was her best friend, Maggie kept her anger under wraps. "So are you saying that he was lying?"

Trick quickly refuted that. "No, I'm not saying that. I'm just saying that the way it all went down seemed a little odd."

Maggie had to grit her teeth. "Well, it doesn't matter how he told me. All that matters is that it was the truth and that he told me."

Trick knew then that he could keep the argument going, but it would only upset Maggie. He assumed he had already done that, so he conceded the point. "You're right. All that matters it that he told you."

Once that unpleasantness was behind them, they played some relaxed one-on-one against each other. When it got too dark to play, Maggie followed Trick into his house. Now that Kenny would be going to prom, she had one more person to convert. It would be much harder now that she didn't have a date for him, but she had to try.

Trick had a message from his dad on the phone. Maggie took a seat in the living room and watched as Trick listened carefully to the message. It amazed her how much Trick smiled while he heard his father's voice. When it was over, Trick erased it and went to the kitchen to grab a drink. He reappeared with something for Maggie as well.

"When is your dad getting back?" Maggie asked.

"I think it's the fifth of May or something like that." Trick replied

"That's quite a ways off."

"Yeah, I know."

"He'll see your graduate won't he?"

Trick nodded his head wildly, "Oh, yeah, absolutely."

Maggie knew how often Trick liked to back out of big public occasions, but this was one that she wouldn't let him off the hook on. "And you are going to go, right?"

"Yes," Trick said annoyed that she even had to ask. "You are my walking partner, and I really don't wanna tick you off at graduation."

She smiled at the idea that she evoked fear in him still. She knew she couldn't do anything to hurt him if she tried, but he always played along. This also gave her a solid segue into her next topic.

"You know what else would tick me off?" Maggie asked.

Trick had an idea where this was going. "No, and I'm not guessing."

"If you didn't go to prom," Maggie answered.

"Can't help you with that one."

Trick quickly ducked out of the room and headed for the stairs to get away from Maggie. Once she realized what he was doing, she was right on his heels. She followed him up to his room and flopped down on his bed.

"Just tell me what would be so bad about going," she said.

"I am not now nor will I ever say that there would be anything bad about going," Trick confessed. "However, if I had the choice, and I do, I would prefer not to go."

Maggie ignored the explanation. "If you don't wanna go alone, I'm sure I could find someone for you."

"That's not it," Trick sighed.

"I'd say that I'd go with you, but I think I'm spoken for."

"Trust me; I'm not saving a seat for Kenny anymore."

Maggie would go on to make several more futile attempts to get Trick to come along. When she had exhausted all options, she left him alone. She didn't leave without warning him that he would be missing out on one of the best nights of his life. He replied that he was young enough that he could make up for it. Besides, she shouldn't be worried about him when there were much more interesting prospects for her to consider.

The next day was a very busy but unproductive day. Much of the day, people recanted stories about the events that had unfolded the day before. So much time in fact that Maggie barely got a word in with Kenny. She could deal with that, however, since she had a class with him the following day.

While the idea was good in theory, it proved much more difficult when the time came. Even though the end of school was almost two months away, Ms. Rutherford had some spring cleaning chores for the class to complete. Maggie and Katie were in the classroom organizing all of the old tapes Ms. Rutherford kept. Jordan and Scott were in the studio resetting the lights after they had fallen the day before. While none of them were pleased with their job, they all were happy to have avoided Trick and Kenny's task. Working in the storage room back in the dark room, they had to go through all the boxes with old yearbooks stacked inside them.

"Okay, honestly, is someone really going to come looking for a yearbook from 1951?" Kenny asked as he lifted the box off the ground.

"I certainly hope not," Trick said, picking up a box of his own. "I'm putting them at the bottom of the pile."

As Trick and Kenny sifted through the boxes, Maggie and Katie were taking all the tapes out of their cabinets. Each time they pulled a tape, they read the label out loud.

"Here's one from 1985," Katie announced.

"Wow, I wonder what was going on in the school then," Maggie said as she examined the tape.

"I don't know, but I bet someone was sporting a mullet."

Maggie laughed as she and Katie ran over to a VCR to check out the tape. At least they were enjoying their job. Since the lights in the studio hung from the ceiling, Jordan had to fix them while on a ladder that didn't quite go high enough to get the job done.

"Stinkin' lights," Jordan whined as he fastened one to the fixture on the ceiling. Meanwhile, below him, Scott had two hands glued to the ladder.

"Hey, be careful man," Scott pleaded. "This ladder isn't too sturdy and you're above the warning label."

"Oh, no!" Jordan cried in a mocking tone. "I'm above the warning label. What ever will happen to me?" Then he dramatically shifted his tone and barked out a command. "Just give me the tape and shut up already."

Scott gazed across the room and saw the tape on the table, but it was out of reach. "I'd rather not let go of the ladder," Scott admitted.

"Just do it!"

"Okay."

Scott let go of the ladder and ran to grab the tape, but the ladder proved to be more unsteady than expected. Before he could get back, Jordan lost his balance and crashed down onto the news desk. Everyone ran to the studio to see if he was injured. Jordan sprung up from the ground, hands up to ease everyone's concerns.

"I'm okay!" he announced.

Everyone started laughing and went back to work. Jordan gave Scott a nasty look.

"I told you you were above the warning label," Scott said.

"I'll give you a warning label," threatened Jordan.

Jordan started up the ladder as Scott contemplated what he said. "What does that even mean?"

"Shut up and hold the ladder," Jordan replied knowing what he just said made no sense.

Jordan's blunder had even brought Trick and Kenny out from the dark room. The muffled sound of a crash of a box ended their fun. Kenny groaned about having to continue, and Trick agreed that he should take a short break. The beginners were working on projects in the computer room. It may not be the most exciting thing in the world, but it gave Kenny some time.

Watching Kenny walk around the room frustrated Maggie. He hadn't said anything to her all day. She was disappointed enough Ms. Rutherford partnered him with Trick. As she followed him around the room with her eyes, Katie could tell what was bothering her. It took some convincing, but Maggie finally agreed to be the one to break the silence between them.

"How's it going, Kenny?" she asked as she snuck up behind him.

Kenny jumped at first but quickly regained himself. "I'm fine; how are you?"

"Fine."

Their brief encounter concluded with some awkward silence. Maggie hoped that Kenny would take over, but he was either unwilling or unprepared to do so. He knew there was still much to say and explain, and he didn't feel that this was the right place to do it. His suspicions were confirmed when he looked around the room and found numerous sets of curious eyes planted on the two of them. Wishing not to be a public spectacle, Kenny went back to the darkroom. Maggie walked away a little disappointed, but at least she had talked to him.

"Can I ask you a question?" Kenny asked when he returned to the darkroom.

"Fire away," Trick replied as he threw yearbooks into a box. One of the older boxes had finally given out. Yearbooks from 1979 and 1980 were scattered all over the floor, but Kenny was thinking about something else at the time.

"Is Maggie expecting me to ask her to prom?"

The question seemed odd to Trick. "Well, she didn't want to do it herself. Why, do you not want to go with her or something?"

"No, that's not it at all," Kenny quickly replied. "I mean…I was going to ask her eventually, but she seems to expect me to do it right away."

"Eventually?" Trick repeated as he tossed the last of the books into the box. He leaned against a stack of boxes a little perplexed by Kenny's thought process. "Don't you think you're spending time you don't really have here? Prom's only a couple weeks away."

"I suppose you're right," Kenny said as if the thought had just registered in his head. "I guess it's just different with all of it right in front of you, ya know?"

Kenny's voice had a slight tremor to it, almost as if he was nervous about asking, but Trick couldn't figure out what he'd have to be nervous about. Kenny admitted the truth just like Maggie wanted, and based on the look on her face when he told her, she was obviously ecstatic that it was him. As long as he stuck to his story, everything would be fine. Maybe that was what was giving him such trouble.

"Everything alright, Kenny?"

"Absolutely," Kenny replied. "Why, does something seem wrong?"

Trick didn't want to honestly answer the question. Of course, something seemed wrong to him. Instead, Trick shrugged his shoulders and shook his head.

"You just seem a little edgy is all," Trick replied. "I'm just trying to look out for my friends."

Kenny smiled and put a hand on Trick's shoulder. "You worry too much, big guy. Tell ya what, I'm gonna go talk to Maggie now. Do you mind if I send Katie back here to help you?"

"Not at all." Trick paused for a moment as Kenny walked to the door. He wasn't convinced that Kenny really wanted this to happen. "You sure about doing this now?"

Kenny chuckled. "Hey, there's no reason to hide anymore, right? I am the guy that saved her aren't I?"

Trick smiled as Kenny disappeared out the door. "So you say," Trick said to himself.

Kenny strolled out to the area where Katie and Maggie were working. His presence caused Jordan and Scott to stop working. They couldn't hear what was going on since the studio glass separated them, but they became deeply interested when Kenny said a few words to Katie and she disappeared.

"No way is he actually going to do this here," Jordan said.

Scott disagreed. "It sure looks like he's going to. He sent Katie to the back to work with Trick. The two of them are basically alone right now. What better time?"

"I could think of a million better times."

Their focus diverted for the time being, Jordan and Scott pressed their ears to the glass. Though not very discreet, they went unnoticed. While it was very difficult to make out what Kenny and Maggie were saying, they could catch the gist of it.

"So, what exactly are you doing out here?" Kenny asked.

Maggie was having a hard time holding back her excitement since Kenny had come to talk to her. She even had to remind herself what she was doing before she could answer Kenny's question.

"It's nothing too difficult," Maggie explained. "Ms. Rutherford just wants us to organize the cabinet and see if there's anything in here not worth holding on to. Katie and I were almost done when you came out."

"Well, I hope Katie doesn't mind that I displaced her, but I kind of wanted to talk to you about something."

Maggie was giddy with the possibilities.

"I...uh...I heard that you still hadn't asked Trick to go to prom with you," Kenny began.

He was about to say more when his nerves got the better of him. He didn't imagine it would be this difficult to ask, especially with no one watching them. At least no one he was aware of. As Jordan and Scott strained to hear every word, Jordan lost confidence in his friend.

"He's not gonna do it," Jordan assured Scott.

"Oh, yes he is," replied Scott. "And if he doesn't, she will."

"Are you serious? There's no way she's asking him."

"You wanna bet?"

"Yeah! I'll give you five if he asks her and ten if she asks him."

"You're on!"

As the silence between Maggie and Kenny grew, Maggie realized that her invitation was slipping through her fingers. She'd like to think that Kenny would be able to ask a simple question, but as she watched him struggle with the idea and even saw beads of sweat start to form on his forehead, she realized she had to step up on this one.

As Kenny mumbled under his breath, unable to form a coherent word, Maggie put a hand on his forearm. It immediately calmed Kenny, and he looked into her eyes. He knew then that she was going to make this easy for him.

"That's true, I didn't ask Trick," Maggie confirmed. "I was trying to convince him to go the other night. I thought about saying that I'd go with him, but then I realized there was someone else I'd rather go with."

Jordan was losing his cool inside the studio.

"He can't let this happen!"

"Just stay quiet, Kenny, and let the woman work!" Scott encouraged.

Kenny smiled when he heard Maggie hint at him. It wasn't subtle in the slightest bit, and he was pleased about that. He couldn't be straightforward about this, but at least Maggie could.

"So, would you be willing to go with me?" Maggie asked.

Kenny smiled, "Yeah, that'd be great."

Maggie smiled and the two sat in silence for a minute. They went back to the tapes as Ms. Rutherford walked by. As close as Maggie and Katie were to being finished before, Maggie and Kenny hadn't gotten any closer in the meantime. They laughed quietly to themselves as they went back to work. Once the threat had diminished, they talked over the plans for that night: where they would eat beforehand, when he needed to pick Maggie up, etc. Since they were going in a group, it was easy for Kenny to fit right in and go with the flow.

Once everything was set, Kenny went back to the dark room. When he stood up, he witnessed the odd sight of Jordan handing Scott a ten-dollar bill. Scott was laughing the whole time for whatever reason, and Kenny shook his head at the two of them. As he stepped back into the darkroom, the smile on his face was blinding.

"I take it things went well?" Trick asked rhetorically.

Kenny grabbed a box and started pitching in. He didn't even notice how heavy the boxes were. "Yep, everything is set."

"Well, good," Katie said. "I hope you appreciate my willingness to come back and lug these boxes around for you."

"I most certainly do," Kenny said.

Kenny's cheery disposition was almost too much for Trick and Katie to handle. Considering everything that had happened, they would learn to deal with it. Kenny was so happy, in fact, that he couldn't accept Trick's plans to skip out on prom. Being on top of the world, he was sure he could change Trick's mind.

"Ya know, Trick, that only leaves you out of this."

Trick stopped mid-stride and rolled his eyes. He had already been through this argument so many times before; he had his excuses lined up. Katie smiled at him, knowing how much he hated talking about this.

"I understand your sudden enthusiasm about the night, but that doesn't mean you can change my mind," Trick said.

"Seriously man, you don't wanna miss out on this one."

Trick looked at Katie trying to get an explanation as to why Kenny was bringing this up all the sudden. He had never argued against Trick skipping a dance. The change of heart wasn't as endearing as Kenny assumed it would be. Katie could only shrug her shoulders and get back to work.

"Say what you will, but it's still just a high school dance to me. I'm not gonna go when there's such a good chance that I'll end up alone most of the evening. I was already planning on that, but at least where I'll be I'll have a pool table and comfortable clothes and a fridge stocked with food."

"But it's going to be so much fun," Kenny said.

As much as Katie enjoyed seeing Trick annoyed, even she knew this was all an exercise in futility. There was no good reason to let it carry on this long.

"Kenny, save your breath. This one doesn't change his mind."

Trick was relieved to have someone backing him up. "Thank you!"

Kenny relented slightly. He would only bring up the idea every few minutes or so. Still, he was determined to get Trick to attend. Unfortunately, Trick was just as determined not to go. Eventually, Trick's determination would win out over Kenny's. After that day, Kenny said nothing more to attempt to change Trick's mind.

Over the next two weeks, the prom hype grew to unimaginable heights. Everyone going fully bought in to the buildup and anticipation for the last dance of the school year. For so many, it would also be the last of their high school years. Knowing that they would all be witnesses to the end of a fairy tale only made the night that much more special. Indeed, it didn't take long for news of Maggie and Kenny's date to spread throughout the school. No one, not even Eric, could balk at the romance of the moment.

So everyone had the date on the calendar circled. The days of school leading up to the event were just a blur. Schoolwork went by the wayside as everyone going had more important matters on their mind.

For Maggie, everything was about the after-prom party. She was certain that Kenny would be too nervous to address the deeper issue of his rescue at prom. Given his tentativeness to this whole issue, Maggie had said nothing about Kenny's candid confession that night. Rather, she decided to wait until the appropriate time and place to address it.

Before she could get to that, she had to make sure that everything would be perfect for that night. She called the restaurant several times to make sure they had the reservation. She called Kenny on a semi-daily basis to confirm all the plans and times. Maggie's parents were very excited to meet the boy that saved their daughter's life, so Kenny also needed to be preparing for the on-slaught they would bring. Every day, Maggie checked her dress to make sure everything was flawless. She didn't dare take it out of the plastic bag, but since it was a clear bag, she could give it a close evaluation.

It was the Thursday before prom when she went to the store to get her corsage. While she was there, she also picked up a few things for her mom. On the way to the checkout line, she ran into a familiar face.

She felt terrible that she had been ignoring Trick these past days, but she had been so busy. Despite a valid excuse, she felt embarrassed running into him here.

"Howdy stranger," Trick said.

He would say something to emphasize her shame.

"I know," Maggie said. "I haven't talked to you in a while, and I feel bad about that. It's just that I've been so busy."

Trick stopped her before she could continue. "Don't worry about it. If I were in your shoes, I'm sure I'd be doing the same thing."

Maggie smiled. If anyone were going to understand or not judge her, it would be him. As they pushed their carts into line, Maggie glanced at Trick's purchases. Among other things, he had a frozen pizza, three large bags of chips, cheese dip, a box of popcorn bags, and a twenty-four pack of root beer. It was the final sign that he wasn't going.

"It's not going to be the same with you not there," she said as a final guilt trip.

"Actually, it is going to be the same," Trick corrected her. "I never went to one in the first place."

Trick started unloading Maggie's cart onto the conveyor belt. Maggie knew he was right. She just didn't know what else to say to get him to go. "I just wish you would be there," she confessed.

"Why?"

"The night would be complete," Maggie replied, not wanting to give her real reason.

Trick knew right away that she was hiding something. He stopped un-loading the cart and faced Maggie. "How so?"

Maggie struggled to find a reason. "For one, I'd get one more dance out of you that I didn't get at my party." Trick smiled, accepting that as a viable reason. He knew it wasn't the whole truth but was willing to let it go at that. Maggie knew that only the truth would be good enough to convince him. "And I just feel more relaxed when you're around."

It wasn't the whole truth, but it was all she could say at this point. She de-cided to go with Kenny. She couldn't risk messing that up by telling Trick the whole truth.

Trick went back to unloading her cart. "Nothing's gonna happen ya know," he vowed. "You've got the happy ending you were looking for."

"I'm not worried about that," Maggie snapped.

"No?"

Maggie paused, knowing that anything she said would only boost Trick's confidence. If she was really going to convince him that she was okay, she had to put all this silliness behind her and move on. With that in mind, she looked back to Trick's cart. The root beer was an odd choice to her.

"Root beer, huh?" Maggie asked.

Graciously, Trick let the subject die. "Yeah, with no one else around, I can drink my favorite and not worry about caffeine."

"I always thought Dr. Pepper was your favorite," Maggie admitted.

Trick shrugged. "I like it just fine, but it's not my favorite."

"Then why have Dr. Pepper all the time?"

"Because that's your favorite."

It was small things like that that made it so difficult for Maggie to hide the truth from him. Even though she was happy that Kenny had told her, there was a small part of her that sincerely wished that Trick had been the one that was hiding behind that mask. She had always had a part of her wishing that so that things would have been much simpler. Knowing that he loved her would make everything seem worth it.

But that was not what happened. That's not how things played out. She couldn't waste time thinking about possibilities that were no longer possible. Kenny was her guardian angel, the one she was going to prom with, and nothing else mattered at that point. Despite her innermost and earnest wishes and desires, she wouldn't dare risk anything affecting what she had so desperately dreamed for for so long.

Chapter Sixteen

Sweet Dreams

As the morning hours before the dance disappeared, the excitement for prom reached a fevered pitch. All over Derby, high schoolers were showering, dressing, and preparing for their night on the town. With the most meticulous care given to the minutest detail, a memorable night surely awaited. Be it a smooth, clean shave and splash of cologne for the gents or the perfect hair, right balance of make-up, and spritz of perfume for the ladies, everything had to be just right. Even if the perfection wouldn't last, images taken on cameras by parents and friends would capture the moment forever. Amid the flashes of those cameras, the bright smiles of young lovers and good friends held the hopes of the night that was to come.

The one glaring exception to the rule was Trick. Already in his garage at five, Trick had a line of food to keep him going all night. He had systematically kept his distance from the partiers throughout the day, fearing a last ditch effort to get him to attend. There was a slight concern in the air as a threat of rain was in the weather forecast, and though Trick knew it wouldn't affect him in any way, he didn't want everyone else's night ruined. As he listened to the weather report, he heard a knock at the door. He didn't expect anyone to stop by but had a good idea of who it was.

"Come on in!" Trick yelled.

The door opened and Maggie, already in her prom dress, walked into the garage. Once he heard the door close, he spun around to see her, quickly mesmerized by her mere sight. Wearing a sleeveless black gown that went down to her ankles, Maggie looked like a masterpiece. The dressed glittered with gold sequins, was back-less, low-cut in front, and had a slit on the left leg up to her mid-thigh.

She had her hair pulled back and wrapped in a ponytail flowing like a golden river. Her skin looked smooth as a silken sculpture. Her smile of pearls illuminated the room. Trick was so taken aback he dared not speak lest he ruin the moment.

His silence said more than words could, still Maggie asked. "What do you think?"

Trick whistled as his approval.

"That good, huh?" Maggie replied, embarrassed by his gaze.

"I do believe that anything I could say would only be an understatement."

Maggie smiled shyly at Trick's candor. "Kenny said it looked pretty good, too."

"Where is Kenny anyway?" Trick asked as he picked out a pool cue.

"He's over at my house talking some things over with my folks. We've been taking pictures for over twenty minutes."

"So what brings you over here?"

Trick started grabbing the pool balls out of the pockets as Maggie slowly walked to where he stood at the end of the table. As she watched him, she couldn't believe it was so stressful to see him before the dance. She knew that she wanted to go with Kenny because he saved and loved her. At the same time, she didn't imagine that her feelings for Trick would create such conflict within her. A part of her that she couldn't ignore agonized over not going to prom with Trick.

She wasn't sure exactly what to say. There really was no reason for her to be there other than she wanted to see him. But the silence was becoming oddly suspicious.

"I only have two reasons, really," Maggie began.

"Which are?"

"Firstly, to show off...."

"Well done."

"Secondly, I just didn't want you to be alone all day. Thought you could use a little bit of human interaction."

Trick smiled at the thought. She would be the only one concerned about him on a night when she had much more pressing matters to occupy her time. As hard as it may be for her to accept, Trick would survive on his own for the night. He had had plenty of solitary nights in the past; he would most likely have more in his future. It was that reasoning that led Trick to believe Maggie had something else on her mind. His initial fear was another dream spooked her confidence, but fortunately, that wasn't the case.

As he placed the balls inside the rack and deadened them so they'd sit perfectly still, Trick waited for Maggie to unveil the real reason. He could see it lingering just behind her eyes. Unfortunately, she didn't feel like being the one to broach the subject.

"Is there anything else on your mind?" Trick asked.

Caught off guard, Maggie stumbled a bit. There was something on her mind, something she couldn't say, and something that would plague her as long as the two of them were alone.

"I don't know," Maggie replied. "Just thought I'd give it one last try to get you to come."

Trick laughed. He thought she had a serious concern, not this ludicrous idea. "Come on, you're gonna be leaving here in a few minutes. I don't have time to get ready or the ensemble for the occasion."

Maggie wasn't going to argue with him this time. Honestly, she just threw out a random thought to cover her anxiety. Getting him to prom wasn't an option any more, but maybe she could get him out of the house.

"Would you come to the after party at least?"

Trick played along more than actually considering going. "Where is it?"

"Where else."

"I'll think about it."

Maggie knew better than to take Trick at his word. She would have to really engrain the idea in him if he was going to give it real thought.

"You're not just saying that so I'll go, are you? You're really going to give it some thought?"

Trick sighed. He could lie some more, put up a front about not going, or just concede the idea. The party wasn't his idea of an ideal night, but after a long day alone, it might be a welcomed change of pace to get out of the house. Aside from that, if he went, then Maggie would be happy. Katie, Kenny, and some others would probably be happy to see him, too. It was all of the fun with none of the hassle.

"Tell ya what," Trick said, "I give you my word that I will be there."

Maggie couldn't believe it but felt overjoyed to hear it. "Really?"

"Yeah, just give me a call when you leave prom so I know when to head over there."

Maggie didn't know what to say. "I can't believe you're gonna go."

"Well, it is the last dance of high school, right? One party won't kill me."

Maggie ran up and hugged Trick, thrilled he would actually be a part of her night. In her wildest dreams, she never would have expected this. When she let go, Trick had a shocked look stuck on his face.

"I refuse to believe my presence is that big of a deal," Trick said.

"You know that's a lie," Maggie refuted.

Rather than dispute the point, Trick smiled and gave Maggie another hug. She had to be on her way as time was running short. They were meeting Jordan, Katie, Ashley, and Scott at a restaurant in Wichita in little more than half an hour. She couldn't dawdle much longer and be on time. Still elated about Trick's promise, she gleefully scampered back across the street and burst in the front door. Kenny was sitting on the sofa with Maggie's mom next to him, and her dad a few feet away in a recliner. From the overwhelmed look on his face, Kenny looked like he needed saving.

"Mom, Dad, we've got to get going or we're gonna be late for dinner. Come on, Kenny let's go."

Kenny quickly shot off the couch and stood at Maggie's side. Maggie's dad smiled, understanding that maybe the two of them had come on a little strong. Maggie's mom put her hands on her hips, not understanding what the problem was.

"Well, this is the first time that I've met the young man that saved my daughter's life," Maggie's mom offered in her defense.

"Yes, I guess we owe you one, huh Kenny?" Maggie's dad joked.

Maggie was becoming more perturbed by the second. "Dad!"

"I'm sorry sweetheart," her dad said with a laugh. "You two have a good time."

"We will."

Maggie and Kenny said their goodbyes and headed for the door. After they had taken a few steps towards Maggie's car, her mom stepped into the doorway. She knew how special this night was for her daughter and wanted to make sure she did everything she could to make it perfect. Of course, she also wanted them to be safe.

"When will you be home?" she asked.

"Late," Maggie replied.

It was an answer, but not good enough for a mother. "How late?"

"Very late!" Maggie yelled.

"Okay," Maggie's mom said, recognizing Maggie's annoyance with the interrogation. "Have a good time."

"We will."

Maggie's mom was prepared to go on, but luckily, her dad saved them. After a roll of the eyes, he stepped up to stop his wife from badgering Maggie anymore. Wrapping an arm around her shoulder, he guided her from the door, much to the delight of Maggie and Kenny.

"Come on, dear. Come inside."

"I just want everything to go well...."

"I know and they'll be fine...now come on."

Maggie's mom reluctantly retreated inside and left Maggie and Kenny to their own devices. After a final wave, Maggie's dad closed the door. They were finally free.

"Sorry about that," Maggie said.

"You gotta expect something like that, I guess," Kenny replied.

"At least it's over now."

"Let's get going then."

Kenny fired up the engine, and they drove off. Derby was south of Wichita by a few miles and on the eastern side. The restaurant they were eating at was located more to the western side by the airport. Maggie had only been there once before for a cousin's wedding. It was very upscale.

During the drive, Maggie took notice of the sky, seeing dark clouds forming off to the north. It didn't look like anything big yet, but that could quickly change. Aware of her concern, Kenny flipped the radio to a station where he'd get the weather report. The chances were at eighty percent that Derby would see rain before the night was over. They could only hope it held off long enough.

When they got to the restaurant, they saw Jordan waiting for them at the hostess table. They walked through the glass double doors into the dimly lit interior. Local artwork adorned the green walls and everyone working there was dressed in a suit or formal dress. The tables looked hand carved, adorned with white tablecloth, an elaborate place setting, and candles. It was a very romantic way to start the evening.

"Do either of you ever show up on time?" Jordan asked as he started leading them to their party. The others sat at the table with menus in hand.

"Oh, stop it, Jordan," Katie demanded. She was wearing a white strapless gown that hugged her curves with her hair pulled back as well. As Jordan sat down, she adjusted his tie for him.

"They're not even late," pointed out Ashley. Her dress was a little more complex. It was a stunning pink number with a criss-cross pattern in the back. Her hair draped over her shoulders. "No one has even taken our drink orders yet."

"Yeah, the wait didn't kill you," Katie said.

"You know what…it did, a little on the inside," Jordan replied.

Katie pushed Jordan away from her, and then motioned for some service. Kenny and Maggie only had a few seconds to select their entrees, but they had no problem choosing. Once the waiter was gone, they all dove into conversations regarding the night ahead of them. The girls regaled each other with the harrowing tales of preparing for the night: Katie couldn't get her hair to agree with her, Ashley almost ran out of nail polish, and Maggie couldn't find her shoes. All crises narrowly averted.

The gentlemen, on the other hand, discussed how uncomfortable they were in their tuxes: Jordan's tie was giving him fits, Scott's pants were too short, Kenny's jacket felt too tight on his shoulders. They were putting up with a lot but getting so much more in return.

After a few minutes, the conversation shifted to more pleasant topics.

"Now, the after party is at Smith's, right?" Scott asked.

"That's what I've heard," Katie replied. "There was some talk about a few smaller parties, but the big one is at Smith's."

"I take it most people are planning on going to that one," Kenny remarked.

Katie nodded. "I talked to Jessica and she said she'd be there with Darren. Cassie said she'd be there with Nick. Whitney and Kevin should be there. If they're going then Kraig, Avery, T.J., Zach, Sonja, Jennifer, Karyn, and Vanessa should all be there…."

Katie carried on through all the names that should be at the party based on their associations through school. It really didn't seem like such a tangled web until Katie spelled it all out. As the others listened to her carry on, they couldn't believe that she managed to keep it all straight.

"...and I think that's just about everyone," Katie concluded.

"I have no idea how you keep all that in your head," Jordan admitted admiringly. "And if I'm lucky, I'll never figure it out."

Hearing everyone's names reminded Maggie about someone else that would be attending. "I doubt you all believe me, but I convinced Trick to make an appearance."

They didn't believe her. "Really? What changed his mind?" Scott asked.

"Who knows," Maggie replied. "Maybe he just wanted to at least have some fun memories of his prom night even if he didn't go. Personally, I think it has something to do with Amy. I guess things aren't going that well between them lately."

The table quieted down as their faces held a remorseful look.

"Poor guy just can't catch a break can he?" Jordan finally said.

A few minutes later, the food arrived. As they sampled each other's orders, they worked their way through their own meals. The food was immaculate, unlike anything they had ever tasted before. Maggie's faint memories of the place hadn't done it justice as not a single scrap of food remained on the plates by the time they finished. Still, Jordan and Scott ordered desserts, Kenny convinced Maggie to share one with him, and Ashley and Katie did the same.

They didn't have much time when they were finished eating. A combination of slow service and inattentiveness caused them to lose track of time. With less than forty-five minutes before the dance began, they paid the check as quickly as possible and then hurried to their cars. It was actually kind of fun to be in such a rush.

As Kenny sped to Derby, the other cars in their party kept pace with him. It was dark outside, but the roads were fairly barren. While Kenny focused on the road, Maggie kept her eyes on the sky. Most likely veiled by the clouds, the moon had vanished. As she eyed the outdoors, a few flashes of lightning illuminated the night sky, slightly startling her. For brief moments, the night became day before reverting back to its familiar darkened look. As they pulled into the parking lot at the high school, a few drops landed on Kenny's windshield.

"Fantastic," Kenny muttered.

"It doesn't matter," Maggie said. "It's not like we're gonna be outside that much."

"Well, let's hurry inside before it picks up."

Kenny grabbed a jacket from the backseat and jumped out of the car. He ran over to Maggie's door and held the jacket above her as a makeshift umbrella. It wouldn't do much, but hopefully it would serve its purpose. Once she was out of the car, they sprinted for the doors. Jordan, Katie, Scott, and Ashley weren't far behind.

On the way, they came across the first set of decorations for the dance. They couldn't stop to get a good look at them, but what they saw was stunning. In front of the door, there was a plaster bridge reminiscent of a medieval castle. Underneath the bridge was a very small moat made up of kiddy pools with fake trees at each end. There were also bright, colorful flowers and small signs along the moat, but they were too difficult to see with the rain falling.

Kenny and Maggie stopped at a small awning by the front doors. As he shook off his jacket. Kenny took one last look at the decorations outside.

"That bridge is awesome," he said.

Maggie concurred. "Yeah, the prom committee did a really good job and I bet that the inside is really cool too."

"Hey, what is the prom theme this year?"

"Sweet dreams," Maggie replied with a smile.

Despite everything that had gone wrong over the past few months, Maggie felt relief from Kenny being there with her now. Everything he was saying took the edge off any possible uneasiness she might feel. It truly was a sweet dream after the nightmare she had been through. Perhaps, it wasn't at all like she expected it to be, but at least she finally had her angel unmasked and at her side.

The rain came down harder as Kenny held the door open for her.

"Yeesh, if it rains like this all night, the moat will overtake the bridge and then we'll be stuck here," Kenny joked.

"If it comes to that, I'll swim," Maggie assured him.

Kenny smiled as they entered the commons. A large silver arch loomed above them. As they passed through it, two volunteers took their tickets and one took Kenny's jacket for him. After handing over their tickets, they passed through another arch hand in hand and entered prom.

As they walked past the arches, they came upon a series of sky-blue pillars decorated in glitter surrounding the steps that dropped down to the commons area. The steps led to a mid-level full of tables. It was one more drop down to reach the dance floor.

The top level of the commons was little more than a hallway surrounding the squared area. Each corner had an entrance to the main floors accentuated by a set of pillars. Across from Maggie and Kenny were the doors that typically served as the faculty entrance. At the third corner was a staircase leading downstairs and at the final corner, an entrance to an auditorium. In each of those two locations, photographers were set up to take pictures. Currently, the line to the auditorium was shorter, so Maggie and Kenny decided to get in line there. As they strolled down the hall, Maggie soaked in everything the scene had to offer.

Atop each of the pillars was a twisting line of streamers connecting them all together. The pink, white, and lavender streams wrapped all around the walkway before leaping out over the dance floor and joining together at a single point in the ceiling. The curved lines coming together made the room seem like the inside of a pole marquee.

Helping complete the illusion of being within a tent was a large lace ornament. Inside, a plethora of white balloons, and colored strobe lights from below danced with the elastic clouds creating a majestic kaleidoscopic effect. It truly was something like a dream.

The chest high walls going around the edges of each level sat decorated with light-strings and colored ribbons. In the dimly lit room, the strands of lights were the only way to see much of anything from a distance. Another strand of lights surrounded a red strip of carpet leading from the main entrance down to the dance floor.

The midlevel of the commons held tables for students to sit at and a small buffet line along one side. There were all kinds of food: chicken, hamburgers, pizzas, chips, dips, cookies, and other goodies. There was even an ice sculpture shaped like the school's mascot. To drink, there was pop of almost every kind, juices, and bottles of water. The piece de resistance, however, was the chocolate fountain with three types of chocolate swirled together to create a veritable waterfall of temptation.

As Maggie looked at it all, her real focus was on the dance floor. The wall covered in green and white wallpaper looked like a castle wall with its decorations. Flower bouquets hung to the walls, and streamers joined one bouquet to the other. The DJ, with his stage and equipment all set up along one side of the floor, worked tirelessly behind his little stage. At his side, a large white screen showed the music videos to the songs he played. Speakers sat at each corner, hidden by small decorations to keep the illusion alive.

Maggie squeezed Kenny's hand, excited for the night ahead of them. He smiled and squeezed back.

The line into the auditorium was moving very slowly. Luckily, Kenny and Maggie got in line right behind a couple they knew well. Darren and Jessica had arrived just a few minutes earlier.

"You guys didn't get rained on, did you?" Darren asked.

"Nothing too much, just a few drops here and there," Maggie replied.

As Darren relayed his relief, Kenny exchanged pleasantries with Jessica. Her dress, a green strapless number, was quite stunning.

"You clean up nicely," Jessica admitted.

"You don't look half bad yourself," Kenny complemented.

"I think this is the first time I've seen you dressed up."

"We all gotta make sacrifices."

"Interesting one for you, isn't it?"

They weren't in line long before Jordan, Katie, Scott, and Ashley joined them. Though they had gotten the worse of the weather, nothing was ruined. Even if something had happened, they felt too enraptured by the scene to care about anything else. It took them a minute to situate themselves with all their surroundings. Despite all their fantasies about what this night would bring, it was something else to see it for real.

As the line neared the auditorium, the girls gushed over the night. The guys kept quiet most of the conversation, happy to see their respective dates happy. Kenny watched Maggie closely. There was something about her that hadn't been there before, a sparkle in her eye he hadn't seen in some time. He thought he understood the importance that October night had had on her life, but he didn't anticipate such a reaction from her now. He remembered the look on her face when he told her, the relief he felt in her embrace. Even that didn't compare to how she looked now. She seemed lifted to a higher level. Whatever cares or concerns she had were null and void. Being here with him was more happiness than she could have hoped for. There truly was something special about prom night.

If there was one thing that could dampen their mood, it was a run in with someone less than friendly. While most everyone had been happy to hear of Kenny's confession, Eric had no reason to feel any happiness for them. So when he and Angela walked by, no one was shocked when a quiet hush came over them. No one knew what to say. Darren and Jessica walked ahead. The others stood their ground with Kenny and Maggie.

Finally, Eric cracked a nervous smile. "Hey, Maggie, how's it going?"

"I'm good, Eric. How are you?"

"Oh, I'm fine...fine."

Maggie and Eric hadn't spoken in quite some time. Ever since their break up and the ensuing unpleasantness between them, they preferred to keep a distance between each other. Maggie still heard about him through friends, and he heard about her as well. He had continued seeing Angela, and they were reportedly very happy together. She was happy knowing that he had moved on.

"How's everyone else doing?" Eric asked acknowledging the others around him.

They all replied that all was well. Katie asked Angela how she was doing, and she replied pleasantly. On the surface, it looked as if everything had blown over. Despite the bitterness and animosity that once existed, Eric seemed ready to let bygones be bygones and try to retain some sort of civility.

And though everything seemed ready to reach a stage of reconciliation, the lingering tension between them remained. After everything was said and done, a certain uncertainty kept everyone from buying into this sudden change of heart.

"Hey, I've wanted to say this for a while. I am sorry about the way things went down between us," Eric said.

Maggie was a little shocked. "It's okay. We all made mistakes. I know I could've done things differently."

"That goes double for me," Kenny added.

Eric shook his head. "That really doesn't excuse the things I did. And I want you to know that I am happy for both of you."

"We both are," Angela said.

Eric extended his hand to Kenny, which Kenny shook. He was surprised but didn't want to do anything to upset the moment. Eric appeared genuine; why question it? A smile of relief broke across Eric's face. They were all relieved at this point. The ugly chapter closed seemingly for good.

"Hey, have a good time," said Eric. "And I'll see you on the dance floor, Maggie. Might even try to steal a dance with you."

"Yeah…maybe," Maggie replied.

Eric and Angela ran off, leaving a bewildered crowd trying to piece together why what had happened had happened. Jordan couldn't help but find the whole performance suspicious. Katie was just as shocked but touched that Eric had made such a gesture. Scott and Ashley stood in silence for a few minutes. Luckily, the tension broke when they had to enter the auditorium.

Set up on the stage was a canvas background with a forest scenery painted on it and a fake wooden stump in front sitting slightly off-centered. It looked awfully cheesy, but that was a common theme among picture backdrops. The line snaked off the stage and wrapped around the seats over to the door. Maggie saw several of her friends ahead of her; all of them were just as excited as she was.

As they stood in line, a girl from their TV class came walking by with a video camera. Though Kelli was only a sophomore, she managed to score a ticket to prom by signing up to film the event. It actually helped her on two fronts because she got a substantial amount of extra credit for class as well. She was very excited to have found Maggie and Kenny.

Kelli narrated the video as she shot. "And here they are, the only couple that most people consider more important than the King and Queen themselves."

Maggie rolled her eyes wanting anonymity more than anything. "Don't you think you're exaggerating that a little bit, Kelli?" Maggie asked.

"No way. You two here together is the talk of the night!"

"Really?" Kenny asked.

"Really," Kelli replied.

The idea of such attention alarmed Kenny to a certain extent. He knew this had been a compelling story throughout the year, but he also thought it ended with his admission. Why on earth would people still be interested?

He didn't have much time to consider it further as Kelli got down to business.

"Come on, say something about prom!" she prompted.

Maggie was first to speak. "I think everything looks amazing here. The decorations are phenomenal. Everyone looks fantastic. It's going to be a perfect night."

Kelli panned the camera over to Kenny and pointed at him to say something. Kenny cleared his throat and said plainly, "Ditto."

Kelli looked up from the camera in disappointment. "Thanks," she remarked.

As Kelli walked away, Kenny started laughing. Maggie didn't want to laugh, but it was just too funny to her. Even Jordan and Katie behind them found it comical. What Kenny did was slightly cruel, considering he was in the same class as Kelli and understood how important good interviews were. However, the advanced students could never pass up a chance to pick on the beginners.

A few minutes later, Maggie and Kenny were at the front of the line. The photographer set them up on the mark. They stood shoulder to shoulder, angled slightly towards each other. Kenny stood up straight and tall. Maggie stood with one leg slightly bent to show a little leg. Taking Maggie's hand with one hand and wrapping the other around her back, he nuzzled in close to her. Maggie smiled ceaselessly as the photographer adjusted them to the perfect pose. After two flashes of light, they walked off the stage still hand in hand.

They waited outside the auditorium for Katie and the others. Once they were all together again, they walked down the steps and onto the dance floor. The music was captivating. The scenery was enchanting. The prospect of dancing the night away was even a pleasant possibility.

While they were on the floor, two friends of theirs, Avery and Sonja bumped into them. Together they were up for prom King and Queen.

"Hey, Kenny good to see you," Avery said.

"Avery, how are things going?" Kenny asked.

"Great, man, how about you?"

"Can't get much better than prom, right?"

As Avery and Kenny chatted away, Maggie had more pressing matters to discuss with Sonja.

"So, you look amazing."

Sonja blushed. "Thank you. So do you."

"Are you excited? You know you're probably going to win."

Maggie's confidence was sweet, but Sonja wasn't sure it was well founded. Everyone up for election had a fair chance of winning.

"I'm not so sure about that," Sonja replied. "With everyone else that's running, I'm not sure I stand a chance."

"Oh, please, everyone I've talked to is voting for you. The two of you are a shoe-in."

"It's too bad Kenny didn't ask you earlier. If the two of you were on the ballot it would probably be a landslide victory."

"That wouldn't have a chance. Besides, I'm just glad he finally told me."

"I could see that. I heard you've been taking it fairly slow since he told you. Are you gonna try to move things along at the party?"

Maggie shrugged her shoulders as Kenny took her hand. She wasn't about to think too far ahead into the night. This would all be over before she knew it, and she had to enjoy every moment that she could. Having her arms around Kenny, around the man that saved her life, was something she had only dreamt about until now. It proved to be more than she could've imagined that she dared not think of what would happen next. She was content to just let it happen.

When the music stopped, a few couples exited the floor for a break. Maggie and Kenny hadn't been out there long, so they stuck around. The DJ announced that it was time for everyone to switch partners. Somehow, in the shuffle, Maggie ended up dancing with Jordan, Kenny was dancing with Ashley, and Scott was dancing with Katie.

"This should be interesting," Maggie said amused.

"Very funny," Jordan said taking Maggie in his arms. "Prepare to be impressed."

The music started again, and Jordan proved to be a sufficient dancer. Maggie didn't say anything though his ability was rather impressive. As they danced, they chatted with a few more friends, sharing compliments on each other's attire. A few more people had questions about Kenny.

"Do you ever get tired of that?" Jordan asked.

"A little," Maggie admitted. "I think it kind of spooks Kenny to know everyone is interested."

"I know what you mean," Jordan concurred. "It's almost like he doesn't get it completely, ya know? Like he doesn't realize what he did."

It was an interesting notion that Maggie never considered. Ever since he admitted what he had done, Kenny had been very low key. Though she couldn't explain it, Maggie took it to be a positive sign. Maybe Kenny was finally dealing with what he had done and more importantly, with what he had said. Whatever angst he had felt before; whatever reason he had for hiding so long wasn't bothering him anymore. Everything was as it should be.

The DJ would call for one more switch. This time, Maggie danced with Scott. He wasn't too steady on his feet, stepping on Maggie's toes a couple times. Normally, Maggie would have been annoyed, but it didn't bother her tonight. Nothing seemed to.

"You look like you're having a good time," Scott commented.

"It's amazing."

Ashley and Jordan came by for a moment.

"I hate to tell you this, Scott, but Jordan's a better dancer than you."

Jordan raised his arm in triumph, and Scott just rolled his eyes. Maggie chuckled as Ashley and Jordan disappeared into the crowd. Only a few minutes remained before the announcement of the King and Queen. When the music paused, Maggie felt a little winded.

"Kenny, I'm gonna go get a drink, you need anything?"

"No, I'm good. I'm gonna talk to Darren real quick."

Maggie trotted off the dance floor and walked over to the drink table. She grabbed a bottle of water, wiped the precipitation off the outside, and started gulping it down. When she turned around, Eric was standing behind her. She almost spilled her drink, she was so surprised to see him.

"Still saving me a dance?" he asked.

Maggie hadn't thought he was serious but had no problem with one dance. "Sure, if you want."

Eric smiled. "Good." He paused for a minute, a little leery about bringing up his next subject. Maggie would soon find out why. "So, how are things with Kenny?"

"They're fine."

"You two…together yet?"

Maggie shook her head. "Not yet, but we haven't really talked about it that much."

Eric nodded and looked out on the floor. He eyed Kenny for a minute, knowing he couldn't leave this stone unturned. "Well, if nothing materializes there, I would really like to give us another shot."

Maggie almost choked as she was drinking. This not only was shocking to hear, it didn't make any sense. Eric was supposedly happy with Angela. The last thought on his mind should be getting back together with Maggie. They had some good times; Maggie would happily admit that. The way things ended however, ended things. She was fine being friends and moving past all of that, but she wasn't about to try it again.

"Eric, you're with Angela," Maggie pointed out.

"I know that," Eric replied, "and part of me hates myself for doing this now. Angela is special to me, but it's nothing like when I was with you."

Maggie knew she had to handle the situation delicately. "Eric…."

Eric was quick to stop her. He wanted all of his cards out on the table before she told him her answer.

"I know that I screwed things up pretty bad when we broke up. Worse than that, I know I haven't been much of a friend to you since. I know it wouldn't be easy to put all of that behind us, but if we really gave it a chance, I think we could. I've never stopped caring for you, and I hate myself for distrusting you like I did. But if I had another chance to show you how much I've changed, you'd see how sorry I am and how much I want to make things right."

Eric stopped and awaited Maggie's reply. He had put his best foot forward and now had to wait. Unfortunately, everything he had said had fallen on deaf ears because Maggie wasn't about to go back to him. Her focus was on Kenny now. The two of them had something going, and she wanted that now more than anything.

"Eric, it just can't be like that," she said. "It's far too late to go back and try to fix something that is better off broken."

Eric tried to say more, but Maggie walked away. She found Kenny as fast as she could. Kenny didn't notice when she found him, but the encounter had noticeably frazzled her. In a way, she was pleased he didn't notice because she didn't want to talk about it.

The distraction that had everyone's attention was the announcement of Prom King and Queen. The four couples up for nomination all stood together on the DJ's stage. The crowd hushed in anticipated silence, waiting for the announcement of the names. As the DJ announced that Avery and Sonja were the winners, the crowd erupted in applause. The cheers continued while the King and Queen were crowned and then led out onto the dance floor for their traditional dance.

"They are such a good couple," Kenny said.

"Yeah, they are," agreed Maggie.

From across the room, Maggie could see Eric longingly staring at her as he held Angela loosely in his arms with a sullen look on his face. Maggie wondered if Angela had any idea what he had said to her. Maggie wouldn't dare say anything to her, it wasn't any of her business. Besides, it may have just been the emotion of the night that made Eric ask. Maybe tomorrow he'd wake up and realize how silly it was to ask what he had asked. In any event, it wasn't Maggie's problem; she had her own night to enjoy.

After Avery and Sonja had their traditional King-Queen dance, the rest of the couples joined them on the floor. Kenny took Maggie in his arms as a slow song played over the speakers. To remove the unpleasant moment from the forefront of her mind, Maggie rested her head on Kenny's chest. He didn't mind one bit.

As the music played and the indelible romance of the evening flooded Maggie's senses, her eyes drifted around the room attempting to capture every moment of this night. As she glanced around the commons, she briefly saw something that almost stopped her in her tracks. She had to look twice to make sure she had seen correctly, but her eyes had not failed her. Leaning over the wall at the top level of the commons was Trick. As he gazed over the scene, Maggie was fairly certain he was impressed. For a moment, their eyes locked. He waved with a smile on his face, which she reciprocated.

"What is it?" Kenny asked when he felt Maggie lift her head.

"Oh, it's nothing," Maggie replied still focused on Trick. "He came."

Kenny wheeled around and saw Trick standing there. Trick's attention was elsewhere at the moment, but Kenny was still happy to see him.

"I told that guy he'd wind up at prom."

"I wonder why he's here."

"Probably just wanted to see what he was missing."

It was difficult for Maggie to think that that was the true reason Trick would show up. He never seemed interested in things like this, and even when she would tell him about it later, he listened strictly as a courtesy. A part of her believed that now that high school was drawing to a close, he just had to know what he had passed up on all those years. Another part told her he was there to make sure everything was okay, which was probably the more precise reason. He did always seem to be there after all. This just happened to be a rare occasion when his services weren't required.

Chapter Seventeen

The Party Rolls On

When the song ended, Maggie promptly left the floor and ran up to find Trick. She sincerely doubted that he'd be willing to come down and dance because, from what she could tell, he was still dressed in jeans and a T-shirt and being around everyone else would kind of make him stick out. Still, she wanted to at least see him and find out what made him come.

Unfortunately, he had disappeared by the time she made it up the steps. Disappointed, she walked back and forth across the walkway looking for him, but everywhere she turned showed no signs of him. She hoped he would at least keep his word and be at the party later. It was disheartening enough that she didn't get to say anything to him here.

Over the speakers, Maggie heard an announcement that the final dance of the night was mere moments away. As much as she wanted to find Trick right then, she couldn't abandon Kenny at last call. Yet, as the music started, she had only stepped foot on the dance floor again, and she hastened her search for Kenny. As she gingerly maneuvered around the couples, she felt a hand reach out and grab hers. When she spun around, Kenny was there with a smile.

"I thought you were gonna miss it," Kenny said.

"Not a chance," Maggie replied.

Maggie wrapped her arms around Kenny's neck as he wrapped his around her waist. Just like that, Maggie forgot everything Eric had said and enjoyed the fleeting moment. It was hard to think that it was over already, for the night had gone by so quickly with a few surprises along the way: some pleasant, some not so pleasant. All in all, everything had been wonderful, and in a way, this ending only triggered a new beginning.

The situation with Kenny had changed drastically. It was a welcomed change though much remained undecided. She had tried to keep that idea out of her mind for some time, but it was becoming impossible to ignore. Kenny had told her that he loved her, and the two of them had to address that at some point. Maggie still wasn't one-hundred percent about her feelings, but she knew enough.

It could have been a product of his actions, or she may have been interested in him due to his heroics though she wanted to believe she couldn't be that shallow. She felt these feelings were genuine, so she would treat them that way. It would take time for all those feelings to mature, but the time seemed relatively insignificant at that point.

As the music concluded, the lights brightened in the room. The DJ thanked everyone for coming and wished them all a good night. There was applause, whooping, and hollering for the wonder of the night, and slowly but surely, everyone started to file out. It was a bittersweet moment, walking out at the end of such a significant and highly anticipated event. It had fit the billing, but no one wanted it to end.

"I sure am glad that's over," Jordan remarked as he loosened his tie.

"Oh, please," sighed Katie. "You know you had a good time. I saw that tear in your eye during the last dance."

Scott and Ashley chuckled as Jordan vehemently denied such an allegation. "Lies! All lies!" he yelled.

Scott put an arm around his friend. "It's alright man. I believe you."

"Thank you. It's good to know I have some people on my side."

Maggie took one last look around the commons as she passed through the archways at the door. She thought about how much her expectations of this night had changed over the year. Originally, she assumed that she would be coming with Eric and a group of his friends. Once they broke up, she assumed that she would be on her own or would have to drag Trick along with her. Now, here she was walking out with Kenny, the man who had pulled her from a lake back in October. It all seemed so strange and remarkable at the same time. Yet, even after such a wonderful night, she couldn't stop herself from wondering what it would have been like had she come with someone else.

The rain had graciously relented for the time being though flashes of lightning promised it would return soon. The ground was still soaked in the aftermath of the latest storm. Couples cautiously walked through the parking lot carefully avoiding the puddles that formed on the ground. Prom may have been over, but the night was still young.

When Kenny and Maggie got back to Maggie's car, they patiently waited for a few minutes before pulling out of the parking lot. The nostalgia of the dance had quickly vanished in the face of the after-prom party. Time was wasting away, so one's thoughts couldn't linger on the past for long.

As they drove to the Smith's, Maggie was thankful that Kenny made no mention of Eric. She knew he didn't know what he had done during the dancing intermission, but his apology could have been an interesting topic of discussion. In some way, maybe Kenny understood Maggie wouldn't want to talk about it. Or maybe Kenny didn't want to talk about it himself. In any event, she was more than happy to let the sleeping dog lie. Eric wouldn't take up any more of her thoughts the rest of the night.

There were quite a few cars parked in the Smith's driveway when they arrived. Scott's car was among them, but not Jordan's. From outside, they could hear music echoing from inside and see some shadows dancing on the white drapes over the windows. Maggie shook her head in disbelief.

"Dancing already?" she asked.

"I guess some people can't get enough," Kenny replied.

Maggie might feel that way in a while, but for now, she just wanted to relax and talk with her friends. At some point, she wanted to get Kenny alone with her.

When they entered the house, they looked for Scott and Ashley. They were sitting on a couch towards the back of the living room by the kitchen. Darren and Jessica sat next to them, and Trick was there as well.

"He came," Maggie exclaimed.

"He told you he was going to, didn't he?" Kenny asked.

"Yeah, but it's still surprising to see him here."

Kenny couldn't argue with that logic. Maggie walked on ahead on him, ecstatic that Trick came. He had his back turned to them, as he was telling a story to the others. Maggie couldn't wait for him to finish and bear hugged him from behind.

"You owe me a dance," Maggie demanded.

"Take a number," Trick responded. "Ashley has called the first dance and Jessica has even asked for one."

Maggie grabbed a seat. "Oh, really. Well, I guess that's the benefit of being the fresh man."

Trick rolled his eyes. "If that's what you want to call it."

"I thought you'd be anxious to dance," Maggie admitted. "After all, you did stop by prom before coming out here."

Kenny was the only other person there who had seen Trick at the dance. Considering how much Trick had rebuked the idea of going, it hit everyone else as curious that he would make an appearance. They all shifted their attention to him, expecting some kind of explanation for stopping by. If he really wanted to go, he should have just gone.

Trick got tired of all the eyes staring at him. "Alright, I'll admit it...the pool got a little boring. I figured I still had some time before the party started, so I dropped by for a minute. I didn't realize showing up would be such a scandal."

"It's not that," Maggie assured him. "It's just that I tried to find you before the last dance and you had already left."

"Well, I don't know if it's that obvious, but I wasn't exactly dressed appropriately for such an occasion. Something about the ratty jeans and tennis shoes seems to clash with everything you all got going on."

While they were talking, Jordan and Katie arrived and joined them. Jordan was happy to get off of his feet for a while. Katie was shocked to see Trick there.

"You realize I may have to steal you for a few dances, Trick," Katie informed him. She nodded her head towards Jordan. "This one has been complaining since we left the school."

"Wow," Trick replied. "My dance card is almost full then."

"I guess I better cash mine in then," Ashley said. "I wouldn't want to keep everyone waiting."

Maggie watched as Trick made his way out to the floor. He truly did look silly in his jeans surrounded by such formal attire, but no one cared at that point. Maggie turned around to find that Ashley wasn't the only one bitten by the dancing bug.

"Come on, Darren," Jessica pleaded. "Just one quick one."

"Not yet," Darren replied. "I want to get something to drink. Maybe Kenny will go."

Jessica looked at Kenny with begging eyes. Before he would consent, he wanted to make sure Maggie was okay with it. He preferred not to leave her by herself.

"Go ahead, Kenny," Maggie encouraged. "Scott doesn't have a partner, so I'll dance with him. I survived once; I think I can do it again."

"Who says I'm going out there?" Scott asked not happy that his name was suddenly up for discussion.

"I do," Maggie replied grabbing his hand.

Once they were all gone, Darren ran to the kitchen to grab a drink. Only Katie and Jordan remained. As she stared intently at him, he became unsettled. He wasn't going out there, and she knew there was no reason to expect otherwise.

"What?" Jordan finally asked.

"You get five minutes," Katie warned. "After that, we're going out there."

"Fine," Jordan replied. "Five minutes, starting…now."

Katie eased back into her chair and watched everyone around them. Trick and Ashley were having a good time dancing. Jessica and Kenny were laughing as well. Maggie and Scott were having a little more trouble but were still enjoying themselves. After a few minutes, Darren returned from the kitchen ready to go.

"Well, Katie, I don't think I'm going to get my date back anytime soon," Darren said. Then he held out his hand to her. "Shall we?"

Katie smiled. "I would love to."

Katie took Darren's hand and popped off the chair. Jordan didn't even bother to move as he was determined to use his five minutes to the fullest.

"Just know that I'll be watching," Jordan called out.

"Come on, man, you can trust me," Darren replied.

"I do trust you. It's her I'm a little iffy about."

"You should be," teased Katie.

Suddenly less concerned about his five minutes, Jordan sat up on the couch as Darren laughed.

"What does that mean?" Jordan asked.

"You'll have to watch to find out," Katie replied.

Darren winked at Jordan, who was still not amused with the situation, as the two turned and ran to the floor.

"That's not funny!" he called after them, but they weren't listening.

As the dancing continued, more and more people arrived from prom. Most of them weren't ready to get back on the dance floor, so they navigated their way around the dancers. Two that joined right in were Avery and Sonja, still on cloud nine from their crowning as King and Queen. Maggie was ecstatic for them.

"I told you, Sonja."

"I'm glad you were right," Sonja replied.

"Congratulations, Avery," Scott said shaking his hand. "You da man."

"Correction, I'm da King," Avery joked.

"Your modesty is overwhelming," Maggie remarked.

"Modesty," Avery repeated. "What about Miss Queen over here? After we won, she started jumping up and down and screaming and junk."

"It was really exciting," Sonja said as her defense. "I couldn't help myself. Besides, Avery, I saw you high fiving guys and chest bumping them."

"Well what was I supposed to do?" Avery asked. "Leave them hanging? I can't do that; it's just not right. What kind of King would I be?"

Away from the King and Queen action, Trick was enjoying himself as he continued to dance with Ashley. It had been quite a while since the two had been together like this, but it proved to both of them that they had moved past the rocky times.

"I gotta say, I was a little surprised to hear you stopped by prom," Ashley said.

"To be honest, I was trying to go unseen," Trick confessed. "All I wanted to do was see how everything looked. I guess it was a bigger deal than I anticipated."

"Don't blame Maggie for being excited. It's nice to see you out and about and not alone in your garage. Besides, Maggie told us things had kind of cooled between you and Amy."

It wasn't a subject that Trick wanted to discuss. The uncomfortable look in his eyes said that much. Still, if he was going to talk about it, he was going to talk to his friends. He could do that much.

"Yeah, the outlook isn't promising," said Trick. His tone was mournful. It was hard to think that way after what he had been through with her. "It's just the distance and all that. We kind of knew it was coming."

"That can't make it easier."

"No, it can't," Trick concurred, "but there are greater tragedies in the world. I'm just glad for the time I had with her."

Ashley smiled. "That's a good way to think about it."

The music faded out, signaling the end of a song. It would only be a few seconds before the next one started up. Ashley would like to have another dance with Trick, but she knew others were in line. Sure enough, Jessica approached them.

"Well, I think I'll go find Scott. I may need another before the night is over, though."

"No problem there," Trick said. "I'm easy to find."

Ashley smiled as Jessica took Trick's hand. Kenny wasn't far behind her and he was looking for Maggie.

"Alright, Trick, it's my turn," Jessica said.

"Maybe, but the pleasure is all mine," Trick replied.

Jessica smiled as the two started to dance. Kenny walked past them and found Maggie still dancing with Scott. He hated to cut in, but fortunately, Ashley wanted her date back as well.

"Thank you for the dance," Scott said with a bow to Maggie. Then he turned to Ashley. "Shall we, dear?" he asked as he offered up his hand

"I'd love to," Ashley replied with a curtsey.

Kenny and Maggie joined together again. Darren and Katie kept dancing together for a while longer. As the music continued to fill the air, even Jordan decided that he was ready to get back into the mix. As he lifted himself off the couch, he straightened his tie and went after Katie. He found her on the dance floor and politely intervened.

"Excuse me, may I cut in?" he asked.

"Of course," Katie said with a smile.

Darren and Katie separated. Katie held out her hand and waited for Jordan to take it. With a coy smile, Jordan bypassed her and grabbed Darren's hands. Surprised at first, Katie could only watch as Jordan prepared to dance with Darren. Though he felt somewhat embarrassed by the situation, Darren played along to be a good sport.

"Sit this one out, Katie," Jordan suggested. "After watching you two, I can tell that Darren's the better dancer."

Katie laughed as Jordan took a few steps away from her, but alas, Darren wasn't as willing to go as far with the joke as Jordan. As result, Jordan tripped over his own feet. Seeing the gag had hit its mark, he let Darren go and went back to Katie.

"Then again, the bad dancers should be paired together," said Jordan.

Jordan and Katie joined the others on the dance floor. It wouldn't be long before the music stopped and several people switched partners. Maggie took her turn with Trick to get her guaranteed dance. Jordan danced with Jessica for a while, while Scott danced with Katie and Kenny with Ashley. The pairings lasted a couple songs before they decided to take a break and sit for a spell.

When they found a spot where they could all be together, Jordan had to reveal his admiration of Trick. He had been thinking about this ever since Trick showed up that night. Now was the time to let everyone know of his brilliance.

"I gotta say, Trick, I didn't understand missing out on prom at first, but I do now."

Though he wasn't entirely sure where Jordan was going with this one, Trick was quite intrigued. Since no one else could tell what Jordan had in mind, they listened attentively. Katie, who didn't appreciate the comment, listened with vested interest.

"Oh, really," she said. "You understand missing out on it? Why don't you explain that to everyone else?"

Jordan ignored her threatening tone. "Gladly. Now, we all criticized Trick for missing out on the actual dance saying that he would be missing out on a once in a lifetime opportunity and all that. But when you think about it, what exactly did he miss out on? He's here now with all of his friends. He's even dancing, which is crazy to do willingly by the way. So what did he miss?"

While the guys felt Jordan had an airtight case, the girls disagreed thoroughly.

"How about the decorations?" Katie suggested.

"Or getting all dressed up and being formal for once," Ashley added.

"Not to mention being in everyone's pictures," Maggie included.

"And just feeling that atmosphere of being at prom," Jessica concluded.

Jordan nodded in agreement. "Okay, so there's that stuff, but is all that really that important? I mean, he still kind of gets the atmosphere being here. He stopped by and saw the decorations at least. And no guy wants to be in that many pictures. To top it all off, he gets to be comfortable the whole night instead of being in this monkey suit."

Tired of the complaining, Katie stood up and wrapped her arms around Jordan's neck. She sat down in his lap and asked him a question in a very calm, albeit intimidating tone.

"Are you saying that you didn't have a good time?"

Jordan realized then and there that he was skating on thin ice. His argument, rock solid as it was, may have proved his point, but it also put into question his time with Katie.

"Of course, I'm not saying that," Jordan replied. "I would never say something like that. It's different for me since I have someone that I really, really.... really wanted to go with. But Trick didn't have anyone to go with, he's all alone...."

"Always glad when that gets brought up," Trick interrupted.

Jordan smiled, hoping to come off as sincere. Katie hadn't totally bought his excuses but was willing to let him off the hook this time. As Katie hugged Jordan and kissed him on the cheek, a wave of relief came over him. The others laughed at how close he had come to disaster.

A few minutes later, the music compelled Katie back to the dance floor.

"Alright, let's go," she said taking Jordan's hand.

"Come on, I just sat down. Let me gather some strength first," Jordan whined. He looked for a scapegoat and found one in Trick. "Take the casually dressed guy. Doesn't he owe you one anyway?"

Katie let go of Jordan's hand and folded her arms. She wasn't happy with his attitude even though he had a valid point. For the time being, however, she could deal with his lackluster demeanor as, with a smile, she turned to Trick.

"He is right, I suppose."

"No time like the present," Trick said.

Katie and Trick headed onto the floor. Jessica found Darren and soon joined them. Scott and Ashley weren't far behind, either. Once the coast was clear, Jordan sneaked to the kitchen to grab a drink. Kenny looked over at Maggie, but she didn't want to dance anymore right now. Kenny wasn't going to force the issue.

"I take it you're enjoying yourself?" Kenny asked.

"Oh, yes," Maggie replied. "It's wonderful. Definitely an improvement over some of the parties I've been to here."

Maggie was referring to the party back in December. It was during that harrowing night that Eric broke up with her and slugged Trick. She remembered distinctly how limited Kenny's presence had been that night.

Kenny didn't like to think about that night, either, though he couldn't ignore it. It was just one more explanation he had to give.

"Yeah, I could see how that night would be easy to top."

"Why were you down by the lake?" Maggie asked.

"I didn't know where else to go," Kenny confessed. "I mean, I heard that Eric was looking for me, and I had a good idea why. Since you didn't know about me at the time, I wasn't exactly looking for an opportunity to explain myself. I thought about getting in my car and driving away, but I was sure someone would see me. Luckily, I was able to sneak out the back, and after that, I went wherever I could.

"For the record, I knew that wasn't the right thing to do, and if I thought things would have worked out better by staying and facing him, I would have. But he sounded a little out of control, and I assumed my being there would send him over the edge."

Maggie understood that. She could still remember the horror she felt when Eric punched Trick in the jaw. Luckily, Eric's friends quickly restrained him, and the matter died shortly after.

"Well, I've been mad about things like that for long enough," Maggie said. "None of it matters now, right?"

Kenny smiled. "Right."

It was truly amazing to Kenny that Maggie could let everything between them drop so easily. Even after he had hurt her like he did during TV class with his adamant denials, she didn't care and was eager to put it behind them. He couldn't believe his luck. He couldn't believe someone could do such a thing.

Maggie moved closer to Kenny and rested her head against his shoulder. Wrapping an arm around her, he watched with her as their friends danced to the festive music. From across the room, Katie's heart was warming at the sight of them together.

"It's beautiful, isn't it?" Katie asked.

"It is quite a sight," Trick admitted.

Since Katie found herself alone with Trick, she desperately wanted to tell him 'I told you so.' She had been the one after all that believed Kenny was the hero all along. Trick had been on Kenny's side, believing his ridiculous fib about Miller's lake. Now that they knew she was right, she had to rub it in his face a little bit.

"So, how does it feel to be so wrong?"

"Wrong about what?" Trick asked.

"You know what—those two. I told you all along that Kenny was the guy that pulled Maggie from the lake, but you were so sure that Kenny would never lie to you. You bought it hook, line, and sinker when he said he was at Miller's lake."

Trick smiled, letting Katie get her shots in. "Yes, it certainly looks like I have some egg on my face now don't I?"

"Seriously though, Trick. How could you not think it was him?"

"Who says I believe it's him now?"

Katie stopped dancing and glared at Trick in the eyes. He couldn't be serious; he had to admit that he was wrong with all the evidence proving as much. As the bewildered look on her face held tight, a smile broke across Trick's face. Katie didn't appreciate being put on like that and grudgingly went back to dancing.

"You're terrible."

Trick laughed. "Come on, I almost got you on that one."

After a few songs, Katie and Trick returned to the couches where Jordan welcomed them back. Maggie and Kenny hadn't moved from before, and it wasn't long after that Ashley and Scott were back with them. Trick seemed somewhat relieved that he had run the gauntlet of dances he owed, leaving him free for the rest of the night.

"So, Trick, anyone else you owe a dance to?" Ashley asked.

Trick looked over the room. "I don't think so. I should be free for anyone else who asks."

Jordan leaned over to Scott. "Ten-to-one says that he doesn't dance with anyone that he hasn't already danced with," Jordan betted.

Scott refused the offer. "Please, I'm on your side."

Trick didn't appreciate the lack of confidence. "I'd bet against you morons, but I don't have any money on me."

Luckily, Trick had back up. Katie and Ashley didn't appreciate the insensitive nature of the bet, and as they stared down their respective boyfriends, they fished five dollars out of their purses.

"Don't worry about it, Trick, I'll back you," Katie said slamming the money down.

"Yeah, me too," Ashley said throwing in her part of the pot.

Jordan smiled, almost laughing at the prospect of proving Katie wrong. On top of that, he had five easy bucks coming his way. "I hate to take money from my girlfriend, but if that's how you wanna go, I'm not gonna stop you," Jordan said.

Katie smiled as Jordan looked over the money on the table. The payout for the girls would be fifty dollars each. It would be a steep lesson for Jordan and Scott to learn, but they would deserve it for going against a friend.

They all shook hands on the deal and then waited to see what would happen. As time went on and no one approached Trick, Scott and Jordan's confidence grew, though Ashley and Katie weren't the slightest bit concerned. Trick on the other hand was.

"Well, I hate to say it, but they may be right. I guess I filled up my dance card too early."

Katie smiled as a girl approached them. "I bet there's room for one more."

Trick didn't know who was behind him, but from the shocked looks on Jordan and Scott's faces, he assumed he was in for quite a treat. Sure enough, when he wheeled around, Sonja, the Prom Queen herself, was standing behind him. Trick smiled, as he turned back to Jordan and Scott.

The beleaguered look on their faces was priceless, and Trick just had to bask in the glory of the moment for a minute.

"Guys, you know Sonja, right? I believe someone told me she won prom Queen tonight." Trick turned to Sonja. "That is just fantastic by the way; so what can I do for you?"

"Well, my date is off bragging to some of his friends about his triumph, so I am without a dance partner temporarily. And since I never did thank you for that video you helped me make for class earlier in the year, I thought maybe I could tell you how it went over a dance."

Trick grinned from ear to ear as Jordan and Scott's jaws dropped. Ashley and Katie high-fived in celebration and picked their money up off the table. Trick looked coyly at his friends who were suddenly out a collective one hundred dollars.

"I'd love to," Trick said.

"Great, let's go."

Trick winked at the others as Sonja took his hand, leading him out onto the dance floor. Katie and Ashley watched in celebration as Trick took in every moment of his victory dance. When they turned back to their boys, they still couldn't believe it.

"I guess that means we win," Ashley said.

"Why do you gotta stick up for him?" Scott asked.

"We like him more than we like you," Katie replied.

Jordan remained quiet. Still watching Trick dance with Sonja, he couldn't figure out for the life of him how this series of events had transpired. Katie was shocked and a little concerned by his silence because she figured he would have been up in arms.

"Don't you have anything to say, Jordan?" Katie asked.

"That's not fair. It's just not fair," Jordan replied.

"What isn't?" Ashley asked.

Jordan over-articulated his dilemma. "Trick is dancing with the Queen of a prom that he didn't even go to. What about that sounds fair?"

Ashley reminded him. "They've been friends for years. It's not like she just picked him out of the blue."

"Besides, Jordan, you've got bigger matters to address," Katie informed him. "I believe you owe me somewhere around fifty dollars."

Jordan and Scott looked at each other helplessly. After they had been so willing to take the girls' money, it was clear Katie and Ashley intended on cashing in. To their dismay, they didn't have the money and didn't want to be out fifty bucks.

Since Scott and Jordan were thoroughly humiliated at that point, there was a small chance Ashley and Katie would be willing to negotiate. Hopefully, they had proven their point and were feeling gracious after their triumph.

"Now, ladies, I know we looked like real jerks when we made that bet," Jordan began. "And we looked like even bigger jerks when we expressed our satisfaction about taking your money. Obviously, we were humbled and taught a very valuable lesson. I don't know if that's enough, but, surely, there is some way to make this go away without any money exchanging hands."

Jordan looked sincerely into Katie's eyes as Scott folded his hands in a begging motion. Ashley and Katie considered their offer for a moment before standing up. After some brief whispers, smiles broke across their faces, which Scott and Jordan took as good signs. That feeling would disappear very shortly.

"Alright, we won't make you pay up," Ashley said. Scott and Jordan smiled and pumped a fist in celebration. "Instead, you're gonna have to dance off your debt."

The smiles quickly dissipated from their faces, replaced by genuine concern. They had never had to work off money by dancing, but were certain it wouldn't be easy. Their inept level of dancing notwithstanding, they doubted sincerely that Ashley and Katie were going to be reasonable about this. Still, they didn't want to pay the money.

Scott listlessly trudged out to the dance floor while Jordan tried to negotiate a rate per dance. His pleas were falling on deaf ears, however, as Katie merely stated that she would let him know when his debt was paid.

Still begging for mercy as Katie dragged him to the dance floor, Jordan started dancing for what he was sure would be an eternity. He watched irately as guys like Trick and Kenny took breaks while he ran his own personal marathon. Between longing looks into the kitchen at the ice chilled drinks and the inviting warmth of the couches, every minute felt like an hour.

By the time he had finally paid up, Jordan had sweat dripping off his brow. His legs were uncontrollably wobbling from the over-activity. He had to loosen his tie to help him catch his breath. In fact, he almost fell down before he got back to the couch. Once he was close enough, he collapsed in a heap with Scott right behind him. Ashley and Katie were still bursting with energy quite satisfied with themselves. Just to ease their suffering, the girls sat next to them and wrapped a consoling arm around them.

"Now, was that so bad?" Katie asked.

"Shhh! Your talking is hurting my feet," Jordan said.

"Would something to drink help?" Ashley asked.

"Couldn't hurt," replied Scott weakly.

Ashley and Katie rolled their eyes as they got up and headed for the kitchen. Jordan and Scott kicked their feet up to get some needed relief. They had closed their eyes for no more than an instant when they felt the couch slump between them. When they opened their eyes again, Trick was sitting next to them with a smile from ear to ear.

"I hate you, Trick," Jordan said.

"Oh, come on now, don't be bitter," Trick said. "All I did was dance. You're the ones that put your respective feet in your mouths."

It was bad enough that Katie and Ashley were rubbing this in their faces; they didn't need Trick to do the same. As Jordan and Scott groaned at his revelry, they moved as far away from him as possible without leaving the couch.

"Why are you even over here?" Scott asked.

"Well, I danced with Sonja, Jessica, a few other girls," Trick bragged. "I figured I could use a break, and who better to spend it with than with my friends."

"Yeah, your sense of camaraderie is overwhelming," remarked Jordan.

Trick laughed as Ashley and Katie returned with the drinks. Jordan and Scott didn't even bother to thank them as they grabbed the bottles and went to town on them. The girls sat away from them in the chairs still laughing at their boys.

"So, Trick, how was the dancing?" Katie asked.

"Oh, it was marvelous," replied Trick. "A very pleasant surprise, ya know?"

"I think I do," Katie said with a smile.

"You look tired," Ashley commented. "I could go get you something to drink if you want?"

While the gesture was sincere, Ashley also asked just to get under Scott and Jordan's skin some more. It worked like a charm as Scott pulled his drink from his lips, almost spilling some down his shirt. Jordan wasn't pleased, either.

"Oh, sure, you'll go get us a drink when we're dying," Scott remarked. "But Trick, who could totally get one under his own power, you'll go get one for him anyway."

Trick laughed and then happily stood up and patted Scott on the knee. He figured Scott had been through enough, he could bite the bullet on this one.

"Don't get worked up, Scott. I'll get it myself."

"You wanna get me one, too?" Jordan asked.

"You've got one," Trick replied.

"It's like half empty. It won't last."

"Alright, I see what I can do.

"My man!"

Trick strolled into the kitchen and opened the fridge to a wide variety of pop to choose from. Grabbing two Dr. Peppers, he slung the door shut to find Maggie leaning against the wall next to the fridge.

"I thought it was Root Beer for you tonight," Maggie said.

"That was before I got roped into coming to this party," Trick replied with a playful smile. "Now that I'm here, I'll need the caffeine boost to stay awake. Guess, I'm still not used to all the dancing."

Maggie laughed. "You are quite a hit for someone who typically flies under the radar."

While Trick was happy to playfully banter back and forth with Maggie, he found it odd that she would be talking to him since the whole point behind tonight had been for her to get closer to Kenny. From what he had seen at prom, she was doing that. Currently, however, the plan appeared to be faltering.

Holding true to form, Trick was willing to give Maggie a chance to air her concerns. As he took a long drink, he scanned her face to find she certainly seemed to have something on her mind. But, also holding true to form, Maggie wasn't going to just start talking.

"So, what are you doing here anyway?" Trick asked. "I figured you and Kenny would be out on the pier by now."

"So did I," Maggie confessed.

Maggie's cheerful tone had suddenly taken a dramatic turn. Trick understood immediately where Maggie's frustrations were coming from. With all that Maggie had told him about earlier in the evening, it was obvious things had become stagnant.

"What happened?" Trick asked.

"That's just it," Maggie replied. "Nothing has happened. When we were at the dance, things seemed to be going perfectly. Then we got here, and he kind of drifted away."

"So reel him in," Trick said bluntly

"You make it sound so easy."

"Well, you've seen how reluctant he is to step up and do anything. Just because he admitted the truth doesn't necessarily mean that would change. If you want something to happen, you may have to step up."

Maggie nodded in agreement, realizing that she had wasted enough time on the sideline. It was time to get into the game. The night was slipping away, but she still had the opportunity to grab hold of it. Leaving the kitchen with determination showing on her face, she tracked Kenny down. She managed to pull him away from the people he had been talking to, and the two of them went into the den, alone.

Kenny was slightly nervous about being alone with Maggie, but she coaxed him into taking a seat on the couch. Once he was reasonably comfortable, she sat down next to him. She knelt down on the cushion of the couch, leaning against Kenny. Her arm was around his neck, and she was gently rubbing his shoulder.

The close quarters were making Kenny noticeably nervous. His hands started to shake a bit, so he quickly rubbed to legs to hide his discomfort. He had expected a lot of things tonight, but not this.

"So, Kenny, I was thinking maybe the two of us could go out to pier," Maggie said.

Kenny wasn't thrilled. "Should we? I mean, it's raining isn't it?"

"No, it let up."

Maggie moved in even closer, which caused Kenny to move over a little bit. This was really going somewhere that he didn't anticipate and quickly. He wasn't entirely sure how to react to this, but he definitely wasn't comfortable with what was happening.

"Are you sure you'd want to go out there when we're so dressed up? Sitting on the wet wood might ruin your dress."

"I'm not worried about that."

Maggie reached over to the end of the couch and put an arm on the armrest, trapping Kenny at the end of the couch. As he slumped back against the edge of the sofa, Maggie practically draped herself on top of him. He frantically looked for a way to escape this sudden madness but had no escape. As Maggie looked down on him with a seductive look in her eyes, he felt his pulse quicken. She could sense his uneasiness and tried to comfort him.

"Kenny, I remember what you told me, and I wasn't sure at first but now I think that I feel the same way."

Maggie moved in to kiss Kenny, but Kenny knocked her over as he broke for freedom. Falling off the couch, Kenny backed away as fast as he could, leaving Maggie stunned and embarrassed on the sofa.

"What are you talking about?" Kenny demanded.

Their interaction had grown loud enough to draw the attention of nearly everyone in the house. Trick was center stage in the crowd with Katie, Jordan, Ashley, and Scott around him. A slew of faces also filled the empty space in the doorway between the den and living room. No one was saying a word as they all tried to grasp what was going on.

"What's wrong with you, Kenny?" Maggie asked oblivious to the crowd.

"Me? You're the one that tried to jump me. Why would you do that?"

The two stood at a standstill as the crowd began to speculate about what this meant. Only a few couldn't see, so some were giving a play-by-play of what had happened. The tension in the room was overwhelming. Eventually, it got to be too much for Katie who needed some answers. There was only one person to ask.

"Trick," she said, pulling on his shirt, "what's happening?"

Trick didn't want to be the one to say it, especially with the crowd around them, but he had to speak up now.

"If I'm reading this correctly, then Kenny doesn't know that the guy who pulled Maggie out of the lake also told her that he loved her."

Kenny's shocked expression affirmed Trick's suspicions, sending the house into an absolute silence. Those who knew of the hero's love proclamation stood shocked at Kenny's ignorance, but others hearing of it for the first time were just as surprised by the revelation. Regardless of their prior knowledge, everyone understood the full significance of the moment. It was obvious that Kenny didn't know what he was supposed to have said and as such, he had lied about being that man for weeks.

Maggie looked despondently at Trick, begging for him to be lying. He looked back at her sympathetically, but the truth remained that Kenny was not the hero behind that mask.

Chapter Eighteen

Hidden Love

The room remained trapped in the silence that shrouded the air. Many people wanted to leave, but the tension was paralyzing. On one side of the room sat Maggie, broken-hearted and despondent. The revelation made in front of everyone solidified that the man she thought had saved her life truly hadn't. The wonder and splendor that was prom night was now just a façade as in one foul swoop, all of the kept promises were broken again. The answers she believed she had were ripped away from her, leaving her where she originally was months ago. Now, there was no clear-cut suspect and the mystery loomed larger than ever.

On the other side lay Kenny on the floor. The finger pointed at him all along only revealed the error in everyone else's thinking. His admission was a fabrication. Those who understood that he couldn't have known the hidden love revealed to Maggie perhaps didn't find his actions to be so heinous. He owned up to something he thought he understood, giving closure to a simple situation that hid a greater complexity than he could possibly have fathomed. Had he known the whole story, surely he would not have owned up then. Because of that, however, another mystery remained. He would not have done this without reason, but what would have compelled someone to lie in such a way?

It was the need to know those answers that kept everyone in that room from moving. They wanted to rid themselves of this even though they did not want to draw further attention to the situation for Maggie's sake and even Kenny's. However, the drive to wash their hands did not overcome the need for some finality on this issue. Whether by choice or fate, they were all a part of this now.

Everything was at a standstill. Maggie sat on the couch, tears in her eyes, waiting for an explanation Kenny didn't want to give. Trick and the others stood frozen in fear. Whatever was about to happen, they couldn't instigate it. They had to be bystanders as much as possible.

Trying to be respectful of the silence, Jordan inched over to Trick. He didn't want anyone to hear him, especially Maggie.

"Uh, Trick," whispered Jordan, keeping his eyes away from Kenny and Maggie. "Isn't what the guy that saved Maggie told her something that Kenny should kinda know about?"

"It should be," Trick replied. "If Kenny was the guy who saved her."

The silence had become too much for some. Katie grabbed Trick's arms and forced him to look her in the eyes. It wasn't an answer he wanted to give, it wasn't an issue he wanted to be a part of, but he was in too deep now. The terror in Katie's eyes was enough to remind him of that.

"You kidding," Katie demanded, her eyes begging for this all to be some kind of sick joke. "Please, for everyone's sake, tell me that you are joking."

Trick looked over at Maggie, her attention captured by the question as well. To him, the question was coming from her and not Katie. Unfortunately, the answer was the same for both of them.

"I'm not," Trick replied. "Kenny didn't do it.

It was at that moment that all the lies, deception, and pain caught up with Maggie. She wasn't going to sit back and cry about this anymore; she was going to get her answers instead. After all this time, Kenny owed her that much. It bothered her before when he denied the accusations, but she was willing to forgive him for that. This, on the other hand, was something else entirely. She was furious beyond reproach that he dared tell her that he was the one that pulled her from the lake, the one that saved her, and the one that loved her. It didn't matter to her that he didn't know—all that mattered was the lie.

As the anger boiled over, she stood up from the couch fists clenched and stood over Kenny dauntingly. He didn't move, totally willing to take whatever she was preparing to dish out. He could almost feel the room shrink as everyone collectively leaned in to see what would happen. Luckily, Maggie was going to make it simple; she wanted the unconditional truth. It was doubtful that it would make her feel better, but at least she would finally have it.

"Alright, Kenny, enough is enough. Tell me the truth, the actual truth. Are you the guy that pulled me out of the lake or not?" Maggie demanded.

Kenny looked up at the ceiling and took a few deep breaths, knowing he couldn't dodge this any longer. As he looked over to his friends and saw the glum, disappointed looks on their faces, he knew he had dug his own grave this time. They couldn't help him out of this one; he didn't want them to.

Slowly, he stood up to face Maggie like a man. He brushed the dust off his pants and took in one final deep breath. It was time to face the music. She knew the answer, but he had to admit it.

"No," he replied.

A collective gasp escaped from the crowd as only Trick stood unfazed. Just like that, the shock resounded through the room again. It had really all been a lie, and the fairytale ending to the story had unraveled. No one knew if it would ever have an ending now.

Unable to deal with the betrayal, Maggie burst out in anger. "You lied to me!" she yelled with the tears already falling from her face. "You told me that you would never lie to me again. You told me to trust you and I did!"

Kenny attempted to explain himself. "You have no idea how sorry I am," Kenny said putting out a hand to console her, "but I...."

Maggie yanked her arms away and backed away from him just as he had done to her moments ago. He could provide no comfort now. There were so many things Maggie wanted to say and scream and yell, but only one thing could find its way passed her gritted teeth and pursed lips.

"Why?"

"What?" Kenny replied, afraid of that very question.

Maggie restated her demands. "I want to know why you did it!"

Kenny violently shook his head. "No, no I can't tell you," he cried out as he turned away from her. Bracing himself against the wall, he could feel everything slipping away from him. Everything that he had worked to keep hidden was suddenly in the spot light. Try as he might, he couldn't hide it any longer.

"You owe me that much!" Maggie exclaimed.

As Kenny tried to find his out, Jessica walked out of the crowd and stood beside him. She placed a hand on his shoulder, which calmed him immediately. When he saw her there with him, he realized what she wanted from him, but he wasn't about to do it. He had guarded the truth so carefully, risked so much that it couldn't come out here, not now; he wouldn't allow it.

But the kindness in Jessica's eyes told Kenny that she didn't want him to hide this anymore. The chaos had to end, and he could do that now. Whatever happened after that didn't matter now that he had backed himself into this corner. There was only one way out, and they would take it together.

"It's okay," Jessica assured him with a smile on her face. "Tell her. Tell everyone for that matter. We don't have to hide this anymore."

It was the 'we' that caught Trick's attention, allowing him to piece the rest of it together from there. The two of them, Kenny and Jessica, were together. It was a secret affair. Something that no one else knew about that for whatever reason they had to keep hidden. Maybe now, even if Trick couldn't condone what Kenny did, he couldn't as quickly condemn him for it, either.

"Will somebody tell me what's going on here!" Jordan yelled.

Jessica and Kenny embraced as everyone looked on.

"They're in love," Trick replied. "Kenny and Jessica are in love."

"But why would they have to hide that?" Jordan asked.

From the back of the crowd, a voice cried out assertively. "Because of me!"

The crowd parted as Jessica's little brother Matt walked through the masses to face Jessica and Kenny. The crooked grin on his face was unsettling at best. For a moment, everyone forgot about the lie and focused in on what was happening between Kenny and Jessica.

"I'm the reason they had to keep this a secret," Matt proudly declared. "I'm the villain behind this!"

Jordan scoffed. "He's a villain? What, is he gonna sit there and twirl his handlebar moustache or something?" Then he grabbed Matt by the collar and pulled him to the side. "Pipe down junior, it's rude to interrupt."

"He's right, though," Jessica admitted. "It was because of him. My parents are very much against my dating. The very mention of it puts them in knots. I've always cared for Kenny, and he's always cared for me. We tried to keep it low key, but then Matt caught us. Ever since, he's always been watching us so carefully that we had to be extra careful and take advantage of whatever opportunity came our way.

"That's what brought Kenny to Miller's lake. We told people we'd be at the Smith's party and then snuck away to be together. Unfortunately, someone followed me that night. Matt somehow figured out where we were and led my parents to us. If they caught us together, the punishment would have been severe.

"Dad warned me that if I tried dating anyone, he'd send me away for college. I planned on going to the same college as Kenny, and the only way I could convince my dad to go along with that was to promise not to date him. In order to keep that arrangement, Kenny had to hide somewhere. It wasn't the best idea but jumping in the lake was all he could do at the time."

The story seemed legitimate. No one was certain that they could trust what Kenny said, but Jessica's reliability was not in question. As Trick gave it more and more thought, it seemed to answer some of the questions that still didn't have answers.

"When you jumped out of Maggie's window, were the two of you upstairs together?" Trick asked.

The idea seemed ludicrous at first. Though with everything else revealed that night, it matched up with the story. After all, Jessica was the first person in Maggie's room after Kenny jumped.

"Yeah, we were," admitted Kenny. "We hadn't been able to sneak away for a while and just couldn't help ourselves."

"What about the Christmas party? Eric was looking for you, but you were nowhere to be found," Jordan said.

Kenny nodded his head. It was another lie that he had told Maggie. Each one piled on the pain he felt for deceiving her so.

"We had snuck out long before Eric came looking for Kenny," Jessica answered. "It wasn't until we got back to school that we heard about the break up."

"How about the project you were working on when we thought you had finished Maggie's tape?" Katie asked.

"That was a tape of the two of us," Kenny said. "All the pictures we had together, everything we did, I had to keep at my house. My parents didn't care and didn't come looking for those things, but Jessica's parents would. I hated that she didn't have anything, so I put it all together for her so she'd have something."

All the pieces were finally beginning to fit and all the circumstantial evidence that pointed to Kenny proven wrong. Only one major problem remained. It was the only question on Maggie's mind. The wave of compassion for Kenny and Jessica had swept up everyone else, but she didn't have the benefit of being able to enjoy such a luxury. Her heart was still broken and left with nothing.

"But why lie to me?" Maggie asked. "Why tell me when you didn't have to?"

It was probably the hardest question to answer. The story up to this point was a sympathetic one. They hadn't yet reached the part where everything took a dark turn, and Maggie wasn't going to let it go unnoticed. Kenny was trying to play innocent when everyone knew his hands weren't entirely clean.

"Matt confronted me in the hallway that day," Kenny said, remembering his admission after school. "He said that he was going to make sure Jessica was sent out of state for college. Even though he had no proof, he assured me that he'd find it eventually. I knew she had the tape I made her somewhere in her house, and I was afraid he'd find it. I needed something to throw him off the scent. I thought that if I could convince him I wasn't at Miller's lake that night, he'd back off.

"There was only one way to convince him I wasn't there. It was already all over school that I showed up at Trick's house dripping wet, freezing to death. If I told you that it was me, which everyone thought anyway, I assumed he'd leave me alone. So if I fessed up to it, no one would question it."

Maggie folded her arms, trying to restrain her anger. Kenny stepped away from Jessica and walked up to Maggie. His eyes held the deepest sincerity, but Maggie didn't know if she could trust them anymore.

"You have to believe me when I say this," he said as a plea more than a demand. "I had no idea how much you had vested in this, and I never heard what he told you that night. I just thought that you would be appreciative of the act, thank me, and then we'd all move on from there."

Maggie couldn't stand to look at him anymore. The tears in her eyes couldn't be held back any longer, and she wasn't about to let him see her cry. She hated him for getting his happy ending while leaving her with this nightmare.

"Well, you were wrong, Kenny...dead wrong," Maggie proclaimed with her voice breaking from the sorrow.

Before Kenny could say anything more, Maggie turned and ran out of the room. She rushed right by Trick who, despite the urge to comfort her, let her go. Fighting her way through the crowd, she freed herself from the scene, escaping out the back door.

Katie looked at Trick to see if he was going to go after her or not. When she realized that he was merely going to stand there with his head down, she decided to go after Maggie herself. She didn't take two steps before Trick grabbed her.

"Let her be," Trick said.

"I can't just let her go," Katie replied.

Trick let Katie loose and looked gravely in her eyes. "She needs time." His tone had been so threatening that everyone took notice. As he looked around at all the concerned faces, Trick calmed himself down. "We all need time with this one," he said.

Katie unwillingly gave in and sat down on the couch. Kenny and Jessica dropped their heads as they held each other. The reality of the moment was back. Even if people wanted to be happy for Kenny and Jessica, they couldn't overlook his tactics. It was too much.

As the crowd started to disperse, a bellowing laughter rang out from somewhere in the crowd. Furious, Trick looked for who would dare laugh at this. Eventually, his search led him to Matt, who was standing in front of Kenny and Jessica.

"Now you're gonna get it!" Matt yelled. "I've got real proof now! I'm gonna tell mom and dad everything. Then you'll be going out of state, and you'll never see Kenny."

Jessica started to tear up. Kenny wrapped his arms around her to console her, but they were standing at a dead end. If Matt told his parents the truth, then that was it. As Trick watched Matt relentlessly taunt his own sister and the guy she loved, a swell of pity came over him. Under similar conditions, it was plausible that Trick would have done the same if he were in Kenny's shoes. It could have happened to any of them really. They'd do anything to protect that which they considered dearest even if they didn't understand the risks. It was only bad luck that it all came crashing down like this.

The longer Trick watched Matt laugh in the face of his sister's pain, the faster the anger built up inside of him. He had already watched his best friend get hurt because her illusions of love dissipated in front of her. Now, more of his friends seemed destined for the same fate. In that moment, he decided that he couldn't let it happen. With everything that had gone wrong, all the tears shed, the feelings hurt, Trick resolved to end it all.

Trick stepped up to Matt, grabbed him by the collar and pushed him back against the wall. Jessica went to restrain Trick, but Kenny stopped her. Trick wasn't going to lose it; he was in control. As Matt tried to wiggle free, Trick held him tightly as Jordan, Scott, Darren, and Avery gathered around him.

"Alright you little twerp, you listen to me," Trick demanded. "It's because of you that my best friend is bawling her eyes out hating my other friends. It's because of you that they lied to her. Now, I've still got the better part of two months left in high school and an entire summer before I go off to college. You even think about ruining your sister's college plans and I...." Trick looked around to see his friends behind him. "...correction...we will spend all of our time making your life unbearable. Do we understand each other?"

Matt was shaking in his boots. Trick was deathly serious, and Matt wasn't about to question his sincerity. He was so scared, his voice cracked when he finally replied.

"Yeah, I understand. I won't say anything. I swear!"

Trick let go of Matt who sprinted out of the house and disappeared into the night. Trick watched him leave before taking a deep breath. Jordan slapped Trick on the back and gave him a hug from the side.

"I am so going to miss those freshmen," Jordan said with a smile.

All five of them smiled and chuckled. Everyone patted Trick on the back for taking a stand, and he proudly shook each of their hands. He had been willing to go it alone but was more than thrilled to have the support of his friends.

He wasn't the only one feeling fortunate in his friends. As Trick, Jordan, and Scott took a seat around Katie, Ashley, Kenny, and Jessica, Jessica had an appreciative smile on her face. She even had a tear in her eye but not a sad one.

"Thanks, you guys," she said.

"Anytime," Scott replied. "You have our number."

Trick was pleased with his actions but still very upset with Kenny. As Trick sat there staring at him, he thought back on all the times he warned Kenny about getting too involved in this. He assured Kenny that there was more at stake than he realized, but Kenny refused to listen to him. Kenny was thinking the same thing.

"I feel terrible," Kenny admitted.

"Good," Trick replied, "you probably should."

It seemed harsh for him to say that.

"Trick...." Katie protested.

"What?" Trick replied. He knew he was justified. "He can cry innocence all he wants to, but that doesn't excuse the lie. None of this reasoning he has does."

Everyone seated there knew he was right. It was nearly impossible having to balance everything that had happened tonight. Kenny's actions were deplorable, yet honorable. He acted out of fear and stupidity. No one would deny it. They all just wanted things remedied.

"How long do you think Maggie will be upset?" Jessica asked.

"A while, probably," replied Trick.

"Should we go talk to her?" Kenny asked.

"What, are you serious?" Trick replied. "No! Stay away from her. The last thing she wants to see is the two of you together."

Kenny sighed. "I just want to make this right."

"Well, you can't," Trick informed him. "No one can make what happened right. It was a mistake of the grandest fashion. I understand why you did what you did, but that doesn't justify it in any way. You decided to walk across fire and burned a lot of people because of it. We all have to live with it now."

Kenny covered his face with his hands. Everything seemed so bleak. The helplessness of the night was devastating. Were they all going to have to live with this empty feeling for the rest of the school year? Would it ever go away or would they have to learn to deal with it as best they could? Would this be how they remembered the last few months they had together? The night revealed several answers, but even more important questions remained unanswered.

As they sat together trying to think of ways to make each other feel better, it got to be too much for Katie. Standing up, she was determined to at least try to make things right.

"I'm gonna go talk to her," she said.

Trick quickly stood up to stop her, "No, I don't think you should."

"Trick, she can't stay out there by herself."

"I agree. That's why I'm going to go." His offer didn't seem to be enough for Katie. "Look, I know it impossible to even consider this, but you all are still on your prom dates. Even though we're focusing on the negative right now, a lot of good things have happened tonight. Don't let this ruin that, too. As hard as it may be, enjoy yourselves because it's what Maggie would want. I'm not saying that it'll be easy to move past this, but we will, and someday, Maggie will even be happy for Kenny and Jessica even if it doesn't seem like she could ever be right now. So just do that much and let us loners stick together."

Again, Katie was unwilling to concede, but she did. Trick started to walk away from them and head for the back door. As he walked away, Katie remembered what Trick had told her when they were dancing. 'Who says I believe it's him now?' he had asked her. She shrugged it off as a joke before, but he was being serious—he really didn't believe Kenny.

"You really never did believe him, did you?" Katie asked.

Everyone stared at her, confused by the statement. Trick stopped and faced her. Katie looked at him and as everyone else's eyes followed, he was more than willing to say 'I told you so.'

"No, I knew that it was a lie all along," Trick replied.

It was a shocking admission really. It was one thing to believe Kenny when he was sticking to his Miller's lake story, but why think he was still lying after he confessed? Since no one could follow the logic to it, everyone faced him, needing to know how Trick knew.

"Alright then, how did you know it was a lie?" Katie asked.

Trick gazed at all the intrigued faces awaiting his answer. He had to chuckle to himself for a minute because the answer was so simple, he couldn't believe none of them had figured it out.

"Well, when you think about it, there's only one way that I could know for certain."

Offering no other explanation, Trick walked away from them and out the door. As they mulled over his cryptic response, the answer to the riddle dawned on Katie. With an exasperated gasp, she bolted for the kitchen without a word. Though no one understood her sudden fervor, the others leapt from their seats in hot pursuit. By the time they reached the door, Katie was staring outside and Trick was stepping onto the pier.

Though not much more than a light shower, the rain had started up again. Through the raindrops, Trick saw Maggie seated at the edge of the pier looking despondently out over the lake. She didn't move even as she heard the wood creak louder and louder before Trick finally took a seat next to her. The rain mixing with her tears made it difficult to tell she was still crying, but he put his arms around her and held her. As soon as she felt his embrace, she wrapped her arms around him as well and pulled tightly into him.

"This is never going to end is it?" she asked.

"Of course, it will," replied Trick.

Maggie pushed herself away from him unable to appreciate the optimism. "No! It won't," she exclaimed. "It's been six months, and it still hasn't gone away. Even if I leave here—even if I try to leave it all behind—it'll follow me. I didn't mind so much when Kenny wouldn't admit it because that meant at least there was a chance that I knew who it was. Just because he was refusing to say yes didn't mean it wasn't him and even if he never did, I could live with that as long as I knew who it was. Now, I don't even know that."

As the rain continued to drop down on them, Trick became overwhelmed with guilt and compassion. He never intended it to go this far. Now that it had, he had to resolve the situation and hope Maggie would be able to forgive him for what he had done.

"Do you know what the worst part of this whole thing is?" Maggie asked before he could say anything.

Trick shook his head. Maggie didn't see but wasn't going to stop anyway.

"He said that he would never leave me if I needed him. Just before he walked out on me forever, he told me that. It was just a lie."

"No, it wasn't."

Maggie rolled her eyes and stood up on the pier. "Really? Are you gonna try to fix this one too, Trick? Are you gonna tell me everything will be okay? Because I'm not buying it! You can't make this right." As Trick stood up to face Maggie, the initial anger in her eyes changed to anguish. "I know you want to, and I know that you only mean the best, but sometimes, that isn't good enough. There's only one thing that can make this better, and it doesn't look like I will ever get that."

Maggie turned away from Trick. She had grown tired of people watching her cry. Even if it was him, she didn't want someone watching her cry anymore.

"He's been with you the whole time, Maggie," Trick replied. "Even if he hasn't been much of an angel, he's been with you."

It was subtle, but exactly the type of thing Maggie would notice...angel. She never mentioned that he had called himself a guardian angel: not to Katie, not to Eric, not even to Trick, yet he knew. How could he know and could the answer really be that simple?

Even if he was the answer to all the questions, she couldn't dare assume it so. She had to hear the truth from him in his own words. Slowly, she turned to face him, and when her gaze met his eyes, her pulse quickened.

As she took a step towards him, she asked, as calmly as she could under the circumstances, "What are you saying?"

As Trick looked into her tear-filled eyes, he felt no fear for the first time in a long time. For the past six months, fear had driven him and kept him hiding behind his mask. He did everything possible to avoid even the slightest bit of suspicion. For the sake of his happiness, he guarded desperately his heroic, yet foolhardy, actions from that night. All his fear, guardedness was gone now because he couldn't do it anymore...not to her. He loved her dearly and couldn't deny that truth any longer.

"It was me," Trick said confidently. For the moment, he did well to hide the shame he felt along with the fear that his most valuable relationship might be breaking.

"It was you?" Maggie repeated in a gasp.

The tension of the moment caused Trick to blurt out his confession. "I panicked. I saw you fall in the lake, and when I got you out you weren't breathing. And as I tried to get you to breathe again I realized that you really might die. I couldn't stand the thought of you being gone and never knowing how I felt about you and how important you are to me. When you were okay, I was so relieved, but I couldn't stop myself from saying that I loved you...."

Hearing him say it was so warming it made Maggie smile, and it was only then she realized the rain had stopped. As she gazed up to the clearing sky, she caught a pale moon and twinkling stars in her eyes. The sudden clarity of the night sky brought to her mind the stunning revelation that she should have known it was him all along. After all, hadn't there been something reassuring in that familiar voice? Wasn't there something comforting about being in his arms? Was it any different that the comfort and assurance she felt when she was around Trick?

Everything that he had done for her, all the times he had been there for her during this trying time had proven to her how she felt about him. Those three weeks he was gone only solidified the fact that she loved him, too. She wanted to tell him as much when he came back, but hearing about Amy had stopped her from doing so. In her mind, she had told herself repeatedly that in a perfect world, Trick would have been the one who saved her. She had what she wanted now, but she would have to have all the answers before she could decide if it was real.

"Why were you out here that night?" Maggie asked.

It was one of the few times in his life that Trick hadn't been able to read Maggie. She had to protect herself right now, and he couldn't tell if she was angry with him or not though he assumed she was. She had every right to be, so it felt justified that she would require all the answers.

"Do you remember the story I told you long ago about when I ran away from home?" Trick asked.

Maggie nodded. Trick stepped out to the edge of the pier and looked to the trees. It was roughly the same area the man…he walked into that night.

"I never told you where I went. You probably assumed I was just out in the yard, but I actually made it all the way out here. The Smith's hadn't moved in yet; it was just country. Mom searched for me for five hours, but she wasn't going to stop.

"After she died, I came out here again and found the tree where she carved the heart. It was fading away, and I could barely see it anymore. I was so terrified that it was going to disappear that I carved it out again. Every now and then, I'd come back just to make sure it was here, but I didn't want anyone to know about it—I wanted it secret. That's why I snuck around and covered my face. If anyone saw me, they'd never know, and I'd still have my secret."

Maggie desperately wanted to believe everything Trick was saying, but the logistics still didn't add up.

Maggie reminded him, "Jordan called you that night,"

Trick stepped away from the pier and looked at Maggie again.

"He called me…on my cell phone. No one has the house number because dad doesn't want me to give it out. I told him I was in my garage; he believed me."

Maggie was still concerned this was gonna blow up in her face like everything else had. "Kenny came to your house."

"Which is why I'm happy I drove," Trick replied. "There's a spot a few hundred yards away from here where I can ditch my car and no one can see it. I got home, changed, and was in my garage by the time he showed up. He was so cold from Miller's lake he didn't really question me when he grabbed the towel I used to dry off. All I had to say was it was a spill."

It all made sense. Even though it all seemed too good to be true, the numbers added up. If all that was true, could it also be true that he was the one that finished her anniversary project?

"Did you finish my grandparents' tape?"

Trick smiled as he nodded. "Kenny wasn't the only one in there all week, but I knew no one would ever be suspicious of me."

With the answers right there in front of her with all the explanation she'd needed, Maggie ran through them over and over in her head, making sure they all held together. After months of searching, she finally had the truth. He was standing in front of her, a man who loved her and had proven that he would do anything for her. He was right that her angel hadn't been perfect, but at least he was finally hers.

As Maggie walked up to Trick, he prepared himself for whatever she was about to say or do to him. He imagined a thousand different reactions, yet he was ultimately shocked when she put one hand behind his head and thrust her lips onto his.

From the kitchen, Katie, Jordan, Ashley, Scott, Jessica, and Kenny could see the kiss unfold. Even though Katie had told them all it was Trick, they couldn't believe what they were witnessing.

"It was Trick?" Scott asked.

"It was Trick," Ashley repeated. "There was only one way he could really know for sure that Kenny was lying. It was because he was the one that pulled her out of that lake."

"All those years they were friends, why didn't we ever suspect him?" Jessica asked.

"I don't know," Kenny replied. "If we just asked the question who would always be there for Maggie, the answer would be him. Despite being the obvious choice, he just managed to stay out of the spotlight and stay hidden behind the mask."

"But it's over now, right? It's definitely over?" Jordan asked.

Katie smiled as they all took their eyes off the pier and looked at each other. "No," she said happily, "it's just beginning."

Once they had all reveled in the moment, they could finally go back to the party. There would be time for celebration later, but after all that had happened, they had to leave Maggie and Trick to their moment.

Even though he was experiencing the moment he'd dreamt about his entire life, Trick couldn't believe it was really happening. He was standing on the pier, kissing the lips of the girl he'd loved more than anyone he'd ever met. As she pulled away from him, only one thing was on his mind.

"How are you not mad at me?"

Maggie smiled as she gently ran her hand down Trick's cheek.

"I've been mad, Trick," she replied, "for a long time. I've been mad, sad, hurt, and a lot of other bad things. Only one thing has truly made me happy during that time, and that was you. I've wanted to tell you every day since you got back from Colorado. I wanted it to be you that saved me. So many things got in the way of me telling you that I'm not going to let anything get in the way of this because I love you."

Hearing her say it was so warming it made Trick smile.

"You love me?" Trick repeated.

Maggie smiled as she nodded yes. Trick tried to say something, but the euphoria within him overwhelmed his ability to speak. As he stood there exasperated, this man of words rendered speechless by the granting of his greatest desire, Maggie laughed to herself. With nothing left to say, Trick reached for Maggie and kissed her again. Never in his life had he felt joy like this—not even in the mountains of Colorado.

What happened next was an afterthought, and where they went from here was completely trivial. To have each other now was more than they ever could have hoped for. All the trials and tribulations they had encountered since that fateful October night suddenly seemed a small price to pay to be where they stood that night. The tears shed, lies told, and anger felt had all been fleeting. This was eternal.